AFTER THE REVOLUTION

AFTER THE REVOLUTION

A Novel

Robert Evans

AK PRESS

ISBN 9781849354622
E-ISBN 9781849354639
LCCN: 2021944651

Please contact us to request the latest AK Press distribution catalog, which features books, pamphlets, zines, and stylish apparel published and/or distributed by AK Press. Alternatively, visit our websites for the complete catalog, latest news, and secure ordering.

AK Press
370 Ryan Ave. #100
Chico, CA 95973
www.akpress.org

AK Press
33 Tower Street
Edinburgh, Scotland EH6 7BN
akuk.com

Cover art and interior illustrations © Tavia Morria
Printed in the USA
Go to https://atrbook.com for more info

This book is dedicated to Cynthia.

I'd furthermore like to thank Sarah and Jeremy, who took me in when I was crazy from grief and trauma. Thank you Moira, for reading my silly book and giving it crucial feedback. Thank you Tavia, for the incredible illustrations and the support. And thank you Sophie, for telling me to stop being a coward and publish the motherfucker.

Last, I'd like to thank Magenta. Without you, and the places we went together, I would not have known the things I needed to know in order to write this at all.

Richardson, Republic of Texas, 2070.

Chapter 1

Manny.

Manny smiled at the way the British journalist's face blanched as the old Toyota hit the pothole. Reggie wasn't used to bad roads, cars driven by actual humans, or the way the heavy metal of the gun mount in the truck bed made the aluminum frame groan. That was all familiar to Manny. He'd grown up in ciudad de muerta, back before the Lakewood Blast. Back when people had still called it Dallas.

The truck's driver veered around the bloated corpse of a large dog lying in the middle of the road. Reggie gripped the truck bed with white knuckles and eyed the swaying ammo-belt of the 20mm cannon like it was a coiled snake. The gunner, Manny's cousin Alejandro, grinned down at the journalist, "The suspension's a little fucked, yeah?"

The Brit nodded, and turned greener when the technical hit another pothole. Manny supposed he should offer a comforting word to the man. That would be good business. But a louder part of him looked at Reggie's brand-new boots and thought, "He can stand a little less comfort." The journalist would brag about this ride for months once he got home.

Escorting reporters from the safety of Austin to the sundry hot spots of the old Metroplex was not Manny's ideal career. Two years ago he'd been working on a bachelor's in business administration from the University of Austin. The plan had been to get a job with Aegis Biosystems, then charm his way into a working visa and a gig in the California

YIELD

Republic. But the fighting had started up again and ruined all that. The culprit this time was the "Heavenly Kingdom," a loose assortment of Christian extremist militias. They'd boiled out from the suburbs of the old Metroplex and all but broken the Republic of Texas.

The autonomous City of Austin had stabilized the situation with the help of an alliance of leftist Texan militias, the Secular Defense Forces. Beating them back had cost a lot in blood and time, and forced Manny to change every plan he'd ever made for his life.

So he'd embraced the situation and started his own business, hiring on some friends as employees. Together they'd built the best network of stringers in North Texas. His boys fed him video, contacts, and news updates, and he sold what he could to the big foreign media conglomerates. In a couple more months he'd have enough saved up that he could fuck off, fly to Europe and apply for a refugee visa.

My odds are pretty good, as long as the war doesn't end too soon.

The technical rolled to a creaky stop in front of a checkpoint that had clearly been erected within the last few days. It was just a collapsible electronic gate and two sandbag emplacements on either side of the battered highway. A street sign nearby announced that they were on the edge of Richardson, formerly a suburb of Dallas and currently a forward position of the People's Protection Army, a local anarchist militia. Manny could see the PPA's red/black triangle emblem stitched onto the jackets of the soldiers guarding the checkpoint.

One of the PPA men walked up to the window and started chatting with Phillip, the driver. Phil and Manny's cousin Alejandro were both with the Citizen's Front, a more-or-less apolitical militia from the suburbs of Austin. Both militias co-existed under the broad umbrella of the Secular Defense Forces. The SDF had been organized by the Canadian government, to lump all of North Texas's palatable militant groups into a single package that could be conveniently armed.

While the first guard talked with Phillip, his partner did a circuit around the back of the truck. The man was big, bulging with muscles so sculpted and prominent they had to be vat-grown, and he moved with the twitchy un-grace of a man who'd replaced his nervous system with circuitry. His weapon was a very old, very battered AR-15 with an M243 grenade launcher below the barrel. The latter was old U.S. military gear. The former had been someone's toy before the Revolution gave America's half-billion civilian guns a new raison d'etre.

The man moved back to the barricades when he'd finished his lap. Reggie looked up at Manny and asked, "Was he, erm...was he 'chromed'?"

Manny smiled. That was always one of the first questions, when any foreign journo saw a trooper with a large enough build, skin with an off-shade, or who just moved a little too fast to seem completely "right." Anything beyond basic aesthetic and medical modifications were banned in civilized countries, like the U.K.

The real chrome, the implants that would let a man lift a tank or take a rocket to the belly, that shit was locked up tight. Few national militaries even used the stuff these days. Not after the Revolution.

"He's got some vat-grown muscles," Manny said, in an off-handed way that suggested such things were common. "Aftermarket nerves too, probably. His stuff is low-grade. That's why it's so visible."

Reggie nodded. His eyes stayed locked on the big man. He was quiet for a while before he spoke again. "You just...you live right alongside them, don't you?"

Manny shrugged. "Everybody's got something out here. And the wetware's what lets us hold back the Martyrs. They'd own the whole city if it weren't for half-vats like him."

The journalist nodded, and his gaze stayed fixed upon the militia-man until a troubled look crossed his face. He glanced back to Manny.

"Are you, ah, 'chromed'?" Reggie asked.

Manny smiled. "I don't expect either of us is stock sapien, eh? But I doubt I've got anything you don't."

Reggie seemed somewhat comforted by this. "Most of what I've read about the really heavy mods says they cause a lot of, well, unstable behavior. That's why..."

"That's why this city's such a shit hole?" Manny asked.

The journalist had the grace to blush. Manny looked away for a moment. His eyes landed on the bones of three large public housing buildings. A barrel bomb had detonated in the center of the courtyard all three shared. It had peeled away the walls, some of the floors, and the resulting firestorm had burned up everything that wasn't concrete, steel, or rebar. For just a moment, Manny felt bad about hoping the war hung on another six months.

"The old government blamed a lot on roided-up veterans with military grade mods," he told Reggie. "Most was just propaganda, fear-mongering. People were pissed after twenty years of plague, disaster, and poverty." Manny shrugged. "It's true though, a lot of chromed-up vets turned on the government. You can't make men into gods and expect them to keep fighting for men."

Reggie pointed back to the bulging militiaman. "I take it muscles there is pretty far from a god."

"Nah," Manny laughed. "He's just a guy with too much meat-money. Gods don't man check-points."

The Brit was excited now. These were the questions he'd wanted to ask since they'd met yesterday. "Do you know where some of those people are?" Reggie couldn't keep the excitement out of his voice. "Could we talk to them?"

Manny didn't have any of those contacts, nor did he know any other fixers who did. He tried to let the Brit down easy. "Most of those folks live, uh, on the road. In between the civilized parts of Texas and the Republic of California."

"Oh," Reggie looked disappointed. From the bed of the truck they could see the wreckage of an old Catholic school. It bore the signs of being fortified, destroyed, re-fortified, and re-destroyed several times.

The Brit was inches from asking another question when the gateman waved them on and the battered Toyota farted its way into drive, belching and complaining past a network of potholes until it hit a relatively straight chunk of asphalt.

"Only a few minutes now, jefe," Manny said. "The PPA's forward position is about five minutes out. You'll be in 'the shit' then. Or at least shit-adjacent."

The journalist's face washed over in an even mix of anxiety and pride. One of the first lessons Manny had learned at this job was that phrases like "the shit" made rich gringo writers unreasonably excited. And excited journalists always called Manny the next time they were in-country. Giving white kids in keffiyahs a lifetime of bragging rights for surviving a couple days in his home killed his soul, just a little bit. But Manny pushed down the anger and told himself that a chip on the shoulder was a lot less useful than money in the bank.

The technical rolled off the old highway. Manny could see "23" and "Spring Valley Road" emblazoned on a weather-beaten, bullet-scarred sign. The technical pulled to the right. The gun swayed in its mount. Manny couldn't help smiling as the Brit instinctively pulled away from it.

They rolled up to what had once been a strip mall and was now a forward operating base for the People's Protection Army. An old laundromat, a bookstore, and a half-dozen restaurants now had their roofs ringed with barbed wire and machine-gun emplacements. Manny could see a line of bullet holes stitched across three of the shops. None of the windows were intact, but otherwise the buildings had weathered the war rather well.

Three M198 Howitzers were parked next to a taco shop that had once served the local college kids beer and cheap grub. There was a flag pole out in front of the shop, and from it hung the blue-and-white starburst flag of the SDF. Three men in uniforms stood, waiting, as the old Toyota rolled to a stop and Manny and Reggie disembarked.

Two of the men were officers in the PPA, Colonel Jakob Milgram and Major DeShawn Clark. Milgram was a boring, tight-lipped, nerdy type, but DeShawn was one of Manny's favorite sources. He was an old infantry guy, a consummate brawler with a face full of scars and three published books of poetry to his name. He actually had a base of international fans, mostly in Spain. The third man was Hamid Mohammed, an advisor from Syrian Kurdistan. The Kurds had been giving aid to the sundry militias of the Secular Defense Forces for years now. Manny considered Hamid almost a local.

He shook hands with Jakob. Since Manny knew DeShawn better he met the man with a full embrace, and used it as an opportunity to palm the Major a packet of his favorite cigarettes. DeShawn gave him a wink and a smile. Manny shook Hamid's hand next, and then kissed him on the cheek. Hamid returned the kiss, clapped him on the shoulder and said, "Emmanuel, my friend, you really should get out of this business. One of these days you'll come up here and it won't be safe."

Manny frowned a little at the use of his birth name, but didn't make an issue out of the matter. "There's still a war on, right?" He smiled at Hamid. "Y'all get that shit under control, and maybe I'll work a straight job again." *Not too soon though*, he thought. *The least this war can do is last long enough to get me out of Texas.*

Hamid smiled back, and Manny introduced Reggie to the officers. The journalist was clearly awkward in that special way Manny had come to expect from new war correspondents. It was the norm for young writers to be intimidated by grizzled military men. Some of them got over that; Manny had worked with a middle-aged *Der Spiegel* reporter last week who'd probably taken as much incoming fire as Major Clark.

Colonel Milgram led them into the militarized taco shop. A brief blast of nostalgia squeezed Manny's lungs. The place had obviously been closed since the Revolution. The drink specials and meal prices printed on the wall were given in U.S. dollars, a currency as dead as the last American president. Manny recognized ads for bands and movies he remembered from his childhood. The glass facade had shattered years ago. The kitchen had been gutted and replaced by wall-length screens displaying maps of the city. At least a dozen uniformed men and women milled around the space in small groups.

He and Reggie sat down at a long picnic table with Hamid and the two officers. Reggie set his camera up on the table. It was just a small silver sphere, but Manny knew it could record everything happening around it at a higher resolution than the human eye.

An orderly brought in three beers, Shiner Bocks from Austin, and one dark brown tea in a glass cup for Hamid. The Brit raised his glass in a friendly salute, "Thank you for meeting with me." And then he started to ask questions. Manny leaned back in his chair and enjoyed a long gulp of cold beer. If he wasn't needed to translate, he generally checked out during interviews.

He used the free time to activate his deck and check in on the two stringers he had working right now. David Allenby was up in Addison today, taking a Californian documentary crew on a tour of an SDF training facility. He'd messaged Manny to let him know they'd gotten through the checkpoints without any issue. Oscar Martinez didn't have any journalists with him. He was embedded with a Republic of Texas police unit, getting footage from inside a neighborhood that had recently been "liberated" from the Heavenly Kingdom.

There were no new messages from Oscar. His last check-in had been the night before. It was probably nothing, but it concerned Manny nonetheless. *What if Oscar got a better offer for his footage?* He'd always been loyal before, but if that fuck from the *Guardian* had gotten to him...

"I'm interested in the Abrams Road bombing," Reggie told the Colonel, and Manny's attention swung back to his reporter. *That's an odd thing to ask about.* The bombing had occurred two weeks back. It'd been big news for a couple of hours. Manny had paid one of his contacts in

Raza Front for a video of a walkthrough of the wreckage. It had brought in about three grand, profit.

"The Abrams Road bombing was not a Martyrdom Operation," Colonel Milgram sounded almost angry.

"Terribly sorry," Reggie said, "you're right of course. There was no driver, so no Martyr. Right?"

"Right," DeShawn Clark said. He pulled a folded piece of white paper out of his pocket, opened it up, and smoothed it out on the table. It was a map of the DFW area, color coded to show the positions of the various militias in the region. "We operate eight checkpoints on that part of the Richardson Line," DeShawn said as he pointed to each one. "Five of them border Republic-controlled territory. The traffic from there is mostly autonomous, and those vehicles slave themselves to our traffic management system before they can enter our territory. The other three checkpoints border territory controlled by the Martyrs. They don't see much traffic, and they're all heavily manned."

Reggie was quiet for a few seconds. Manny could almost hear the gears turning in the journalist's head as he struggled to find the words for his next question.

"Would it be fair to say the autonomous checkpoints are less secure, then?"

DeShawn smiled a thin, quiet smile. Hamid grimaced. Colonel Milgram responded in a terse voice, "The autonomous checkpoints have fewer defenders. But they border Republic territory. The Martyrs haven't pulled off an attack on one in quite some time."

"Was Abrams Road not one such attack?" Reggie looked eager now, like a hound following a scent.

"We don't know who bombed Abrams Road," Colonel Milgram said. "No one's taken credit, but we doubt it was the Martyrs."

"Why?" the journalist asked. Manny leaned in a little, interested in spite of himself at where this was all going to lead.

"Perhaps," Hamid said, "you should read a bit more about this 'Heavenly Kingdom.' They reject all autonomous technology. They even use remote human pilots for their drones, like its two-thousand-and-fucking-three. That's why our skies are always clear. We jam them."

Reggie asked, "Is it possible they found some way to hack your defense system?"

Hamid laughed. "We bought this system from the Israelis. If you're telling me one of the Martyrs' Brigades has a hacker who can crack that, then I'm the King of Albuquerque."

"But something still went wrong," Reggie insisted.

Hamid's smile turned cold. "This is war, Mr. Reggie. It's mostly things going wrong."

That's where the line of questions petered out. Reggie asked them for access to the security footage from the destroyed checkpoint, and Colonel Milgram agreed to send it over.

"We'd like to speak to the survivors as well, if possible," Manny interjected, not waiting to see if the journalist would ask. He knew those men were all stationed behind the line now, which would make for a safer, easier rest of the day than heading up to the wire.

"Of course," Colonel Milgram said, with a smile to Manny. They said their goodbyes, and then Major Clark walked them out to their waiting Toyota. The Texas heat hit like an oven as they exited, and Manny was glad they'd be spending most of the rest of their day indoors.

DeShawn clapped a hand on Manny's shoulder as he lit one of his new cigarettes. "It's good to see you again Emmanuel," he said. And then he smiled at Reggie. "And it's nice to meet you, my British friend. I'm sorry you've come to the front at a boring time."

"Why?" Reggie asked.

"Because this," DeShawn gestured at the gun emplacements and loitering militiafolks of the command post, "this is not war, not really. Your job is to help your people, children of peace and plenty, understand what is going on here. You must teach them the language of war. And to paraphrase a dead poet, the language of war is a language made of blood. To be spoken, it must be earned."

There was an awkward pause. A little bit of the blood drained from the journalist's face. *You old nutty fuck,* Manny thought, with more amusement than fear. "Classic DeShawn," he said, and laughed to ease the tension. The Major bid them both a good day, hugged Manny, and sauntered off back to the command post. Smoke from his cigarette curled up into the air behind him as he walked. Manny's eyes lingered on it for a second before he turned back to Reggie.

"Ready to go?" he asked, chipper as he could manage.

Three hours, a handful of interviews, and one short drive later, Manny and Reggie arrived at their home for the night: the Richardson Autonomous Project. Once a Walmart, now a twenty-two-year-old experiment in sustainable urban living, the Project was the furthest island of "civilization" on the SDF's side of the front. Its militia steadfastly refused to involve themselves in the region's greater conflicts. They'd been targeted a few times by the Heavenly Kingdom. The SDF, by contrast, left them alone. So when a fixer like Manny found himself on the wrong side of the LBJ Freeway after dark he could usually trust the Project to provide food, booze, and shelter. For a price, of course.

Sleeping arrangements in the Project were broadly communal. The bulk of the old Walmart had been converted into an indoor meadow with grow-lights hanging from the rafters and a wide, lush field of native grass sprawling across most of the inhabited space. Fruit trees, bushes full of berries, cannabis plants, and copses of bamboo lined the edges of the space. The center of the field was dominated by a large, circular kitchen surrounded by a handsome oaken bar. Tables, gazebos, and sundry personal structures dotted the field, along with a pair of dance floors.

Reggie's face lit up when he saw the bar. By the time Manny had dropped off their bags and paid Charlie and the driver for the night, the journalist was already three beers in. The Brit wasn't precisely drunk or sober, but at that productive twilight in between. He'd unrolled a portable screen and had a holographic display up, looping four separate sections of the security footage Colonel Milgram had sent over. The journalist alternated between typing furiously, scrawling notes in his journal, and taking huge gulps of something brown and foamy. He stopped working when he saw Manny approach and waved him into the adjacent seat.

"Hey brother, check this out."

Manny pulled up a seat and the journalist directed his attention to a six-second loop of footage, from immediately after the bombing. It showed two man-sized silhouettes standing on top of an old garage; Manny remembered the building. It stood maybe two hundred meters from the Abrams Road checkpoint. One of the silhouettes had a rifle. The other held a short, squat tube that Manny recognized as a camera lens.

"Notice anything?"

"Spotters," Manny said. "Probably trying to get a kill count."

"Nah, man. Look at where he's pointed. That cunt's not looking at any post. He's looking straight back, deeper into the old town. And I'll bet you he's high up enough to be staring right at Colonel Milgram's command post."

Manny looked again. He thought about the angle. "OK, so, what?" he asked. "You think this was a probing attack for some big action?"

The journalist shrugged. "Maybe. It's something new, is what interests me. Two years of martyrdom operations that all look more-or-less the same and now this weird one. An autonomous vehicle bomb from a group of fanatics who think autonomous vehicles are the devil."

"Yeah," Manny agreed, "that does seem weird."

The bartender walked up and offered Manny his pick of the finest liquor in this particular warzone. Manny ordered a Shiner. It was the one beer a drinker could find across both the Republic of Texas and the Austin autonomous region. He looked back at the looping footage. They both watched it twice more. Then Reggie spoke up again.

"What have you heard about Pastor Mike?" he asked.

Manny stiffened a little bit at the name. He'd heard it, of course. Vague stories of rioting in Kansas, a fundamentalist uprising inside the southernmost territories of the United Christian States. He hadn't thought much about it at first. But two years ago Pastor Mike had moved to Texas, shortly before the Heavenly Kingdom had declared itself. It was hard to say exactly what role the preacher played within the organization. But he was certainly its most visible "face."

"I know who he is," Manny said. "I know the Republic let him in because they thought his followers might provide a buffer against Austin's influence. I know that blew the fuck up in their faces." Manny took a long drink and continued. "That's an old story around here, the Republic using those god-fondling nut-fucks to push back against the leftists."

The journalist raised an eyebrow and Manny instantly regretted his crude response. He didn't really care about religion one way or the other, but whenever he came out to the front it was hard to not get a little angry. Especially after a drink.

"Sorry," he said, "it's been a long day."

Reggie looked down, coughed and took a sip. He looked back at Manny, took another sip, and said, "You know that's another subject I'd rather like to cover."

"What?" Manny asked.

"Anti-Christian sentiment in North America."

Manny grunted and looked down at his drink. The Brit barreled on.

"You're not the first North American I've heard express anger toward Christians," he said. "In California, Cascadia, the North American Federation, I've just seen a lot of hate..."

"Look," Manny interrupted. "Me, I'm a man of peace. I love everybody. But this continent's been torn apart and bleeding out for the last twenty years. Lotta people hate Christians. The ones that don't hate Christians hate leftists. And everyone outside the American Federation hates capitalists. Hate, hate, hate."

Manny took a gulp of his beer and set it down, a little harder than he'd intended. He looked Reggie in the eye and finished, "There's exactly one thing all the broken bits of this continent have in common. Hate."

The journalist arched an eyebrow at Manny and returned the gaze. He had the look of a man peering into the enclosure of a particularly exotic zoo animal. Manny wanted to resent it, but he'd been doing this job long enough to know this was just how journalists looked at people.

Reggie downed his drink. He reached a hand up to signal the bartender and then looked back at Manny. "Can I buy you another round?"

Manny shook his head. "No thanks. I'm tired, and I don't want to drag ass at the front tomorrow."

He downed the last of his beer, bid Reggie a good night, and headed over to the spot of turf where he'd set up his sleeping bag and gear. He popped off his shoes, his pants, and his shirt and rubbed himself down with a handful of wet naps. Then he grabbed a nightshirt and sweatpants from his bag and slipped them on. Manny considered clean pajamas a necessity.

He fired up his deck again once he was swaddled in his sleeping bag. There was a juddering start, and then the corners of his vision were populated by a series of small, partly translucent screens. Each one bulged with updates; friends asking about his weekend plans, spam from his college, notifications about new video uploads, and headlines from the local news. David had messaged him twice more, to let him know he and his journalists were headed back to Austin and, then, that they'd arrived.

Oscar still hadn't responded. Manny's initial concern was over his loyalty: *I got that fucker started as a stringer. If he sold that video and cut me out of the deal I'm going...going to...* But the longer he thought about Oscar, the more Manny worried that something might have happened. He'd been working in Plano today, near a very stable chunk of the front. But this far out, almost anything could happen...

Manny closed his eyes, sighed, and tried to purge the anxiety from his mind. There was nothing to do now, other than get to sleep so he could wake up tomorrow and make more money. That thought prompted Manny to pull open his banking app and check on the status of his saving's account. The numbers glowed, fat and happy, in the space right in front of his head. *Another five months in the field, maybe six. Then I buy that plane ticket.*

He started to think about the pictures he'd seen of Dublin and Berlin and Barcelona, all the places he thought he might live if this war would just hang on a little longer. He soon fell asleep, and slept pretty well until the first mortar landed.

Chapter 2

Roland.

He woke up, suddenly aware of two pressing problems:

The acid's worn off.

And,

Eight people are here to kill me.

Both of these facts concerned him equally. He couldn't remember his name or where, exactly, he was, which made the impending kill-team all the more worrisome. He opened his eyes. His vision was blurry and unfocused. His head felt filled with sand.

Roland (*–Oh shit, that's my name! Roland!)* wondered how long he'd been asleep. He reflexively triggered his deck before the dim firing of a synapse reminded him that he'd permanently disabled his data connection...well, a long time ago.

Five million two hundred twenty six thousand minu–

His "hindbrain," what Roland called the acres of microscopic processors and databanks spun into his blood, spat the knowledge out unbidden into his conscious mind. Roland tried to curse but wound up spitting out a wad of brackish phlegm instead. His eyes settled on a quarter-full bottle of fungus whiskey. He grabbed it, drained it, and rooted around on the table where he'd found it until his digging turned up a sheet of acid. He ripped the sheet in half, ate one half, and pasted the other on his sweat-damp chest.

Roland's brain didn't wait for the acid to do its job; nanomachines couriered the lysergic diethylacid direct to his synapses. The drugs

took hold in a manner of seconds. Acid softened the world around him. His hindbrain's running commentary faded into a sort of generalized hyper-awareness of the world around him. He sighed, relaxed, and remembered.

A woman hovered over him, her hands on his shoulders, her knees on either side of his body. Sweat dripped down from her short black hair onto his face and chest. Her pupils were the size of dinner plates. She smelled like acid and desire. She smiled, revealing a row of damascus-steel teeth–

Roland pulled himself out of the memory. He felt the strike team advance. His hindbrain generated a map of the approaching assassins. They were still a solid minute from his hovel.

There were six men and two women on the team. If he'd wanted, a microsecond's focus could've told him which members of the group were vegetarians, where two of the team were on their menstrual cycles, and how recently each of their firearms had been cleaned and oiled. But Roland didn't care about that information. He was trying to remember where he'd left his gun.

The one-room hut Roland occupied was best described as "squalid." He knew he'd lived there for quite a long time, although he wasn't sure if the home was "his" in any legal sense of the word. Its one room held a filthy mattress, a hot plate, several dozen empty bottles of liquor, and a tinkling carpet of spent whippets. A large knife was embedded in the door. Roland couldn't remember why. He knew he'd had a gun at one point, even though he couldn't currently find it. He stood up, still wobbly from the massive dose of GHB he'd taken with his nightly tequila, and started kicking at the piles of bottles and drug paraphernalia in the hope that one of them might contain his gun. He found some bullets after a few second's search, at the bottom of a Folger's Coffee tin that was half-filled with marijuana.

Next to the tin was a large metal bowl of stagnant water. Roland glanced in and caught sight of his own reflection. His black skin looked ashen and clammy. *Unusually pale*, he thought, but he didn't recall enough about himself to know if that was really true. His face was long and drawn, with wide jutting cheekbones and a patchy uneven beard. His head was covered in stubble. The center of his face was dominated by a crooked, heavily scarred nose. Roland had no recollection of why it was scarred, but he knew the injury must've happened back before the Army filled him with chrome.

He turned away from his reflection and continued his search through the house, scattering food-encrusted plates, empty coke bags, and old-fashioned print pornography into even less-organized piles. No dice. *Did I pawn it?* he wondered, as his machine-assisted eidetic memory warred with his profound intoxication. Roland was now conscious enough to remember that not remembering much was normal for him, and that he should really worry more about the assassins coming to kill him.

Oh shit, right!

The strike team was just fifty meters out now. He felt a gust of wind and, in the same way, felt as two of the men began to assemble a large sound cannon behind a rocky hill that faced his hovel. He guessed it was a Callahan Mk. 38. Roland didn't know how he knew the weapon's name, but he knew it could burn out even his armored synapses with a few seconds of continuous fire.

One man was on overwatch for the Callahan team. He carried a two-bore Ruger Falchion anti-vehicular rifle. The mingling odors of fear-sweat and baby formula wafting off him triggered sense-memories of someone holding a newborn infant. Roland guessed the man must have a kid back home. *A kid he's scared of leaving fatherless if some chromed out acid-head fillets him.* That was useful data. He filed it away in the chunk of his brain least likely to lose that information over the next four seconds. Roland's memory was real good in four-second chunks.

Over the next picosecond he caught equally informative whiffs of the others. It was enough to suggest that the two women in the main assault team were lovers, and they'd both had milspec sub-dermal armor implanted recently. The acrid scent of fresh sutures hung heavy in the air around them. Roland could also tell that one of the men in the assault party took heavy testosterone supplements, either because of a genetic abnormality or because he'd been assigned female at birth. The fourth man was moderately addicted to ephedrix and riding into battle on a high stimulant wave.

The last member of the assault team was the only one to give Roland any pause. He could guess the man's height and weight (*six foot five, two-hundred-forty pounds*) from the sound of his footfalls. Roland could smell the Sig Sauer .500 submachine gun in his hands, but otherwise the man was a sensory blank. No sweat, no hydraulics, and black to thermographic sensors. The man was chromed. Not so heavily as Roland, of course, but the competent and well-armed squad he led might be enough to narrow the gap.

Where in the shitting shitshitshit did I leave that gun?

The static balance in the air changed as the overwatch team warmed up their sound cannon. The assault team was close now, barely a hundred feet out, waiting in the cover provided by several large boulders at the base of the rise that held Roland's ramshackle home. He knew how this fight would go. They'd unleash the Callahan for a good five seconds while the kill-team moved into position and kicked in the door. Next the big bruiser and the two women would enter while the remainder of the assault team fanned out to cover the sides.

Textbook post-human kill-team tactics, he thought. He didn't actually remember any of the fights this conclusion was based on. But he'd clearly lived through similar encounters. And if he trusted his body and hindbrain he would again.

Roland finished searching the apocalyptic ruin that was his kitchen sink. The pile of plates had been large enough to hide a short-barrel AR-10, but his gun wasn't there either.

"Fuck-nuts," he cursed. The profanity brought a tiny serotonin spike, and Roland felt himself calm down even as the noose tightened around him. His combat wetware did most of its work in the moments before meat met metal. So Roland closed his eyes, slumped his shoulders and relaxed while it cross-indexed his memories of past firefights with his current sensory data. A moment later, Roland was presented with three potential counter-assault strategies.

He selected the one that sounded like the most fun.

The Callahan fired, blanketing his home and much of the area beyond it in a web of noise designed to assault and eventually fry the synapses of anyone dumb enough to stand too long in its wake. Pain lashed from Roland's inner ear and sparked out to every nerve in his body. It would've been enough to leave a strong man curled on the ground, shitting his guts out. But Roland just felt a distant ache. His experience of the damage was more akin to seeing the check-engine light on a car than true agony. He was aware that if he waited too long the sonic weapon would blow out the pain dampners on his spinal nerve gates. Luckily for him the assault team didn't wait that long.

Roland felt the big man arc his leg up to kick in the door. It crumpled in and Roland lunged left. This helped him avoid the first spray of covering fire as the chromed man and both women barreled inside. Roland flung himself into the hovel's main structural support beam, which ran up the building's left wall. He hit it with the rough speed and force of a light truck going twenty miles an hour. His momentum carried him and half the left wall into the rocky ground outside.

Roland's filthy little home tottered and swayed. It collapsed first on the left side and then on the right as the whole structure failed. Roland was already up with a jagged piece of two-by-four in his hands. He rushed the ephedrix addict holding down the left flank. The man got two shots off and, to his credit, both hit right where Roland's original heart had been. And then Roland was on him. He shoved the wood into the meat of the man's face. It gouged off enough flesh to fill a pint glass and shattered the poor fellow's jaw. He went down, hard.

Roland smelled the familiar scent of anti-hemorrhagic nanomachines as they rushed to save the man's life. He caught a slight sour whiff of the cheap clotting agents in the man's blood. Roland guessed it was TrauMax brand, which was convenient. TrauMax had based their whole line off of a piece of Brazilian military wetware that itself was based on a crude synthesis of horseshoe crab blood. The organs worked well enough, unless you happened to be an amphetamine addict who'd suffered massive tissue damage. Then your TrauMax unit would flood your synapses with adenosine to knock you out, rather than risk pushing more amphetamines on your stressed heart.

Something in the smell of the man's blood set off a powerful sense memory buried deep in Roland's hippocampus—*vines slashing his face, boiling jungle heat, and his fist connecting with the face of a heavily armed young woman. Her orbital bone broke under the blow, he smelled her blood meet the air and she dropped, dropped, dropped*—the memory flashed by, free of context, in the time it took the other man to hit the ground.

It was frustrating to only remember the "what" of an action, and not the "why" or the "after." It was like knowing how to ride a bike without remembering who'd taught you and when, only for everything. Roland found it somewhat unsettl–

A 12-gauge slug hit him in the thigh. It dug deep, hit reinforced bone, and stopped. The little machines in Roland's blood were already cutting it apart by the time he stopped musing and bounded over to the other flank-man. Roland chucked the two-by-four hard as he ran.

The wood impacted above the assassin's temple with an audible crack, shattering the man's sphenoid bone.

The battle drugs started to trickle into Roland's synapses now, a cocktail of endorphins, oxytocin, serotonin, and epinephrine concocted to make violence as addictive as a fat rock of crystal meth. Roland instantly wanted more, and he knew he could trigger a greater dose by stomping on the downed man's skull and ending his life. He fought down the urge and, instead, grabbed the man's AA-32 combat shotgun and rolled for cover behind a red-rock boulder.

He was almost fast enough. But either the overwatch man had some aftermarket parts Roland hadn't smelled or all the hardcore drug abuse had done long-term damage to his reflexes. *Maybe no more crack binges,* Roland thought as a massive two-bore slug blew most of his left shoulder out into the desert behind him.

Roland belted out several fuckwords as pain flooded the banks of his dampeners. And just that second, with truly exquisite timing, the Callahan crew swiveled their weapon around and poured sonic fire at him from above.

For a fraction of a second everything went dark. Roland's world was riotous red pain and little else. If his body had required the input of his conscious mind, he would have been in a real pickle. During the milliseconds it took for his dampeners to cut through the pain haze, Roland's body dove ten feet to the left, enough to take him out of the Callahan's spray and behind an outcropping of rocks. Two rounds cracked into the rock above his head. Roland came back to himself as the shards cut into his skin.

He glanced down at the ruin of his shoulder. His little blood robots were already hard at work, rebuilding the muscles, bones, and sinews blown out by the giant slug. A couple seconds more and the limb would be usable again. But Roland had a better idea.

He used his intact arm as a flesh-catapult and flung himself up over the boulder, toward the Callahan and its three guardians. The man with the two-bore fired again. Roland had known he would and his hindbrain had already calculated the ideal motions to avoid the dozen most-likely shot patterns. He sailed over the half-pound bullets with ease and used the hand of his intact arm to rip his wounded arm free at the shoulder.

Roland landed hard in front of the Callahan. He swung his own severed limb like a club and knocked the barrel to the left. Then he laid into the gun's crew with a mix of pounding swings from the arm and stomps to the other men's knees and ankles. Bones shattered. Assassins screamed. The man with the two-bore and the newborn child at home wavered and broke. Roland had expected this. Many normal humans, even hardened veterans, found it nauseating and unsettling to see a man move as fast as he could move. Add "beating their friends half to death with a severed limb" and, well, he'd predicted the guy would break.

It's not your fault buddy, Roland thought as he watched the man run. *Don't feel bad.* He'd wanted to say that out loud but he was having trouble working his vocal cords.

In roughly seven seconds, Roland had eliminated five out of eight threats in the kill-team. His hindbrain predictions had given him six more seconds, at least, before the entry team cleared themselves from the debris of his collapsed hovel. But the other post-human, the man who'd shone blank on most of Roland's senses, had freed himself faster. Roland realized this when a trio of .50-caliber slugs burst into his chest cavity. He dropped, avoiding the last three rounds of the burst, and rolled behind another pair of boulders with his severed arm in hand.

The two female assassins were close to freeing themselves now. Roland could hear them struggle out through the vibrations of their bodies in the red sand. He couldn't see the other post-human, but he'd triangulated his most likely location. Unfortunately, the other fucker had him dead to rights. If Roland broke cover, he'd be shot to pieces, maybe more pieces than his trauma organs could put back together.

Alright, old boy. Do we eat a bunch of lead and charge the bastards? Deploy the meat rockets and run for a gun while they're blind? He suddenly remembered the spring-loaded assault razor embedded in his left forearm, and then the 22mm grenade pistol buried in between his small intestine and his sigmoid colon. (*Did I remember to load it before shoving it in there?*) But before he could take any action the firefight was interrupted by an oddly familiar voice.

"Hey Roland, how's it swingin'?"

Roland hadn't smelled or heard this new man coming. The voice was very familiar. Roland felt a name on the tip of his tongue, but it just wouldn't come.

"Weapons down, lads and lassies. I've seen enough to guess the end."

Roland smelled frustration waft off the two women, now free and angry. The other post-human smelled like nothing, but Roland felt him lower his weapon. Some gray, dead strand of memory pulsed in the back of Roland's brain and he guessed that it was safe for him to stand up now. So he did, and put eyes on the mystery man.

The fellow had a lopsided, square-ish jaw with a very deliberate five o'clock shadow. His nose was thick and bulby. His red hair was tangled into dreadlocks that were more the result of inattention than stylistic choice. He was tall, muscular but lean, with a bare chest that was covered in tattoos of black snakes. They writhed in time to the beating of his heart. He wore nothing but a pair of red leather chaps and a broad, calm smile. His bare penis swung pendulous in the breeze. Both of his palms were extended, out front and visible. It was the kind of gesture one used to calm an animal.

Roland's synapses fired and misfired and a string of fragmented memories ran through his mind. He recalled a really good hot dog on a sunny day, push-ups in the mud, searing pain in his genitals, and the taste of shitty ditch weed. These memory fragments were all somehow tied to the man in front of him.

It took Roland a moment, but as soon as he got a full look at those coal-gray eyes, the man's name clicked into place.

"Oh shit," he croaked, "Jim?"

Roland hadn't spoken to a person in...months, at least. Maybe longer. He sounded more like a suffering cat than an English-speaking human. But Jim understood him.

"Ayep," he said.

Roland sighed, looked at his severed arm, and crudely shoved it into place. It had clotted a bit, and his stub burned as the tiny robots in his blood got to work re-attaching his once-and-future limb.

"Jim," he said again, sounding a bit less like a frog after a six day coke binge. "You fucked up my house, man. That's not cool."

Roland didn't know how long he'd known Jim. He couldn't even pin down the man's last name. But he was pretty sure they'd fought together, back before the Revolution. And he was certain they'd had a threesome with a devilishly handsome Spetznaz man. He couldn't remember that guy's name, or why they'd all been in Panama, but he didn't expect that was the sort of experience past-him would've shared with someone who wasn't a friend.

"You remember me?" Jim asked.

"Basically," Roland answered.

"Good. Cause I got a favor to ask."

Chapter 3

Sasha.

The drone gun rotated on its axis and brought a new, slightly different chunk of cityscape into view. The world was a dull green-gray color through the lens of the weapon's camera. Once again, there were no humans in sight. That was the norm, but Sasha still logged in for her scheduled gun-time every day. Her parents would have been mortified if they knew how she was spending her few hours of free time. But she had a good VPN, or at least it was good enough to hide her activity from her non-tech-savvy elders.

She doubted they'd ever suspect her of something like this. Sasha was a good student. Her grades guaranteed her admission to the American University in D.C. At one point she'd had a shot at being her high school's valedictorian, and maybe of gaining admission to Stanford. But then she'd discovered the true Gospel and given herself to Christ. Her grades were still good, but probably not good enough to earn her an educational visa to the California Republic. The extra time the old-her had dedicated to school was now spent glued to a guncam, browsing live feeds from various Christian militias, and reading everything she could from the few pastors brave enough to preach the Word.

The new-her didn't want to go to school near San Francisco, capital of what Pastor Mike had called "the world's most sinful nation." Sasha didn't even really want to go to college in D.C. What was the point?

"Sash'," her dad called from the kitchen, "dinner's on. Cheese enchiladas!"

There was still nothing in her line-of-sight. For the eleventh month in a row she was spending sixty-five AmFed dollars for the privilege of staring through a camera at nothing for a half hour a day. Sasha had been warned about this when she'd signed up to support the Woodlands Martyr's Brigade. Their drone guns didn't see much action; the front had been stable for the last year. Rumor said the number of backers who'd even gotten to fire during their turn was under a dozen. Sasha had hoped she'd be a special case.

Something moved!

Just as she thought about killing the app and going downstairs, something moved across her drone's field of vision. It happened again, and Sasha realized that the somethings were armored soldiers, sprinting past her weapon. She locked the drone on one and, for the first time ever, selected the "Fire Approval" button. A second went by, then another, and then a red box replaced her firing reticule.

Target Declined: Friendly Fire!

"Sasha!" her mother called up, in that grating voice that meant she was almost frustrated enough to start yelling, "Get down here!"

She stared at the box for a long moment. *Friendly fire.* That made sense, as she belatedly realized the men had been rushing out of territory occupied by the Martyrs. *Good thing they check up on us before we pull the trigger.* Her heart pounded a little at the thought of killing the wrong soldier. But at the same time she noticed something odd; the men were still coming. They rushed past the drone camera in waves, ten feet apart, ducking low and hefting heavy weapons. She must have watched at least a hundred of them pass before she realized what this meant.

A new offensive. Oh God–

"Dial Alexander," she told her deck. A comm window popped up about six inches in front of her hand, to the left of the large drone control screen that hovered above her. Anyone without a deck would've just seen a seventeen-year-old girl, lying on her bed and poking at the air. But Sasha saw the space in front of her as a giant screen curved around her body. She opened another window and flung it up on her right side. It was populated with links to the camera feeds of all the personalities she followed. Most of them were located somewhere in the Republic of Texas, and more than half of the feeds were dark. It was hard to tell just what was happening on the others. Sasha decided she'd get a faster update on the situation through her news aggregator. She reduced the other windows and shifted them to her periphery, then she opened a new window and waited a half-second for her curated newsfeed to populate. Her deck kept ringing Alexander while she scanned the headlines.

Reports of Explosions Across The Dallas Front
Texas: Extremists Advance into SDF, Republic Territory
Reports from Dallas Suggest New Offensive By "Heavenly Kingdom"

A half-dozen rings later, Alexander picked up.

"Sasha?" he asked. His voice sounded distant. There was noise on the line. After a second or so Sasha heard a boom and then a strange cracking sound that had to be gunfire. It didn't sound like it did on the movies, or even in the few VR shooters she'd played. Sasha's heart had started to pound by the time she responded.

"Yes, Alexander! I was just on my drone, and it looks like something's happening. The media's saying it's another offensive."

"They're right, for once," said Alexander. "And they're still wrong at the same time. This is something new, Sasha. I'm sorry I couldn't tell you before. But it'll all be clear soon."

"Is this just the Martyr's Brigade?"

He smiled, and Sasha's face went red.

"No. Sasha, something wonderful is–"

"Are you near the front? Are you part of the fighting?" Sasha interrupted. She'd never have done that normally. But she could hear what sounded like gunfire over his line, and Sasha was scared.

"I'm with the second wave," he said. "The 'tracks are moving us into position now. I'll probably have t–"

Whatever else he'd been about to say was cut short as all of Sasha's deck apps closed at once. Her digital world was replaced with a red box that read, "PARENTAL LOCKDOWN: Come to dinner, Sasha!"

"Moooooooooooooom!" she screamed down the stairs as her eyes welled up with tears at the unfairness of it all. Alexander, the man she was pretty sure she loved, was going into battle for the first time. He was fighting right now to re-establish the Rule of God on Earth. *I should have read him a poem or said something beautiful and stirring. Something about how my love for him was as everlasting as God's own love.* It should have been a powerful moment, but her heretic whore of a mother had ruined it for enchiladas.

Sasha stormed downstairs, ripe with fury but unable to vent it. Her parents couldn't know she'd been giving money to a militant group. They wouldn't have to drop in on her talking to Alexander to know what she had planned. Six kids from her high school had already left for the Republic of Texas to fight in one militia or another. It was a problem across the American Federation, but here, in Virginia, parents were particularly wary. The border of the United Christian States was just an hour's drive from her front door. Ratlines in the UCS brought thousands of young volunteers yearly from the heart of corporate America to the various militia groups that battled across Texas.

"Sasha Marion, what did we interrupt that was so important you had to yell?"

"I was praying, Mother."

It wasn't really a lie. Pastor Mike had said that every deed done in support of the Heavenly Kingdom was an act of prayer.

Gwendolyn Marion frowned back at her daughter. She was a stern woman, with a broad Germanic face and dirty blond hair pulled back into a severe bun. Faint crow's feet trickled out from her eyes, but those were from choice rather than time's formerly inevitable march. Gwendolyn was the chief of surgery at Annapolis General Hospital. She'd been taking JuvEn treatments since she was twenty. She'd only decided to let the crow's feet through once Sasha had turned seventeen.

"You can pray as much as you want, honey. But right now it's dinner time and this is something we do as a family."

Sasha thought JuvEn was unnatural. Heretical. God had created each human to age a certain way. Using science to disrupt that natural process was an act of blasphemy. She yearned to say something cutting, hurtful in response, but she fought it down.

"*You don't have to obey your father and mother, if they try to keep you out of the Kingdom of Heaven*," words from one of Paster Mike's weekly 'casts rang in her ears, "*but the Lord God still calls on us to respect our parents.*" He'd added that well-behaved kids were the ones who caused the least suspicion, and had the best chance of successful escape.

"Yes, ma'am," was all she said as the family settled into their chairs.

Her brother Ian was just five and unusually quiet for his age. He smiled at her as their father doled him out an enchilada.

"Sash', who's Alexander?" he asked, and Sasha felt the blood run out of her face.

Their father, Tony, smiled wryly at the remark as he spooned a proportionally larger serving onto his own plate.

"Alexander, huh? Maybe this means another boyfriend. It's been, what, four years?"

Tony had opted for fewer cosmetic JuvEn treatments than his wife. Sasha loved her father's receding hairline, his slight jowls, his graying hair. He was still a heretic, but at least he wasn't a vain one.

"He's not my boyfriend, Dad. Just a boy I talk with sometimes. We pray together."

Gwendolyn rolled her eyes a little.

"Such an exciting adolescence you're having," she said. Sarcasm swelled every word. Sasha didn't rise to the bait. Her self-control was iron now. She wouldn't give them any cause to worry or call the authorities. It was better, even, for them to think Alexander was some boy from school. If they thought her principles were thawing, they'd be less likely to suspect what she had planned.

The Marion family ate companionably for several minutes. Tony talked about some "cockeyed nut" who'd come into his office at Deutsche Bank looking for a loan.

"He wanted three million, at 19 percent, to—get this—build a blimp to take tourists from AmFed to Louisiana without crossing UCS territory. And I'm like, first of all, I can name a hundred boat charters that do the same thing, and second..."

Sasha tuned most of it out and tried to focus on eating. But knowing Alexander was out there, facing death for his faith, killed any appetite she otherwise might've had. She ate mechanically, without really tasting it, until her plate was almost clean. Sasha was already planning her exit when her mother spoke up.

"By the way, the school called today and said you still haven't been by to get sized for your graduation robes. They need at least forty-eight hours to print them out. You're running out of time."

"Sorry, Mom," she said, "I know that's important. I've just had a lot on my mind lately. The FST was last week."

Sasha had gotten very good at telling her parents what they needed to hear without actually lying. The Federation Standardized Test had been last week, and she'd certainly had a lot on her mind lately, but the FST hadn't been keeping her up at night. It was little more than a rubber-stamp for a student like Sasha.

"That's OK, sweetie," Gwendolyn said. "I know how important your school work is to you. I just want you to have a fun graduation experience. That's important."

There's a war going on a few hundred miles from your door. Men are dying for God's Kingdom, and you think school matters to me?

But Sasha just smiled, told her mom she loved her, and went back upstairs to her room as soon as it was politic to do so. She re-activated her VPN and popped her deck into "stealth" mode, which displayed a curated selection of websites and chat apps for her mom and dad, in case they came by. She drew a new private window about two feet in front of her face and split it in half, between a face-comm with Alexander and a newsfeed full of her favorite militia press offices.

Her jaw dropped.

Voice of the Prophets' main headline was, "Republic of Texas Forces Clash With Martyrs!"

"Judgement day is here!" she read in a social media post from one of her favorite sources in the area, a twenty-something mechanic who lived on the fringe of the Republic and supported the Heavenly Kingdom. He'd posted a picture of the Governor's Mansion in Plano. It was burnt around several of the windows and riddled with holes. Gone was the Republic's flag, replaced by a white banner with a burning black cross in the center. Sasha sent out another call request to Alexander and switched over to Al-Jazeera's feed to learn more.

It galled her to use a news source run by Muslims, but she'd learned from experience that Al-Jazeera had the best reporters on the ground in the Republic. They'd negotiated coverage deals with several of the militia groups, including Alexander's. The first thing she noticed was that their last article had gone up well over an hour ago. But the titles of the four most recent articles painted a vivid picture.

Republic Capitol in Galveston Burning: Military Coup?
Republic Media Feeds Go Dark: SDF Under Attack in Dallas
Pastor 'Mike' Donaghan Announces New Offensive for 'Heavenly Kingdom'

How could there could possibly be a new offensive against the secular forces in Dallas? The Richardson line had been locked in a stalemate for the last year. Alexander had told her often how outnumbered and outgunned the Martyrs of the Heavenly Kingdom were. "We're holding our own, but only by the grace of God," was his usual refrain. The idea of them advancing again on the SDF seemed impossible.

"Nothing is impossible with God," she could almost hear Alexander's voice echo in her mind's ear. She glanced over at his chat screen, but it still just showed the standard "Dialing" symbol. Frustrated, Sasha brought up her militia newsfeed. This was one of her most cherished possessions: it had taken months for her to sort out the most influential Christian militias in the area, find their official spokesfeeds, and cross-index them based on which groups agreed with the strict neo-Calvinist doctrine that she, Alexander, and Pastor Mike all knew to be the One True Word of God.

And for the first time since she'd started the feed, each and every militia she followed had posted the exact same message.

The First Battle of Armageddon Has Begun.

Sasha was confused for a minute. She'd done her homework, she knew the final battle of the End Times was supposed to occur at Mount Megiddo, in Israel. But she thought back to Pastor Mike's sermons. He had talked about the "battles of Armageddon" many times. The coming end times and the central place of the Heavenly Kingdom in the world's last battles were constant refrains in his sermons. Sasha had always believed the battles of Armageddon would come. She'd just thought she had more time.

Sasha was frustrated and a little hurt. Alexander must have known this was in the offing and kept it from her. She understood, of course. But she was furious at herself for being so far away from the action that he'd been forced to hide this from her. The first battle of Armageddon was beginning, just a few hours south of her bedroom. She could either stay here and rot in the American Federation or prove God with her devotion and move there. It didn't even seem like a choice, really. If good men were fighting and dying to restore the Kingdom of God on Earth, it fell to her to travel there and support those men.

She thought of Alexander. His liquid green eyes, his scraggly beard, the way his still-boyish voice broke in excitement when he lost himself in the Spirit of the Lord. Her beloved was out there right now, fighting and maybe bleeding to bring the Truth back to the world. The least she could do was join him.

Weeks ago, Alexander had given her the contact information for a man named Brother Andrew. He'd called the other man a "deliverer." Sasha knew her parents and the AmFed authorities would've described Brother Andrew as a people smuggler. She hadn't reached out to Brother Andrew yet. In her fantasies, she'd always waited to graduate before escaping to the Heavenly Kingdom. She was still a few weeks shy of her eighteenth birthday, and had hoped to at least spend that with her parents before setting off.

But now, as she scrolled through articles about the Martyr's breakthrough and immersed herself in snapvids of cheering soldiers raising cross banners over newly captured neighborhoods, Sasha felt a powerful anxiety overtake her. She *needed* to be there. There was no other option.

Sasha flicked open a window on the left side of her viewspace, typed in the address she'd memorized for Brother Andrew, and sent him a message.

"I'm ready to go."

Chapter 4

Manny.

Manny woke up needing to piss, and also to the sound of explosions. He couldn't quite tell which was more to blame for his sudden, unwelcome consciousness. His lizard brain woke up and shouted, *"Get the fuck out of there, you asshole!"* a second later. Manny got to his feet, grabbed his gear bag, and looked around for the journalist.

Reggie still seemed asleep. But he stirred just as Manny started toward him and another thundering "boom" shook the world.

"Christ! What was that?" Reggie asked in a slurred voice, heavy with sleep.

"Mortars," Manny explained. "I think I heard rockets, too."

"Shit," the Brit exhaled sharply. "Is this bad?"

Manny shrugged. "Those sound like small mortars. Very short range. But we're miles behind the line, so–"

A deafening explosion shook the world. It was loud enough that Manny didn't even properly hear it. He felt it, hard and hot against his skin. The sheer impossible noise of it pulled the air from his lungs and the thoughts from his head.

The next instant he was flat on the ground. His eyes darted left and right for cover. He spotted something: an artificial cave, built into a corner of the main room, perhaps a hundred feet away. It looked like some sort of shrine or temple. Manny could see the walls were thick with melted candles, colorful drawings, and a variety of brass symbols.

He grabbed Reggie by the shoulder and shook, hard. The other man jerked, locked eyes with Manny, and mouthed, "What?"

The fixer pointed toward the shrine, pulled himself up, and sprinted toward it. The journalist followed, and soon both men were huddled in the little substructure, staring out at the devastation that had overtaken the RAP. They could see two holes in the roof. The huge circular kitchen/bar looked like it had taken a direct hit. Beer spurted from shattered taps, and Manny could see what looked like blood staining the white oak of the bar counter. Flames licked somewhere off in the distance, on the other side of the vast structure. The air smelled of smoke and burning grass.

More blasts sounded in the distance, including a few that were just too loud to be mortarfire. Now that he focused, Manny could also hear the chatter of machine guns. It was distant, but not nearly as distant as it should've been.

Manny dug into his pocket, found where the deck was clipped inside, and thumbed the power button. Static flashed at the edge of his vision as his implants started up. He nearly always ran in minimalist mode, which gave him access to his maps and his communications suite and nothing else. He selected his address book and subvocalized his cousin's name; "Alejandro." It rang.

And rang.

And rang.

"Hey man?" Reggie said, his voice oddly calm. "I think we might need to get the fuck out of here."

Manny looked over at the Brit and then toward the flames. They were bigger now, and closer. He could see a dozen or so men and women fighting the fire with hoses and extinguishers. They didn't seem to be winning. Elsewhere, he saw small groups breaking cover to run for the exits. The sound of alarm bells echoed across the big structure. Alejandro hadn't responded, which meant he was fighting or dead. Either way, Manny and Reggie would need to find their own ride out of this mess.

It had been a while since the last mortar had landed on the complex, and the small-arms fire still sounded distant. This seemed as good a time to make a break for it as they were likely to get. So they ran until they hit the nearest exit doors, shoved them open, and staggered outside into the balmy Texan night.

The asphalt parking lot outside was filled with newly minted refugees, perhaps two hundred of them. Most carried at least a go-bag. A few had managed to drag out more. They were ringed by a widening cordon of armed men and women, fifty at the most. The militia clutched antique weapons, mostly small arms, and stuck like glue to the Hesco barriers that ringed the old parking lot. Here and there Manny caught sight of a man with an RPG, or a light machine gun. It was a force meant for scaring off bandits. The rockets still thudding in the distance told Manny these men and women faced considerably more than their match.

A green blink of light caught his attention. Reggie had engaged his lapel camera. The Brit fixed him with a look that said, "Dude, what did you expect me to do?"

Most of the survivors were probably recording to their decks too. But Reggie's little camera could do considerably more: it scanned the world around him in a 360-degree arc. It also recorded the journalist's own physical data: his heart rate, his respiration, his adrenaline levels. Everything he saw and felt was being recorded for later consumption. The Brit was carving out a little slice of the war for safer parts of the world to binge watch.

Vehicles started to arrive. The Project's motor pool included three tracks built to carry large groups of people in semi-armored semi-safety. The commune's rapid reaction force set to work, loading children and wounded up first. There was no panic, no hysteria, just an exhausted efficiency that spoke of long practice. Manny saw glassy eyes and clenched jaws, but very little open rage. *They're so very used to it,* he realized. Scattered throughout the crowd, Manny saw people whose bodies rattled with the sort of palsied shock that artillery leaves in its wake.

Reggie just stared out at them, mouth slack. His left knee twitched, the foot below it pumped against the ground. Manny guessed he was caught between the urge to step out and talk to some of them and the voice of sanity in the back of his head that knew how tone deaf that would be. Manny put a hand on the journalist's shoulder.

"We need to get the fuck out of here, and our ride is off comms," he said. "I'm gonna suggest we hitch with the RAP. We're their guests, they'll make room for us. But if you'd rather drag ass I know a safe neighborhood about six miles into the city. We could probably hire a ride there."

"It looks like they're a little short of room as-is," said the Brit. "Those tracks can't hold more than twenty or thirty people each."

Manny smiled a little, "Twenty-four. But that's just if you're attached to things like 'seats.'"

Ten minutes later, Reggie and Manny clung to the hood of the track as it barreled down the broken streets of ciudad de muerta, bound for a staging area in Deep Ellum. The fighting sounded much closer by the time they left. Manny guessed the small-arms fire couldn't be more than a couple of blocks away. He and the journalist held on with white knuckles and tried not to linger long on what would happen if they lost their grip.

"The Martyrs are past the command post!" the Brit shouted in sudden realization. His voice strained to be audible over the roar of engines. "Holy shit, they have to be, right?"

Manny thought about the geography for a moment. It was possible the Martyrs had only broken through in a few chunks of the line. But that would mean DeShawn and the others were alive and surrounded or fleeing. Those were the best case scenarios.

"I think we might be fucked," Manny said, stunned by the realization. For the last year Major Clark had been his most reliable source in the SDF. That post had seemed immovable, impregnable for its significance in his little chunk of the world.

The track creeped slowly. Parked facing them were two smaller, armored SDF tracks with swiveling cannons on their roofs. Soldiers scurried around them. They pulled sections of thin, frosted gray Stihlglass barricades off the vehicles and started setting them up to form a new defensive line. Manny watched two militiawomen wrestle with a large olive-green case covered in boxy Cyrillic script. They pried it open and Manny saw a huge metal tube and what looked like a lot of antique optical equipment. It was probably an old wire-guided missile launcher, something that had been an antique before the Revolution. He'd never seen the SDF use anything that old. They had drones half this size that carried even more firepower.

Had them yesterday, at least, he thought.

The track slowed to a cautious stop and honked. Manny glanced back at the driver. She had her hands in the air in a universal "Please don't shoot us" gesture. Two of the soldiers peeled off from their efforts and approached, weapons in hand but not aimed. The driver opened her door and shouted something down at them. One of the men responded and gestured vaguely downtown.

Manny couldn't make out exactly what was being said, but the driver's face contorted in a fury that was impossible to miss.

"Something's fucked," Manny said to the journalist. "I think we're all about to lose our ride. Look!"

He pointed to the makeshift barricade, and the dozen or so soldiers who filtered past it and toward the track. The driver yelled and one of the other passengers near the front started to shout. The soldier's face remained impassive but he put a hand on his sidearm and repeated a command Manny didn't even need to hear. A few seconds later a soldier with a megaphone arrived and addressed Manny, Reggie, and the new refugees.

"Citizens, your vehicle has been requisitioned for medical use by the SDF. Please dismount in an orderly fashion. Injured and pregnant individuals may stay aboard."

The man repeated the order, this time in Spanish.

Reggie's jaw clenched. Manny could see fear in his eyes, but Reggie just nodded and started to climb down off the track. Manny did the same. Not all of the track's passengers were as compliant. There was a lot of shouting and even a few shoving matches between the militiamen and the passengers. But in the end, the SDF got their way. Manny gathered fairly quickly that they planned to send the civilians a mile or so back, to a holding area behind the new line. That was the last fucking place in the world he wanted to be, so he approached the officer who'd been arguing with their driver.

The man had no rank insignia on his uniform, but that wasn't unusual for militia. His fatigues were old U.S. Army issue. His armband identified him as part of the Citizen's Front. Manny found that odd: most of the militia at this barricade were with Raza Front or the PPA. This much intermixing wasn't normal. It pointed to a lot of casualties among the SDF.

"Disculpe, señor–" Manny started,

"Chico, no ahora mismo. I don't have time to debate–"

"No, señor. My cousin Alejandro is with the Citizen's Front, 9th Battalion. He was our ride. We were taking this journalist," Manny jerked his head toward Reggie, who stood a few feet back, "...and we got caught up in the attack."

The officer nodded, then grunted. Manny studied his face for a moment. The man was middle-aged, with a weak chin and enough extra meat on his bones to suggest that this was his first frontline duty in a while. His eyes were bloodshot, his hands clenched. His attitude softened a bit at Alejandro's name.

"Alejandro Hernandez?"

"Yeah."

"He's a good man. Or was," the officer said darkly. "All our frontline units were wiped out, or near enough. The whole SDF's been pushed all the way back to ciudad de muerta. If he's alive, he's a prisoner." The man shook his head. "Sorry, chico. There's not much I can do for you or your friend."

"We need to get to Waco. I know there's a hospital there; that must be where you're sending the serious injuries, right? Dallas doesn't have anything left with a full ER."

The officer nodded. "These tracks are headed to the field hospital, in Oak Lawn. But we've got a couple deuce-and-a-half's loading up at Firebase Jiminez. If you can get there on your own I'll radio ahead and ask Major Peron if he's got space.

"I know Peron!" Manny almost shouted. "I went to school with his nephew, Hector." He couldn't stop himself from wincing as he said, "If you'd give him my name, that might help."

The other man's eye cocked up in a *really, motherfucker?* look. But then the soldier asked, "And your name is?"

"Manny Sanchez."

He nodded. "Good luck then, Manny. I'll radio ahead. You and your friend get to the firebase...rapido, comprende?"

Manny nodded and turned to Reggie.

"We've got a ride. But it's going to be a bit of a hike."

It was less of a hike and more of a panicked jog. The streets around them were filled with dozens of people carrying their possessions in bags and rusted old shopping carts. Manny had never seen Dallas this crowded. Less than a million people still lived in the old metroplex but most of them seemed to be out in the streets to watch the world end. Sirens sounded, courtesy of the city's old civil defense system, mixed every few seconds with the distorted voice of a woman reminding them that all motor-vehicle-use was prohibited.

"Any civilian vehicles on the road will be assumed hostile and targeted."

The road traffic was all military. There was less of it than Manny would've hoped to see. In the space of a few seconds, he watched three pairs of Cougar assault vehicles race up toward the front, carrying squads of armored troopers in their open beds. He also saw one convoy of five anti-drone tanks. Each was the size of a four-door sedan, with two linked chainguns on a turret that scanned the sky in fast, jerky arcs. There was a troubling amount of dead space on the road between the two units.

By the sound of it, the fighting had only grown more intense throughout the morning. The crack of small-arms fire had been almost drowned out by the all-consuming roar of close-support drones in the sky above them. The only noises to rise above that din were the stippling bangs of mortar fire and the pop-pop-popping of cluster bombs.

Firebase Jiminez was about two miles back from the new front. It was mainly a staging area for the SDF's Autonomous Artillery Division. The AAD was made up of men and—mostly—drones from all the secular militia groups active in the Dallas area. The firebase itself wasn't well-fortified. The only physical defense was a fence topped with razorwire to keep civilians out. That wouldn't be much of a barrier for a determined assault. Until a couple of hours ago, Jiminez had been far enough from the front that an assault wasn't considered possible.

After an hour of mixed jogging and running, Manny and Reggie took a left onto Park Lane and the firebase came into view. It had been built in the bones of an old apartment complex. Several buildings had been converted into offices and the rest left as barracks space. The apartments were situated across the road from a tall, very thin, parentheses-shaped building that looked out over a large field dotted with landing pads. The name "Top Golf Driving Range" was still visible on one side of the building.

Several hundred militiamen were hard at work throwing up defenses. Stihlglass sheets had been set up to screen a dozen machine-gun nests. Further back, soldiers piled sandbags in front of two howitzers. Manny and Reggie weren't the only civilians trying to gain entrance. Fifty or so people clustered by a checkpoint in the middle of the road, a hundred yards ahead of the construction efforts.

The checkpoint was new, just a sandbag machine-gun emplacement manned by six fighters in powered body armor. They were overwatched by a pair of ancient Abrams tanks, positioned on either side of the road. The soldiers in the middle checked documents and let the occasional civilian through. They turned most people back. There were a lot of shouts and violent gestures on the part of the civilians. While Manny watched, one of the guards raised their rifle up and fired it just to the left of a screaming man's face. He recoiled in fear and pain, clutched his ears, and staggered away from the checkpoint.

The wait was only about ten minutes, though, with the thudding artillery at their back, each of those minutes felt like an hour. But soon they stood face-to-mask with one of the armored militiafolks. Reggie went stiff at once, his pupils the size of dinner plates. He had never seen powered armor up close before. Manny couldn't blame the man for being unnerved. The reflective, bug-eyed ballistic glass of the helmets and inhumanly broad shoulder armor made the wearers look like Cronenbergian gorilla/mantis hybrids.

The shortest armored soldier was well over seven feet tall and almost as broad as two men. Their gender was impossible to discern. But a feminine voice leapt from the speakers.

"State your business," she said. "If you're looking for shelter, you'll have to head to North Park Center; we don't have room for you."

"I'm Emmanuel Sanchez. Major Peron should have my friend and I on your list."

The woman was silent for a little while as she called up the list. She clucked her tongue between her teeth, and the high-fidelity mic in her suit made it sound like she'd done it next to his ear.

"Well, hell, there you are."

Her helmeted head bobbed at them.

"Alright, you're in. Come through quick. You stop being my fuckin' problem as soon as you're inside."

They made their way toward the actual front gate of the firebase, passing squads of militia struggling with Hescos and setting up firing positions behind the Stihlglass palisade. Manny and Reggie walked past it all and to the firebase's front gate. They were let in without any fuss, which surprised Manny a bit, but he wasn't about to question it.

On the other side of the gate they found themselves adrift, unescorted and surrounded by pure chaos. There were other civilians inside the walls, huddled in small groups around piles of backpacks. They sat, wide-eyed and shaking, and waited for whatever deliverance the SDF could provide. Soldiers rushed through the clots of humanity in groups of two or three. Often their arms were filled with machinery, or paper, or even crates of munitions. Everyone's eyes were wide and full of fear.

For a while, Reggie and Manny milled around with no real aim, unable to enter any of the buildings. Manny found them an unclaimed place to sit that looked like it would be easy for Mr. Peron to find. And then they just sat there. At one point Reggie offered him a protein bar. Manny tried to eat it, but three bites in he accepted that his appetite just wasn't there.

What do I do if Dallas falls? He ran through his finances over and over again, mulling over which European visas he could afford, and how long he'd be able to survive in each country. *I could make it a year, maybe eighteen months, in Croatia.* He'd been studying German for the last year though. *I can learn Croatian in a year*, he tried to convince himself.

He also tried to ignore what he'd be leaving behind if he hopped the next flight from Austin to the E.U. He didn't want to think about Oscar's wife and child, how they'd get by without their dad's income. He didn't want to think about his own father, or the rest of his family, and how they'd fare if Austin fell. *You can only afford to take care of YOU here, Manny.*

It was two hours before Major Peron found them.

The older man's skin was a deep, sun-charred brown that seemed at odds with his narrow face and thin wire glasses. He had the look of a high-school history teacher who'd been transplanted into a warzone. There was something drawn and strained in his expression that spoke of deep exhaustion. His eyes were bloodshot and his nose was swollen slightly red. Manny could remember seeing that same face, a bit younger and wearing a t-shirt rather than digicam, at a hundred different slumber parties. Mr. Peron was Hector's dad. Mr. Peron made them kettle corn and let them watch violent movies on the family projector.

Major Peron, Manny had to remind himself, *he's Major Peron.* The Major favored Manny with a sad smile. "Madre de dios, Emmanuel. It's fucking good to see you. Have you seen your cousin, Alejandro?"

"He was with us last night," Manny said. "Before the attack."

A pained look crossed the Major's face.

"OK," he nodded and forced a smile back across his lips. "I hear you boys need a ride?"

"Yes," Manny said. "If you could get us back to Waco I have enough connections in the area to get him," Manny nodded back to the journalist, "into Austin."

"And what is your name, sir?" Major Peron asked the journalist as he extended his hand.

"Reggie," the Brit responded. "Thank you so much for helping us."

"I'm afraid there's not much I can do right now. The situation is still very fluid. We've set a new defensive line running from the Lakewood Crater to Love Field. With any luck, the Martyrs have spent the bulk of their strength and we'll hold them there."

"And if not?" Reggie asked.

Mr. Peron laughed and scratched his head. "Well, if the line breaks then I'd guess our collective pooch is screwed. We'll begin the evacuation if it gets much worse. But right now we're still waiting for convoys of wounded to get back through the lines." He gestured out at the considerable amount of fenced-off open space in the firebase. "This whole place is about to be a big open-air hospital." He gave Reggie a severe look. "I won't tell you not to record them, because quite frankly everyone here is too busy to police that. But I will ask that you show tact and respect in your documentation."

"Of course," said Reggie, with enough sincerity that Manny believed him.

"Alright," he clapped Manny on the shoulder and, after a second's pause, embraced him. "Hold on out here for a while. I'll try to send some food in a little bit."

Manny and Reggie both thanked Major Peron, and he trundled off into the old Top Golf building to do his part in coordinating the defense.

"So what now?" Reggie asked.

"We wait," said Manny.

Three hours passed. More and more wounded men streamed into the base, carried on stretchers and in ambulances and, in several cases, stacked like firewood on flatbed trucks. The wounded were set up on cots and piles of blankets in the grass and, wherever possible, in paved sections of the driving range's old parking lot. Medics, far too few medics, hustled from soldier to soldier at a frantic, manic, unsustainable pace.

For a while, there was nothing to do but follow Reggie around while he interviewed the wounded men and women who were stable enough to talk. They all reported shock at the speed and ferocity of the attack. Their testimonies drove home the fact that this was something new. Tendrils of fear crept up Manny's spine. It was all he could do to keep moving with his journalist.

"Hey man," Reggie said, "look at that fellow." He pointed to a soldier with the top half of his head wrapped in blood-soaked bandages. Something about the man's broad and square chin looked familiar.

"Isn't that one of the men we met yesterday?" Reggie asked. "The Major?"

Holy shit. Reggie was right. That had to be DeShawn Clark. Manny ran over to him. As he drew closer it became clear that DeShawn was in even worse shape than he'd looked at a distance. His shirt had been ripped open, exposing a muscular chest drenched in blood. Three white plugs of hardened celox wound spray were visible across his abdomen. He'd been shot repeatedly and had what looked like a shrapnel wound on the side of his head. *At least he's breathing,* Manny thought.

"Major Clark?" he said, and, to Manny's surprise, the warrior poet stirred.

"...Manny? Sweet Jesus, is that you?" DeShawn asked in a slurred voice.

"Yes sir," Manny said.

"You know, I was damn sure you'd been killed. Haven't had that much time to think about you in the last few hours, of course. What with everyone dying and all."

"I'm glad you're alive," Manny said. And he was; Major Clark had always been good to him. "Do you know what happened to Hamid? And Colonel Milgram?" Manny asked before the thought had fully crystallized in his mind.

Major Clark tried to lift his head and almost cried out from the sheer agony of the movement. He didn't speak for a few seconds, he just took deep, slow breaths. But then he started to whisper.

"The last sunbeam lightly falls from the finish'd Sabbath, on the pavement here, and there beyond it is looking, down a new-made double grave."

"What?" Manny asked, confused.

"Walt, actually." Major Clark laughed, winced, and then explained. "Walt Whitman, that is. Sorry, imminent death makes me go for the deep cuts."

"So they're dead, then?" Manny asked.

Major Clark coughed and, again, his lips curled up in an agonized cringe. "...I think so," he managed to say. "I think everyone from the command post is dead. I was out grabbing a smoke when they hit us. Came out of nowhere. Drone artillery. Heavy stuff. The whole place lit up like Christmas."

Two loud booms sounded in the distance. Major Clark tensed up. Reggie cringed. To Manny, the whole situation seemed almost too unreal to justify a reaction.

"Like that," Major Clark said. "After, I grabbed who I could and tried to save as many men as possible. Fighting retreat, you know? We linked up with as many fighters as we could but every time we'd set a line they'd break through. They had so many damn drones. I've never seen Martyrs use drones like that."

"What do you mean?" Reggie asked.

"Well they've always had drones. But usually just as defensive aids, for when we'd make a push. We've got enough jammers that their hardware was no use in our territory, since none of their shit goes autonomous."

"So what," the journalist asked as he drew in a bit closer, "do you think they've changed their minds on autonomous drones? Or is this something else?"

Major Clark rolled his head, just a little. It seemed to be the only gesture he could make without hurting himself.

"I don't know, kid," he said. "Whatever's happening, it's totally new. And it's totally fucked us."

Major Clark was taken by another coughing fit. This one lasted a long time. Blood bubbled up and out from the corners of his mouth. Manny wanted to call for a medic, but he couldn't see any of them who weren't dealing with patients who were even worse off. Eventually the coughing subsided, and Major Clark drifted off into unconsciousness.

They sat with him until the night fell and Mr. Peron finally came to get them. He looked exhausted and somehow broken. His skin was sallow and so pale it was almost yellow. His uniform was soaked with old sweat stains and he had two lit cigarettes in his mouth when he found Manny and Reggie. Manny wasn't sure he'd ever seen the older man smoke. Mr. Peron noticed his surprise.

"I've taken up smoking again," he said with a hollow laugh, "since I don't expect to survive to the end of the week."

"That bad?" Manny asked.

"Worse," he shook his head and then seemed to notice the Major. "Is that Deshawn Clark?"

"Yes sir," Manny said.

"Is he...?"

"He's alive. And he seems to be stable, for now."

Major Peron looked relieved.

"That's one spot of mercy, then. Hopefully we'll get him out in time. On that note: I've confirmed that we've got a convoy of wounded heading out tomorrow AM, as soon as our scouts clear the route. You'll both have a seat in that convoy."

"Thank you so much sir," Reggie started. Mr. Peron cut him off.

"It's no problem, son. Do your job and tell people what's happened here."

"What are you going to do, sir?" Manny asked.

Mr. Peron looked into his eyes. He'd always had an intense stare. His edge had been evident even when he'd been driving the boys to soccer practice or taking them out for pizza. Now his eyes bored into Manny's heart so deeply that the fixer finally understood what that phrase meant.

"I'm going to die here, Emmanuel," he said. "I'm going to die here, like your cousin Alejandro died here, because it's the only thing I can do that might protect our home."

Manny felt an intense urge to look away, to cast his eyes down. But he didn't. He held Mr. Peron's gaze and braced himself for what came next.

"What about you?" Mr. Peron asked. "What will you do if they reach Austin?"

"Wait, is that on the bloody table?" Reggie interrupted.

Mr. Peron paused for a moment and considered his words. "I don't know," he said. "No one does. But the Martyrs just broke through at Lakewood. We won't hold Dallas for another day."

He pulled Manny in for a hug and kissed him on the cheek. When he pulled back, he kept his hands on Manny's shoulders.

"I've always been proud of you, Emmanuel. I think that what you do here," he nodded to Reggie, "has value. But there are times when our homelands require more of us. What are you prepared to give for Austin?"

Manny clenched his jaw. *I plan to be on a plane out of there in the next twelve hours, if possible.* But "I don't know, sir" is all he said. It was hard to meet Mr. Peron's eyes. When he did, he was sure the older man saw the guilt in them.

Mr. Peron didn't say anything though. He just led Manny and Reggie over to where the convoy was assembling and slipped them a pair of MREs and some bottled water. "The best I could do," he said apologetically. He left them at the disembarkation point. Manny's last clear sight of the man who had helped raise him was of his slumped, sweat-stained shoulders trudging back to the firebase's command center.

They sat there for hours. Neither of them talked much. One by one the wounded men were loaded carefully onto the assortment of old half-tracks, buses, and trailers that made up the convoy. Once they were seated, there was another two hours of wait time before the convoy got moving. Both Reggie and Manny found time to nap, but neither of them were really rested when the dawn broke and the convoy set forward.

By the time the ramshackle assortment of trucks and broken soldiers started on its way to Waco, the sound of mortarfire was so constant it had almost become white noise. The small-arms fire wasn't as loud, but it was also clearly much closer than it had been when they'd arrived at Firebase Jiminez. As the convoy rolled out onto the old access road that led, eventually, to Waco, a flight of drones roared past them and toward the new front line.

"Those aren't SDF drones, are they?" Reggie asked, without actually looking at Manny. His gaze was focused on the two medics in the back of the truck as they moved from soldier to soldier.

"No," Manny confirmed. "Those are Austin Civil Defense forces."

The Brit whistled through his teeth.

"So, you think this means the SDF ran through their drones?"

"Could be," is all Manny said. The track, and its escort, lumbered through cracked remnants of the old highway system. They accumulated hangers-on, civilian vehicles piled high with refugees, as they rolled along. The civilians stayed back, leery of the convoy's guns but trusting in its presence for protection. By the time the convoy finally left the Dallas sprawl, their tail stretched back to the horizon line.

Manny had seen similar sights before, when his parents had fled the DFW area for Austin's relative safety. Here and there, on and in the cars behind them, he saw small figures that had to be children. Kids like he'd been, fleeing the same city he'd had to flee for the same basic reason. Manny's stand-out memory from that time wasn't the terror of seeing a mortar land for the first time, or anything about their flight out of the city at all. Instead, it was from the next day, at their first refugee camp, when he saw his father in line for their daily ration of food. A journalist had passed by, taking the sort of pictures Reggie's lapel camera now snapped mindlessly. Manny's dad had been crying, ashamed that he'd needed "charity" and even more ashamed to have fled the family home.

More than anything about that time, Manny remembered how his father had hidden his face from the photographer. The gesture had told Manny more about their new status in the world than anything an adult had actually said. Behind him now were cars full of mothers and fathers and children, who were about to have their own searing experiences. Manny hated how familiar this felt to him. He hated that, for Reggie, it counted as the adventure of a lifetime.

Manny looked at the journalist, at the awe and innocent excitement in his eyes, and tried to imagine Reggie's life back home. None of the individual pieces of that life would be new to Manny. His world also had bars and parties and apartment leases and term papers. The thing he couldn't imagine was the sense of security. Living life without the constant threat of war.

He'd been so close to securing that life for himself. *If they'd only waited six months.* But they hadn't. And now Manny had a choice to make: stand and fight, or run with what he had and hope for the best. Manny leaned back, as much as his precarious seat allowed, and stared out at the burning city that had once been Dallas.

"Goddamn," he muttered to himself, "I gotta get the fuck out of Texas."

Chapter 5

Roland.

Twenty years ago Camelback Mountain had towered over a wealthy suburb of Phoenix, Arizona. Then had come the civil war. Power, food, and water shortages made the city's 130 degree summers insufferable for all but the hardiest or most chromed. Millions fled for less vicious climates, or simply died from exposure and starvation. Now Phoenix was a looted, crumbling ghost. But Camelback Mountain still hosted a version of human civilization.

CamelToe was a city-state of roughly five thousand. The name had come about because the settlement's founders, homeless teens, thought it was funny. A few hundred orphaned or abandoned kids had settled in the McMansions clustered around the mountain's western side and foothills. They'd scrounged grow lamps and engines and weaponry and, today, the denizens of "the Toe" had the strongest city-state between California and the Kingdom of Albuquerque.

Roland was their guardian.

Mind you, they'd never asked him to guard them. The polis had been doing quite well, thank you very much, when he'd shown up and built his shack in the middle of their only park. A delegation of armed Toe-ans had shown up to politely evict Roland and he'd been forced to carve off their foreskins as a show of dominance. They'd sent a single negotiator next and worked out a thoroughly beneficial arrangement: Roland would aid in the city's defense in exchange for his now-departed shack and, twice a year, all the narcotics he could carry home from their harvest.

It was an arrangement Roland had enjoyed. He was frustrated that Jim's men had forced him to destroy his beloved hovel. But it was hard for him to be angry, all the same. The sun was out now, and it was early enough that the day's heat had yet to set in. The great red desert and the carcass of Phoenix stretched out around them and, to Roland's eyes, it was all beautiful.

Once Jim had called the fight, a pair of boxy, armored heli-transports had flown in another squad of his men. They'd assembled a brunch spread, complete with a table and two wicker chairs. Roland hoped his old friend was doing this to show off and not planning an actual meal. The acid twisted Roland's guts into knots and effectively killed his appetite. He was still high enough that familiar boulders around his home seem to flex and wobble like great mounds of red jelly.

Jim's face, however, was rock solid. Roland focused on it while the rest of the world blurred. A towel came into his hands, and he realized a moment later that Jim had handed it to him. Roland wiped the crusted gore from around his shoulder, where the tiny robots in his blood had finished re-attaching his arm. It was a messy process that involved a lot of shuffling bad blood out of the skin in sludgy red globs. The globs looked a bit like the boulders, now that he thought about it.

Jim's mercs were over by one of the aircraft, getting worked over by a medical team that must've been waiting in the wings this whole time. The acrylic stink of fear wafted off them from thirty feet away.

Once the table was up and the spread was set, Roland and Jim sat down to watch the last rays of sunrise turn into boring old daylight. A lackey handed them both steaming mugs of coffee. Roland took his black and Turkish, so thick it was almost pudding. Most humans made it too weak for his taste, but this cup was perfect. He sipped deeply, and the warbly acid-lines straightened and grew just a little bit thicker.

"It took forever to teach them how to make it right," Jim said. "Having human orderlies is a bit of a trial. I think there's something about us that breaks their brains, just a bit." Jim sipped his coffee and added, "I got a theory about that, by the way."

Roland let out a harsh, phlegmy exhalation that meant, "I don't care." Jim continued all the same, sipping his coffee and then launching into a spiel.

"My theory," he said, "is that Homo sapiens just aren't built to acknowledge a higher form of life. Not one that's flesh and blood and staring them in the face demanding service. I think deep in the human brain there's the race memory of running up against Neanderthals. They were bigger and stronger and faster than humans. But we...they still wiped the Neanderthals out. I think humans look at us the same way their ancestors looked at Neanderthals."

Roland grunted, because that was easier than talking, and because he really wasn't listening. His eyes were focused on the shimmering surface of the coffee. Sober, his brain kept his thermal vision on a different mental track from his color and infrared vision. But while he was tripping they all sorta bled together into one multi-tone mass of information. So he stared, enthralled, as red heat bled off into the white air around them. The math of it all was rendered as a beautiful swatch of colors, some of which weren't even visible to human eyes. Roland lost himself for a moment.

"If you were any other man I'd prick you with a sober stick right now," Jim said, clearly irked. "It's been a long time since someone's ignored me."

"Not ignoring," Roland managed to say. The words came out wet and mushy. He'd taken a round to the lung apparently, and the repair efforts played hell on his throat. His eyes were still locked on the psychedelic sprawl of color lifting off from his coffee. He had to force himself to take another sip. The mild stimulant surge helped him break off his perseveration and he met Jim's still weirdly solid gaze.

"Sorry, but this coffee's more interesting than your bullshit," Roland explained. "Blame the acid."

Jim laughed. The snake tattoos on his torso curled and corkscrewed in simulated excitement. "Y'know," he said, "there's a new movement in the post-human, ah, community. Started up in Idaho, in one of the intentional communes. They take a pretty strong anti-narcotic policy. Apparently it distracts us from the important work we should be doing."

"Fuck that," Roland said, and spat on the ground for emphasis.

"I don't disagree," Jim nodded, and produced an enormous and very phallic blunt. He lit it, pulled deep, and passed it over. Roland took a long drag and eased into a slump as the THC did its slow work.

"So, Jim," Roland said after a few more passes, once the acid and weed had time to push his brain into a hazy new equilibrium, "why are you here?"

Jim gave an eloquent shrug, popped the blunt out of his mouth and stared at the curling smoke. Roland stared too. In his eyes, it was wreathed in a chartreuse-black halo of heat that seemed to almost vibrate near the cherried tip.

"To catch up," Jim said, "and to offer you a job."

"Job?" Roland snorted. "I need not your filthy lucre. Look at this wealth that surrounds me," he made a broad gesture that encompassed the broken remains of his hovel. "What could you possibly offer?"

"Well," Jim said, "for starters I can replace your hot plate. I think Bigsby broke it with his body."

"So I'll steal another one," Roland said. "What do you really have?"

"I'm gonna guess a few million won't pique your interest?"

Roland blew a fat, wet raspberry. "I don't even care what currency you're talking about. What good'll money do me?"

"Not even Cascadian scrip, eh?" Jim asked with a grin.

"Cascadia?" Roland had heard the name, of course. Last he remembered, the Pacific Northwest's premier independence movement had been agitating to secede from the Coastal Pact. "Is that a thing now?"

"As of six years ago," Jim said. He took a deep pull on the blunt, handed it back to Roland, and exhaled a thick white cloud as he spoke. "And they just finished their own civil war, so the value's skyrocketing. You really don't get out much these days, do you?"

Roland's response was another deep gulp of his coffee.

"Anyway," Jim continued, "I know you don't care for cash. But there is something I think you might want, and I can buy it back for you if you'll help me out."

"Wait– buy it back? Buy what back?"

Roland recognized the snake-man smile on Jim's face. He had the vague sense that he'd seen it before, enough that the sight of it set his hackles arise and sparked an itch in his left trigger finger. He took a deep hit from the blunt and handed it over to Jim.

The other man took the blunt with his left hand and made a gun shape with the fingers of his right hand. He pantomimed a shot to the head. His lips made a barely audible "pow."

"Memories," Jim said. "I know you're only playing with half a deck, maybe less. Surprised you remember my mug to be honest."

Jim took a final drag from the blunt, which was barely the length of a thumbnail now, and passed it off to Roland.

"But science, eh, she's kept right on lurching forward the last ten years. There's a neuro team up at MIT, they reckon they've made a breakthrough. Alzheimer's research, initially. But they think they've figured out how to straight-up recover memories from damaged brain tissue. Their tech has reversed a lot of injuries the old science said was permanent."

Roland felt a painful tugging sensation in his chest. He thought back to the woman from his dreams, with the damascene teeth. He saw her every few weeks, trapped in some foggy memory or another. Her name felt like it was always on the tip of his tongue. He didn't know what she'd meant to him, but the thought of her twisted his heart into knots. It was maddening, not even knowing what she'd been to him, or he to her. Roland frowned, turned his head and locked eyes with Jim.

"You think a bunch of fed-funded school scientists are going to help me?" Roland asked. "I got a strong feeling nonc of the governments on this continent are fans of me."

Jim waved a careless hand. "Less the issue," he said. "Those AmFed motherfuckers are pragmatists. I've been in and out of the Northeast a half-dozen times, just this year. You do work they value, and they ignore a little terrorism."

"Memory's hazy," Roland said, "but I know 'little' isn't accurate. I think we killed a skyscraper."

"Ha! You don't remember that? The Dimon building, in '41. A hundred and twenty floors of rich pigs wallowing in shit. We slipped a bomb in during an austerity summit led by the CEOs of the Big Four. Bugged their conference room so we could hear 'em scream when that first blast cut the support beams. It was better than sex."

There was a peculiar joy in Jim's eyes. His chest-snakes writhed in orgiastic glee. Roland felt queasy.

"Roland," Jim added, "the sons of bitches had it coming."

"Maybe," Roland said, "but I know we didn't just kill CEOs. I remember other times, kids..."

"Not kids," Jim insisted. "Heirs. Young enough to take full advantage of JuvEn. The future undying Lords of Capital. They had to go."

Roland shivered. "Even if they did, I'm sorta glad I don't remember it."

Jim shrugged, swirled his coffee cup, and stared into it for a minute. If he'd been anyone else, Roland would've been able to read his emotions by the scents coming off of him and the microexpressions on his face. Most post-humans were just as easy to read as regular humans. It took a mix of very specific surgeries and a hell of a lot of time spent in practice to hide anything from Roland. It said a lot that Jim had considered the expense worthwhile.

"Violence is the coin that buys the future," Jim said. "There was a time when you explained that to me."

"I don't remember that conversation," Roland said. "But it's been years since I've taken a life. A couple of foreskins, one guy's hand, sure. Sometimes a point needs making. I haven't killed anyone in a long time though. That's why all the folks you sent to my door are still alive. And I mean to stay on the wagon.

"Killing's not wanted on this mission," Jim assured him, "just property destruction. I need two or three days of your unrivaled shit-up-fucking expertise."

Roland flicked a suspicious eyebrow at his old friend.

"Property?" he asked.

Jim nodded, "A couple guys might need crippling along the way. But no killing."

"So what's this gig?" Roland was interested now, in spite of himself.

"Sabotage." Jim's lips curled up in a feral grin. "Over the last few months, we've noticed a substantial build-up among the radical Christian militias in North and Central Texas."

"We?" Roland asked.

"My own organization, and the AmFed's Central Intelligence Agency."

Roland couldn't help but laugh, "I remember enough of the old days to appreciate the irony of you working with the CIA."

Jim's head cocked just a little to the left. He grimaced. Roland wasn't sure, but he thought his friend might be little embarrassed and defensive.

"Anyone who lives long enough becomes a hypocrite," Jim said with a shrug. "I'd hoped to hold out longer, but their satellite coverage is fucking phenomenal. I'll send you the intel–"

He made a flicking gesture toward Roland with his right index finger, and then frowned in annoyance. "You might be the last darkbrain on this continent, you know that?"

Roland wasn't sure why he'd disconnected himself from the Internet. It seemed to annoy other people, but he rather enjoyed it. His hindbrain had absorbed petabytes of data before he severed the link, so he'd never found himself needing to consult a Wiki to remember the equations behind the Coriolis effect, or a bullet's trajectory. He could have walked from Canada to Venezuela without encountering a plant or animal, his distributed mechanical brain couldn't name. The only downside to his situation was that he couldn't keep up with politics or bleeding-edge military technology. He only gleaned that sort of information by experience or conversation. And, being a creepy, god-like being who sometimes circumcised trespassers, Roland didn't have many conversations.

One of Jim's aides ran up and handed Roland a paper-thin tablet. Jim directed him through a dozen satellite images of what looked like vehicle and ammunition depots. Roland's hindbrain recognized the Dallas road systems immediately. A surge of sense memory hit him–

–FIRE so much fire, the smell of it only drowned out by the intense stink of thirty-thousand people panicking at the same time. Roland felt bullets dig into his flesh. He saw hate in the eyes of the advancing cops and felt a corresponding surge of glee as his brain started to pump out battle drugs. He squeezed his trigger–

Roland shook his head and pulled his mind back into the present moment. Jim frowned but didn't say anything. He just pointed back at the tablet. Roland focused again. It appeared to be a satellite image of a defensive line in Dallas. He noted a large number of military vehicles piled into several parking garages.

"What's going on here?" he asked.

"Suit carriers," Jim said. "A couple dozen of them."

Roland shook his head. "Impossible. That'd be enough to support, what, six-hundred power-armored fighters? Those are nation-state numbers. I know the Republic of Texas is a shit-show, but there's no way they'd let some insurgent militia build an army like that in their borders."

"Maybe not," Jim said, "maybe so. Truth told, I don't care what's parked in those garages. You blow 'em up, I get paid, and you get your fancy surgery."

Roland felt uneasy. The job itself seemed too simple. The kill-team Jim had sent to wake Roland up probably could've done this job with a few reinforcements. It seemed weird that some nutbar extremists could get their hands on that many suits. Roland just didn't trust the whole situation.

"Jim?" he asked. "Can you promise me this memory thing will work?"

"Fuck no," Jim scoffed. "I can't even promise you'll survive. This is a bleeding-edge mad-science operation. The AmFed is willing to break international law to work on a wanted terrorist. I'm half sure they just want to see what happens when they start poking around your skull. You might be making the worst mistake of your life here. But at least you'll die after blowing up a bunch of gear owned by Christofascist assholes."

Roland considered for a long moment, and then nodded his assent. "Alright then, you've convinced me. I'm in as long as this stays a sabotage mission. No killing."

"No killing," Jim agreed.

They both stared out at the vacant desert for some time. Roland found himself humming along to a song he couldn't name, or even remember hearing. Jim hummed along with him. He put a hand on Roland's shoulder. That felt good. There was something about human contact that none of the machines in his head could replicate. They sat for a while longer. Then Jim squeezed Roland's shoulder and stood.

"Time for another peaceful war, then," he said.

Chapter 6

Sasha.

"History is a messy thing, class. Even a question as simple as 'When did the Second American Civil War begin?' doesn't have a clear answer. Some scholars say the first shots were fired during the failed Montana secession movement in 2040. Others will name the Dallas water riots of 2041, or the bombing of the Dimon building six months later by leftist militants. You can make a good, evidence-based case for any of these."

Mr. Dane was a good lecturer, with a rich baritone voice and a habit of animating his lectures with vibrant hand gestures. He was Sasha's favorite teacher and one of her favorite people. Mr. Dane was a heathen, of course, but he was still a sweet man. She appreciated his even-handed perspective and his commitment to the unbiased study of history. It broke her heart that no one else in her Advanced Placement Continental History class seemed to appreciate him.

The other twenty-four students stared ahead with slackened jaws and unfocused eyes. They were all deep in their decks, messaging friends, browsing snapvids or playing whatever game was popular right now. Decks were far too entrenched in modern life for the schools to force them off during class time. Instead, the school filtered the WiFi and forced students to download apps that restricted access during school hours. This had led to a thriving underground trade in apps that countered the school spyware and covertly lifted the blocks.

The district IT team was locked in a perpetual, losing battle to spot and crack these programs. But on a practical level, the teachers, like Mr. Dane, just had to accept the intrusion. The students didn't ignore him entirely. But very few of them gave him their full attention. They didn't give anything their full attention, really. Most of her peers went through their days half-reading two or three conversations, playing games, and scrolling through several social media feeds even when they were out in the world, surrounded by people.

Pastor Mike called it "the death of joy." That was the name of the essay in *Revelator* that had first turned Sasha onto the Heavenly Kingdom. He'd railed against "distraction culture," which he said not only robbed mankind of a relationship with God, "but it also robs us of the little moments. The quiet joys of living are drowned by a flood of data. It's a mosquito bite on the human soul, and the masses have convinced themselves that the abatement of discomfort from scratching this itch is the same as happiness."

All around her, classmates scratched their itches while Mr. Dane lectured. He looked so lonely up there. They all looked lonely.

"So," Mr. Dane cleared his throat in an attempt to pull at least a few of his students out of their stupor, "as we close this unit I'd like to ask you all a simple question: what should we call the war that split the United States? Your textbook calls it 'The Second American Civil War.' In the Northwest and the Christian States, they call it 'The Revolution.' By next Monday, I'd like each of you to upload an essay arguing which name is more appropriate. One thousand words, please."

The bell rang. The other students got up slowly, in twos and threes, and made for the door. Sasha was one of the first up. But Mr. Dane called to her before she reached the exit.

"Ms. Marion, would you mind holding back a moment?"

Sasha stiffened. She glanced, involuntarily, up to one of the government's propaganda posters on the wall. It showed a young man with a brightly-colored backpack surrounded by burnt-out buildings and rubble. A green rocket hung above him like the Sword of Damocles, an instant away from impact. Next to the young man were the words, "Think Again. Step Back."

"Yes sir?" she asked as she approached his desk.

Mr. Dane fixed her with a kind smile. He looked around forty, although that was no guarantee of anything. His eyes and lips were creased with smile lines though. She liked that about him.

"You seemed a little bit distracted today, Sasha. That's not uncommon for most of my students," he gave a slightly forced laugh, "but you're normally so engaged. I just wanted to make sure everything's OK."

Over the last year Sasha had started building up a stockpile of what she called "Defensive Smiles." She had one for when her parents were worried. Another for her (few) friends, and another for the school administrators. The smiles were calculated to reassure everyone that she was still normal Sasha, and she certainly wasn't planning to escape to the Heavenly Kingdom.

But she'd never worked up a smile for Mr. Dane. She genuinely enjoyed his class, so it hadn't seemed necessary. She decided to go with her "Friend Smile" and hope that worked.

"I'm OK. I'm just, y'know," inspiration hit her, "...the news today is so scary, what's happening down in Texas. I'm worried."

Mr. Dane visibly relaxed. "Ah, yes. I can see why you'd be troubled by that. I think it's taken everyone a bit by surprise." He paused and struggled with his words. "I...expect it must be somewhat more difficult for you than the rest of the class, being a Christian."

Her smile faltered a bit. She knew she was supposed to act like one of the tame preachers the government trotted out, the men and women who'd claim Christianity was all about peace and love. They'd say that the Lord's truth could co-exist with the "equal truths" of other faiths, and with the secular world of the AmFed. That all felt wrong to her. But a little imitation was worth avoiding suspicion.

"My faith is stronger than a handful of terrorists," she said to Mr. Dane. "There are a lot of Christians in the Secular forces, you know. They'll win in the end, won't they?"

Mr. Dane's smile remained unchanged, but his eyes bored into hers. Sasha was more comfortable with eye contact than most teens but she found this deeply uncomfortable. Invasive, even. After several long seconds he spoke.

"I fear it's going to be a long, bloody fight before that happens. We're very lucky to be insulated from all that madness. You know," he sighed. "An eleventh-grader over at Jefferson High was killed fighting in Dallas yesterday. The news just broke."

Sasha hadn't been aware. *But thank God for him, and his sacrifice,* she thought.

"That's awful," she said. "I can't imagine what his parents must be going through."

"No, you can't," he agreed. And then Mr. Dane broke eye contact. He looked down at the ground, and his voice dropped an octave as he asked, "Did you know I had a son?"

Genuine surprise passed over Sasha's face. "No sir, I didn't."

He shrugged and gave up on his smile. It wasn't much more than a ghost now, anyway.

"I married young. I was a dad at nineteen. And by the time he was nineteen, the whole country was coming apart."

He reached down to his desk and picked up a small, rather battered-looking red button. It had the letters "rj" printed in lowercase letters across the front. Mr. Dane stared at it. Something twitched, under his left eyelid. He bit his upper lip. He was silent for a long beat. Then he swallowed and looked up at Sasha.

"Do you know what this is?"

"No," she said, reluctant and pretty certain she ought to have known.

"In the years leading up to the revolution, there were a lot of different activist movements founded and spread by anonymous radicals. They'd organize flash demonstrations and coordinate direct-action campaigns. The pins were one sort of 'ID badge,' so when you showed up for a flash demo you could quickly identify your comrades."

He shook his head ruefully.

"It sounds silly now. All I can say is, at the time, it made sense and it felt meaningful. The anonymous voice I listened to was a guy named Red John. He had these videos about history, politics; he explained the whole world and what was wrong with it in a way that just felt right. I started playing his stuff for my boy, Mikey, when he was thirteen or fourteen. I just wanted him to know what was going on. I thought I was doing the right thing."

Mr. Dane's eyes looked watery, and heavy with the ghost of old tears. He seemed to have trouble keeping his voice steady.

"Mikey grew up believing hard. And when the fighting broke out he was young and strong, and so very ready to fight for the world he believed we all deserved."

Mr. Dane set the pin back on the desk with its cover facing down. His eyes were red. "He died in Denver," Mr. Dane said, and his voice broke a little, "shot through the head when the National Guard pushed into Westminster."

Sasha put a hand on Mr. Dane's shoulder. It was an instinctive move, blessedly honest. She silently thanked God for this moment of connection to the educator she so admired. He smiled back at her. "Thank you. I don't mean for this to be a lecture. I don't think those tend to work. Just..." He glanced back at the table, "just be careful about putting your faith in charismatic men and their ideas."

"I will," she said.

A minute later, as she left the classroom, a notification pip lit up at the top right corner of her vision. She wink-clicked it and saw a message from Brother Andrew.

"Bus stop 23A. 4:30 PM."

The rest of the day passed normally enough. In the afternoon they had an assembly about the suicide of a classmate. It was the third this year. Principal Hargrave delivered the same platitudes they'd all heard a hundred times. There was a lot of talk about suicide hotlines and chatrooms, of all the counseling services the school had available. Sasha knew none of it would help. Almost 20 percent of teens in the AmFed would attempt suicide. Every year that number ticked up a few tenths of a percent, and the government had no idea how to stop it.

Pastor Mike blamed the rash of suicides on the emptiness of secular life, the spiritual hole at the center of capitalism, and the self-worship it fed. Sasha thought he'd hit that right on the money. Even the United Christian States still engaged in global capitalism, and in doing so "fed a dark god in permanent opposition to the Lord Almighty" (Pastor Mike, again). She knew Principal Hargrave's lectures were pointless, but she sat through the assembly and gave the right smiles to the right people the rest of the day. She focused on her studies as best as she could despite the growing anxiety in her gut.

Two weeks ago, she'd read a Pastor Mike article in *Revelator*, "Don't Talk Yourself Out of Heaven." It had clearly been written for the conflicted faithful, just like her.

"I've received messages from hundreds of you who say, 'I'd love to open myself up to martyrdom, but I'm a doctor, or a police officer, or an engineer, and I think I can do more to glorify God where I am right now.' Brothers and sisters, *these are the doubts of the Serpent.* Don't be fooled. No one stays in comfort because they want to bring glory to the almighty.

"Our Lord does not speak to us from comfortable places; he spoke to Moses in a desolate desert, from a burning bush. He delivered His greatest sermon atop a mountain. Jehovah wants our souls to be so on fire with devotion that our own lives mean nothing before His flame. The Heavenly Kingdom is that cleansing flame. What a gift that it is here, now, in your lifetime! What a tragedy it would be to miss this chance at salvation."

She recited that passage again and again, throughout what she now knew would be her last day at school. The words steadied her as she waved goodbye to Mr. Dane at the end of the day (*"these are the doubts of the Serpent!"*). They calmed her when she looked into her backpack, which held the small "go-pack" she'd put together that morning. It was just a change of clothes and handful of hygiene items. That seemed woefully inadequate, but anything more would've looked suspicious.

Leaving. I'm leaving.

It was only now, on the cusp of leaving, that Sasha realized how much she was going to miss movie night with her friends, central heating in the winter, reliable Internet access...

Our Lord does not speak to us from comfortable places.

It took her an embarrassing amount of time to find the bus stop. She was scared to use her deck—she'd shut it off as soon as she left school—and she didn't know the city bus system very well. She'd taken buses to school for years but her parent's car had always driven her around the city. She was ashamed of how anxious she felt about riding a city bus. Here she was, on her way to a warzone and possible martyrdom, scared of public transit.

"Be strong and courageous, and do the work," she recited David's advice to Solomon. "Do not be afraid or discouraged, for the Lord God, my God, is with you."

That helped a little. Thinking of Alexander's smile, his green eyes, and the strong lines of his jaw helped more. Sasha didn't like admitting that to herself. It felt too carnal, almost sacrilegious. But she knew that what mattered to God were her actions. Even if her flight to Zion wasn't done with a completely pure heart, God would forgive her. Her sacrifice to build the new Jerusalem would outweigh the sinful part of her mind that couldn't stop imagining how Alexander's strong arms would feel when they finally wrapped around her.

She waited at stop 23A. 4:30 came and went. By 4:45 PM, her chest burned with barely restrained panic. She was sure the people passing by all knew her secret plans. A pair of police officers passed her at one point. One of them, a woman not much older than Sasha, flashed her a smile. For a long time she was convinced this had been a sign, that her communiques had been intercepted and the police or the FBI were onto her plan. But the police didn't come to stop her. And, after a quarter hour that felt like days, a brown sedan rolled up to the bus stop. Its window peeled down and Sasha locked eyes with a care-worn young man in the back.

"Sasha Marion?" he asked.

"Yes?" she said. "Are you Brother Andrew?"

"As I was with Moses, so will I be with thee."

That was the passphrase Alexander had told her to expect. It was all Sasha could do to stop from bawling right then and there. She got into the car.

The man inside was exactly what she'd have expected of a man in Brother Andrew's profession. He had long, straw-colored hair and a ragged beard. There were deep pockets of exhaustion under his brown eyes, and well-creased smile lines around his lips. He wore a simple black suit with no tie. Everything about the way he looked and the way he dressed spoke of quiet devotion and humble service. Here, finally, was a man of God: not a pressed, preening dandy like the pastor at her father's church. Not a "hip" young pretender like the Baptist Minister who'd given a speech on "inclusion" at her school last year. Here was a real, road-weary man of the Lord.

"I know how you must feel right now, Sasha," he said. "You're relieved. You never thought you'd make it this far. You didn't know if you'd have the courage to take the final leap of faith. But you have now, child, and your soul is secure."

Sasha melted. The knot of anxiety that been twisting in her guts suddenly untied itself. Her eyesight blurred, and she realized that she'd started to cry. It was all she could do to look over to Brother Andrew and whisper, "Thank you."

Together, they drove to a little white-walled suburban house, maybe five miles away from the only home she'd ever known. The car stopped, but Brother Andrew gestured for her to stay in the vehicle while he stepped out and knocked on the door. Another man, shorter and balding, stepped out. They both hustled back to the car, their eyes darting left and right. As soon as they made it inside, the car sped off fast enough that the acceleration pushed Sasha back in her seat.

The new man sat across from her in the autonomous car's second row of bench-seats. He was older, in his fifties if he hadn't taken any JuvEn treatments. He had tired eyes with deep bags beneath them. While Brother Andrew radiated calm self-satisfaction, this man seemed nervous and a little frantic. He clutched a small briefcase with white-knuckled hands. Sasha smiled in an unconscious attempt to calm him. He smiled back. Brother Andrew spoke.

"Ms. Marion, this is Brother Brian. He's going to disable your deck. It's the only way we can get you across the border to our people in the Christian States."

Brother Andrew smiled and put a hand on Brother Brian's shoulder. The other man took this cue to open up his suitcase. He started to assemble something small, silver, and intricate. Brother Andrew kept speaking.

"All it'd take is one phone call from your parents or your school and the police could spot your precise position from the GPS unit in your deck. This car is a deadzone, so you're safe inside it. But as soon you exit you'll be back on the map. So we need to remove your deck before that happens."

"Will it hurt?" Sasha remembered how it'd felt when they'd first implanted her deck, like having a new tooth forcibly inserted into her jaw. She'd been four or five at the time. Her head had hurt for days.

Brother Brian didn't look up from his briefcase as he answered her. "Yes. I've got a topical anesthetic, but nothing stronger. It'll hurt."

Sasha nodded gravely. She had anticipated this. A little pain was a small price to pay to become one of God's elect few. She thought of Paul and Silas, stripped and beaten with clubs on the orders of a heathen magistrate.

God shows his love through salvation. We show ours through sacrifice.

The memory of Pastor Mike's words helped to ease her fears. She'd miss her deck. But Alexander had said there'd be replacements in the Heavenly Kingdom. In another minute Brother Brian had finished assembling the tool. It looked like a cross between a syringe and a handheld shopvac. At Brother Andrew's urging, she moved over to sit on the bench seat next to him.

"Now lay across my lap, and angle your temple toward Brother Brian."

A pang of fear flitted across her heart. These were men of God...but they were also men she didn't know, who were both much older and larger than her. She had to fight down the urge to panic and flee. *You're trusting these men to smuggle you across a border, dummy.*

She hesitated for a few sweaty seconds, but eventually Sasha nodded and lay down in Brother Andrew's lap. Her heart beat so loudly she could hear it crashing in her skull like ocean waves. Brother Andrew put his strong hands on her. He tightened his grip. *He's holding me down,* she realized. And although he tried to restrain her in a comforting way, the liquid mass of panic in her chest almost boiled over.

There was a sudden, sharp pain as Brother Brian plunged the needle in through her temple and then a dull, throbbing feeling like a migraine. Sasha felt dizzy, disoriented, and then nauseous in turns. She blacked out for a few seconds. When she came back to herself she realized she'd been vomiting. The floor of the car was coated in the remains of her lunch. Some of it had gotten on Brother Andrew's pants leg.

Brother Brian looked disgusted. But Brother Andrew was all smiles and comfort. "Jesus hears your suffering, sister. He knows what you are giving up in his name. You will reap the dividends of this investment in your soul."

He helped her up and guided her to the opposite bench, where she laid down and continued to clutch her throbbing head. She drifted off, or passed out, and when she came to, the interior of the car had been scrubbed clean, leaving behind only a brown stain and the lingering smell of sick and antiseptic. Sasha guessed an hour or more had passed, although, without her deck, it could have been more. They were in the woods now, driving along a country road.

Brother Andrew explained that they were just a few minutes away from the border, and almost as far as an automobile could take them. Soon they'd stop in the town of Franklin, right on the border of the UCS, and she'd meet the men who would help her on the next stage of her journey,

"The main border stations are blanketed with cameras," Brother

Andrew said. "But we're right in the thick of the Blue Ridge Mountains here. They can't watch every inch of 'em. We have some coyotes here who know where the 'holes' are. One of them will spirit you across."

"Coyotes?" Sasha asked.

"It's an old term," he said. "A coyote is someone who helps smuggle people across national borders. Usually the phrase has somewhat... mercenary connotations. But the men we work with are true believers, soldiers in the Army of God. You needn't fear, Miss Marion."

A few minutes later, they rolled into Franklin. She'd never heard of the place before, but a quick look around told her most of what she needed to know. Most of the buildings were empty. The storefronts were boarded up. The City Hall was in disrepair, and the skeleton of a once-mighty Walmart Supercenter dominated the south side of town. There was clear fire damage around its roof and entrances. Twenty or so years ago, when the Civil War had been at its height, Franklin had swollen with refugees. When the war had ended, the refugees had gone elsewhere, and the city had been left gutted and exhausted in their absence.

The car stopped outside of a public park. Sasha noticed that the grass was overgrown, and the sidewalks around it were cracked and broken. She shared a quick prayer with Brothers Andrew and Brian, and then they bid her farewell. The car pulled away and Sasha was alone. She'd been told to find a park bench and wait "just a few minutes." So that's what she did.

"A few minutes" turned into ten, then fifteen, then twenty. Sasha began to worry again. That was when she really started to miss her deck. Normally she'd have been able to catch up on the latest news from Zion, read one of her favorite issues of *Revelator*, and maybe even touch base with Alexander. Without it, she only had the throbbing pain in her head to keep her occupied. Sasha's mind wandered to the rolling mountains on the horizon. She'd never spent so much as a night out camping before. The wildest animal she'd ever seen was a squirrel.

And there are bears out there.

That scared her more than the prospect of being arrested, or even the fear of what might happen to her nearer to the fighting. Dying in a drone strike or from a sniper's bullet would be quick and expected, given where she was going. She'd spent a lot of time thinking about dying from sudden violence. It had acquired a patina of romance in her mind's eye. But dying on some mountain, to a slavering monster from another age?

Sasha shuddered, seized by a chill entirely at odds with the extreme heat of this August day. It was 109, at least. Sasha rooted through her bag and pulled out a small leather-bound Bible she'd received as a Christmas gift from her dad two years ago. She opened it at random and found herself in the book of Jonah: "In my distress I called to the Lord, and he answered me. From deep in the realm of the dead I called for help, and you listened to my cry."

She read on through the rest of Jonah's cries, to the whale vomiting him up onto the shores near Nineveh. The word of God calmed her. She grew so engrossed in her scripture that she was taken completely by surprise when the coyote found her on the park bench.

"Miss Marion?" A man's voice, weathered and gravelly, said from behind her. "You'd serve us both well by putting that book away. This is not a safe place."

She looked up at the coyote. He was older than she'd expected, in his mid-forties at least. He had a mop of greasy blond hair, a round face, kind blue eyes, and a slight paunch that spoke more to his age than inactivity. He had thick biceps and forearms that bulged with corded muscle. His thighs were large, too. He had the look of a man who spent a lot of time on his feet.

"Mister...?" she asked.

"Jonah," he said. "You can call me Jonah."

And again, the knots in her stomach melted away. She rejoiced inside. Over and over her faith had flagged, and over and over the Lord had sent her signs of his love and approval. *That's what trusting in reason gets you*, she admonished herself, *fear and pain. God is watching out for me.* Her childish fear of bears faded away. Suddenly the world, and her future, felt bright and exciting again. After years of delay she was finally on the doorstep of Zion.

"Jonah, I'm ready to go. You lead the way and I will follow."

It took about an hour for Sasha to decide that she liked camping, and then two more hours to decide that she never wanted to camp ever again. By the time they stopped for the night she'd gouged herself open on half a dozen different tree branches, smashed her left toe into a rock and somehow managed to draw every allergen on the east coast into her nose. The headaches from her improvised surgery and her throbbing sinuses warred for dominance. She couldn't sleep, food had no taste, and her hands were too grubby and, generally, snotty, to allow her to read her Bible.

Jonah was not as talkative as Brother Andrew. He'd given her a brief run-down of things to avoid out in the Blue Ridge Mountains. He told her how to recognize timber rattlers, diamondbacks, and copperheads, although for some reason she had much more trouble retaining that information than she'd had memorizing the Pythagorean theorem, or the date and importance of the Battle of Hastings. She was supposed to watch for pointy heads, she knew that. But every time a snake slithered past her, it moved way, way too fast for her to tell the shape of its head.

Other than that quick lecture and a few admonishments for her to "step lightly," Jonah hadn't said much. He'd given her food, protein bars and nuts mostly. He'd been kind enough to let her snuggle with the heated blanket he'd brought along. She knew she'd gotten snot on it but he never complained.

When they settled into camp on the second night, Sasha was surprised to see her coyote start to gather wood and build a fire. He laughed when he saw the dumbfounded look on Sasha's face. He pulled out a small yellow bottle of lighter fluid, squirted it onto the wood, and then lit the edge of it with his lighter. The fire leapt to life, burning away at the pine needles until they caught the smaller sticks and limbs stacked in a small box. Next, he pulled two silver pouches out of his backpack and handed both to her. The labels informed her that one contained Chicken and Dumplings and the other Macaroni and Cheese. Her mouth was watering before the first "and."

"Tonight, Miss Marion, you get a fire and a hot meal. We're over the line."

And that was how Sasha learned she'd crossed the border into the United Christian States. She had successfully fled her country, and the secular rule of law entirely. The UCS wasn't a true Godly state, not by her standards. Its multi denominational acceptance was a denial of the harsh truth of God's love. Not everyone who called themselves a Christian truly lived in such a way as to earn God's gift of salvation. But just being in a country that acknowledged the primacy of God Almighty in their law and public policy was enough. For now.

There's no abortion here, she thought with awe. *No atheists on television mocking the Lord. No callow acceptance of premarital sex.* She felt a thrill at being in a place that was so much closer to her conception of "right." It didn't even matter that she was still stuck in the woods.

"Jonah?" she asked. "Do you live here?"

"Most of the time, yes." He had a quiet, soulful voice that made him seem even older than he looked.

"What made you decide to start smuggling people out of the AmFed?"

He stared into the treeline as his hands stuffed thin sticks into the base of the growing fire. Sasha watched his jaw clench and unclench, as if he was mentally rehearsing his response before he said it out loud.

"I was a United States Army Ranger once. I've been a Christian my whole life, though. Southern Baptist. I grew up in a country just as lost to sin and vice as yours is. And when the fighting started I saw an opportunity to bring my nation back to its Godly roots."

Hands emptied, Jonah rooted around in his bag and pulled out a kettle. He filled it up with water from a heavy fabric bag and placed it on a flat rock on the edge of the fire. Then he stood up, gestured for her to follow, and walked over to a nearby copse of trees.

"I joined a local militia in Marietta, near Atlanta," he said. "Most of us were vets, like me, and either Baptist or Pentecostal." He crouched down next to a tree that had been cracked in half by lightning. It was dead, and very dry. The ground around it was littered with tree limbs and thick slabs of bark. He started gathering up some of the larger pieces,

"C'mon, get down here and help. Some of these are a little damp, but we'll stick 'em around the edges to dry out. Most important thing right now is to get some middlin' sized logs in there, so we can build up a little bed of coals."

Sasha wiped a runnel of snot from her face and knelt down to help. Jonah continued his story while they filled their arms.

"Anyway, things heated up. The Army started calling in their deep reserves, guys like me who'd been out for dadgum near a decade. This was after the feds nuked Dallas, so goin' active duty again didn't sound good to anyone."

He lifted away a fallen limb, and revealed a massive log, roughly the size of Sasha's torso. Jonah shifted everything he'd gathered over to his right arm and then hefted the log with one hand. He nodded at Sasha's much smaller pile. "We prolly got enough," he said.

They headed back to the campsite. She could see Jonah was doing that twitchy jaw thing again, thinking carefully about every word.

"I grew up real patriotic, y'understand? I loved my country, fought for it down south. But I also grew up with a Confederate flag on the back of my dad's truck. I wasn't on board with those Marxists who started the civil war. So when Governor Galen had his referendum on secession, well, that felt right. I was on board with the UCS back before it was even born."

They sat around the fire again. Jonah started to add in larger branches. He slowly built the fire in a u-shape around the flat stone.

"Now I was never a fanatic. Went to church most Sundays, but I had Jew neighbors. There were a couple Muslims in my unit, good guys. I wasn't real political, y'know? But Pastor Elgins gave a speech, the only time I saw him in person, he said diversity wasn't making us strong anymore, 'A melting pot's all well and good, but the quality of the soup depends on the recipe.' That made sense to me."

He sat back, popped the kettle onto the rock, looked over to Sasha.

"The idea was, a Christian 'recipe' would make for a stronger nation. But the UCS wound up being a dadgum prosperity gospel pile-a-nonsense. Better than the AmFed, sure. Maybe we got less queer politicians, less rich Jews running things, but it's still corrupt here."

Sasha really wasn't sure how to handle this...disclosure. She'd run into similar attitudes among believers online; uncomfortable references to Jewish, gay, or gay Jewish conspiracies. That sort of nonsense had always gotten on her nerves, but she'd written off its purveyors as edgelords and trolls. Part of her thought that they might be CIA plants, hell bent on making the Kingdom look bad. But she knew they didn't speak for the actual heart of the movement.

Sasha wanted to speak up, but she held her tongue. The fact that Jonah had been nothing but kind and respectful to her didn't change the fact that he was twice her size. Who knew what he might do if he got agitated? Sasha fought for calm and recalled a specific passage from *Revelator*, in one of their guides for young women emigrating to the Kingdom.

"Know, daughters, that our Lord made your brothers and husbands both strong of body and quick to anger. It is your job to soothe, not incite. And if his wrath falls upon you in a sudden burst, remember the forgiveness and patience of our Lord. Let His example guide your reactions."

So she smiled at Jonah and said, "Tonight, I'm happy enough to be in a Godly land."

He smiled back. Sasha hoped God was proud of her for being meek as Mary. When she thought about it that way, the rest of the night was surprisingly tolerable. The food wasn't "good" by her normal standards, but it was hot and savory and after days of protein bars it was exactly what her suffering stomach needed.

Sasha wasn't aware of when she drifted off to sleep.

Jonah woke her up the next morning, not long after the crack of dawn. He handed her a box of wet napkins and walked off into the woods for a few minutes while she cleaned herself off as much as possible. When she was done, he led her down the mountain and into a small town on the border. It was Sasha's first real look at life in the UCS, and it did not disappoint.

In the twenty minutes or so they were outside she saw nine churches. There were crosses on every house, in a dizzying variety. She saw Bible quotes printed on windows of shops and cafes, and the strangers who passed them in the street all flashed warm smiles. A few offered her blessings. Sasha had never seen such public display of religion. She floated through those first few minutes on a cloud of giddiness unlike anything she'd ever known. The architecture and the environment were similar to what she'd grown up with. But everything else seemed alien in the most exciting way possible. Sasha felt so light she could almost feel the Holy Spirit lift her up. Her gleeful reverie only ended when Jonah led her up to the door of an unassuming brown, stone house.

They were taken in by another man, whom Jonah introduced as Saul. Saul looked a little younger and a lot less weathered than Jonah. He had the thin arms and stooped posture of a lifelong scholar, and his conservative white button-up shirt made him look more like a youth pastor than a people smuggler.

"Welcome, sister." He smiled, but his voice sounded more haggard than warm. "You'll want to get inside, please. There's no sense tempting the law."

Saul's house was packed to the rafters with toilet paper, jugs of water, bins of freeze-dried food, and bags upon bags of clothing. The house had almost no furniture, and no decorations aside from a large wooden cross above the hearth. There were a couple of stools arranged around a crate on the ground, which seemed to serve as an improvised coffee table. Saul sat them down, left for a moment, and came back with a hot French press filled with coffee.

"I'd suggest drinking your fill. It's hard to come by in the Kingdom right now. Most things are, I'm afraid."

"I'm not scared of hardship!" she said, a little too loud. *You sounded like a little kid. Keep your stupid mouth shut or they'll think you can't handle it.* Saul was conspicuously silent, but Jonah spoke up. "She handled herself well out in the woods," he said. "Not bad, for a city girl. Didn't have a lot of woodcraft but did have an open heart. Y'took to it well, ma'am."

Saul chuckled as he began to pour and hand out cups of coffee. First to her, and then to Jonah. Sasha wasn't entirely sure why, but she waited until both men had taken their first sips to take hers. She didn't know much about coffee, but she was pretty sure this wasn't the beverage at its best.

"Would you like to pray with us, Ms. Marion?" Saul asked.

"Uh– of course."

He extended his hands out on either side. So did Jonah. Sasha took Saul's left and Jonah's right.

"Heavenly father," Saul began, "bless this young woman who comes to you with a full heart from a land of sin and shirk. She's given up all pretense of control and yielded herself fully to your grace, Lord. Please guide her in this next journey. We pray that she makes it safely to your Kingdom and into the arms of her husband-to-be," Sasha almost peed. *Where did he hear that?*

She and Alexander hadn't even met yet. There'd been no proposal. Was he just speaking in the general hope that she'd get married, or had Alexander told him something?

"...May she obey him as she does you, Heavenly Father, and may you quicken her womb like Rachel, so that she delivers a new Joseph to our cause."

That didn't sit well, either. Sasha wanted children very badly. She knew they were in her future. But not now. Certainly not soon enough that'd she'd be praying for them already. She was grateful that they had their heads bowed in prayer; if any of this had come up in conversation first she was sure she'd have reacted in obvious shock. But Sasha calmed herself, thought of her duty to God, and centered her mind just as the prayer ended.

"And may I say, m'lady, it's a brave thing you're doing," Saul said as he reached for his cup and took another sip. "Even here, in 'God's country,' not many are willing to answer the call. Oh, sure, they'll all tell you it's the drone strikes that scare them—'I can do more good by working my job and sending money!'—as if the Lord asked Abraham to sacrifice a bag of gold in His name."

Saul kept talking, but Sasha's attention drifted. The spot on her head where the deck had been itched, all of a sudden. She scratched it, and for the second time she found herself truly missing the gadget. If she had her deck she could call Alexander and find out what was going on. But instead she just squirmed a little in her chair and hoped the men didn't notice how uncomfortable she'd become.

"Miss Marion, you alright?" Jonah had noticed. Of course he had. Sasha cursed herself and then cursed herself again for cursing.

"Yes, sorry. I'm kind of tired, even with the coffee. And I'm, um, worried about my friend in the Kingdom." She definitely stressed the word "friend" too much. "Do you think I'll be able to find a deck once I'm there? I've heard a lot of different th–"

"Ma'am," that was Saul, and his voice had no more feigned mirth. "You're about to be smuggled illegally across a heavily fortified border. There are all sorts of worldly goods in the Heavenly Kingdom. We're not paupers or savages. But as to whether you'll get a deck, well, that rather depends on what our Lord wants for you."

Sasha lowered her head a little in submission. This wasn't the time to press further. Maybe that time would never come. *You knew there'd be sacrifices,* she reminded herself.

"How are you going to smuggle me across the border?" She asked.

Saul finished his coffee and set his mug down on the makeshift table. "I'll show you," he said.

He led her past the living room and into a spacious and much cooler garage. There, a trio of workers with face masks were busy sealing up large crates of unfinished wood. She couldn't quite make out the words stamped on the sides, but the blocky font looked military.

"There was a time when it was easy enough to sneak the faithful across on foot," Saul explained, "but international concerns have forced the government to take a rather hard line. I'm afraid this is the best way to get anyone across the border."

"Wait," Sasha's gut went sour. She felt the acid in her stomach churn in a greasy boil, "Are you trying to tell me I'm going to be nailed inside a crate?"

Saul's face turned. There was no pretense anymore; he was disgusted with her. Sasha didn't really know why. All she'd done was ask questions. But then Jonah was there, with a hand on Saul's shoulder and a calm voice in her ear.

"Think of this as a blessing," said Jonah. "Most people never test the 'blind' part of blind faith."

He was right, darn it. And there was something freeing in the idea of just giving herself up to Providence. She'd done everything God had asked of her. Now he would either deliver her to Zion or the arms of the law. Either way, she'd done everything she could to obey the call of her faith. All the little sins of her life, the cursing and the anger and those dark, gnawing desires she still struggled to tamp down, those would all be forgiven. She was truly giving herself to Christ now, so nothing else mattered.

"You're right," she said, "I'm sorry I questioned it. I'll do whatever it takes to reach the Heavenly Kingdom."

She took another hard look at the cramped wooden box and the piles of aid supplies surrounding it. How was she going to fit in there?

"Whatever it takes."

Chapter 7

Manny.

Manny was used to war. He wasn't quite as used to being on the losing side of one. As chaotic as things got in ciudad de muerta, his guys had always held the upper hand. Manny had come to expect safe supply lines and reliable transport to and from the battlefield. During past offensives, the Martyrs hadn't controlled the skies.

His first hint that this had changed came when the .50 caliber machine gun atop their transport fired into the sky. It was soon joined by the echoing boom of the lead vehicle's 20mm cannon, and a sparking whoosh as anti-drone rockets arced up into the sky.

"Nuts!" Reggie yelped as the gunfire jolted him awake. He'd drifted off a half hour or so into the ride. Manny grabbed onto him and looped his own legs around the bench seat for stability. An instant later, the transport veered off of the road and into the high grass surrounding the highway. There was a flash somewhere to the left, followed by the roar and heat of an explosion. When Manny looked back, he saw the smoldering wreckage of one of their escort vehicles.

"Drones!" he shouted into the journalist's ear over the blistering gunfire.

Manny scanned the skies as their transport plowed through the tall grass. Wounded soldiers screamed as the vehicle banked and bounced and sent them slamming into each other. He caught sight of a small drone, maybe the size of his torso. It was matte black and an almost perfect oval. The only break in its seamless form was the bulge of a missile pod on its belly. A red light blinked above the weapon. The drone slowed to a stop maybe a hundred feet above them.

There wasn't time to think. The fixer shoved his journalist, hard, off the back of the transport, and then leapt off himself. He hit the ground with a painful thump that knocked the air out of his lungs and the sense from his mind. For a second the whole world was stars and shock. Manny rolled to a rough stop against what felt like a large rock. Something cracked inside his chest.

And then there was another explosion, this one louder and closer than the last one. The heat hit him like an ocean wave. Manny was vaguely aware of the scent of burning hair. His hair.

He cried out but he couldn't hear his own screams. Manny's ears rang like the inside of a church bell. It was several moments before the pain and shock subsided enough for him to open his eyes. He looked down at himself first; his pajamas were scorched and his arms were scraped and bloody from the fall. His backpack was gone. But there were no signs of serious injury. None of his bones seemed broken.

What remained of the transport smoldered half-a-football-field away. He saw a few writhing, burning shapes inside. Manny's stomach turned.

Reggie.

The pain of the fall had, momentarily, wiped the journalist from his mind. Manny scanned the field and found the other man curled into a fetal ball a dozen or so feet to his left. He ran over, gave the journalist a quick scan and determined Reggie wasn't seriously injured either. A small sliver of shrapnel had pierced the other man's bicep. He was just as scraped and bloody as Manny, but also basically intact. Except his eyes didn't quite focus when Manny looked into them. Maybe a minor head injury?

The journalist said something, a lot of somethings in fact, but Manny's hearing was all tinnitus. There was no time to talk anyway. He hoisted Reggie up by the armpits, ignored the other man's pained expression and pulled him along as he beat feet away from the flaming wreckage and the ongoing firefight. Another blast wave rolled over him, this one more distant, and then another, coming from somewhere above them in the sky.

The extent of their injuries meant their "run" was more like a hobble. Reggie had dislocated his unshrapneled arm. Manny had fucked his knee up in the fall and done something awful to his ribs. The two stumble-staggered as fast as they could manage, toward an abandoned gas station by the side of the old highway. They reached their temporary salvation and took cover inside the dusty, cobwebbed building.

"Cuntcuntcuntcuntcunt!" Reggie screamed as he slumped down against the wall. It took Manny a second to process the fact that he could hear again.

"You're alright!" he shouted. "You're fine. We're going to be OK." Manny had no idea if that was true, but he knew managing fear would be critical to their survival.

The gas station had been abandoned for a decade or more. Most of the glass was gone but the basic structure of the inside counter was still intact. He and Reggie took cover behind it, careful to avoid the piles of shattered glass and shrapnel. There were old bullet holes in the wall all around them. At one time there'd been a plexiglass window on the inside wall behind the counter, with a little bucket in it so the cashier could do business at night without letting customers inside.

Most of the plexiglass had been removed, leaving a gaping wound in the building's concrete hide. Manny stuck his head out of the hole and looked out at the site of the massacre. Both transports had been hit. Much of the field was aflame. The sick-sweet smell of burning human flesh wafted over them like a dense fog. Manny saw two of the escort trucks still firing into the sky. There was another flash above as one of them hit a drone. It corkscrewed out of the air, burst on the ground, and ignited the dry grass.

"What the fuck do we do?" Reggie shout-asked. There was panic in his voice, and quite a lot of pain, but the journalist didn't seem to have lost his wits.

"We need to get out of here," Manny said, "while those drones are still occupied."

The highway was a couple hundred feet away. The civilian vehicles following them had scattered when the attack began. Some of them had clearly been hit by machine gun fire from one of the drones. Others had crashed, rolled into ditches, and been abandoned by their occupants. Manny spotted one, an ancient white jeep, that looked like it had taken a round through the window. He could see blood inside the vehicle, but the engine and wheels seemed intact. The treeline of a sparse forest was just on the other side of the highway, a half-mile away. If they could reach it.

"Reggie," he put a hand on the journalist's shoulder. The two men locked eyes, and Manny tried to force all the fear out of his voice, "When I say so, run. Very fast. Straight toward that white jeep. Understood?"

The Brit brought a hand to his dislocated shoulder and winced in intense pain. But then looked back to Manny and let out a sharp sigh.

"Fuckin', alright. Shit. Yeah."

Manny took that as a yes. He glanced back at the firefight in the field. The "fire" part was literal now. At least a full acre was aflame. The smoke seemed to have interfered with the drone sensors. That was probably the only reason their last two escorts had stayed unfucked for so long. Manny watched in horror as large beetle-black drone buzzed down low and opened up with a machine gun. He saw bursts of red as the rounds tore into the escort's gunner and flung him off the truck's bed.

"Time to go!" Manny slapped Reggie's uninjured shoulder and sprinted as fast as his janky ankle could carry him. It was increasingly obvious that his leg was supremely fucked. The middle of Manny's back itched the whole run, in anticipation of a bullet. That peculiar sense was even louder than the pain.

They reached the jeep. Manny went for the driver's side door, pulled it open, and jerked back as the soupy remains of a pulped human being oozed out onto the asphalt. He heard Reggie start to retch behind him.

It was fucked in there, for sure. The man—he was sorta sure it had been a man—had taken a couple rounds from a very large weapon. Manny guessed they'd been .50 caliber mass-reactive bolts because the impact had torn the man apart. He wasn't sure if additional rounds, or bone shrapnel, had hit the two kids in the back seat. But they were all exceptionally dead.

Manny pulled his shirt off and did his best to wipe the corpse from as much of the seat as possible. He hopped in and glanced over to the journalist. Reggie retched outside.

"Hey, get the fuck in! We don't got all–"

A concussive blast echoed from the field. That was one more escort down. The fight was as good as over. Manny felt a tinge of panic rise up in the base of his spine. Reggie still hesitated.

"Dude, either deal with some gore on your clothes or stay here and die. Your choice."

The Brit snapped out of it, went for the passenger door and hopped inside. Manny wasn't a great driver, or even a very good one. But this was a simple vehicle and he was blessed with the motivation of not wanting to die. He turned the car back on and the engine woke up with a rich electronic hum. The fixer flipped the vehicle into drive and gunned for the treeline.

The jeep bounced and swayed over the lumpy grassland terrain. Reggie puked out the window. Manny felt nauseous too. He honestly wasn't sure if it was more from the pieces of people scattered inside the vehicle or sheer motion sickness. Fifteen seconds went by. Thirty. A minute. Manny allowed himself to think they might make it out of this alive.

And then he heard the buzz. That sickening, familiar machine hum that every warzone kid knew as well as the sound of their own mother's voice. A drone. Closing in.

Manny jerked his head out the window and scanned the sky. The jeep hit a pothole and his head slammed up into the top of the window frame. He saw stars and almost lost control of the vehicle entirely. It veered to the right and lifted up onto only two wheels. He righted the jeep, spun it back to the left and gunned it again as he turned the other way. He stuck his head out again and scanned behind them.

There it was. The black beetley fucker, buzzing toward them. It was close enough that he could see the glint of its camera optics and the barrel of the heavy machine-gun slung underneath it. Manny knew it was picking up speed to compensate for the recoil of its weapon. It would be low on ammunition now. It'd probably wait to fire until it was too close to miss.

The treeline was so near he could almost grab it. Another fifteen seconds and they'd be there. But the drone was close. They didn't have that long.

He looked over to the journalist.

"Get ready to bail."

"Get ready to wh–?"

Manny saw the muzzle flash, and in the same instant he spun the wheel hard to the right. The drone's first round chunked through the back of the jeep, cracked the axle and blew apart the left tire. But the jeep was in the air an instant later. It flipped over like a drunken dolphin and the rest of the drone's shots blasted chunks out of the ground where the jeep would have been. By the end of the burst, the recoil had robbed the drone of its momentum and brought it to a spinning halt in the sky.

The jeep rolled twice and bounced Manny and Reggie around like rocks in a tumbler. It hurt. It hurt shitloads. But Manny was high enough on adrenaline and fear that he could almost ignore the pain. Blood streamed from his forehead. Something ached terribly in between his shoulders. When the jeep came to a stop he was deeply surprised to be alive.

"Let's go!" he shouted to Reggie, not even 100 percent sure if the journalist had survived the crash. Manny pulled himself up out of the open window and then reached his hands back, blind, into the jeep, while he scanned the sky around them. He felt Reggie's hand, from his good arm, grip his own. It was wet with sweat, maybe blood, probably both. Manny squeezed, pulled him up. The two hopped down, quick as they could with their sundry wounds.

The drone had probably veered around and started another loop so it could build up the speed for one more accurate burst of fire. Manny couldn't quite hear the buzz yet but he couldn't hear much of anything over the sound of his pounding heart. Reggie pulled ahead of him in a lopsided run. Manny tried to pick up speed but his knee just wouldn't let him.

Hrmmmmmmmmmmmmmmmmmmmmmmmmmmmmmmmmmmmmmmmmm–

Ah. There it was. He had three, maybe four seconds before that big gun opened up again. The treeline was only about a hundred feet away. So close, and yet too far for him to possibly make it in time. *I really didn't want to die here. I was so close to getting out.* He thought of a picture he'd seen of the Bavarian alps, white snow-filled valleys and rich pine forests. *I'm never going to see that. Or anything else.*

Reggie looked back as he reached the treeline. Manny appreciated the hesitation. It was dumb as fuck, though.

"IDIOTA, RUN!" the fixer bellowed at the top of his lungs. The journalist didn't hesitate this time. He bolted past the treeline and disappeared into the wooded thicket.

Manny felt a weight lift off of his shoulders. He was about to be torn apart by some nutfuck Martyr with an itchy trigger finger and a joystick.

But he'd done his job. He'd gotten his journalist to safety. *Well, not quite "safety,"* he thought, *but whatever. Best I could do under the circumstances.*

The hum grew louder. Manny tried to coax a little more speed out of his wounded leg, even though he knew he was too far away now to make the treeline even at a dead sprint. *It would've been nice to see Berlin. Or Paris. Ah well.*

KRUMP! KRUMP! KRUMP!

He heard the thumping sound of heavy gunfire and braced himself for the instant of agony that would precede his end. But instead, he heard the sound of impact and crunching metal behind him, followed by a high-pitched mechanical whine. Something heavy and black crashed into the ground ahead of him.

He made it to the treeline, pushed through the underbrush, got perhaps twenty feet into the woods, and collapsed against a tree.

For a few seconds he just let the pain wash over him. His knee. His shoulders. He could feel something stuck deep in his back, too. Maybe a shard of glass? Or some shrapnel from the start of the firefight? He had quite a few deep cuts. The trauma nanites in his circulatory system had clotted most of them, but the deeper ones still oozed blood. It was hard to tell just how injured he really was, since his body was also covered in blood and viscera from the jeep's previous occupants.

Espere, he thought, *how am I alive?*

His brain gradually spun up to meet his body. Someone had shot that murderbeetle out of the air. But who? Reggie? Where would he have gotten a gun? And the man was British. He couldn't shoot.

"Reggie?!" he shouted.

"Over here!" the Brit called back. He sounded weirdly cheerful, "I, erm, think we've made some friends."

For the first time in his life, Manny found himself face-to-face with two post-humans.

The first appeared to be a lady. She was hunkered up in the branches of a tree and she cradled a very large gun in her arms. Most of her body sort of faded into the forest. She was only easy to see now because of her smile. The shine of her teeth was quite unlike anything he'd ever seen. They appeared to be made of some sort of strange, swirling-colored metal. Where a normal person would've had incisors she had long, curved fangs.

The other chromed was a Black man. He was of average height, with a muscular body and a wide build. His head was shaved and he had a plump, friendly face and round cheeks that accentuated his broad smile. He wore a red kilt and silver breastplate over his muscular chest. It gleamed in the afternoon sun. His only weapon appeared to be an enormous sledgehammer larger than Reggie's entire body. He smiled and nodded at Manny. His whole body twitched as he stood there, as if a constant stream of electricity buzzed through him.

Reggie stood in front of the man. It looked like the journalist had run into the post-humans during his flight from the drone. He looked terrified, in the friendly sort of way only the British could manage.

"Hey...y'all," Manny said. He wasn't really sure how nomadic half-god warrior people preferred to be addressed. "Y'all" seemed a safe bet.

"Hey guy," said the woman up in the tree.

"Sup," said the kilted man.

"Um. Can we help you?" Manny asked.

The man chuckled. He had a deep, throaty laugh that bounced off the trees and seemed to get louder as it reverberated.

"Naw, buddy. You guys look pretty near death. I'ma guess you don't have anything I want. Nice pajamas, though." He pointed down to Manny's blood-soaked and burned pajama bottoms. The fixer's face turned red with embarrassment.

"They might have whiskey," said the woman. "Ask if they have whiskey."

The big man smiled, lowered his maul, and spoke.

"The name's Skullfucker Mike," he said. "The lady who shot down your drone is Topaz MacMillan. Do you guys have whiskey?"

Manny didn't. But Reggie did. ("Holy fuck," he shouted, "I actually do!") Somehow, the journalist hadn't lost his backpack in the chaos. He unzipped the main compartment, dug around for a few seconds and produced a small metal flask. Reggie passed it off to Skullfucker Mike, who took a belt of it and let out a dog's bark. He didn't bark *like* a dog. It was the exact sound of a large hound barking.

Skullfucker Mike passed the flask up to Topaz. She took a pull and cooed appreciatively.

"Alright Skully, I like these guys. They get a ride."

"A ride?" asked Reggie. "A ride to where?"

"To Rolling Fuck," she said. "To the city of wheels."

Chapter 8

Roland.

"So you were there, right?" Sardar asked. "You saw the White House burn?"

Sardar was Jim's mechanic. He was a short, slightly pudgy kid with a wide, handsome face and skin a couple shades darker than Roland's own. This was maybe his twentieth question since Jim's aircraft had dropped their transport off two hours ago. The other members of Jim's team hadn't said so much as a word to Roland. They'd all listened though. He could see the tension in their shoulders and feel the vibrations in the air as their ears twitched and their eyes darted over to watch his replies. The fact that they were all cramped together inside the armored confines of a Mattis APC made it easy to read the room.

Roland wasn't 100 percent sure if the young merc had been put up to the task of questioning him or if Sardar was just an inquisitive soul. Roland smelled a light drizzle of nervousness waft off the boy. He'd caught several glances between Sardar and Bigsby. But neither of those facts were proof of anything. Nervousness was a perfectly natural reaction to hanging out in a cramped metal box with a guy you'd just been trying to murder.

"I remember pieces of it," Roland replied. "Fucking someone in the Lincoln Bedroom. Stealing liquor from the kitchens. Shitting in the ball-return of the White House bowling alley."

Sardar shook his head.

"That's fucking loco. You're like a history book. I bet I read about shit you did back in high school."

"Probably," Roland said with a shrug. He had about nine clear memories of his life before the shack on Camelback Mountain, and none of them felt very historic.

"Can I get your autograph, man?" Sardar asked.

Bigsby, the post-human Roland had been about to arm-club into submission a day ago, shook his head and groaned in embarrassment. One of the women he'd buried in his collapsed hovel grunted out a laugh. Her name was Nadine, or something with an N, anyway. She and her partner, Azime, were both close assault specialists. Like the rest of the crew, except Sardar, they'd been cold to Roland ever since he'd beat the living hell out of them. Something occurred to him.

"Hey, I've got a question for you," he said to Sardar.

"Yeah?"

"Your crew's been real pissy to me this whole ride." Roland nodded at Bigsby. "How exactly did you guys expect that fight to go down?"

Sardar pursed his lips. He seemed at a loss for a second. Then he said, "Jim framed it as a standard kill-team action. We've done that sort of thing a couple times. Last year there was this chromed out Nazi in Ida–"

"So he tricked you, then?" Roland interrupted. "Convinced you this was just another assassination, when all he really wanted to do was get my attention?"

Roland looked around, and realized the rest of the transport was glaring at him. Bigsby spat on the ground in front of Roland's foot.

"We'd have iced you if he'd given us another minute."

Roland just laughed, and turned his eyes back to Sardar.

"It's clear you and the other guy," he gestured at the young man next to Sardar, "are the only smart bastards in the unit, since you didn't get back up when I beat you down."

Sardar squirmed a little, clearly uncomfortable.

"Me 'n Pedro," he gestured to the other man, "we're just engineers. We don't go toe to toe with, uh, whatever you are."

All this conversation, the most he'd had in years, made Roland feel uncomfortably lucid. He rooted around in the tattered old backpack he'd brought with him. It contained one rusty Mateba Autorevolver that he'd found under the floorboards of his collapsed shack and five-point-oh-eight-seven kilograms of assorted narcotics. Mostly opiates.

Roland remembered how fun it was to watch things explode while high on oxy.

He pulled a pill bottle out of the sack—dilaudid—and poured half of it into his mouth. Roland swallowed, then guzzled the second half.

"Jesus," said Will, the man he'd stabbed in the throat with a piece of wood yesterday. "This is the guy who kicked the shit out of us?"

"I am sorry about that," Roland said. "If I'd known we were going to wind up sharing an APC, I probably would've just choked you out."

Krump. Krump. Krump.

Mortar fire. Incoming. Roland's hindbrain ran the calculations, estimated it at around eight miles out. He sat up straight, senses focused toward the sound of the fire. Bigsby and Azime reacted the same way. They'd clearly splurged on the good ears. The rest of the team didn't seem to have heard.

"There's shooting ahead," Azime said. "60mm mortars."

"Kit up, folks." Bigsby added as he pulled his own S-30 Barrett assault rifle from its resting spot on the wall behind him.

Krump. Krump. FWOOM! FWOOM! FWOOM!

"The fuck was that?" Azime cocked an eyebrow. Her left ear twitched. Her tan, lean face flushed red with excitement, "I don't recognize that one."

"Me either," Bigsby grunted. The other post-human looked to Roland with clear frustration. "You recognize that?"

Roland did.

"It's an M142," he said. "Mobile rocket artillery. Antique, U.S. military issue."

Will looked over to Bigsby, confused, "I've never heard of anything like that in the SDF's armory."

"It's not the SDF," Roland explained, slurring his words more than a little. The opiates had just started to hit. *Holy shit I love dilaudid,* he thought. "That's incoming. Can't you tell?" he asked.

"Not, uh. Not from this distance." Azime answered. She glanced awkwardly over to her partner. Nadine put a hand on her thigh and squeezed.

"Could you not be monstrously fucked up when we're about to go into battle?" Bigsby asked. He seemed angry. Roland debated offering one of his handfuls of pills. He decided he'd much rather save them for later.

"First off, I didn't sign up for battle," he explained as he popped and chewed a pair of morphine tablets. "Second, we still got about, almost eight miles before we hit the front. Plenty of time to sober up."

"Eight miles?" asked Sardar. "The Richardson Line is fifteen miles out."

More mortars krumped in the distance. Roland heard blossoms of heavy machine-gun fire too, and the hum of dozens of assault drones.

"Hey Bigs?" the voice of the APC's driver crackled over the vehicle intercom. "There's a lot of craziness coming in from the main SDF channels. It sounds like a major assault. The Martyrs have pushed all the way to Deep Ellum. Some of the field commanders are talking about a full retreat."

"Jesus–"

"–Shitting–"

"–Christ."

Will, Bigsby, and Nadine all cursed at the same time. Roland thought it was cute. It tugged at his heart strings a little. He missed being part of a close-knit team. Some of his stronger memory fragments involved really good times he'd had during and after the war. He remembered blowing up an armored school bus with a guy named Mike, and throwing rotten oranges at a government sniper with Jim. His brain also brought up snatches of late-night drinking sessions and watching cartoons on an old projector in the desert. When he closed his eyes he could smell the burning manzanita smoke of their campfire. Pain tugged at his heart, but he was jerked out of his reverie by the sound of an explosion.

It was big, and close enough that everyone in the APC heard it, even though Roland's hindbrain put the distance at over seven miles away.

"VBIED," Bigsby and Azime said at the same time.

"Real big one," Azime added.

Roland could tell that the explosives-rigged vehicle had been an E-Series Mercedes truck, but he didn't bring that up. No one liked a know-it-all.

Bigsby's mouth opened and closed, the tell-tale sign of someone having a subvocal conversation through their deck. Roland could've read his lips, but that would've been rude. Instead he looked over to Sardar.

"If the gig gets called on account of war, you wanna go get shitfaced in Austin with me?"

The kid blinked, and then replied. "I mean, of course. But I'm pretty sure bossman's gonna want us to do the job even if it's hot out there."

Roland growled a little, without thinking, and Sardar cringed.

"I did not sign up to defend against an active invasion. I'm here to fuck up property, not people."

"Jim says that's still the plan. You fuck up the property," Bigsby grunted, "my fam and I are here to fuck up the people."

A red hot cherry of anger bloomed in Roland's heart. "That wasn't the deal," he said, "and Jim knows it. One of you call him and loop me in on your screen. I'll set this right."

"Call him yourself," spat Bigsby.

"He can't," Sardar pointed out. "He's got a dead deck. No signal at all. True null."

"Why the hell would you go null–" Azime started to ask. Bigsby interrupted her.

"It doesn't matter why this asscopter's null. I'm on with Jim, and he says you're under contract still. We'll make sure you don't have to kakk anybody."

For a moment, Roland focused his attention outside the little APC. His hindbrain collated the bursts and vibrations that echoed out around the battlefield. It compared them with his petabytes of stored combat data and the last map of Dallas he'd downloaded before severing his deck. In a couple seconds he had what his hindbrain assured him was an 80 percent accurate projection of the current fighting. It didn't look good for the defenders.

"And what if it's too much for you guys out there?" Roland asked. "You gonna expect my ass to murder a bunch of strangers to get you 'n your 'fam' home safe?"

Bigsby rolled his eyes. "It's a bunch of fucking Martyrs. Maybe they caught the SDF with their pants down, but they'll lose steam soon enough. Those savages are all baseline sapien. We got chrome on our side."

Roland shrugged. "If you're wrong, I'ma take one of your nipples home with me. Just a heads up."

The other post-human's face turned purple. It grew purpler still when Sardar laughed at the remark.

"Sorry, Bigs. It's fucking funny, man."

"It wasn't a joke," Roland assured them both.

They hit Dallas proper ten minutes later. Their arrival was heralded by the sounds of car horns, squealing brakes, and frustrated shouts. The songs of a city at war. Flashes of memory, from this same city, in a different war, shot through Roland's mind. They kept him occupied while Bigsby and his squad prepped their combat gear. There was something almost comforting about the sound of men and women arming for battle. He remembered the way Mike ran through the lyrics of "Eye of the Tiger" before every op, and the careful way Jim had loaded his pre-battle meth pipe.

The krump of mortar fire and the boom of heavier artillery grew louder and louder. The sour scents of gamma-aminobutyric acid, cortisol, and epinephrine filled the cabin. Bigsby's team had good game faces, but they were nervous.

"Bigs," the driver's voice crackled over the intercom, "I'm seein' a shitload of hostile drone activity. Sky's fucking angry right now. Might be best to dismount h–"

Roland smelled the fuel burning off in the wake of the Hellfire missile roughly a second before it hit. He knew the archaic munition didn't have the ability to penetrate a Mattis APC, but he still warned his fellows.

"Missile's a'comin."

"What?" Sardar asked.

And then it hit. The impact rocked the vehicle on its axles and bounced its hapless passengers into the hard metal edges of the cabin. Roland bounced with them, although, for him, the pain of impact was more curiosity than actual discomfort. The driver braked hard. Roland heard and felt as the APC collided with what sounded like the outer wall of a large concrete building.

He smelled blood on Sardar and Nadine. From the sound of the blast and the resulting crash he guessed the APC's front axle had splintered. Ryan, the driver, was unconscious. He'd hit his head hard enough that the trauma nanites in his bloodstream had knocked him out while they worked to stop the swelling in his brain.

"Out! Out! Move it, motherfuckers!" Bigsby shouted.

There was a hiss as the rear and side exit hatches of the APC fired open. Light streamed into the vehicle. Bigsby was out first, his very large rifle at the ready. Nadine and Azime followed behind him. The former had a Juggernaut auto-shotgun, the latter had an M14 sniper rifle.

There were no infantry nearby, not yet. But Roland closed his eyes, concentrated, and after a second his hindbrain guessed that the nearest ground troops were a quarter of a mile away. Six men in Ares-pattern powered armor followed by fifty unmodified human soldiers, a half-dozen technicals, and two drone-carriers.

The men in the Ares suits were the only thing that concerned him. Powered armor couldn't make an unmodified human into a true match for a godfucking monster engine like himself. But it could give a squad the firepower they needed to do some real damage. If they could hurt Roland, they could kill Bigsby and his team. His hindbrain told him the power armored soldiers would be in weapon's range within two minutes.

Just enough time to roll a blunt!

He grabbed a blunt wrap and a bag of ground weed out of his backpack and started to roll as he walked out of the abandoned APC. Sardar and Pedro had taken cover behind the vehicle and started to administer basic first aid to their wounded driver. Will was a few meters ahead, on overwatch, covering them all with his heavy M-94 belt-fed grenade launcher. The others were nowhere to be seen. Roland heard them though; about fifteen meters west of the stricken transport. He felt them take up firing positions.

Should I warn Bigsby about the armored guys? Roland wondered. He shook his head and said "Nah" out loud. Sardar stared at him.

The weed was dry and slightly yellowed with age. Roland had certainly smoked better. But he'd smoked worse often enough not to complain. He drizzled the crumbled herb into the blunt wrap and rolled it between his fingers. He licked the seam and sealed it as he watched Sardar shoot a stim capsule into Ryan's neck. The driver started to regain consciousness. Roland lit his blunt, took a hit, and offered it to the man.

"Welcome back to the land of the waking," he said with a cheerful grin. "Pot?"

Sardar gave him a stern look. "Is this really the time?"

The screech of a rocket-propelled grenade filled the air. Outgoing fire. It must've been from a nearby SDF position engaged with the advancing Martyrs.

"Of course there's time," said Roland. "We've got a solid ninety seconds until they're here. Might as well get high."

The kid rebuffed his offer. Roland would've been a little hurt if he hadn't secretly hoped they'd turn him down. It took a lot of pot to get him high. One whole blunt was about the right amount for where he wanted to be.

Thump-thump-thump-thump-thump.

Bigsby opened up with his heavy machine gun. A vague worry started to grow inside Roland. The armored Martyrs had moved faster than anticipated. *Am I going to have time to finish smoking?* He was thankful that he'd at least loaded up on painkillers before reaching the front.

The machine gun was joined by the sharp crack of Nadine's sniper rifle, and the rich bellow of Azime's auto-shotgun. It sounded like she was firing tungsten-core penetrators rather than the explosive Dragon's Breath rounds she'd loaded during the assault on Roland's shack. That was probably smart.

"Are you going to do something?" Sardar asked. Roland could smell as fear wafted off him like a fine mist. He heard the heavy hum of a suit-mounted rotary chaingun, and then another. Incoming fire. A few rounds arced and ricocheted off the body of the APC. Sardar and Pedro dove for cover and pulled Ryan with them. Roland didn't move; his hindbrain had plotted the trajectories of the errant rounds as soon as they'd left their barrels. There'd been no danger. Well, no danger to them. By the sound of it, the power armored Martyrs had pinned Bigsby down. Roland could smell Nadine's blood in the air. She was alive, but injured.

Will started to fire, and pumped a steady stream of explosives out in a high arc in front of the Martyrs. Roland felt as the men scattered. He also felt the footfalls of dozens of normal infantry, two hundred meters behind the power-armored vanguard. He heard the rich "thunk" of recoilless rifles being bolted into the ground.

Roland puffed on his blunt as he considered the tactical situation. Bigsby and his team seemed to have knocked out one of the armored Martyrs. But they were alone and unsupported. The SDF was in full retreat, and the small squad didn't have the firepower, or the chrome, to hold off what was coming.

Roland did.

But he very much disliked the idea of murdering several dozen brainwashed idiots. These kids weren't responsible for anything beyond buying into artful propaganda and lofty promises. He didn't see them as worse than any other gaggle of armed eighteen to twenty-two-year-olds in the history of war.

"Hey Sardar, you got a wrench?" Roland asked.

"Wha–...yes?" Sardar replied.

"Can I borrow it?"

"Um," the young mercenary raised an eyebrow in confusion.

"It's not a sex thing," Roland assured him.

"I, ah, never assumed it was," Sardar said.

"Then can I have it?"

Sardar stared at him for a long beat and then said, "...OK."

He handed over his wrench. It was nice. More than two feet long, and made from 15.4 pounds of stamped steel.

"This is perfect," Roland told Sardar.

"Perfect for what?" Sardar asked.

"Wounding," Roland replied.

And with that, he was off. Roland could break thirty miles an hour at a dead sprint, but with all the painkillers and weed he'd just taken that didn't sound super fun. So he strolled along at a brisk eighteen miles per hour, darted by Will and zig-zagged his way past a few hundred errant rounds the armored Martyrs fired to suppress Bigsby's squad.

THOOM. THOOM.

Two of the big recoilless rifles fired their giant, explosive-tipped munitions. Roland reached Nadine and Azime's position. The former was down, bleeding from multiple gunshot wounds. Her lover fired from cover. Roland felt as one of the explosive rounds arced toward their position. The other was headed toward Bigsby. Roland's hind-brain guessed that Bigsby would survive the hit. Nadine and Azime wouldn't.

He jumped forward and grabbed them both while still airborne. In the instant before missile met masonry, he threw them back out of the blast radius. He knew the landing would hurt, but both women were chromed enough to survive.

After he tossed them, Roland slid to a stop on top of the pile of ruined bricks they'd hidden behind. The rocket-propelled munition hit about three feet below him. The 75mm round contained half a kilogram of hexogen, enough explosive power to tear a hole in the side of a small tank. It detonated and turned the pile of bricks into a shrapnel volcano.

Roland hopped again. His hindbrain made it clear that he wouldn't avoid all, or even most of the shrapnel. Metal and brick tore through his biceps, his gut, his legs, and his pectorals. Most of the shrapnel stopped at the sub-dermal carapace that protected his vital organs. A few pieces went further. They tore one kidney in half and pierced one of his hearts. But Roland had multiple redundant back-ups for every important organ. His medical nanites had already started to purge the foreign matter and repair the damage when he hit the ground.

The battle high rolled in and Roland's synapses flooded with endorphins, serotonin, and enough morphine to kill a middle-weight elephant. The chemical elation of imminent combat filled his senses. Roland wasn't just high on war, he was tripping balls.

Sweet shitting fucks, I've missed this.

Roland flipped a jaunty salute to Bigsby as he sprinted forward, past the man. This time he let his legs pump as fast as they could and rushed toward the five advancing armored Martyrs. In the quarter-second before contact, Roland had his first solid look at The Enemy.

Their suits were definitely some iteration of the basic Ares design. They had the familiar insectoid helmet with its bulbous eyes and heavy nasal sensor blister. The shoulders, chest, groin, thighs, and shins were heavily reinforced. These were breaching suits, meant to lead an advance and absorb an enormous amount of incoming fire.

The armor was painted the dull yellow of a Texas grassland. Roland could see red and blue on the edges of the pauldrons; Republic of Texas colors. But the suits had clearly been painted over, repurposed by their new owners. Two of the men had large, white crosses daubed across their chests. One man had a cross painted over his face-plate. The paint jobs seemed new. These suits had been captured—or handed over—recently.

Their wearers moved like competent fighters who weren't used to the capabilities of full powered armor. Two of the Martyrs had shoulder-mounted missile pods with angry-looking rockets inside them.

Three of them mounted rotary chain-cannons. Between their targeting systems and reflex-augmentation hardware, they could have hurt him if they'd had their shit together.

But they didn't, and he hit the point man like a bag of concrete thrown by a gorilla. Roland didn't even bother to swing the wrench yet, he just let his substantial body weight turn him into a post-human battering ram. The first soldier hit the ground, Roland atop him, with a whine of pistons and internal motors. He tried to bring his assault cannon to bear on Roland but the barrel was too long. Roland slammed Sardar's wrench into the man's crotch eleven times in the space of a second. The suit's groin armor was rated to stop a .50 caliber rifle round. It caved in on the third hit.

Stop, he shouted inside his own mind. *Stop! You're going to kill him!*

Roland pulled back with considerable effort. His brain wanted more, and every impact fed a few more endorphins into the hopper. But he managed to stop himself before he did irreparable harm. This hesitation made him a target, though. One of the armored Martyrs shot him four times and ripped deep gouges in his torso.

Roland rushed the man and slapped his weapon aside. The drugs flooded into him again as he swung his wrench up, under-handed, into the poor fellow's chin. Bone shattered on the first swing.

Bigsby fired. Roland felt one of the other armored Martyrs go down, knee-caps and throat shot out. The two remaining Martyrs opted to retreat. But it was a fighting retreat. They bounded backward and launched a flurry of rockets toward Roland as cover fire. These he had to avoid. Roland could eat small-arms fire all day. Rockets were not small.

He shoved the wrench into his waistband and threw himself into an elegant backflip (he maybe wanted to impress Bigsby a little). He landed fourteen feet back from his prior position. In the same continuous motion he picked two fist-sized chunks of concrete off the ground, flipped back again, and launched both improvised missiles at the retreating Martyrs.

The rockets impacted, one after the other, in spaces Roland had been a millisecond before. Shrapnel from the detonations tore at his skin and penetrated his less critical organs. Roland's hindbrain registered at least thirty new injuries. None of them were serious enough that he felt actual pain. He back-flipped again, definitely show-boating, and landed eight feet ahead of the last rocket, and right in front of Bigsby's fighting position.

Right as he landed, the chunks of concrete he'd thrown impacted the face plates of both Martyrs at around eleven-hundred feet-per-second. That impact wouldn't be enough to kill men in Ares armor, probably, but it was enough to break most of their suit sensors and shatter a lot of the bones in their faces. Roland fixed Bigsby with an evil grin as the last two power-armored men staggered back, wavered on their feet, and collapsed.

"Son-of-a–" Bigsby started to curse in a low, awed voice.

"Guess I'll be taking that nipple now," Roland interrupted him.

Chapter 9

Sasha.

They unloaded her in Plano. The porters who cracked open her crate, two men in dirty jumpsuits, seemed disappointed she wasn't food. One of the men was tall and balding, the other shorter and still fairly young. They had white skin, burnt reddish by the sun, and neither of them looked liked they'd bathed in quite some time. Their faces were gaunt. Sasha didn't see any extra fat on either of them.

"Aw dang," said the tall man.

"Welcome," said the short one. "I hope yer ready fer what this is."

They were not exactly the welcome crew she'd expected. Saul had told her a man named "David" would be waiting. But neither of the porters knew who David was. They seemed much more frustrated than joyous at her presence. The building wasn't what she'd expected either. It looked like an old FedEx facility, with all the branding covered by red spray paint.

There was trash everywhere, mostly food waste from crates of aid supplies that had been opened too late. The spoiled food had been shoved into large piles and left to rot in one corner of the large room. Sasha guessed this had once been a loading dock, where delivery trucks would've dropped off and received packages. The room was filled with a mix of aid crates and miscellaneous boxes, stacked into piles by a ragged army of tired-looking men. Like the two men who'd greeted her, they all looked malnourished and skinny.

The only people not dressed in blue jumpsuits were a pair of armed guards. They stood in the back of the room, near a door that seemed to lead deeper into the facility. Both men had white-paint crosses daubed across the body armor on their chests. Both carried very large black rifles. One of them ran over once he saw her emerge from the shipping crate.

"Welcome to the Heavenly Kingdom, ma'am," the boy drawled. He looked young enough to have come from her own high school. There was a dusting of acne on his unlined face and his round cheeks still held a bit of baby fat.

"Thank you, sir," she said, and pointed to the cross on his chest. "It's good to see that!"

The young Martyr smiled.

"Yes, ma'am. We wear the cross here." He glanced at the porters and narrowed his eyes. "Most of us, anyway."

He extended his hand. Sasha took it and he helped her take her first few steps into this strange new world. Her legs felt wobbly and unstable after so much time crammed into a crate. She was grateful for the help.

"I'm looking for David," she said. "Do you know where I might find him?"

"No David here, ma'am," the Martyr replied. "But Darryl's the team leader for this receiving yard. He'll set you to rights."

They walked through the rear door and into the building proper. Sasha's escort guided her past old offices and break rooms and to what looked like it had been a waiting area for customers. It had been transformed into an office. The only occupant was a single man surrounded by four folding tables, each piled high with a mix of paper shipping manifests and folding e-paper displays. He sat in the middle of it all and scrolled feverishly on a heavy government-issue tablet computer.

This man, Darryl, was tall and broad-shouldered but stooped forward. It looked as if his spine had been bent at the mid-shoulders. Sasha relished the deep lines in his face, the bags under his eyes, his receding hairline, and even the way his joints "popped" audibly as he stood when she entered. No man she'd met in the American Federation had aged so honestly, not even her father. Sasha realized with a start that this was the first older man she'd ever really seen. He must be fifty, at least.

"Hello, sir," she started.

"Nuts," he spat. "Not another one'a you."

The man had a thick drawl, he sounded "country" in a way Sasha had only heard in movies. Her voice caught in her throat as she tried to respond, "Sir, I'm...I'm looking for David."

"Ayep," he grunted, "you'n every other teenager what's come through my depot. I'll tell ya the same thing I told them others: ain't no David here."

Sasha's eyes widened. She squeaked and immediately hated herself for it.

"No...no David?"

Darryl must have seen the fear in her face and taken pity, because his tone softened.

"Listen, I uh..." he glanced at a small screen wrapped around his wrist, tapped it a couple of times and looked back to her. "I got about fifteen minutes left here before I got a meeting downtown. I can drop you off. Folks there can help you get set up, if'n you decide to stay."

"I would appreciate that very much," Sasha said. Her face reddened again when she asked, "Is there a restroom I can use around here? I'd like to clean up a bit."

"Ayep," the man grunted and nodded toward a red door in the back of his office. "That one's private. No shower, but the water runs."

Sasha couldn't really smell herself anymore, which she knew meant she probably smelled terrible. The thing she wanted most was a long, hot shower with shampoo. *Holy God*, she realized, *shampoo is amazing*. She was so preoccupied with the thought of clean hair that she didn't even chastise herself for the blasphemy. Sasha knew she wouldn't find shampoo in this restroom, but any kind of clean was better than her current level of filth. She thanked Darryl and stepped into his bathroom.

Sasha told herself it wasn't the worst bathroom she'd ever seen, even though that was a clear lie. The floor, once white tile, was so crusted with black and yellow she could only tell there'd ever been tile by the slight suggestion of square-ish shapes underneath the filth. The toilet had been shattered almost completely; all that remained was a little circle of busted ceramic around a hole in the ground. It seemed to function as a squat toilet, now. The sink was intact, but it also looked like it hadn't been cleaned at all in the last year. The metal of the faucet was green where it should have been silver.

Sasha held her nose, turned the hot water on, and hoped for the best. It took her a round minute to stop hoping for hot water. Of course this place didn't have a functioning water heater. *This is a warzone, you stupid girl*, Sasha cursed herself. She felt tears at the edge of her vision but fought them down. Slowly, deliberately, she pulled off her top, undid her bra, and hung both from the doorknob. As she did she thought of the Book of Romans.

"...we rejoice in our sufferings, knowing that suffering produces endurance, and endurance produces character, and character produces hope, and hope does not put us to shame, because God's love has been poured into our hearts through the Holy Spirit who has been given to us."

The word of God gave her some comfort. But Sasha's stomach still churned. As she scrubbed the grime from her body she confronted the fact that this was all Real now. She'd fled her home and her family, traveled to a warzone and now she was here. It was done, her great sacrifice was now real, not theoretical. The excitement she felt at that realization was marred by an anxious kind of horror at the things she'd never do now.

She hadn't really thought about that before she'd left. But now Sasha realized that she was never going to graduate high school. She'd never go to college. She'd never see her father's face again–

She started to cry. It surprised her a little. For days now her emotions had felt stunted, buried under the very immediate concerns of escape and survival. But as soon as she had a minute to breathe, everything she hadn't been able to let herself feel flowed out of her, eyes first. She tried to fight it. But then she remembered something Pastor Mike had written in one of his columns for *Revelator*, "Embrace your pain, for you will hurt again. Embrace your grief, for it is a gift. Lean into the wounds the world gives you. Have faith that the Lord God does not send us burdens we are too weak to bear."

She'd left behind a world where people denied their age with science, salved their pain with narcotics, and fought the natural order of the world the Lord had built. Sasha had wanted authenticity. She'd wanted to live the truth of Christianity without compromise. That meant leaning into this pain and letting it lift her up into the arms of God.

So Sasha leaned in. She sobbed and sobbed and sobbed, shook and shuddered with a pain more profound than any she'd known before.

And then she stopped. She dried herself off, pulled her one fresh pair of clothes out of her backpack, and got dressed to go and meet the Heavenly Kingdom she'd sacrificed so much to join.

Darryl banged twice on the door, right as she slid on her socks.

"Ma'am, I gotta get movin'. Maybe do the make-up later?"

Sasha shoved her dirty clothes into her backpack, zipped it up, and opened the door.

The Heavenly Kingdom included rather more shit and bullet casings than Sasha had expected. She'd known, of course, that it was a warzone. The whole Kingdom was less than two years old. Plano had been taken just days ago. It had all been won by blood and violence. She'd just...sorta figured the Army of God would've cleaned up after itself.

Darryl's truck was the oldest vehicle, and the first non-autonomous one, she'd ever ridden inside. It was frightening to think that one person's movements were the only thing that stood between her and a grisly death. But her fear at that soon faded into anxiety at the state of the world around them.

The signs identified this as Plano. She knew the center of that city had been a stronghold for the Republic of Texas and its corporate masters. They'd been content to leave many of the surrounding cities in the hands of the Heavenly Kingdom, since that had meant more work for the SDF and Austin. Despite its proximity to the front, Plano's status as a stronghold for some of the Republic's wealthiest citizens and corporations had made it seem unassailable. The notoriously stingy Republic had spent heavily on the city's garrison.

Sasha still didn't know what had happened, how a Republican stronghold had fallen so fast. But she saw evidence of how the fall had gone down all around her. The city was devastated. They drove by a police station that was filled with bullet holes and burnt black around its windows. They passed an elementary school that looked as if it had been barricaded, turned into a fortress, and then blasted apart with rockets. The streets they rolled over had been cracked and broken by shellfire. Sasha stared out with wide, excited eyes as they passed mansions that had completely collapsed under the weight of heavy bombardment.

And all around them the streets were filled with soldiers. There seemed to be a checkpoint every two or three minutes. The Martyrs who manned those checkpoints looked impossibly young. That made Sasha feel a little less lonely. *This is what it looks like when a generation comes back to God,* she thought. At each stop Darryl pulled a laminated paper ID out of his pocket. The soldiers would take it, look it over, and then ask him about her. None of them met her eyes.

"Just arrived today," Darryl always said. "She's here to help build the Kingdom."

"Thanks be to God," was the usual reply. Some of the men at the checkpoints were enthusiastic, and shouted it with all the joy she'd expected to hear. But a few of them just looked at her with eyes that were half sullen, half hungry.

"Darryl?" she asked, twenty minutes and three checkpoints into their drive. "What...exactly happened here? I left home the day after Plano fell. It felt like, just, such a miracle. It seems impossible for things to change so much, so fast."

Darryl fixed her with a look that Sasha couldn't quite read. It made her nervous. The next words jumbled up as they left her mouth.

"It's just, erm. Um, I mean– I know all things are possible through God but...how? How did we win here? From what I read on the news–"

The older man laughed. "Well there's yer problem, trustin' the news. Y'ain't gonna read much true 'bout Texas there. All those foreign papers love the SDF," he stressed each letter, pronouncing it "Ess-Deee-Eff," and then spat out the window for emphasis. "And they treat the Republic like a real government, not like a collection of robber barons and their hired guns. Truth is, their position was always rocky. People 'round here would rather live under God's law than the rule of the rich, or those prancing Austin faggots."

He spat again, and somehow made the gesture look like an apology. "Sorry fer the curse, Miss Sasha. It's been a minute since I spent much time 'round a woman."

She smiled in response because she wasn't sure what else to do. And then they turned a corner, past a mostly intact line of shops and a sign that welcomed them to downtown Plano. The wide streets had been cordoned off by sandbags and what looked like enormous fabric cubes filled with rocks. Several dozen armed men milled about and, in the center of the broad thoroughfare, Sasha saw what could only be a gallows built right in the middle of the two-lane street.

It was her first gallows. Capital punishment was illegal in the American Federation. She stared, horrified at the way the six corpses strung up there swung to and fro with the breeze. Sasha squeaked, just a bit, in shock. She was glad the bodies weren't very close.

Darryl seemed to notice her discomfort. He looked down at her with a mix of pity and understanding,

"Ain't always pretty, what we're doin'. But it's the Lord's work."

The truck rolled to a stop outside of a large red brick building that reeked of government. Sasha couldn't tell what it had once been; the sign was too thoroughly burned. A new sign, made of white vinyl, identified this building as the "House of Miriam."

"This'd be your stop, ma'am," Darryl said.

"Th- thank you." She forced a smile and then asked, "Should I just go in?"

"I'll walk ya in. How's 'bout that?"

Sasha nodded her gratitude. She wasn't 100 percent sure what was supposed to happen at this point. *Revelator* had claimed that every man and women who journeyed to the Heavenly Kingdom would be given "meaningful work, food, and as much shelter as the Martyrs can provide." She knew she could expect to be housed with other young, unmarried women, at least until she and Alexander were finally together.

But this trip, and the Heavenly Kingdom, was already so very different from everything she'd expected. That was reinforced when she stepped out of the truck and directly onto a pile of spent bullet casings. There were burnt cars in the street; burnt buildings all around her, and a vague but persistent smell of sour milk in the air. The feeling of dread that had built inside her since she'd left the crate hit a new crescendo.

And then Darryl took her inside the House of Miriam and everything changed again. Sasha saw a middle-aged woman sitting behind a desk in a big white room while younger women sat and lined the walls around her. The older lady had loose, friendly jowls and a mop of gray hair tossed into a lazy bun. She looked exhausted until the moment she fixed her eyes on Sasha. At that moment, her eyes lifted along with her lips into a smile that was the truest thing Sasha had ever seen.

"Praise be to God!" she cried. "You've made it!"

And then a sea of girls rose up around her. Most of them appeared to have been sewing up military uniforms. But at the woman's call, every one of them set their work down and rose up to meet her. Sasha was swarmed by a sea of smiling faces as girls pressed their hands to hers, or embraced her, or prayed over her and chanted in tongues. A dozen people told her their names at once. Sasha went stiff at first, shocked and a little mortified by the mass display of physical affection by so many strangers.

But then the older woman made her way through the crowd and put her hands on Sasha's shoulders. She brushed a stray hair out of Sasha's face and fixed her with a smile that was more motherly than Sasha's actual mother had ever been.

"It's alright now," she said in a voice that was pure comfort. "I'm sure you're probably feeling frightened, and overwhelmed. But you've reached the Heavenly Kingdom. Loose yourself from the chains around your neck, O captive daughter of Zion. You're home now."

Something about the woman's voice and the way her hands felt broke through the anxious wall around Sasha's heart. She found herself in the older woman's arms. She sobbed. And then she felt the press of bodies close against her. The mingled scents of lavender, citrus, and human beings filled her nose. It comforted Sasha in a way she'd never quite known. The anxiety and fear were gone now, but so was any sense of motive inspiration. She let her sisters guide her to a pillow on the ground.

The room got very busy. Girls scattered, they heated up water and prepared food and generally bothered themselves with every aspect of Sasha's comfort. Soon she had coffee and buttered muffins and a heavy jug of gatorade. A fan was moved into position where it could blow more cool air on her face. The older woman sat down next to Sasha and started to speak.

"My name is Helen," she said. "I watch over the newcomers here and I help them adjust to life in the Heavenly Kingdom. The most important thing for you to know is that you are loved and wanted here. You'll have food and shelter and a purpose. Do you understand that, darling?"

Sasha tried to smile, but realized her face was still stuck in the same absent grin she'd worn since the greeting. After a long pause she managed to nod and speak, "Yes. Erm. Sorry. Sasha. My name is Sasha Marion. I'm from Virginia, in the American Federation."

"Sasha," Helen said. "Just Sasha. We have no last names here, and no nationalities beyond our allegiance to God and his Heavenly Kingdom. Do you understand?"

Sasha nodded. "Yes, I mean. Of course. I read every issue of *Revelator* before coming here. I know that nations and states are a worldly concept that only serves to separate us from God Almighty. I memorized Pastor–"

"It's one thing to read the truth. It's another to live it. Don't worry, child. It'll take some time to unlearn your old habits." Helen had cut her off, but she'd done it so gently that Sasha didn't even take it as a rebuke. She just nodded again. And then she remembered something.

"I need to find a young man. His name is Alexander. He's in a mechanized infantry unit. I think he's a corporal, and I have a picture of him printed out in my bag if it'll help."

"Dear," Helen's voice dropped an octave, "I know this is hard to hear, but the Martyrs have important work to do. They fight that we might build the Heavenly Kingdom. If the Lord sees to deliver him safe from the fray..."

Sasha really didn't like the way she said "if."

"...then we will find him, and reunite you two."

"Re–?" Sasha gave a nervous laugh. "Oh, no. We've never met. Except for online. He convinced me to come. I mean, I didn't come for him, but I was really on the fence until I met him."

Helen's expression shifted. She looked...was it anguished? Or angry? But Sasha didn't detect any anger in her voice when she replied. "I know it's hard, love. But you're going to need to wait to hear from Alexander. For right now it should be enough that you're here. You're safe. You've done it. Do you know what this means?"

"It means I didn't get caught."

Helen laughed. She had a beautiful laugh. Sasha wanted to curl up and fall asleep inside it.

"No. I mean, well, yes of course," she said. "But more than anything, it means that for all time, for ever and ever, you're a person who made the choice to be brave. You took a leap into the dark and trusted that God's light would rise to meet you."

There were tears in her eyes. Genuine tears, wrapped up in genuine wrinkles and laugh lines that had never felt the touch of a surgical laser.

"That's the most beautiful thing in the world," Helen said. "I want you to know that."

Sasha started to cry too. Helen embraced her, held her close, and Sasha was certain she'd never been happier.

Chapter 10

Manny.

It couldn't have been much past ten in the morning when they arrived at the City of Wheels. Topaz and Skullfucker Mike had helped him and Reggie into an open-topped red buggy they'd apparently driven out to the ambush. The old vehicle beat the hell out of walking but it had not been built with comfort in mind. Every bump and jostle on the road sent pain shooting up from Manny's fucked knee to what felt like a small forest of tears in his shoulder muscles. Mike, the driver, kept the vehicle at a conspicuously slow pace, but he hurt all the same. The ten minute drive was agony.

But then Rolling Fuck came into view and all thought of pain faded from Manny's mind. The main structure of the city had once been a colossal Bagger 288 strip-mining machine. It looked like a sideways, skyscraper-sized spider made of scaffolding and cranes. At the center of the vehicle was a four-story building on a massive set of treads. Four spindly towers rose up out of that main structure in a giant half-circle in the air around it. A gantry way the length of a football field connected the spindles to a mighty steel arm at the end of the structure. It had once housed an enormous wheel-bucket mining apparatus, but that had been replaced by a queer cube structure. It sat high in the air, and gleamed in a shade of black that made Manny's stomach hurt.

The overwhelming motif of Rolling Fuck was "aftermarket." The spindle-towers had originally looked like scaffolding, and mainly

ARIZONA
HONKPLZ
FUCK YER DAY

existed to offset the weight of that titanic arm. But they'd been built on and added to with a series of treehouse-looking contraptions. He saw people, hundreds of them, climbing from door to door via a series of ladders, ropes, and what looked like vines. Below the main body of the city, a series of vehicles surrounded the vast, rolling building that made up the city's foundation. Manny saw long-haul trucks, deuce-and-a-half army transports, and at least one old Abrams tank. Hundreds of sets of solar panels glistened under the Texan sun.

"Good god," Reggie whispered, awe temporarily overwhelming his pain. "I didn't realize any of the road tribes were this large."

There were easily two or three thousand people visible in the sprawling camp. Mike glanced back at Reggie, a somewhat stern look on his face.

"This is not a tribe. It's a city."

"Oh," said Reggie, "that's just how a lot of people back home refer to–"

"I get it," Mike interrupted. "But there are actual Indigenous tribes out on these roads. Comanche bands in the Panhandle, roving up from New Mexico to Colorado. We've got defensive and trade agreements with a few different groups of Apache out west. The Navajo have the only stable territory south of Mormonland and north of Albuquerque."

Mike glanced back at the road long enough to steer around a pot hole and turn them in the direction of what looked like a greeter station. Then he continued, "Anyway, there are tribes out west. But we're a city. The fact that we don't hold any land or control any territory is important to most of the folks here. Think of it as a kind of rebellion from people born to a settler culture."

"Ah," Reggie nodded, "that's absolutely fascinating. I have so much I want to ask–"

"In good time, buddy," Mike said. "Let's get y'all settled in first."

Manny knew that every foreign correspondent he'd ever met would kill to have the opportunity Reggie had just lucked into. The road people were a popular topic in world media. He supposed that wasn't surprising. They all led visually spectacular lives. Rolling Fuck was just the grandest variation on a theme.

Rolling Fuck was famous across the West for having the highest proportion of post-human citizens. Something like a third of them were chromed enough to no longer fit in the "Homo sapiens" category. Manny had never heard of them traveling this close to Dallas before. They were banned in all of the Republic's cities. People with military-grade mods were uncontrollable. That, and cultural-PTSD from the war, made them pariahs pretty much everywhere.

The main structure of the city was encircled by a ring of thirty-ish large and heavily customized RVs. A few dozen smaller vehicles, many of them bearing sundry armaments, were scattered throughout the campground. The only thing that resembled a checkpoint was a tidy little one-room trailer with a bright "WELCOME" sign above it. Mike steered them in to park in front of it.

The guard who approached them was a shirtless, dreadlocked person with dusky brown skin and an automatic shotgun. Topaz kissed them. Then the guard greeted Manny and Reggie.

"Welcome to Rolling Fuck. Rules are: don't start no shit, won't be no shit. Cool?"

Manny nodded. So did the Brit.

"Alright," they said, "enjoy!"

Manny was a little shocked by how loud it was. Several of the camps appeared to have been built mainly out of speakers. There were a handful of open-air bars outside the main structure of the city, heterogeneous mixtures of tiki-torches, brightly colored silk shade structures and scrap-metal bar tables. Despite the early hour, quite a few people were drinking and dancing. Manny noted more people were doing the former than the latter. Most people were either naked, or wearing a few pieces of light, ornamental clothing. Nearly everyone carried a firearm.

He looked over to the journalist and noticed that Reggie was blinking rapidly and working his jaw. His arm was still dislocated and it seemed to pain him as much as Manny was pained by his leg. Manny's sense of professional pride lit up again, and he leaned forward to speak to their hosts.

"I don't mean to seem ungrateful," he said, "but is there some way we could see a medic? We're pretty shredded back here."

"Ayeah, ayeah," Skullfucker Mike grunted, "Topes and I got some medishit in our trailer. We'll getcha. Just suck it up a bit longer and—Oh!" He popped open the glove compartment. Inside it Manny could see a handgun, a battered can of Miller High Life, and a large bottle of pills. Skullfucker Mike passed the bottle back.

"Oxy. Printed 'em out myself like, two weeks back. Probably shouldn't take more than two or three unless you've got a robust fuckin' narcosuite in your brainmeat."

Manny took two. Reggie took four. Topaz guided the little buggy through the organized chaos of the encampment and toward a big silver airstream parked about a dozen feet away from what Manny guessed was the backside of Rolling Fuck. He guessed that because someone had bolted a twenty-foot tall license plate to that end of the city. It said, "HONK PLZ," in glowing white letters.

The buggy slowed to a stop and Skullfucker Mike hopped out. He put out a hand as Manny and Reggie started to stand.

"Hold up, guys. Y'all're just covered in pieces of dead people."

He went up into the Airstream and came out moments later with one arm full of towels and a large jug of hot, soapy water. Manny and Reggie washed their hands and faces, pulled off their shirts and scrubbed the blood from their chests. The Brit looked over at Topaz when it came time to take off his pants.

"Erm," he said when she made no motion to hide her face.

"Hmm?" she asked.

"Would you mind turning around?"

"Oh!" She seemed surprised. Her face went a bit red, but not with embarrassment at their impending nudity. "I'm so sorry; I didn't even think about it. You people come from the world."

She turned. Reggie and Manny scrubbed most of the blood off their aching, wounded bodies. Skullfucker Mike brought them a pair of fluffy white robes, bundled them up, and ushered them inside the airstream.

It was tame by comparison to the grand, weird, wheeled city above them. The gleaming silver vehicle had been modified with a rooftop greenhouse that was filled with pot plants and some squat bush with red berries Manny had never seen before. The back had been extended and the stainless steel replaced by an enormous bay window. As he entered Manny was hit by a wave of cold air and the strong smell of marijuana.

Roughly half of the trailer's interior was taken up by a huge papasan bed covered in velvet blankets and dozens of furs. A circular table started right where the bed ended, and the rest of the trailer was a large, glass-walled combination bathroom/bar. There did not appear to be a kitchen.

Manny's leg had started throbbing as soon as he stood up to exit the buggy, so he dropped into the first seat he could find, a little padded bench by the table opposite the bed. Reggie sat down on the other side of the table. Manny noticed then that he looked nervous. Sweaty. The journalist's hands shook just a little. His skin seemed pale.

Topaz came in after them, followed by Skullfucker Mike. She hopped over the table with the grace of a deer jumping a fence and, in one smooth movement, spun 'round and settled into a cross-legged sit on the plush mattress. Skullfucker Mike walked up to the bar and pulled down a large white bottle with the word "ROOFIES" written across it in black marker. He took two pint glasses, filled them three-quarters up with the white liquid, and then added a splash of cranberry juice to each glass.

"Skully." Topaz sounded reproachful. Mike stiffened, then dropped his shoulders in contrition. He turned toward them.

"Sorry guys, my manners're burnt out. Would either of you like a G-tini?"

Neither of them answered for a long second. It was Reggie who finally responded.

"G...tini?"

Mike laughed. "Yeah, that's what Topes and I call GHB and cranberry juice. It really hits the spot after shooting something. I can make you guys some, uh, human-sized portions."

"No, thanks," Manny and Reggie said at the exact same time.

The big man handed one glass to Topaz and belted down the other himself. The woman took two gulps to finish hers. She handed her cup to Mike, and he walked back to the bar to fill both glasses again. Reggie looked shocked.

"I'm fairly sure you both just ingested enough GHB to kill two normal humans."

"Eh," Topaz shrugged. "I'd say what we've had so far is only about 70 percent of a fatal dose for someone of your size, metabolism and modifications. Skully's better at drugging people though."

Skullfucker Mike finished pouring two more G-tinis and nodded. “She’s about right. The Brit drinks more, though. I’d say he could take a heavier dose than– what’s your name again?”

“Manny,” Manny gasped out. “And, um, would it be too much to ask for like, some medical care? We are both in tremendous pain.”

Topaz and Skullfucker Mike looked ashamed.

“Ah jeez,” Topaz sighed.

“Fuckin’ hell guys, we’re so sorry,” added Mike. Then he grabbed a long knife from his belt and gouged it deep into his wrist. Reggie damn near jumped out of his chair. Manny kept still. The pills had started to help but he was in too much pain to react to anything with gusto.

“It’s alright,” Topaz assured them in the kind of voice Manny remembered his mom using on their cat when it was sick. “I know it looks weird, but he’s helping.”

“Helping–?!” Reggie gasped as Skullfucker Mike positioned his open wound over a shot glass, jammed the knife slightly to the left, and let a thick strand of his syrupy red blood fill the glass. He filled a second one in the same manner. Then he pulled the knife free, set it on the bar counter and handed the shots to Manny and Reggie. By the time he reached them Manny noticed that the big man’s wounded arm had already scabbed over.

“Don’t worry,” Skullfucker Mike smiled, “my blood’s pretty sterile. And it’s full of good robots. They’ll take care of ya.”

Manny took the shot right away. He knew it was working when he felt pain from the wounds in his back again. That meant Mike’s blood had fixed whatever godawful thing happened to his knee well enough that it barely throbbed.

“Mierda santa,” the curse slipped out. Manny felt better. Great, in fact. But kinda queasy at the same time? He felt somehow…in motion, almost as if his whole body were shifting and burbling like the contents of his gut. The fixer glanced at his journalist and nodded to the empty shot.

“It’s, ah. It’s good.”

Reggie looked terrified. His knuckles were white. The journalist gripped the edges of the table like he was holding on for dear life.

“I. Am. Fine,” he gritted out.

“Aw dammit, Skully,” Topaz said. “You’ve scared the poor kid with your damned wizard-blood.”

"Shit," said Skullfucker Mike. "Sorry. We were tryin' real hard not to trip your head."

Topaz nodded. The gesture looked a little telegraphed, as if she were out of practice with making it.

"Stock sapiens, like yourselves, don't always do well around folks like me'n Mike. We move too fast, or we've got too many weird extra parts, I dunno. It's probably different for every one of us. But your brains definitely read 'monster' when you see us."

"Oh," Reggie croaked. "You're not monsters. You've both been very, erm, polite. Perfect hosts."

"Ah," said Mike, "it's got nothing to do with how nice we are or aren't. It's how your brain reacts to the way we look and move..."

"It's because we're fuckin' monsters, Skully." She fixed her eyes on the journalist. "I don't mean that in a bad sense. But like, we've taken a big damn step out of anything near to nature. Nothing is supposed to be the way we are. It's normal for humans to feel weird when they're around us for the first time."

"Oh, well," said Reggie, "maybe don't slice your wrists open in front of company in the future. Or at least do it behind a screen?"

Mike nodded as if that had been a profound suggestion. Then he handed Topaz her second G-tini and belted down his own. They were both visibly intoxicated now. Topaz's eyes looked unfocused and she sprawled out backward on the bed and cuddled absent-mindedly with one of the fur blankets on her bed. Mike drifted off too, tapping his foot to a beat Manny couldn't hear and drumming his fingers on the bar top to what looked like a completely different beat.

The journalist stared at his blood shot. It looked like it had begun to clot. A thin rind had formed across the top. Reggie was in obvious pain, but he was just as obviously too squeamish to drink a stranger's blood. Manny felt a lot better though. It was weird how fast Mike's blood had worked. He found himself worrying at the scab on the gash he'd received on his forearm, only for the scab to fall away and reveal clean new skin underneath. An hour ago it had been a bleeding wound.

"It really works man," he told Reggie. "Just trust me. Choke it down."

Reggie didn't look convinced.

"Think about what a story this'll make for everyone back home," Manny said. "You escaped a killer drone and drank the blood of an immortal. You'll dine out on that for years."

Reggie still looked pale and rather disgusted. But he put his fingers around the shot, closed his eyes, and then gulped it down. Manny heard him retch once, and then twice. Tears beaded at the corners of the journalist's eyes. But then he swallowed and slumped back in his chair.

Skullfucker Mike was hard at work mixing up another batch of cocktails. These ones seemed to just be normal gin and tonics, four of them. "There's not anything fucking crazy about those drinks, is there?" Manny asked.

Mike shrugged. "Two shots of gin. Splash of tonic. Nothing you normies can't handle."

"Neither of us asked for a drink," Manny said.

"Yeah," Topaz yawned from her place stretched out on the bed, "but you almost died today. You should always have a drink after almost dying."

"Listen to Topaz," said Mike as he passed out the drinks. "She's almost died more than almost anyone I know."

Reggie came alive as his hands touched the drink. He gulped it down faster than either of the post-humans. Manny took a couple slight sips of his own (it was heinously strong) before he sat the glass down and asked, polite as he could manage, "So, uh, why are we here? And why were you there? That kinda luck doesn't just happen. And now we're just, what, all gonna hang out in your trailer getting lit?"

"Would that really be so bad?" asked Mike.

"Skully," Topaz said in a warning tone. "He's right. And it'd be rude for us to pretend we've got altruistic motives here." She looked Manny in his eyes. It was a little unnerving, because her left eye was a notably different shade of brown than her right one. And then there were her metal fangs.

"Look kid," she said, "we got a duty to help strangers in immediate need. It's Rule #1 for all the monsters here. But we were out there because we were looking for someone like you."

"A fixer?" He felt dumb as soon as he asked. To her credit, Topaz just smiled.

"A citizen. Of the Republic of Texas."

"One who's not afraid of dangerous work," Mike added. "And judging by the day you've had, I'ma guess you've a certain familiarity with danger."

"What about me?" Reggie asked.

Mike put a hand on the journalist's shoulder. Manny guessed it was meant as a calming gesture, but the Brit still flinched at the contact.

"Don't worry guy," said Mike. "We'll get you back to Austin, or wherever's got an airport that'll fly you home. Your friend's the only one whose help we need."

"What help do you need?" Manny asked.

"The best person to take that question is up in the city," Topaz said. "You guys up for a little bit of a trek?"

Manny stood halfway to test the strength of his knee. It felt good. As good as new, in fact. His back and shoulders, which had been peppered with shrapnel, just itched now. He didn't even feel particularly tired. On the other side of the table, Reggie looked to be doing well too. He worked his formerly-dislocated shoulder in its socket and gave Manny the thumbs up.

"Apparently so," he said.

Rolling Fuck had not been built by the minds, or for the comfort, of mortal men. That much was obvious the second the elevator doors closed. The narrow metal box launched up with the force of a rocket. It climbed six stories in the space of about a second. By the time it stopped and the doors slid open with a pleasant "ding," Manny and Reggie were both on the edge of vomiting.

"Ah shit, Topes," Mike said. "You forgot to drop the speed back down to normal."

Topaz looked genuinely distraught. "Fuck me with a splintery dick," she cursed. "I'm sorry, guys. This is the nearest elevator to our trailer. It doesn't normally take humans."

"The city's got an elevator under each spindle," Mike explained. "There's also a big lift under the main roller—that's what we call the big building on treads in the middle—and another behind the rear roller. Humans tend to stick to the rollers. It gets weird up in the spindles."

"Weird?" Reggie asked.

"Weeeeeeeird," Skullfucker Mike leaned down and hissed out the word into the journalist's ear. He winked at the Brit in a way that somehow suggested both coitus and violence. Topaz punched Mike's shoulder in annoyance. She gestured for Manny and Reggie to follow her down the narrow metal walkway.

"We live life on a different scale than the rest of you," she said. "We see more colors, hear more sounds, most of us have at least a thousand times as many nerve endings and no fear of mortality to draw the line between pleasure and pain. The kind of environments we enjoy can be...intense, to unmodified humans."

Right as she said "humans," the group emerged from the hallway into a wide, open gantry way. There was no ceiling above them now, and a huge rectangular metal frame loomed over them, connected to the other spindles of the vehicle-city via thick, metal tension wire. The surface of the spindles had been covered in colorful bits of metal and wood, welded and nailed into dozens of crude structures that stippled up the iron frames like technicolor mushrooms. Everything was covered in lights and screens and buzzed with the hum of a thousand speakers.

Reggie's pace slowed. The journalist's jaw was slack. He mouthed what must have been a curse and then asked their guides, "Is it OK if I record?"

Skullfucker Mike grinned and clapped him on the shoulder, "Of course it's OK. If y'ask nice, I might even let you film me in one of the Fondleboats."

"What the hell is a–" Reggie started to ask. But then the first Fondleboat came into view. At least, Manny assumed that's what it was.

A very large lifeboat hung off the gantry, as if it was the deck of a cruise ship. The interior of the boat was all soft cushions, pillows, blankets, and about two dozen writhing naked people. Some of them were surely having sex, but it was hard to tell exactly what was going on. Manny saw several tails curled around limbs or jerking spasmodically in the air. His eyes were drawn to one mechanical limb that looked like a large metal chicken's foot. He watched it kick, repeatedly, into the chest of a young woman. She cried with joy at every impact. The whole mass of coiled post-humanity gleamed wet in the morning light, coated with a mix of blood and what looked like motor oil.

"...Christ," Reggie whispered. Manny was at a loss for words. He felt a bit nauseous. He'd never considered himself a prude, but something about what was going on in the Fondleboat just seemed wrong. In the physics sense, not the moral sense.

"Probably best not to watch," said Topaz. "It can make humans sick."

"Er. Yeah," Reggie coughed. "Is that a common sight?"

Mike shrugged, "It's not uncommon. We try to keep stuff like that on the outside spindles, away from the rollers. As a courtesy."

They walked on, past the boat and through another covered section of the gantry way surrounded by a half-dozen little buildings that looked like shops. Manny saw fruits and vegetables hanging in one, an assortment of labeled decks and other electronic gewgaws on tables in another. It had the look of a Middle-Eastern bazaar, but with no shopkeepers present.

"Y'all want food?" Topaz stopped and gestured at the shop filled with produce.

Manny held up his left hand, which had his cash-chip implanted in it. "I've got Republic of Texas currency and some Californian crypto, if you guys take either."

Mike and Topaz both laughed, and then Mike grabbed an apple and tossed it Manny's way. Manny caught the fruit, although it was a near thing.

"We don't use money, not within the city," Skullfucker Mike explained. "We do sell a lot of what we grow for foreign monies, but that's mostly used to book bands or buy stuff we can't make. Nothing costs anything here. Not to us, and not to our guests."

"Y'all're guests," Topaz clarified.

Manny hadn't really had time to think about his stomach in the hours since their explosiony wake-up call. They'd been on the run and in danger the whole time. But now that he had a moment to think, he felt a mild gnawing sensation in his gut. The journalist must've been in the same way, because he immediately set to piling fruit, bags of nuts, and a paper sack of vat-grown jerky into his arms. Manny went for a bag of shelled pistachios himself, and the two munched as Skullfucker Mike and Topaz led them across the spindle's gantry and down toward the main roller.

The main roller had once held the control center and engine room for the gargantuan strip-mining vehicle. In its conversion to Rolling Fuck, two new levels, built from a half-dozen sorely abused airstream trailers, had been added to the top. Four of the spindles met on the roller's roof, which also hosted a lively cafe. There were around a dozen patrons drinking at the circular center bar, and perhaps another dozen lounging on cushions around low-slung, morrocan-style tables. Most of the customers looked human to Manny's eye. They wore an assortment of colorful loose-fitting garments: sarongs, skirts, long shirts, and keffiyehs. Most of it looked hand-made although Manny was hardly an expert on such things.

As they walked past the bar, Mike scooped up four pint glasses of dark brown lager. He kept them in one hand as he opened a metal hatch on the rooftop. Manny could see a ladder that led down into semi-darkness. Mike nodded toward the ladder.

"Down you go. Beer at the bottom."

Manny and Reggie descended into a luxurious conference room. It was candle-lit, dim enough to seem intimate but bright enough for human navigation. A single redwood table dominated the space. It was twelve feet in diameter and low to the ground, like all the tables he'd seen in the cafe. Cushions and other colorful, lumpy soft things surrounded it. One man and one woman were already seated cross-legged around the table. Manny was shocked to see they were both quite old.

The man was heavyset, with a lot of curly black hair piled atop his head and around his craggy, lined face. Startlingly bright blue eyes stood out over the flickering candle light. He wore an old-fashioned suit with a necktie and everything. It was the kind of suit a banker might have worn fifty years ago, if the old movies Manny'd watched were close to accurate.

He looked to be in his sixties, while the woman next to him seemed considerably older. Her face was so lined, and her skin so thin, she almost looked fake, like some kind of animatronic creation. No one looked that old anymore. The Austin autonomous region wasn't wealthy but basic JuvEn treatments were cheap and heavily subsidized. Even the poor could afford to combat the worst side-effects of aging. Things were different in the Republic of Texas proper, but none of the poor there lived long enough to look like this woman.

She wore high-waisted, purple yoga pants and a very tight t-shirt with a faded print of a five-fingered Bart Simpson flipping the bird. Her hair was completely white and bound behind her in a tight ponytail. She smiled at Manny when he looked at her. The old woman's teeth were as white as her hair.

"Hello there, young men," she said in a voice that evoked the Platonic ideal of a grandma. "Hello, Topaz. Mike."

"Skullfucker Mike, ma'am," Skullfucker Mike corrected her as he came down the ladder. He handed Reggie, Manny, and Topaz each a beer and then found a cushion large and plush enough for his bulk and dropped down. Manny took his cue and found a seat. Reggie grabbed the cushion next to him. Topaz leaned against the back wall but stood as she introduced them.

"This is Manny Sanchez, he's a fixer from the Austin region. And this is Reggie Sullivan, he works for the BBC. Manny, Reggie, this is Nana Yazzie. She's our Eldest. And the less-old fart is Donny Farris. He's a guest. And a Brit, too."

"Wait, *the* Donald Farris?" Reggie asked. "The guy who made–"

"*Visions of Blood*? Yes," said the old man. "Did you actually watch it? Or have you just seen a handful of ten-second clips in your media feed over the years?"

"Both, actually," Reggie replied.

"Mmmph," Donald grunted.

Manny had heard of *Visions of Blood* back in school. It was a documentary, released a year before the Second American Civil War caught fire. It followed two Navajo special-forces veterans as they organized a massive direct-action campaign that started in Sante Fe but spread throughout the Southwest. His textbook had called it one of the major seeds of the old U.S.'s collapse.

Reggie was clearly star-struck by Donald. Manny was more curious about the old woman. No matter where he turned his head, he couldn't quite seem to escape her eyes. She had this strange way of staring at him, without really staring. It made Manny feel somehow naked and, vaguely, comforted all at the same time. "Nana" meant "grandma," which made sense. But he wasn't sure what the rest of her title meant, exactly.

"Are you in charge, then?" he asked her. In response, everyone but Reggie chuckled.

"No one is 'in charge' here," said Nana Yazzie. "That will become increasingly clear the longer you stay. I'm the Eldest, which means exactly what it sounds like. I'm old as dirt, and older than any of the other dirt around here, too." She eyed Donald Farris, and continued.

"When I give advice or have an opinion some people listen. This is not a state, and I am not a head of state, but sometimes I play one for the folks outside. Foreign policy, diplomatic relations, that sort of stuff. Mainly because no one else can be arsed."

"By the way," she added, "welcome to the City of Wheels. Or," she frowned a little, "Rolling Fuck. I argued rather strenuously against that name, but I was outvoted."

"I like the name," said Skullfucker Mike. "It's fun. Cities shouldn't take themselves too seriously. That's when the problems start."

"So why are we here?" Manny asked. "I mean, I'm grateful and all. We're grateful," he nodded to Reggie. "But I know y'all aren't just being nice. Mike said you had dangerous work."

"Skullfucker Mike," Skullfucker Mike insisted again. Nana Yazzie ignored him and replied to Manny.

"We do have a job for you, mijo. You are not required to take it though. If you say no we'll still return you and your journalist friend to Austin. And if you do help us, you'll be compensated."

"So what is it you need?"

The old woman snapped her fingers. A projection screen hummed to life on the wall of the room that faced Manny and Reggie. It displayed three faces: two women and one man. They all looked young, though that meant very little. One woman was white and kept her hair in a bright purple mohawk. The other was as bald as Skullfucker Mike, with round cheeks, green, scowling eyes, and skin a little darker than Manny's. The young man was very pale. He appeared to be of Chinese descent, and his exposed skin was covered in scarified symbols from a language Manny didn't recognize. It definitely wasn't Chinese.

"From left to right; Marigold Fulton, Tule Black Elk, and Rick Hartford. They're all citizens, and they act as our negotiators when the city is in the Southwest. Two days ago they arrived in Plano to negotiate a trade deal with the Republic of Texas. We have quite a lot of processed coffee and we were hoping to trade it for..." She trailed off a bit and her cheeks reddened. Manny thought she looked embarrassed. "For snacks."

"Snacks?" Reggie asked.

"Yes," she nodded. "The Frito-Lay Corporation is—or at least was—still headquartered in Plano. The junk food they produce is harder to find out west."

"We mostly wanted cheetos," Topaz licked her lips. "For whatever reason, the imitations we print out here just don't cut it."

"We barter everywhere we go," Nana Yazzie continued, "and since post-humans aren't welcome in most populated areas, our negotiators are all pretty close to baseline. They traveled unarmed into Plano. The city fell six hours after they arrived."

Reggie grunted. "Two days ago people were telling me the Kingdom was on its last legs."

"Yes," Nana Yazzie said, "it would appear they are not quite the paper tiger everyone expected. We're still scrambling for good data, but it's safe to say they've pilfered the majority of the Republic's heavy equipment and converted as much as half their standing army. At the same time Plano fell, dozens of Christian militias across the state launched fresh offensives. Galveston is still holding, but that could change at any moment. Houston blew their levees and flooded half the city to save the other half. But that also means the Kingdom can move on to Austin without worrying about their flank. They've pushed the SDF entirely out of ciudad de muerta, so there's nothing left between them and your home."

Donald Farris spoke up, grave and gravely. "We know that the offensive started with dozens of autonomous car-bombings at checkpoints and fortifications. We don't know how they managed it."

"What's important now," Nana Yazzie continued, "is that three of our people have been captured."

Manny fought down a spike of anger. "With all due respect Nana," he said in a deliberately neutral tone, "they just conquered the city I was born in. I've probably lost a dozen friends and these godfascists are only, what, two hours away from Austin?"

"Ninety minutes," Donald said. "They seem to be holding position now. Digesting their meal. But they'll be on the march soon. I expect the vaunted Austin defense forces will be able to hold them off for, oh, a good four or five days. Maybe a week. Unless." He glanced over to Nana Yazzie. She nodded in agreement.

"Unless?" asked Manny.

"Unless," Nana agreed. "Unless our militia comes to their aid. We're not in the habit of fighting other people's battles. But we're not in the habit of letting regressives win, either. I asked for a vote once we learned our people had been captured. Our fighters, most of them, agreed to stop the Heavenly Kingdom's advance and give your people enough time to coordinate a proper defense. But there's a catch."

"Ah," Manny was starting to get it. "If you step in, they'll kill your people."

Nana Yazzie nodded. “Yes. And none of our fighters are willing to risk that.”

“Well I’m not sure what you want from me,” Manny said. “I’m a talker, not a fighter.”

“A talker is exactly what we need, Emmanuel,” Nana Yazzie assured him.

Manny winced in irritation at the use of his full name.

“Manny,” he insisted, in the same tone Skullfucker Mike had used a little earlier.

“As you say, mijo.”

“What kind of talking do you want me to do?” he asked. “I’m sure you’ve got better negotiators than me.”

“Perhaps, but you’ve got something none of our people possess. You’re a citizen of the Republic. And the Heavenly Kingdom has just issued a general amnesty for all citizens willing to repent and declare allegiance. You know how the people in this region talk. You won’t arouse suspicion if you enter.”

“So you want me to find your people. And then what, break them out? I can barely shoot straight. I don’t think I’m the man to execute a prison break.”

“They’ve got plenty of fighters, son,” Donald Farris growled. “But if Topaz and Skullfucker Mike haven’t keyed you in on this, the chromed aren’t exactly good at ‘blending.’”

“He’s right,” Nana smiled sadly. “We’ll pair you with someone who can do the violence. But we’ll need you to get them close enough to find our people and effect an escape. You’ll need to help our person maintain their cover.”

Manny felt a powerful anger boil up inside his belly.

“So, basically, you and your ‘militia’ are holding my homeland hostage? And if I don’t risk my culo to save your negotiators, Austin dies?”

“Mijo. It’s nothing as sinister as that. Our people want to fight, but...”

“But,” Donald picked up, “we’re all family here. And family comes before corrupt, fractious foreign militias and equally corrupt, fractious foreign cities. All told I’d say it’s a good deal for you.”

“What was your plan before this meeting?” Nana Yazzie asked.

Manny opened his mouth to respond, but realized he didn’t have a clear answer. He hadn’t exactly had much time to puzzle that out. And any time he'd tried, he thought about Oscar, his missing stringer, and that made him want to panic. *He's dead, or worse. And there's nothing you can do about that. What you can do is buy a fucking plane ticket and beg the Germans to take you in as a refugee.*

That seemed like a good plan. Or at least the best of a bunch of shitty options. But then a scornful voice rose up from the dark recesses of his semi-withered conscience. *What about his wife? Are you just going to leave her broke and widowed? You have to at least give her something...*

"I'm flying to Germany," he said, "or maybe France. Wherever I can get the cheapest ticket, either in Austin or El Paso."

"How much money do you have saved up, son?" Donald Farris asked. "They won't issue a long-term visa unless you've got at least sixty grand, Californian."

Manny had a little more than half that. Less, once he paid off Oscar's wife. *Widow. Fuck, man, you sent him out there.* The uncertainty and despair must have been obvious on his face. Both Donald Farris and Nana Yazzie gave him the kind of looks normally reserved for wounded kittens.

"I may be able to help," the old Brit said. "I do have some connections in Germany. People who might sponsor your visa. If you help."

The thought of a visa, the mental image of seeing one stamped in his otherwise-worthless passport, was intoxicating. Manny'd never traveled outside of Texas but he had kept, at all times, an active passport. It had been the physical anchor for his wildest dreams. And now Donald Farris was telling him he could make something as magical as a visa real. Manny almost swooned.

"Do I have to decide now?" he asked, careful to keep his tone as calm as he could manage.

"Of course not," Nana Yazzie said, "that would be terribly unfair. You should get some sleep and then a proper breakfast. There's certainly enough time for that. And you look exhausted."

He was. Now that the excitement of the morning had faded, he felt gripped by a bone-deep weariness that was not at all helped by the dim lighting and comfortable cushions around him. Reggie should have been even more tired, what with jet lag. But the journalist looked alert, jittery despite the bags under his eyes.

"If it's possible," Reggie said, "and you have one, I could really use a high speed data connection. My deck's been spotty since the shooting started. I've got a lot to upload to the company servers, and I should probably check in with my editors, let them know I'm not dead, et cetera..."

"That won't be a problem." She stood, and her knees popped audibly with the movement. "Ooh," she grunted and then continued, "Topaz and Mike–"

"Skullfucker Mike."

"–will show you to a nice, relatively soundproof room. They'll help you get onto our data tower too, Reggie."

"Thank you."

She looked at Manny again, and fixed him with her sad grandmother's smile.

"We'll give you as much time to decide as we can. We expect the Kingdom to hold for a few days. But we didn't expect them to launch an attack like this. So take that with a grain of salt."

"I'm Texan, Nana," Manny said. "I take everything with salt."

Chapter 11

Roland.

Roland loved to fight men in powered armor. The increased firepower and durability gave them an outside chance, which made it fun. And the sheer expense of modern suits made it feel a little like wailing on rich kids with fancy toys.

But Roland did not like fighting normal humans. He'd hoped the infantry coming up behind the armored troopers would run like hell once he popped their vanguard. But instead, they'd insisted on a fight and started shooting at him with very large guns. One explosive munition had hit nine yards ahead of his position and the other had impacted close enough to pepper Roland's torso and face with shrapnel.

So, regretfully, he charged the enemy. The Martyrs shot back, they hit him a few times, but Roland paid their bullets as much mind as he would a mild rain.

He drew close enough for visual contact. These Martyrs were a motley sight. Several of them fought shirtless with white crosses daubed across their chests. Most of them wore body armor, very little of it modern. Roland saw a lot of old pre-war plate carriers and surplus police vests. That crap wouldn't stop military-grade rifle rounds. Although, since the only weapon in Roland's hand was a big-ass wrench, how these men were armored hardly mattered.

They were mostly armed with old M4s and a smattering of newer assault rifles probably pilfered from the Republic of Texas. Fifty men.

Six technicals. Two drone carriers. Roland hit their skirmishing line before the teams on the recoilless rifles, his first target, could reload.

Roland's wrench broke jaws and orbital bones, it cracked pelvises and shattered thighs. He dispatched the rifle teams and then danced through the onrushing mob of militia like some sort of compound-fracture-dispensing ballerina. And as he fought, Roland felt the familiar sunlight warmth of serotonin flood his synapses. He remembered a little of how the Army had explained the battle drugs now flowing through his brain: "a guarantee of sustained aggression." The longer he fought, the harder it would be for him to stop fighting, and to avoid killing.

Roland felt his self control begin to fade as he knocked out his dozenth Martyr. He started swinging harder. His blows increasingly connected with clavicles instead of coccyxes, and jaws instead of elbows. His hindbrain warned him as the kill likelihood estimates jumped from four to six percent, up to twenty, thirty, forty percent. He felt his conscience fade beneath the euphoric red haze of narcotic splendor.

Before he knew it, the whole platoon of martyrs was either on the ground or fleeing for the relative safety of their technicals. Roland laughed a madman's laugh, tickled that they thought a bunch of old Toyota trucks with machine guns in the beds might slow him down. He put a fist through the engine block of one and ate a burst of .50 caliber fire from the other as he pivoted and launched his wrench through the driver's-side window. The improvised missile connected with the face of the driver, who spun his wheel hard to the left. The truck flipped forward onto its cabin. Something about the wet crunch it made sounded so familiar–

"–Oh God, oh dear sweet Jesus please sir–"

The National Guardsman was nineteen years old. Randall Wallace was his name. Roland knew that because his hindbrain had sucked in every piece of publicly available data on the boy once it had scanned his face. It had done that with all the occupants of the humvee in the four seconds before Roland had blown it on its side. Wallace was just the only member of the crew unlucky enough to survive.

"Please sir–"

Roland stepped toward the broken, bloodied boy.

–He came back to himself, a bit disoriented but none the worse for wear. His hindbrain and a lifetime of combat memories had kept his body fighting in his mind's absence. Now wrenchless, Roland used his bare hands to tear open doors and break faces. The gunners on the remaining technicals tried to fire back, but their maneuverability was limited by the rubble-choked streets and their own fleeing infantry. One minute after first contact, the Martyr contingent had been reduced to a dozen shell-shocked soldiers piled hastily onto the tops of their retreating drone carriers.

Roland hopped onto the last of the technicals. He disabled it by pulling the driver out through the front windshield and using the man's body to beat the gunner into unconsciousness. Roland tore the vehicle's 20mm cannon free from its swivel-mount and sighted in on the fleeing troops. His synapses promised him more chemical rewards, if only he'd pull the trigger.

But something in Roland's forebrain stopped him. Under the joyous miasma of the battle drugs his conscience re-asserted itself. He lowered his weapon and watched as his enemies beat hell for leather in the opposite direction. His hands shook, and he felt the first symptoms of withdrawal as his heart-rate dropped and the adrenaline drip slowed its flow. Roland closed his eyes. He breathed in and out and centered himself.

The crash came.

Now that the fighting was done Roland had time to process the sense data he'd pulled from his enemies. He knew what the driver he'd ripped out of the windshield had eaten for breakfast. He knew which of the militia he'd crippled were fathers. He knew which had wives, or at least girlfriends. He could smell traces of football leather on some of their hands. One man he'd wrenched had smelled of rosin; a violinist.

Roland couldn't fight a man without learning much more about him than any killer should know about their victims. That knowledge crashed down on him in a hailstorm of guilt. Roland dropped the cannon into the truck's bed. He hopped down, pulled Sardar's wrench free from the wreck of the second technical, and, with a heavy heart, headed back toward Bigsby and his squad.

Nadine and Azime both looked pretty seriously wounded. Bigsby was helping to carry them both back to the APC while Will handled overwatch with his grenade launcher. Roland caught up with them and fell into step. Bigsby looked over at him and grunted, "You gonna try to take my nipple now?"

Roland shrugged. He wasn't in the mood. His brain was in the dark ugly place it always went after a bloody fight, when the raw data about all the men he'd killed or battered lingered in his brain like a fart in the back of a humvee.

They reached the APC. Sardar gasped when he saw them. Pedro vomited. Roland was confused until he realized Bigsby and Will had also started to stare. Roland looked down at himself and saw that he looked like a literal dead man walking. He'd been shot forty-seven times, by his hindbrain's best count, and peppered with shrapnel on top of that. He had ribs showing through, holes blasted in his biceps and his belly, and the bone on his left thigh was completely exposed.

"It looks worse than it is," Roland said.

"It looks like you should be dead about five times over," Sardar replied.

Roland looked Sardar up and down. His hindbrain did the math.

"Eleven times, if I were you."

"Jesus–"

He handed Sardar the wrench, now dented and bloodstained. A large clump of hair and scalp was still stuck to the heel jaw. The mechanic took his tool with one hesitant hand. He stared at the gore on it until Bigsby started to yell again.

"Oi, fuckos. In case you've forgotten there's an army breathing up our asses. Sar', you good to drive man?"

Sardar nodded.

"Then let's get the wounded in the cab and power the fuck out of here. Will, stay on watch."

Will grunted and jerked his head at Roland. "This fucker oughta cover us. He just took out half a company on his lonesome."

"You trust him to watch your six?" Bigsby asked.

Roland only half-heard them. He stared off into the distance, worked his jaw, and clenched his left fist so hard his fingernails drew blood. He was lost in his head, scanning scent-memories and analyzing the men he'd just beaten. He was drawn, again and again, to the memory of one man in particular. He'd worn a tattered U.S. Army issue vest and an M16 that posed as much of a threat to Roland as a drunken hornet. He'd had the scent of a woman on him. He wasn't alone in that, but the rich wave of oxytocin that had poured off him was intense and real. In his memory, the man's face kept twisting and morphing into the face of Randall Wallace.

Roland started to cry.

Bigsby and Sardar loaded Ryan, Nadine, and Azime into the transport. Will just stared at him. His gaze locked on Roland's tears as if each one were the Loch Ness Monster. Roland didn't care. His hindbrain kept up its glitchy feed of data, a mix of information on the men he'd just killed and men he'd killed years ago.

Once the wounded were loaded up, everyone filed into the Mattis APC. Will popped the top hatch and sat gunner with his grenade launcher. Inside the APC, Bigsby and Pedro did their best version of first aid on their wounded companions. There wasn't much for them to do, though. Everyone in the squad had fairly advanced healing suites.

Roland trudged into the APC and took his seat. No one made eye contact with him. Sardar kicked it into gear, and off they went.

Waco had always been one of the worst cities in Texas. In the late 1800s, it had been a refuge for former Confederate loyalists. In the 1900s, it had developed a reputation as a haven for kooks and religious extremists. Caught between the economic powerhouse of Dallas and the relative cultural mecca of Austin, Waco was a second-rate college town at best and, at worst, a meth-filled rest stop between Texas's good cities.

The Revolution had changed that. After the Lakewood Blast, Dallas had bled 60 percent of its population. Most of those people had fled to Austin, since constant flooding had rendered much of Houston uninhabitable. But half a million of them, ish, had swelled Waco into something resembling a worthwhile place to exist. The city had thrived in the post-revolutionary years. It was nominally controlled by the Austin Regional Government, and so it had been spared the worst of the Republic of Texas's corruption.

But now it looked like Waco would be the next city eaten by the expanding Heavenly Kingdom. Roland could smell the stink of fear in the air when they were still a half-dozen miles out from the city limits. Once they hit the city proper, their convoy halted at a military checkpoint. Power-armored Austin Republican Guardsmen opened the side hatch of the Mattis APC and inspected the squad. Bigsby spoke for them, beamed over some credentials from the SDF, and they were waved in.

They stopped at a fueling depot with the rest of the SDF column and Roland hopped out of the APC to stretch his legs and roll another blunt. He picked a cherry-apple wrap he'd dipped in a vat of extra-strength hydrocodone syrup earlier that morning. As he rolled it tight and sealed the seam with his saliva, he watched the SDF unload hundreds of wounded warriors from half-tracks and APCs and the beds of flatbed trucks. Many of the walking men and women looked wounded too. Most of the vehicles were damaged.

Roland lit the blunt and stared off toward Dallas. It was still early morning, and the sky was streaked with red and orange. On the horizon black smoke rose to meet the sunrise. Roland was struck with a powerful sense of déjà vu. This wasn't the first time he'd watched a great city burn in the light of the rising sun. According to his hindbrain, it was around the thirtieth time. He recalled a few of those cities—Denver, Baltimore, D.C., Richmond—but the particulars of each calamity were lost to his memory.

He wondered, not for the first time, if his broken brain might be a blessing.

"Oi."

It was Sardar. He approached from the rear and stepped up to Roland's right side. Roland offered the mechanic his blunt, now half-smoked, and Sardar accepted it. He drew in a deep lungful of medicated smoke, held it in his lungs for three long seconds, and then exhaled with only a small fit of coughing.

"This tastes like fucking cough syrup, man."

"Ayep," Roland agreed. "There's enough opiates on that to kill a small cat."

"That's a weird thing to say."

"Ayep," Roland agreed.

Sardar took a second hit and then passed the blunt back to Roland. They stood in companionable silence for a minute and watched the distant smoke mingle with the morning light. Sardar spoke first.

"Jim's on his way out here. He's flying in with three more squads. Austin's approved emergency funding to stabilize the front. Apparently a chunk of that's coming our way."

"Grats," said Roland. And then, "What's the money mean to you?"

Sardar shrugged. "Cascadia, probably. Been saving for a couple years now. Fifty grand to buy residency, another hundred grand or so to set me up for the first year while I find work."

Roland finished another deep pull on the blunt and offered it to Sardar. The other man declined with a polite wave of his hand.

"No thanks."

Roland puffed again and asked, "So what's the Pacific Northwest got that you want?"

"A future," Sardar said. "I mean, that's what it always meant in my head. I grew up in El Paso. Got trained up by that army, blooded in their first little civil war."

"The Albuquerque Secession?"

Sardar nodded. "Didn't see much action then. But I got Jim's attention. He made me an offer when my term of service expired. The idea was I'd be with him for five years and retire with enough money to make a new start out West. I always dreamed of a life in Portland. It seems nice there."

"It is," Roland agreed. "Or at least, I've got nice memories. I met a girl out there when I was...younger. I remember watching the fog roll in with her."

He ran a hand over the stubble on his head. It was weird to him that he'd been given so much control over his bodily functions and yet still found himself making nervous gestures. For some reason talking about her made him want to cover his face. The impulse was wired into him, deeper than the carbon fiber that laced his bones.

"That sounds tough," Sardar said. He managed to look concerned without showing pity. "I can't imagine having all these memories floating around with no throughline to connect them together. It must hurt."

Roland shrugged. "What hurts most is knowing that it should hurt more. I don't remember enough to give the pain its proper due."

They were quiet for a bit. Roland finished the blunt and put it out on his right index finger. Sardar pulled a bronze flask out from his jacket pocket, took a belt and then offered it to Roland. It was Laphroaig whiskey. Even if he hadn't been chromed to the gills Roland would've recognized that smell from three feet away. He took a gulp from the flask and passed it back. Sardar broke the silence again.

"Look, maybe I'm reading things wrong but...we've got some tents set up near the APC. You up for a fuck?"

Roland looked the man up and down again. Sardar was a good looking guy. Short, broad with muscular arms and a comfortable belly paunch. He had a neat-trimmed beard and curly black hair.

"Yeah, alright."

It was pretty good sex. Nothing to blow Roland's mind but the release provided a quantum of chill to calm the pangs of memory. Afterwards, Sardar fell asleep nuzzled into his shoulder. Roland didn't particularly feel like cuddling but he sensed the other man needed the human contact. So he laid there with him for a couple of hours, rolled and smoked two more blunts and tried not to think about the lives he'd ended that morning.

A little after noon, Bigsby came by and knocked on the tent flap.

"Sar', Roland, el jefe's here. Clean up your fuckstink and meet us by the APC."

They did. Five minutes later, the whole squad had assembled around the Mattis. Ryan looked more or less recovered from his injuries. Azime also seemed good as new. Nadine was still pretty bandaged, and her eyes were lidded and unfocused from blood loss and opiates. Will had brewed up a large French press of coffee. He busied himself pouring measures of it out into hemp-foam cups. Roland took one and drained it in a single mighty gulp. It was proper post-human strength coffee. The caffeine rush mingled with the opiates and THC already flooding his synapses and brought him to a lovely half-lucid state of quasiwareness.

"Did you guys fuck?" Pedro finally asked, after about a minute of staring at Roland and Sardar and asking the same question with his eyes.

"Yes," Bigsby and Nadine both replied.

Sardar laughed at that. So did Roland. For one beautiful moment, he felt nice. A kind of nice he was pretty sure he hadn't felt in a long time. And then came a familiar pattern of bootsteps, tickling Roland's ears.

Jim.

Roland turned just as Jim walked into view. His legs were covered by a pair of armored red leather chaps. His groin was wrapped up in a thick kevlar thong but his pelvis and ass were otherwise unguarded.

He wore a double-shoulder holster with a pair of bone-handled wheelguns under his arms. The snake tattoos on Jim's chest and shoulders danced to a melody Roland eventually recognized as "La Cucaracha."

"Your ink looks real good today, boss," said Bigsby.

"Ass-licker," said Sardar.

"Takes one to know one."

"I don't lick ass," Sardar replied haughtily. "I eat it like a starving hyena."

More laughter, and another fleeting moment of community that was broken when Jim addressed the squad.

"Alright. So several bunks have been humped here. This Heavenly Kingdom's got at least ten thousand effectives in-theater, with armor, artillery, drones—the works. Our new employer, Austin, has about three thousand fighters here in Waco. Plus now the fifteen of you lot. I flew in with Ajax and Florin. They're prepping their squads now."

Bigsby spat. "Ajax fights about as well as a drunk dog in a burlap sack."

Will replied: "You're just sayin' that because he choked you out in the Blood Dome last year."

Bigsby responded with a double middle-finger.

"Ahem," Jim ahem'd. "Plenty of time for dick-measuring later. Time enough for the rest of you, at least. This city doesn't have a ruler long enough for my dick."

He paused for a laugh. No one obliged. Jim rolled his eyes.

"Assholes. So, look, we're in a bad position, with fuck-all for reinforcements coming in. Austin might be able to scrape up a couple of battalions if they suddenly clear out the Houston front, but that don't look likely. Enemy has another ten thousand men there."

"Fuck." Sardar was the only one to actually say it, but everyone else in the group mouthed the word or some equivalent curse.

"How is that even possible?" Azime's voice was still a little slurred from the painkillers, but her eyes were focused now.

Jim shrugged. "Hard to say, exactly. Mass defections from the Republic of Texas. Intel suspects the UCS probably sent in some spec-ops guys, I dunno. Some sorta skullduggerous bullshit went down. The 'how' of it ain't really our problem today. For now we've gotta deal with the reality."

The snakes on Jim's torso stopped writhing. He locked eyes with Roland, and Roland felt compelled to meet his old friend's gaze.

"Can we count on your help?" Jim asked.

"Fuck no," Roland said. "I've killed enough naive young men today. I don't aim to kill any more."

To his surprise, Jim nodded in acceptance.

"Understandable. This kind of fighting was a violation of our contract. I regret that, Roland. If I'd known this was going to be a meat grinder I wouldn't have interrupted your retirement."

Roland wasn't sure he believed that. But he kept his mouth shut as Jim continued.

"I'd like to propose a renegotiation of our contract. In light of the changing situation on the ground."

"I'm not blowing up anything else for you."

"That's fine." Jim put his hands out in the sort of placating gesture one would use on an angry dog, "I don't need your killyness. I need your sneakiness. You can still take faces, right?"

Roland's memories of his time in the army were as patchy as his memories of everything else. He didn't remember much about how they'd used him. But he knew that some of the wetware they'd installed allowed him to modify his skin and bone structure to fool facial recognition scanners, thumbprint readers, and, of course, human beings.

"Yes," he said, "but..."

Jim cut him off, "You don't need to kill anyone. The face you'll need is already dead."

"And what do you want me to do with this man's face that isn't more murder?"

Jim's lips curled up into a grin. The expression sent shivers arcing down Roland's spine. He felt like he'd seen that grin before, never preceding good things.

"Rolling Fuck is nearby, and in the City of a Wheels are six hundred or so real scary bastards. I have it on good authority that they'd be happy to throw down on our side. But it turns out some of their negotiators were captured, back at the start of all this shit. No one in the city will risk fighting until they're pulled out safely."

Roland raised an eyebrow, "So, a rescue mission then?"

"That's right." Jim grinned in a way Roland didn't quite trust. "You'll be saving lives."

Roland's gut twisted into knots. The shades of a thousand memories spoke up and warned him not to trust Jim at his word. But those shades also drove him to take Jim up on the offer. He wanted his memories back. Jim smiled that hackle-raising smile again.

"You don't have to agree yet. Come to Rolling Fuck with me. We'll talk things over with their elders. You can do some of their fancy space drugs. And then you can make your decision."

"Alright," Roland sighed. "But only 'cuz you said 'fancy space drugs.'"

They flew to Rolling Fuck in Jim's heli-craft. It had been military issue originally, but the interior had been redone to Jim's tastes. That mostly meant a lot of velour and a full wet bar. There were four beers on tap, just to the right of a double-barreled 35mm grenade launcher mounted beside the door. Roland drank for the duration of the ten minute flight.

"You know," Jim said, "Topaz lives there now. Been with the city a while."

"Topaz?" Roland asked.

Something shuddered in his gut. He felt his hippocampus flicker with the dim light of recognition. He saw that face again, the woman from so many of his dreams and a few of his shattered memories. So that was her name. It felt right, now that he knew it again.

"Do you remember her at all, Roland?" Jim asked, his voice uncharacteristically tender.

Roland nodded and swirled the beer in his hands to buy some time.

"I remember snatches of her," he said. "I remember loving her. I remember enough that it hurts sometimes. Mostly it hurts that I don't remember enough to be as sad as I oughta be."

There was a spark of real sorrow in Jim's eyes. The other man's hand twitched in a way that made Roland think he might've been about to reach out to him. But Jim kept his hand to himself.

"I'm not sure how much I should say," he said. "I'm sorry."

There was something in Jim's face when he said that. It resembled regret, or guilt. But it passed quickly. And nothing else was said during the flight. They landed on one of the top spires of Rolling Fuck, on a landing pad that doubled as a nude bar. He and Jim grabbed another round of drinks before they proceeded down, through the infinite party that was the City of Wheels and onto the top of the main roller. They grabbed another round of drinks there and sat at the bar table while Jim waited for the word to go down.

It was late afternoon by this point, and evening had started to close in. The normal boiling Texas heat was cut by a cool breeze. White clouds rolled in above them. Roland's hindbrain told him there was, at best, a 12 percent chance of rain. But the clouds were still welcome. He and Jim drank in silence for a few minutes until the other man tapped his shoulder and said, "They're ready for us."

They stood, a bit unsteadily, and headed toward the ladder down into the main roller. They reached the ladder just as two other people came up it, a man and a woman. The man's face triggered a flurry of memory fragments: fighting back to back in the choking streets of Baltimore, drinking heavily on the edge of a canyon in the Arizona desert, charging a riot line with pipes and hammers in their hands. A name bubbled up from inside the memories.

"Mike!" he shouted before he really thought about it. "Hey brother!"

Skullfucker Mike froze. Roland was already halfway to a hug when he realized Mike wasn't feeling it. And then he caught his first good look at the woman coming up the ladder behind him. She had short-cropped teal hair, damascene fangs, and eyes so loud he could almost hear her thoughts. Topaz.

"R–" she started to say his name and then her voice caught. He heard the ghost of tears beneath it, and then she finished, "...Roland."

"Yes," he said, not sure of what else to say.

"Do you remember me?"

"No," he admitted. Part of him wanted to lie. But he couldn't. The broken scraps that remained of his love for her made it impossible. So he gave the honest answer, and he watched her die a little inside.

Topaz nodded. She closed her eyes for a second, bit down on her bottom lip, and then she put a quick hand on Mike's shoulder before she walked away, up one of the gantrys and into the chaos of night in Rolling Fuck.

Roland looked to Mike.

"I'm sorry."

Skullfucker Mike smiled sadly back.

"I know, buddy."

And then he left too. Roland felt confusion and a distant hurt. He had a feeling that he should have been crying. But, for some reason, he couldn't. And so he didn't. Instead he took a fistful of Oxycontin and stumbled down the ladder, following Jim.

Rolling Fuck's conference room was sumptuous, elegant, and surprisingly professional. Two old people sat at the far end of a conference table. Roland had a vague memory tingle of having met the man before, long ago, but neither of their faces brought a name to his mind. Jim introduced them but their names fled his head a few seconds later. In fact, the first minute or two of conversation flowed around him in an indistinct haze.

That may have had something to do with the softball-sized mass of Oxycontin he'd eaten as he'd climbed down the ladder with Jim. Roland had assumed the drugs would help him focus through the boredom. Apparently he'd miscalculated.

"So," the old lady said with a hint of finality, "that's the situation we're in. Are you willing to help us?"

In response, Roland blacked out. Just for a few seconds. He was awoken by the thud of his head hitting the conference room table. *Fuck that's good Oxy.* He wished he could remember where he'd gotten it.

"Oh dear," said the lady.

"He's fine," Jim sighed, "but we're probably going to need to start over."

The lady brought him some coffee and re-introduced herself as "Nana Yazzie." Thanks to the coffee and Roland's clearing head, her name stuck this time. It was hard not to marvel at her age, and harder still to stop his hindbrain from calculating how much longer 'til her human heart gave out.

Roland smelled cancer on the old man. Not serious cancer, nothing basic medicine couldn't handle, but all the same the odor that wafted off him brought Roland a sort of primal discomfort. Or maybe it was the old man's eyes that made his guts warble. It was hard to say. There was something disconcerting in the way he looked at Roland.

"Roland!" Jim shouted. Roland shook himself out of the haze and refocused on Nana Yazzie.

"Sorry," he grunted.

"It's fine," she said, and set into her spiel again. She showed him pictures of her captured friends, Tule Black Elk, Rick Hartford, and Marigold Fulton. She explained the dire situation in North Texas and the Doom that marched toward Waco and Austin. It was a sad story, but not one that compelled Roland to action. Other than Topaz and Skullfucker Mike, the citizens of Rolling Fuck were total strangers to him. Austin was just another little ailing Republic in a continent full of them.

"I'm sorry for your people," he told her, "and I'm sorry for Austin. But I really don't see how any of this is my damn business."

Jim took those words as his cue.

"Tule and Topaz are close," said Jim. His voice was low, his tone smooth as silk. "Like sisters, from what I hear. Marigold vouched for Topaz and Skullfucker Mike when they joined the city. She's all fucked up over this."

"From what I hear," he added.

"So let her do something about it then," Roland muttered. "She's got enough chrome to choke a river. Shit, this city's got enough monster-people to burn the Eastern Seaboard. Why do you need me?"

"Because the Martyrs aren't stupid," Jim said. "They're scanning for chrome, for biomods, for everything but the shit you've got. Because no one left alive is packing the shit you've got."

Roland grunted again, his nostrils flared. There was something strange about the words Jim had chosen. *No one left alive.* Had there been others? He knew his mods had come courtesy of the old U.S. Defense Department, but he didn't remember which unit he'd been a part of or what he'd done. There was a bit of memory, hazy and fragmented, that popped into his dreams from time to time–

He was stuck inside a long, cool metal pod. The cold black of space unfolded around him. Roland felt warm bodies to his left and right, smelled the comforting scents of Men He Trusted. Red lights blinked above his field of vision. Something tugged at his belly, there was a powerful feeling of inertia–Roland closed his eyes, leaned forward, pinched the bridge of his nose and groaned just a little bit. When he came back up Nana Yazzie stared at him in confusion. Jim looked, perhaps, worried? It was hard to tell with that guy.

"What's going to happen if I don't do it?" he asked Nana Yazzie.

"To you? Nothing."

Roland shook his head. "Not to me. What are you guys going to do if I don't help?"

"Oh," she frowned. "I suppose we'll have to mount an assault. Send in a small team, four to six commandos, and try to pull them out."

"It'll be bloody," Jim said.

The old man frowned at that. He opened his mouth like he wanted to say something, but the lady put her hand on his and gave him a significant look.

"That's true," she said, "it will be bloody."

Roland felt a twinge of anger, but he couldn't blame Nana Yazzie for trying to manipulate him. The lives of her friends were on the line. Roland knew himself, though, and he knew that missions like this always went wrong. If he took this job Roland knew he'd take more lives.

"You'll save lives by being there," Jim insisted, smiling. *That fucking smile.* Roland was sure that smile had tricked him into dumb, violent things in the past. "You're the only one who can handle this with a minimum of death."

Roland didn't believe that and, at the same time, he had to admit it was technically true. He just didn't trust himself, or reality, or Jim. And yet–

"I'll do it," he said. "I'm sure I'll regret agreeing to do it, but whatever. I'll do it."

Jim looked satisfied with himself. Nana Yazzie looked relieved. The old man looked, somehow, angry?

Most of Roland's reason for agreeing to help came down to Topaz. He hated to admit that, even to himself, but it was true. The thought of her in pain twisted something in the center of his heart. He wasn't used to pain there and his tolerance was pretty low. *This is so dumb*, he told himself, *you couldn't even remember her name this morning.*

He and Jim and the old woman shook hands on the deal. Then they let him loose in their city, to imbibe and fornicate and test the limits of his wetware.

"We have things to plan," she said.

Chapter 12

Sasha.

The Lord did not mean for Sasha to be a cleaner. That was her first big lesson as a citizen of the Heavenly Kingdom. She was good enough at it, and she had too much self-respect to complain, but the work felt so unrewarding that she knew it must not be what God wanted for her.

She'd spent her first night in the Kingdom being pampered and provided for by her fellow Sisters in the Faith. They'd fed her, cleaned her, found her fresh clothes and given her all the emotional reward she could have ever wanted. And then the next day Helen had woken her up at seven in the morning to help clean out an old Republic barracks that was being transitioned over to housing for soldiers of the Heavenly Kingdom.

She knew it was honorable work, she knew it was necessary work, and she knew from the issues of *Revelator* she'd read that establishing the Kingdom of Heaven was a job that would not be accomplished easily or without pain. She'd accepted this when she'd made the choice to venture down here. But by the time she'd scrubbed her twelfth toilet of the day, Sasha had decided that her mind and her loyalty were better used elsewhere.

Oddly enough, something her father had told her about the corporate world stopped her from whining.

"Never complain, never speak ill of your colleagues, and always ask if there's more work you can do."

It had been his advice to survive and thrive in business. But she took it to heart here, and by the end of her first full day in the Kingdom she'd scrubbed more toilets than any other girl. She hated the work, but she also took a perverse sort of pride in it. That brought a little guilt, because she wasn't here to serve her pride. But also, wouldn't the Lord God be happy to see her commitment?

I'll ask Helen about that, Sasha told herself. *She'll tell me how much of my pride is justified, and how much isn't.*

She didn't see Helen again until the end of that day, when a truck came to gather up all the girls and take them back to the House of Miriam. They all washed up and then sat together around a large oaken table while Helen led them in prayer. She read a chunk of the book of Isaiah and then gave a quick lecture on the value of physical labor ("Each callous on your hands is a kiss from God") before inviting them to tuck in.

The dinner wasn't luxurious by Sasha's standards: just biscuits, a thin brown gravy, and a palm-sized slice of beef for each of them. But they had oranges for dessert, which was a treat, and Sasha felt more comfortable than she'd ever have believed among her new sisters.

Caroline had fled from Florida, North America's Banana-est Republic. She'd been shot in the arm making her way to the Heavenly Kingdom. She said almost nothing—Sasha wasn't sure she even spoke English—but Caroline worked hard. There was an intensity in her eyes that was a little scary and humbling at the same time.

Then there was Susannah, from the Blackstone Nation. Sasha couldn't help but notice she was the only Black girl there. Susannah had spent most of their work day singing to herself. She had a beautiful singing voice.

And then there were the three other AmFed girls: Emmeline, Rosie, and Anne. They'd all left a few weeks before Sasha had made her own journey. Anne had actually gone to the same middle school as Sasha.

She wasn't great with names, so most of the other girls in her group were still more of a collection of smiling faces than real people at this point. But they'd all been so warm to her. There was a real effort, from all of them, to make regular physical contact. They put hands on each other's shoulders and cheeks. They hugged constantly. Sasha experienced more touching in her first twenty-four hours here than she'd experienced in her last five years in the American Federation. There was something intoxicating about being touched and feeling so cared for.

The only girl she didn't like was Mae. Like Sasha, Mae was within spitting distance of age eighteen. She'd fled from the UCS and she had a gift for letting everyone around her know when they fell short of God's standards. During their work day she'd spent more time policing the other girl's posture than she'd spent scrubbing toilets. When Anne had hitched up her shirt sleeves, it was Mae who'd scolded her for immodesty. When Susannah took off her shoes and socks during their lunch break, Mae had yelled that she was "an unfair temptation" to the young soldiers walking by on the street.

Sasha knew it was unfair and definitely unchristian to feel this way, but Mae LOOKED like someone who lived to tell other people what to do. She had the pinched features, squinting eyes, and high-pitched voice of a born snitch. Mae kept her hair tied up in a bun so tight and short it looked military. She never smiled and never seemed to relax. And there was something about the frenzied way she'd pray, alone, quietly in the corner throughout the day that made Sasha leery.

She hated that she'd noticed those things. She knew God didn't want her focusing on what other people were doing wrong. *And besides,* she told herself, *what are you really angry about? That she's TOO serious about her faith? Isn't that why you left home?*

"Gluttony is a sin too, you know," Mae said.

Sasha realized with a start that Mae had addressed her. She had been eating her orange and, absent-minded and tired after a long day of labor, she hadn't realized how messy she'd been about peeling it. Her hands and sleeves were covered with the sticky juice. She looked around at the table and noticed that the other girls had been much more careful with their desserts.

"Sorry," Sasha started, "I wasn't thinking..."

Mae rolled her eyes and started to say something else, but Helen cut her off.

"It's quite alright, dear. None of us is perfect," she cast a reproachful eye at Mae, "...and we all lose ourselves in thought sometimes. Especially in the wake of great change. The Lord understands."

She looked out to the rest of the table with a gaze that seemed to take in each of the girls collectively, and individually. Then she spoke.

"We are all here because we recognize the primacy of God's word on earth. But we are no more perfect, and no more beloved by our Lord, than the enemies we face. Never forget that girls. Our foes are as dear to him as we are. They must be purged when they seek to interfere with God's will, but we should feel sorrow for such losses. And we should never, ever," her eyes went to Mae again, "let our fortune in hearing God's word bleed us of compassion or lead us to arrogance."

Sasha's heart swelled at this. She'd never admired a woman more. Helen had a way of imparting wisdom without judgement, of shining a light on the truth without seeming like it was her truth alone. Helen wasn't a preacher, but Sasha had never heard anyone speak the word of God with more conviction.

After dinner they had an hour of free time to read their Bibles, share a few stories of their old lives, and drink a single cup of sweet lemon tea. By nine o'clock it was bed time. Sasha was rankled a bit by the fact that she and her fellow young women were being ordered into bed at a set hour. But she was so exhausted by her day of labor that she couldn't work up much frustration over the mild injustice. Perhaps when she'd had more time to adjust, she'd bring this up to Helen.

She collapsed in her bunk bed certain she'd fall asleep in an instant. Instead she lay awake for the better part of an hour thinking of Alexander. She'd still heard nothing more from him, or about him. She'd asked Helen a couple times today and the older woman had almost seemed angry. Somehow Sasha knew the anger wasn't toward her, and that was doubly confusing.

"Sasha?"

Anne's voice broke her reverie. The other girl was situated just below her on the bunk bed. Sasha was surprised to hear her, still awake.

"Yes. Is something the matter?"

"No," Anne said, "I just couldn't sleep. I thought maybe you were awake, too."

"I guess we're both in the same boat then." Sasha kept her voice low, more to avoid waking any of the others than out of fear of breaking the rules.

"In more ways than one," Anne said. "I'm waiting for a man I love too."

Sasha's heart beat a little faster. It was like that with everything that made her think of Alexander. Her mind didn't need a great deal of prodding to turn toward him.

"Your love is at the front too?" Sasha asked.

"I think so," Anne said. "I was lucky enough to get to see him, twice. I arrived in Coppell first, back before the Kingdom took Plano. We met once then, and once more after the city fell and they moved us into the House of Miriam."

Jealousy seized Sasha's heart. She tried to replace it with gratitude in the Lord. He'd sent her someone who could understand her pain and frustration. Wasn't that a blessing?

"That must be hard for you," she said, "getting to see him and then being separated." The words came out a bit stilted and cold. She hoped Anne hadn't noticed.

"It is," Anne said, "but it isn't half so rough a place as you're in. I can't imagine how anxious you must be, arriving here and not seeing him."

"He's not the only reason I came," Sasha said, a bit defensively, "but yes. It's hard. I'm...scared. I don't know why I feel so silly admitting that."

"It's certainly not silly," Anne assured her. "But I get it. Everyone here is so focused on gratitude and God's wisdom, it almost makes you feel like a traitor for feeling afraid. Or unhappy." Anne's voice dropped a few decibels, as if she was ashamed of her next words: "I almost feel like a liar when I smile."

"I don't think the Lord wants us to be liars," Sasha said. "But I think being happy, or trying to seem happy, is a sacrifice we make for the Kingdom. It helps keep everyone else around us strong."

"Hmm," Anne said, and then yawned. Her voice sounded heavy with sleep. There must have been something contagious in the sound, because Sasha felt her own eyelids start to droop. "That's a nice way to look at it," Anne said. "I like the way you think, Sasha."

Helen woke all of them up the next morning. She was gentle with it—a hand on each girl's shoulder and a word in each of their ears, but there was no mistaking that she meant Now. So Sasha got up. Her feet hit the floor just as Anne took her first steps forward, toward the dining room. They all filed in, silent and groggy.

The girls took their breakfasts in the form of a thick, tasteless protein shake and then they were loaded onto a heavy military-looking bus and driven off to a large red-brick office building. According to the bullet-pocked signs, it had once been an administrative building for the corporation that had run most of the Republic's schools.

Sasha swept up bullet casings and shattered glass. She scrubbed toilets and wiped the blood off the walls and tried not to think too hard about how it had gotten there. Conversation wasn't forbidden, but there was a lot of ground to cover and Mae was quick to scold anyone who dawdled. Sasha and Anne both kept moving, but they passed each other in the halls often. Each time, the other girl would favor Sasha with a supportive smile and Sasha would return it.

They broke for lunch a little after noon (stale cheese sandwiches and orange juice), but instead of getting back to work after their meal they were met again by the bus that had taken them there. They were told to file inside. Sasha wound up in between Anne and Susannah in the middle row of the bus. It was hot, the air circulation was bad, and the smell of sweat was thick on the bus. But the windows were down and, once the bus got going, the air that blew in felt like heaven.

"Lord God, I've been waiting for this all day," said Susannah. "I'd stay on this thing all night if they'd let me."

"Yeah," Anne said, "this is actually a lot more comfortable than the bunkroom, even when the power's working and the fans are on."

"Does the power go out a lot?" Sasha asked. She felt dumb for even giving voice to the question. But her seatmates didn't treat it like a stupid question.

"Not a lot," Anne said, "but we'll lose an hour or two most days. And it can be out for quite a while when Austin gets a drone through."

"That doesn't happen often," Susannah assured her. "I've been in the Kingdom ten days, and we've only had to take shelter once."

"Twice for me," Anne said, "but I've been here almost three weeks."

"I'm not scared," Sasha assured them, "I'm just curious."

"You should be scared," Susannah said. "It sucks."

It wasn't a long ride, and Sasha was embarrassed at how long it took her to realize the destination: this was the same route they'd taken from the House of Miriam, just in reverse. She and the other girls were being taken downtown. Once she got a good look at the gallows she understood why. There were six people lined up in front of the little stairway that led to the platform. They looked like prisoners.

Susannah looked just as confused as Sasha. But Anne seemed to understand what was going on. She scrunched her face in disgust.

"Oh no," she said, "I hate it when they make us watch this."

The two Martyrs who'd guarded them all day opened the doors and told them to form up outside of the bus. Sasha did as she was told while grabbing as many long looks at the gallows as she could manage. None of the people who stood out in front of the platform looked like soldiers or robber barons or much of anything at all. They just seemed young and scared.

"Fags," the Martyr standing next to the driver at the bus door grunted as Sasha stepped past him. He waited until the other girls had all filed off the bus before he stepped around to stand in front of them. Sasha hadn't paid the man too much attention during the day because, in truth, he scared her. He looked old, over forty at least, and his face was heavy with scars and tattoos. There were faded blue crosses inked on each of his forearms. There wasn't much skin visible under his armor and helmet, but the skin she could see was tanned red like leather. His eyes were cold and seemed fixed into a permanent squint. When he addressed the group, it was with a voice that sounded like it came to them through a filter of gravel and glass.

"These people," he said—and spat after the word "people"—"are gender traitors." There were a few gasps from among the crowd. He continued, "It took us a while to crack into the Republic's old files. But we finally got a list of all the fags who refused to accept their God-given gender. They thought surgery could hide 'em, but there's no hiding the truth from the eyes of God or his true servants. And there's only one fair punishment for someone who turns their back on natural law."

Sasha's heart started to pound. She'd known, of course, that Pastor Mike didn't approve of transgenderism, of gender-change surgery, of homosexuality, or of anything else that didn't fit into the Biblical lines of what a man and a woman ought to be. But he'd always phrased his objections with such compassion. Queer and trans people weren't monsters, deserving of death. They were victims of the fallen secular world, same as anyone else. Sasha agreed they needed re-education, but this...

The crowd, perhaps three hundred strong, cheered as the prisoners were led up to the gallows. Sasha's heart beat like a bass drum. She couldn't hear anything else. The voices of the crowd, of her sisters, faded behind the beating sound of the blood that coursed through her head. But her eyes continued to work, and she watched in horror as they fit nooses around each victim's neck.

The young people cried and screamed and begged, but the Martyrs paid them no mind. Some of them chanted in tongues while they prepared the killing machine. Sasha saw the joy in their eyes. She found it revolting. Before long, they'd finished their preparations and six people were strung up on the gallows before the brays and cries of the crowd.

Sasha didn't think it was possible for her heart to beat any faster. But it kept speeding up. She felt light headed and nauseous and a little like she needed to go to the bathroom. Her knees grew weak and she found herself leaning on Anne. The other woman looked almost as scared as Sasha did, but she weathered it better. She put an arm around Sasha, supporting her, and the two of them looked on as the executioner called out and pulled the lever that sent six human beings dropping down to dangle until they were dead.

The snap of their necks was the only thing Sasha heard above the sound of her own pounding heart. She watched them twitch and jerk for a second, two, and then her body grew too light and her legs collapsed beneath her. The world went black.

She awoke back in the House of Miriam. Her sisters knelt or stood around her. Sasha was gratified to see she wasn't the only one who'd passed out. Anne lay next to her, clearly disoriented, along with two other young women whose names Sasha hadn't quite memorized. Helen sat in between them, wet washcloth in her hand, and stroked their faces.

"There, there, dears. You've had a terrible shock. And there's no shame in your reactions."

"No shame?" Mae spat the words. There was a glow to her face and a manic glint in her eyes. "Ma'am, with all due respect, I don't know how these girls can call themselves committed to the Heavenly Kingdom if the sight of divine justice hurts them so much."

Sasha saw anger in Helen's eyes, but the older woman didn't let it carry over into her voice. Instead she fixed Mae with a cool gaze and said in an even tone, "Miss Mae, one can believe in our Lord's justice and still regret the pain that comes with it. That does not signal a lack of devotion. It signals compassion, a trait Jesus Christ had in abundance."

Mae frowned and pursed her lips, but she kept them shut for now. Helen turned back to Sasha and the other girls who had fallen.

"Death is never easy to witness, girls. It should be a horrible thing to witness," she glanced back to Mae, "...and we should all be worried if a day ever comes when we can see such violence without pain in our hearts. But these are dire times. The world has fallen too much for pacifism to bring back the rule of God. And so we must use violence. Do you understand?"

Sasha nodded. She heard the other girls give stuttering, hollow replies. Even the girls who'd managed to stay standing looked shaken. Mae was the only one who wore a smile. They gave her a wide berth the rest of the day.

Whoever was in charge of their schedule paid some deference to the fact that they'd been forced to watch an execution. There was no more cleaning that day. They spent the rest of the daylight hours seated around the common area in the House of Miriam, sewing uniforms. Sasha had never sewn before, but Anne sat next to her and taught her the basics.

Her hands were still shaking when they got to work, but Anne helped her and, eventually, focusing on the meticulous task allowed her blot out the horror. Once she got a good grip on the basics of what was required of her, she was able to lose herself in quiet productive flow. She was almost disappointed when Helen called them to dinner.

They ate the same food as the day before. They prayed. And then they had an hour of relatively free time. They couldn't leave the House of Miriam since it was after eight. But they could talk. Sasha gravitated naturally to Susannah and Anne. The topic of conversation turned at once to the execution.

"Is that what it's always like?" Susannah asked.

Anne nodded. Her voice shook a little when she said, "I passed out last time too. I thought it'd be easier the second time around. But it really wasn't..."

"It feels wrong," Sasha whispered. She glanced over to Mae, who was holding court with a few of the other girls at the other end of the common area. "I'm not saying it's OK, what those people were doing. But surely they deserved a chance to repent."

Susannah nodded. "I don't think Jesus would want us to murder people just for being wrong. It's one thing to kill an atheist or an apostate who's attacking you. It's another thing to just," her voice caught a bit, "hang people."

Anne shook her head in an absent sort of way. "Kyle told me it was necessary."

"Kyle?" Susannah asked.

"My intended," Anne said. "I watched the first execution with him. When I passed out, he was so sweet. I came to and he was holding me, petting my head." Anne's eyes shone with love, and Sasha had to fight hard to keep the jealousy from her own face.

"He explained that the Heavenly Kingdom couldn't afford to reeducate the fallen. They are too many, and we are too surrounded. If someone is capable of changing, God will know. And He will ensure they get their just reward in Heaven."

Sasha was not entirely convinced, but she also wasn't willing to argue with Anne. It felt a little dicey just admitting her continued discomfort with the executions. So she stayed quiet and the talk turned to more comfortable matters; what they expected from the next day's work, and what sort of lives they'd lead when the fighting was over and they were settled down with the gallant warriors they knew they'd marry. Soon the girls all filed off to their small, snug beds.

After a long day of work and stress, the bed felt so good that it made Sasha feel guilty. Alexander was fighting right now. He'd surely seen more death than she had and he didn't have the option of fainting or crying about it. As she drifted off to sleep again Sasha promised herself that she would never faint or cry out in the face of death again. If this was the way God had ordained his Kingdom must come, she owed it to herself and to her Lord to stand and see it.

The next day they went back to the same battered administrative building as the day before. Sasha scrubbed and swept, ate her lunch, and got right back to work. She forced herself into enthusiasm for the menial labor with the same discipline she'd used when it had been time to study for an exam in a class she hated. The same tactic worked in both high school and the Heavenly Kingdom.

About two hours before the end of their workday, Sasha's rhythm was interrupted by the sound of a crash and a scream from one of the girls in the bathroom next door to the room she was in. Sasha dropped her scrub brush and darted over. She was the first one into the room.

It took her a moment to piece together what must have happened. Susannah had been scrubbing a sink that had been badly damaged by shellfire. The sink had collapsed while she scrubbed it and a jagged edge of porcelain had torn open the girl's hand. There was already an enormous amount of blood by the time Sasha arrived. Susannah looked pale. She'd backed up against the wall and was just screaming, wordlessly.

Sasha had taken three semesters of pre-med classes in the last two years. She had a good basic instruction in first aid. She pulled her shirt off over her head and wrapped it around the gash on the other girl's hand. It was the spare shirt she'd brought from home, and it had an antimicrobial weave that should make it relatively safe as a wound dressing. She pulled it tight, wadded the extra fabric up over the wound and applied as much pressure as she could. Susannah kept screaming but the flow of blood from her wound slowed.

"Breath with me," Sasha told Susannah as she stared into the other girl's eyes. "In," she inhaled, "and out," she exhaled. She repeated this several times, until Susannah stopped screaming and started breathing in time with her. Several of the girls had crowded around the entrance to the bathroom at this point. When Sasha glanced up she could see Mae's face in the back of the crowd. She looked disgusted, probably at the fact that Sasha had torn off her shirt.

"Please call for the Martyrs," Sasha asked no one in particular. "Tell them Susannah needs medical attention. I don't think she has any clotting agents in her blood."

No one moved. So Sasha locked eyes with Anne and told her, "Please go now. We shouldn't take any chances with a wound like this."

Anne nodded, broke away from the gawking group and stumbled off to find help. Sasha looked back to Susannah. She coaxed the other girl to sit down against the wall and sat down next to her, applying pressure to her hand the entire time. Sasha's shirt was now soaked through with hot, sticky blood. Her hands were wet too. But she didn't feel squeamish about this. She'd expected to after her reaction to the hangings, but somehow the sight of all this blood actually calmed her. She knew what to do here. It felt good to take effective action.

The Martyrs arrived a minute or so later, with a medic close behind. By that point Susannah's bleeding had stopped entirely. The medic was impressed, and he said so.

"Do you have some kind of training, ma'am? You handled this very well."

"Three semesters of pre-med," she'd answered. "It was only high school pre-med but they made us do a lot of first-aid drills."

The medic gave her a significant look and then asked, "What's your name, miss?"

"Sasha Mar–", she started before correcting herself. "Sasha."

Susannah was taken off to whatever served as a hospital for the Heavenly Kingdom while Sasha and the rest of the girls finished their work day. It was uneventful after that, but the other girl's attitudes toward her seemed to have shifted. Anne had given her a big hug, of course. But everyone was more respectful. Several of them came to her to ask minor things, advice on how best to clean a room or clear a pile of rubble. At one point Sasha had divided four girls up into two teams to remove a huge amount of shattered glass. While she'd directed the effort Mae had walked by the room and butted her head in.

"Just because she knows a little first aid doesn't make her a foreman," she sneered.

The other girls didn't pay Mae any mind. They left for the day at the usual time and arrived back at the House of Miriam in the early evening. Helen was waiting for them at the door. Behind her stood an older man in a white lab coat. He had a cross pinned to his lapel and a larger red cross on his armband. As the girls all filed into the building Sasha saw Helen point to her and whisper something to the man. He nodded.

"Miss Sasha?" he called out as she headed to her seat at the dinner table. Sasha peeled off and approached him. Helen stood nearby, distant enough to make it clear this conversation was between her and the man, but close enough that her presence provided a warm kernel of certainty and support.

"Yes?" Sasha asked.

The man had a sharp, narrow jaw and a long nose. There were deep bags under his eyes and his hair was at the grayest end of pepper-gray. He wasn't very large but he used his physicality well. He moved like he was used to controlling the room.

"Sasha, I'm Dr. Brandt. One of our medics was very impressed with your work earlier today on the injured girl."

"Sir, all I did was try to stanch the bleeding. Anyone could have handled that. It didn't require any special knowledge..."

"No," he interrupted her, "it did not. The knowledge of how to stem bleeding is not rare or special. But the willingness to jump in during an emergency, and to get blood on one's own hands, is rather rare. I understand you have some form of medical training?"

"Very little, sir. I took three semesters of pre-medical courses in high school. I was thinking about a medical career before I–"

"Yes, well, three semesters of any kind of training almost makes you a doctor here. We're not exactly flooded with qualified medical experts."

Dr. Brandt lacked Helen's gift for interrupting without seeming rude. He was clearly a busy man. And the fact that he'd offered praise made it hard for Sasha to take offense.

"Miss Helen," he snapped back at the older woman, "I'm putting this one on special duty. Would that be alright?"

"Of course, Dr. Brandt," Helen said. She smiled at Sasha, and there was honest pride in that smile. More pride than she'd ever seen in her mother's eyes. Sasha resisted the urge to tear up in response.

Dr. Brandt turned to Sasha next and asked, "What do you know about the People of the Road?"

She frowned. Post-humans were a popular topic of discussion in her high school. Sasha had seen *Wasteland Warriors* a couple years back and been as enthralled as everyone else. But her school curriculum didn't talk much about them, and definitely downplayed their influence in the rest of the continent. Her father had called them, "A bunch of idiots dancing around the desert, doing drugs and robbing people." She decided to use a variant of that for her answer.

"They're drug-addled pagans, fornicating and spurning the Will of God."

Dr. Brandt smiled. He had such a serious face and such stern features that Sasha was shocked by the honest kindness of that smile.

"I'd say that's basically accurate," he chuckled, "perhaps even a bit charitable. It turns out one of these groups sent some emissaries into Plano just before the city fell. They were on some trade mission. They wound up getting stuck in a pen with a few other prisoners. We didn't even realize who we had until their people contacted us and demanded their release."

Sasha's eyes widened. All she could think of were the grainy video fragments from one section of *Wasteland Warriors*. It was supposedly a recording of an attack on an Aegis Biosystems convoy headed from Milwaukee to Denver. The convoy had been well-armed, but it had been taken apart in a matter of seconds. The assailants moved so fast that the documentarians had needed to slow the video to make them visible as anything but flashes on the screen. *How could something that fast and that deadly be captured?* Dr. Brandt answered her question before she could ask it.

"I'm going to guess you're wondering how we managed to capture three of those Frankenstein abominations."

"Yes sir," Sasha said.

"Well," Dr. Brandt popped the glasses off his face and buffed the lenses on his shirt while he spoke, "most members of any given group aren't quite like that. Oh, they're all pagans or atheists or some other kind of heathen. They have a lot of aesthetic modifications, LED tattoos and body lighting and some sensory upgrades. But few of them have military-style implants."

"I see."

"As you know, cities and civilized nations tend to ban those implants within their borders." Dr. Brandt slid his glasses back into place on his nose. "So the People of the Road have to send their less-modified citizens out to negotiate, etcetera. Which means we've got a bit of a tiger-by-the-tail situation here."

"What do you mean, sir?" Sasha asked.

"Well, the stories about these types are absolutely true. Some of them have hundreds of warriors packed to the gills with nightmare technology. There are individuals who are capable of taking on entire companies of human warfighters. The 'tribe' these particular captives hail from, well...their name is quite obscene. 'The City of Wheels' would be the most polite variant. They're as lost as it gets when it comes to the word of God. But they've got about six-hundred post-human citizens."

Sasha thought back to what a dozen of those things had done to that convoy. She tried to imagine the carnage six-hundred of them could unleash upon the Heavenly Kingdom. A shiver ran down her spine.

"Exactly," Dr. Brandt nodded at her. "Like I said, we've got a tiger by the tail. They might not intervene while we have their people. So we've got to make sure our captives are well taken care of. That's where you come in."

"Me?"

"Two of the captives are women, Sasha. They'll need to be inspected by someone besides me. We do have some qualified female nurses. But an SDF drone hit one of our troop transports about two hours ago, and I'm afraid they're both in the thick of that mess. So you're coming with me to handle this job."

"I'm proud to do it, sir." She wasn't sure what else to say. And besides, it was true.

The first captive sat on a small concrete bench in the back of an eight-by-ten cell. Her hair had been shaved into a mohawk, but the purple hair was deflated and greasy now. There was stubble on the sides of her head. Her face was round, but lean. There were slight laugh lines at the corners of her cheeks and the edges of her eyes. She wore a sleeveless purple-and-black dress that was, by now, filthy. Her arms were covered in a strange series of tattoos: dozens of branching lines that each terminated in a box. They looked almost like circuit diagrams. Sasha quickly realized that each "box" held a little LED screen. Most of the screens were set to a dull red color, but once she stepped into the woman's cell they flashed bright orange. The woman looked up and snarled at Dr. Brandt.

"The fuck do you want, shitbird?" She looked over to Sasha and then added, "Sorry, shitbirds."

"Sasha," Dr. Brandt sighed, kneading the bridge of his nose, "meet Marigold Fulton."

"Jesus fucking Christ. What are you, six-fuckin'-teen?" Marigold said to Sasha. Then she looked to Dr. Brandt, "That's fucked up, man."

Dr. Brandt winced at both curses. Sasha glanced down and saw that his right hand was balled up into a fist and clenched tight.

"Marigold, this is Sasha," he said through gritted lips. "She'll be performing your intake exam. We need to make sure you're uninjured, noninfectious, and not hiding any weaponry. I would recommend compliance."

"Your kind always do," the woman spat back.

"Sasha. You've got this." Dr. Brandt gave her a curt nod, turned on his heels, and headed back out of the cell.

There was an armed guard just outside the cell. As Dr. Brandt had instructed, Sasha pulled a long privacy screen out from the far end of the wall and clasped it to a set of hooks on the other end. The captives were being held in the old Plano jail, which made this one of the rare buildings in the Heavenly Kingdom being used for its intended purpose. Sasha was grateful for the privacy screen. She was also unbearably nervous about what came next.

"I'm going to have to ask you–"

In one smooth motion, Marigold pulled the dress up over her shoulders and off of her body. She wore nothing underneath it. Her pert breasts, her little belly, her pubic mound and its shock of purple hair were suddenly just there.

"You gonna do your job, or are you just gonna stand there and jill off?" Marigold asked.

"I– what? Jill…?"

Marigold gave a harsh laugh.

"It's synonym for masturbation. Lady masturbation. You don't do that, do you, sugar? I'm gonna guess the Heavenly Kingdom frowns on girls having fun without the help of boys."

Sasha grimaced. "The Heavenly Kingdom doesn't frown on women having fun. But it does encourage self-control. Mastur– what you're talking about, it's a distraction. It's worldly."

Marigold whistled in mock-surprise and said, "Spoken like a lady who truly needs an orgasm."

"What I need to do is draw some of your blood, and some of your saliva. And, erm…perform a cavity search."

Marigold's lips curled up into a catlike smile. She opened her legs. Sasha had seen other women's vaginas before, but only in textbooks and movies. This was the first time she'd found herself staring directly down the barrel of one, so to speak. She gulped.

"Ah, darlin', am I your first? Don't be scared. I got some chrome in me, but I never wound up putting defensive teeth in there. Now, my friend Topaz…"

"Stop. I know what you're trying to do. Just stop."

Sasha hadn't thought the woman's smile could get any wider, but it did.

"And what am I trying to do, child?"

"You're trying to...to fluster me. To distract me."

"Oooooor," Marigold rolled her eyes as she replied, "I'm bored. You fucks have kept me in one holding area or cell or another for almost a week. I spent three days shitting in the corner of a gym. But at least Rick and Tule were there too."

The woman's smile softened. For just a moment she looked troubled, vulnerable.

"You don't have any idea where my people are, do you?"

Sasha shook her head. She felt guilty for some reason. That was stupid—she hadn't done anything wrong. But she felt the need to assuage the other woman's fears.

"I don't. I'm sure they're alright, though. We wouldn't execute them just for being in the wrong place at the wrong time."

Marigold snorted. "Maybe you wouldn't, luv. Your friends, though? I've seen your gallows. It doesn't seem like the kind of thing someone builds just for show."

"We...have a right to enforce our laws. God's laws." *What am I doing, defending the Kingdom to someone who's clearly blind to the Word?* Sasha shook her head. She opened the blood testing kit Dr. Brandt had given her and stepped toward Marigold.

"Look, I've got to do this. Just hold still and it'll be quick."

It was. The other woman offered no resistance. When Sasha told her to stand, she stood. When Sasha reached a gloved hand up inside her to search for foreign objects, Marigold said nothing. She didn't even flinch. Instead, she kept her eyes locked on Sasha's. The other woman barely blinked. In about two minutes, Sasha had finished her examination and collected her samples. She started to step back, but Marigold's hand shot out whip-fast and grasped her around the wrist.

"Listen."

Sasha stopped and listened. She wasn't sure why. It was something about the other woman's tone. She'd heard the term "command voice" before. Sasha hadn't understood what the term meant until now. When Marigold spoke again it was in a hushed tone, barely more than a whisper.

"I don't know what brought you here, but you're obviously smart. You don't have those dead zealot eyes," she jerked her head in the direction of the guard outside. "When I mentioned the gallows you looked fucking ill. I'm going to guess you haven't been here long. You're probably having second thoughts. Help me get my people out of here. If we can get back to my city, you'll be safe. We'll take you wherever you need to go."

"I..." Sasha wasn't sure what to say. She should've slapped the other woman, or spit in her eye. But she didn't.

"Don't say anything. You'll be back here. I promise. Think about what I've said. Think about where you are. Just fucking THINK."

She let go. Sasha stepped back. The two women locked eyes for a long moment. And then Marigold grabbed her slip dress off the floor and slid it back down her thin frame. Sasha unclipped the privacy curtain and headed back out into the hallway.

The other woman captive, Tule, was tall and muscular. She had a wide face with cheekbones so sharp they were almost jagged. Her skin was a dusky brown. Her eyes were alert, and moved rapidly between Sasha, Dr. Brandt, and the guard who led them into the room.

"Her name is Tule," Dr. Brandt said, "and she's probably going to threaten you. Pay her no mind." He turned away and left, while the guard stayed behind and kept a close eye on the tall woman.

Sasha was scared to approach Tule at first. The woman's forearms were corded with muscles, and she had biceps that looked as broad as Sasha's thighs. But the woman didn't move an inch, or say a word, the entire time Sasha worked on her. Tule didn't even blink. She complied to every one of Sasha's requests without eye contact or any other form of acknowledgment. The woman seemed dead to the world.

Somehow, Tule's quietness and seeming stupefaction were more uncomfortable than Marigold's aggressive words. Sasha finished her work in short order. Once the last vial was sealed and her gloves removed, she took a final look at the captive.

"I hope you get to go back to your home soon." Sasha immediately regretted the words. *This woman is The Enemy. Why would you try to comfort her? She won't even look at you.*

Tule let out a dull laugh. She had been so silent earlier that it shocked Sasha. The other woman turned her head and stared at Sasha.

"I will return home soon. And fire and blood will come to this place, because you've held me here. You're a dead woman walking. Enjoy the last beats of your heart."

Sasha didn't know what to say. What could you say to that? So she took her samples, and left.

Dr. Brandt dropped her off outside the House of Miriam and told her he'd send a jeep out tomorrow morning to take her to the hospital. Sasha thanked him and headed inside.

The other girls were already almost finished with dinner when Sasha sat down and joined the group. She gave a quiet smile to Susannah and nodded at the other girl's bandaged hand. When dessert (a banana this time) was over, Miss Helen took Sasha aside while the other girls broke off to read their Bibles and drink their nightly tea.

"I have some news for you."

"Yes, ma'am?" Sasha asked.

"Alexander has been rotated back from the front. And..." that strange look of mingled frustration and anger crossed Helen's face again, "you'll be able to see him tomorrow. After lunch."

Sasha's heart pounded, an excitement that made her feel guilty and elated at the same time.

"I'm afraid it won't be a long visit," Helen continued. "But you'll have a bit of time with him."

And then Helen sighed again, just a little. Sasha was sure she wasn't supposed to have noticed it. Miss Helen's eyes looked a bit watery. Sasha was so happy, so excited, that her brain glossed over this fact. Instead she gave Miss Helen a hug. It wasn't nearly the first one they'd shared, but this was the first time the older woman had seemed hesitant in returning it. But she did, after a moment, and Sasha's joy-drunk brain wrote over any sense of doubt she ought to have felt.

Sasha buzzed with uncontained energy the rest of the night. Sleep was near impossible. She tossed until the small hours of the morning, turning over her memories of chat conversations she'd had with Alexander. His face felt so clear and real in her memory that she could almost touch it. And tomorrow she'd be able to do just that.

Sasha finally passed out about two hours before Helen came around to wake them up. She should have been exhausted. Instead, she found herself out of bed, feet planted firmly on the ground, before her mind was even fully awake. Her subconscious was that eager to start the day.

She rinsed herself with extra care that morning. Mae seemed to notice the added effort she put into primping and called her out for it.

"You're not working at the hospital to snag a doctor," she sneered. "You know that, right?"

Sasha tried to ignore the comment. Susannah, whose hand was still bandaged from her injury the other day, spoke up in her defense.

"There's nothing wrong with being extra clean, Mae. It's probably important for the work she's doing over there. Sasha's dealing with wounds and stuff, she's not scrubbing toilets like you."

Sasha was gratified by how that made Mae's face flush. She flashed Susannah a grateful smile and shuffled out of the washroom as quick as she could manage. She headed outside and took in her first deep gulp of the cool morning air. "Cool" might have been too strong a word to use. But the fresh air felt good on her skin.

It only took her a few seconds to spot the battered and dirt-specked jeep Dr. Brandt had sent to pick her up. A young man, maybe as young as her, with a weak chin and an acne-pocked face sat behind the wheel. Sasha waved to him, ran up, and hopped in.

It wasn't a quick ride to the hospital. Large sections of the road were destroyed, blocked by rubble, or jammed with traffic from refugees entering the Heavenly Kingdom. Seeing that had gratified Sasha. *More souls coming to God,* she thought. For the most part, she lost herself in thoughts of Alexander until, forty minutes later, the jeep rolled to a creaky stop in front of the Medical City of Plano.

The enormous hospital complex looked badly damaged, and largely abandoned. Many of the windows had been shot out or shattered by large blasts. Several buildings had chunks of wall and roof that had fallen in. But there were lights on in many of the windows, and the hum of generators filled the air of the front courtyard. Dozens of people milled about, filled with purpose, running wires, and wheeling patients.

Sasha was excited at the thought that she might get to do some actual work in a functioning emergency room. When she found Dr. Brandt, he quickly disabused her of those notions.

"We're doing alright today. What I need you to do is come in here and help me catalog which medicines have spoiled."

The power had gone out during the fighting for the city, Dr. Brandt explained, and the medical storage room had been without refrigeration for almost two days. He showed her how to check medical vials for signs of spoilage, handed her a clipboard to mark her findings, and told her to get to work.

It was a menial, painstaking task and Sasha found herself missing the heck out of cleaning. She hated it, but she devoted herself to the work and, minute by minute, the time passed. Eventually it was time for her meeting with Alexander. Sasha pulled herself away from the rows of vials and jars and blister packs and headed outside, to where she knew the jeep would be waiting.

Her driver that afternoon was a different Martyr, slightly older but still quite young. She was so preoccupied with thoughts of Alexander that she almost forgot to greet the man. He didn't seem to be in a talkative mood either, though, and they rode in silence back to the center of town. Sasha was so focused on the butterflies in her stomach and trying to catch glimpses of her hair and face in the rearview mirror that she didn't notice the crowds thronging downtown until the jeep rolled to a stop and it was time for her to disembark.

A familiar sense of queasy dread gripped Sasha's guts as she exited the vehicle and looked out over the crowd. They were converged around the gallows once again. Sasha craned her neck, and she was able to see four men in filthy, tattered rags standing before the killing instrument. It took her a second to recognize two of the men as the porters who'd first unloaded her from her crate. An older, bearded Martyr in jet-black body armor stood before them. He held a Bible in one hand and a formidable looking handgun in the other. Sasha started to push her way through the crowd for a better look. She hadn't made it far when the bearded Martyr addressed the crowd.

"These four men were all once employees of the secular abomination that called itself the Republic of Texas," he said in his booming, stentorian voice. "The Heavenly Kingdom offered them mercy, in the form of indentured servitude. All we asked..." he scanned his eyes across the crowd, the left corner of his lip curled up into a slight growl, "All we asked for was their honest, obedient labor. And they repaid this mercy by stealing food and supplies meant for the Heavenly Kingdom's brave soldiers."

He lifted his big pistol up into the sky and fired off four shots in quick succession.

"These men stole from God. There is only one proper punishment for such a sin."

He turned back toward the gallows and nodded at a hooded Martyr who stood behind him with a hand on the thick wooden lever that operated the whole grim apparatus. The other man pulled downwards and the four bodies on the scaffold dropped with a sickening chorus of snaps. Sasha felt her stomach turn sour. This time, though, she watched. She didn't take her eyes off the gallows until the last man had ceased his twitching.

"It's not a pleasant sight, is it?"

That voice. Sasha recognized it immediately. It was the voice she'd heard a hundred different times over her deck, hidden up in her room back in the AmFed. It was the voice of the first man she'd ever really loved. It was Alexander.

Sasha turned around and her heart nearly burst at the sight of him. He was tall, broad, and muscular in a way that somehow seemed comforting and not scary. His mop of curly brown hair, lopsided smile, and round, prominent jaw line were all exactly as she remembered from their dozens of chat sessions. He wore olive-green fatigues that looked stained and burned in a few places. His hair was greasy, and there were great big bags under his eyes. But he was here. He was real.

She collapsed into him. Before she realized it, she'd started to sob.

"I love you I love you I love you I thought you were dead I love you!"

He hesitated for several long beats before he returned her embrace. But he returned it with gusto. His hands crept down, from her sides to her buttocks. He squeezed her. It was a gesture she'd fantasized about several times in her weaker, more carnal moments. It was not something she'd expected a Godly man like Alexander to do out in public, surrounded by people, in the immediate aftermath of an execution.

Sasha pulled back and coughed in surprise. She didn't say anything though. She didn't want to mar their first meeting with that. And she also remembered something Pastor Mike had written in *Revelator*, that the "beastly nature of a man must be salved by the goodness of women." Alexander had just spent several days up at the front. He must have seen terrible things. It was understandable that his self control would not be at its peak right now.

Still. She didn't like the way he looked her up and down. There was something of the wolf in his eyes. It was not the look she'd dreamed of seeing. But then he spoke.

"Sasha. I'm so proud of you. I didn't know if I'd ever see you here. I wasn't sure if you'd be willing to truly commit yourself to our Lord. But I prayed that you would and now, by the Grace of God, you're here. And you're even more beautiful than you looked online."

Sasha blushed. How could she not?

"Look," he waved a hand toward the gallows, and the bodies, "things are still sort of a mess around here. But I know one cafe nearby is up and running again. I've got enough ration tokens to get us both a cup of coffee. What would you say to that?"

"I'd say yes." She smiled at him. Her earlier reservations dissolved as she took his hand and followed him down the street, past the gallows and the dispersing crowd and toward the cafe. In a minute they were there. It was a small place, one rectangular room with a coffee maker, a half-dozen tables and an outer patio area with another half-dozen tables. There was a generator, power and air-conditioning inside, so they sat there. Alexander ordered them two large cups of black coffee. He sat down while he waited for their order and stared into her eyes. She stared back. For a while, that was all they did.

"It's so good to see you," Sasha said. "I've been working at the hospital and I've seen so many wounded men. I couldn't stop thinking I was going to see you there in one of those beds, broken and bleeding..."

He smiled at her. Then he reached his left hand out and sat it on top of hers. Sasha shivered, she couldn't help it. Things stirred inside her. She felt a sudden, powerful urge to possess his body, to hold him and squeeze him and be explored in turn. She clamped her mouth tight and focused on trying not to give all her thoughts away through the blush in her cheeks.

"Sasha," he said, "it brings me such joy to see you here. And don't worry. I know the situation at the ladies' barracks is rather primitive. But I'm talking to my commanding officers. As soon as we get married, you'll be a part of my household. We'll be able to live together. We'll build a life and that life will help build the Heavenly Kingdom."

She was stunned for a moment. Sasha began to tear up and all she could do was nod at him. This was like a dream. It was, of course, rather different from her actual dreams, which had involved Alexander and a house but not so many bleeding and dying men, nor a gallows.

Their coffee arrived. Alexander took a sip and she followed suit. He continued.

"I know you're working at the hospital now. I'm sorry about that. I'm sorry you had to spend so much time scrubbing toilets. As soon as I can get you off those duties, I will–"

"Oh no!" she interjected, "I love working with Dr. Brandt. It's important, and I want to do my part to help the Kingdom thrive."

Something passed across Alexander's face. It looked like irritation, perhaps at her interruption. But it was gone quickly, and his smile returned.

"That's admirable, Sasha. You're a remarkable young woman. If that's what you want, I'm sure you can continue to help out there until you're with child."

"With...child?" Sasha felt guilty for the horror in her voice. Of course she wanted children. She just didn't want them now. Or particularly soon.

Alexander nodded, "We must be fruitful and multiply so the Heavenly Kingdom can remain and expand." His smile was so warm, so kind. "I know you've read more of Pastor Mike's writing than I have, Sasha. You're a very smart girl. But God made you to bring forth more children. You wouldn't want to delay your purpose, would you?"

Maybe a little, she thought.

"No..." she lied.

"Good," he smiled again. "And don't worry. You won't have to do it alone. Malia already has a child, and Adelaide's two months pregnant. They'll help you, too."

The world stopped. At least it did for Sasha. She could tell people were still moving around her, but Sasha's reality had shrunk to the pounding sound of her heart and a twisting in her gut.

"A– Adelaide? And Malia?"

Alexander gritted his teeth. There was something almost practiced in the way he said what came next.

"Adelaide and Malia are my wives. As you will be."

"Wh–? Alexander, you didn't say anything about other wives. You never mentioned them at all. Why are... How can you be telling me all this now?"

His smile turned sad. Or at least it gave the illusion of sadness. Sasha was still too shocked for anger. She felt like a hole had just been knocked in her heart. She knew she should be angry. But she also felt like there must be something missing. Something she didn't understand yet. Alexander was a sweet boy, he wouldn't do this to her.

"Look," he said, "I'm sorry. This is never easy. You understand how important the Heavenly Kingdom is, Sasha. Nothing in the world could matter more. And the Kingdom will not survive without people like you. One of my jobs here is to push young women like you to take the terrible risk of coming here."

"And so you lied?" she croaked, barely able to believe what was happening. "You bore false witness, Alexander. I–"

"I did not lie." His voice hardened and so did his eyes. "I did not tell you about every aspect of my life here. But I did not lie." He sighed, took a sip from his coffee, and continued.

"I'm part of a special unit within the Kingdom, formed on the order of the Pastor himself. He calls us Jacobians. It is our job to seed the next generation of Martyrs. We take personal responsibility for the Kingdom's expansion. Finding you and bringing you here was one part of my work in this great cause. If I'd told you every detail about life here, every single thing, you wouldn't have come. And your soul would have stayed in jeopardy."

He took another deep, arrogant sip of his coffee.

"I'm sorry if this hurts you. But it was for the greater good. We must sometimes do distasteful things to serve God's design."

Sasha's vision went red. She stood and, without thinking, grabbed her now-lukewarm mug of coffee and splashed the whole thing in Alexander's face. He yelled at her and sputtered like a goldfish. But she was already up and heading for the door. She flung it open, walked out into the crowded street and lost herself in the press of the crowd and the boiling waves of her own anger.

Chapter 13

Manny.

Manny woke up feeling like his mouth was filled with cotton and his head was filled with spiders. It took him a few long seconds to remember where he was and what had happened to bring him here. He activated his deck and was shocked to see that more than a day had passed since he'd dropped into bed. His first guess was that he was suffering some side-effect from Skullfucker Mike's blood. He couldn't think of any other times he'd slept that long, although he also couldn't think of any other times he'd survived a drone attack and an intentional car crash in the same minute.

"Mierda!" he cursed, and then called out, "Reggie?" He looked over to the cot the journalist had been sleeping on. It was dark in the little room Nana Yazzie had provided. He could see the outline of Reggie's empty cot and not much else. The room was just one ten-by-ten section of an old shipping crate. Manny knew the only things in the room, besides their cots, were a table with a built-in coffee maker and a pair of folding chairs.

Manny sat up, groaned as every poppable thing in his body popped, and then rose to his feet. As he stumbled to the door his deck started to populate with messages from friends and family back in Austin. By the time his hand touched the knob there were more than fifty translucent messages hovering at the edges of his field of vision.

He blink-selected a mass-response template, filled it with the names of everyone who'd sent him something, and typed out an update:

"Not dead. Details later."

He almost sent it, but then he noticed one of the names: Aisha Martinez. Oscar's wife. He could only see the first few lines of the message without opening it, but what he saw made it clear she was terrified for her husband. Manny de-selected her from the list, and sent the mass-message off to everyone else, and then scrolled through his messages until he found Oscar's message stack. The other fixer still hadn't said anything, not since the assault had begun.

Manny opened up Aisha's message. He tried to read it, he really did, but his brain wouldn't let his eyes focus on the words. His heart started to pound. His gut curdled. And, instead of reading it, he typed her a quick response.

"I'm alive. I'm so sorry, but I don't know where Oscar is or if he's made it out." And then he typed a sentence he knew instantly he'd regret.

"I will do everything I can to find your husband."

Then he sent the message and stepped out of the room, into the dying light of the late North Texas afternoon. Rolling Fuck unspooled around him. It was crowded, or at least more crowded than it had been yesterday. Dozens of people and non-human people were packed onto the gantry ways and into the sundry buildings added around the rollers and up on the spires. One building that jutted off the rear roller looked like a carousel ride, with little rocket ships instead of horses. It appeared to function as a spinning bar. Drunk people rode the little ships while bartenders in the middle kept them liquored up. Someone shoved by him, a heavily-chromed person with three tails, each topped by the fully-articulated and seemingly sentient head of a cat. One of the cat heads belched a small puff of fire at Manny as their wearer passed.

He shook his head and squeezed his way over to the main roller. It helped a little to pretend he was just pushing his way onto the Austin Metro. While he walked he noticed a message from Reggie. He blink-clicked it open and heard Reggie's voice in his ear.

"At the rooftop bar, drinking my way through some research. Find me when you wake up. I'm onto something."

Of course Manny had already been on his way there before he'd seen Reggie's message. That was the simple reality of British journalists: if it was possible for one to be drinking, that's what they'd be doing.

The walk took about ten minutes. He crossed a combination of gantry ways, staircases, and even one webbed net. The bar was packed when he arrived but it was easy enough to pick out Reggie. Both his holographic screens were up and active on the bartop in front of him. He was seated next to Skullfucker Mike, and they were deep in conversation when Manny walked up.

"Hey, brother," Reggie said, "you've been out for a long time."

"Yes," Manny said. "Nothing like that's ever happened to me before. How long were you out?"

The journalist thought for a moment and then answered. "I'd guess like a day," he said. "Mike told me that's not weird."

"Yeah," the chromed man chuckled, "all medicine's got side-effects. My weird-ass blood's no different. Y'all cute lil' humans ain't made for it."

Skullfucker Mike and Reggie were both clearly drunk, and just as clearly not as drunk as they planned to be by the end of the night. Mike flashed a grin at Manny and offered a hug that the fixer accepted awkwardly.

"Guy, it's good to see ya," Mike said. "I gotta tell you I'm kinda jealous of your nap. I miss sleep like that. With all this chrome in me," he waved a hand vaguely over his head, "I can't get exhausted like that anymore. You miss it when it's gone. I gotta drink like, thirty of these fucking things—" Mike gestured to the half-full drink in front of him. It looked like a pina colada. A strange incense-y odor wafted up from it—"just to pass out like a normal person."

Reggie was drinking the same thing. He offered his half-full glass to Manny.

"These things are the best man. Vodka and opium coladas."

"They got a liiiiiiiiiil' bitta THC in 'em too," Mike added in a high, sing-song voice.

Manny waved them off.

"I'm good, thanks. I just woke up a minute ago. I probably shouldn't immediately take three different drugs."

Reggie and Skullfucker Mike both looked at him like he was an alien.

"Weird," they said at exactly the same time. Mike laughed, and Reggie looked back at his screen as a push-notification popped up with a cheery "ding."

"Shitting tits," he cursed.

Manny and Skullfucker Mike leaned into the screen. The notification was a newswire update from a journalist who must've been embedded with either the SDF or Austin's forces. The title said it all:

> As the Heavenly Kingdom prepares for another assault, SDF and Austin abandon Waco.

"I'm not surprised they're pulling out," Mike said. "Your people are good enough fighters on a normal day. But the SDF's built to dominate a buncha squabbling militias. They were never gonna hold off a sustained assault from a real army."

The sleep was fully banished now. Manny was awake, and the gravity of what had happened over the last few days sank in again. Hamid and DeShawn were probably dead. So was Mr. Peron. And Alejandro. And Oscar. *Oh holy shit, holy shit, what am I going to tell Aisha?* And then the darker, more selfish thoughts: *Am I going to have time to fly out of Austin?*

"How the hell did the Martyrs turn into a real fucking army overnight?" he asked, with more fear in his voice than he meant to display.

"Well," Reggie said, as he gestured to a series of curated social media posts from people in and around ciudad de muerta. "Best as we can figure, they sorta stole most of the Republic's army. There are a lot of reports of entire units of Republic soldiers, thousands of fighters, turning at once."

He gestured to a live-updating political map of Texas. It was a map Manny consulted regularly. The Heavenly Kingdom's territory was outlined in red. There was a lot more red on the map today. It seemed impossible that...

"Son chorrados," Manny breathed, "Galveston?"

"Yeah," Reggie gave a grim nod. "Fell about ten hours ago. Heavenly Kingdom's pushing into the Lake Houston suburbs right now. They're holding position in Dallas though. Digesting their gains still."

"Ain't gonna be long before they hit Austin," Mike said. "Maybe a week. Maybe two."

Manny stood there for a moment. He thought about his father, his friends. He thought about the house where he'd grown up and the view of Austin's sprawl from his roof. He imagined golden cross banners flapping in the breeze above burnt-out buildings. He pictured gallows filled with people strung out along sixth street. A knot of nausea started to build in his belly.

What will you do, Emmanuel? He heard Mr. Peron's voice echo in his conscience. Manny shook the dead man's words away.

"I need to get back home," he insisted. "Is there some way you can get me a ride?"

Skullfucker Mike took a long pull from his drink. He squinted at Manny and the chromed man's eyes focused. One iris looked a lot larger than the other. Mike swayed a bit in his seat but he seemed lucid. Mostly.

"And what're you gonna do in Austin?" he asked. "Pick up a gun and die fighting? Unless you're hiding some serious mods under that skin, I don't think your help will make a rat's shit wortha difference."

"I know. I'm not going there to fight. I need to–"

"What, fly away? Go to fuckin' California? Try your luck in Europe?" Mike shook his head. "You've got a chance to actually do something. Help us get our people out of Dallas and we can fuck the Kingdom's advance. Maybe even throw them back."

Manny thought about it, sighed, and said, "I think I do need a drink."

Skullfucker Mike nodded. He pointed over to a table lined with a dozen different beer taps.

"The normal stuff's self-service. I recommend the Wheat Haze. Pretty mild, but it's good for stock humans like y'self."

Manny got up, grabbed a glass from a dispenser at the edge of the bar and walked over to the beer table. Each keg had a thick strip of white tape across the front. The only details given about each beer were vague, almost illegibly scrawled names. Manny found two labels that both looked like they might say "Wheat Haze." He picked one at random, then headed back to the bar and sat next to Reggie.

Mike looked impressed for some reason. "Good choice," he said with a nod. Manny took a sip. It was really good, a mild pale ale with just a hint of sour. He leaned in and looked at the maps and scrolling updates on Reggie's screen. The journalist finished writing down a couple of notes and shook his head.

"I'm really sorry man. Truly." He gestured toward the live map, "This is so fucked."

"You gonna stay here to cover the fall?" Mike asked. Reggie shook his head. He looked frustrated.

"Got a message from my editor a bit ago. They're trying to work out an extract for me. Gonna send a team out here to drive me west, to El Paso. I guess it's not safe to fly out of Austin right now, so..."

He trailed off. The three of them drank in silence for a minute. Skullfucker Mike gulped down the last of his glass and ordered another, along with three shots of bourbon. Manny started to turn down the shot, but it was soon apparent that Mike wanted all three shots for himself. He downed them all in the space of around a second, belched loudly, and then returned to staring at Reggie's screen.

"Fuck," he sighed out again. "Fuck, fuckedy fuck."

Manny was halfway through his beer when Donald Farris approached. The old documentarian wore a burgundy velvet waistcoat underneath a slightly battered but well-tailored tweed jacket. He had a glass of probable whiskey in his hand and the soberest eyes Manny had seen that day.

"Hello there, gentlemen. Skullfucker Mike. Getting caught up on the latest catastrophes, are we?"

"Yep," said Mike. "How ya been?"

The older man shrugged and took his seat at the table. He gulped his whiskey and looked down the table at Manny. It was strange to see an actual old person this close up. The creases in his forehead and around his lips were so deep they could have been carved with a knife. There were spots on him, a clear sign he'd taken no JuvEn treatments at all. His voice had a deep craggy richness that lent every word he said a certain vague majesty. Donald Farris spoke and Manny felt compelled to listen.

"You can help this you know. We're stuck negotiating with the Kingdom now, and they are most recalcitrant. But the Fuckians–"

"Wait a second," Reggie interrupted. "Fuckians? Really?"

Donald and Mike exchanged a look, and then a laugh. Donald replied, "This city's not exactly famed for consistency. Almost any collective noun you can think of would be appropriate."

He took another slip from his glass and set it down on the bartop with a "clack." Donald Farris leaned in at that and eyed the glass as he rotated it around on the table. He tapped it again, smiled, and looked back up to the group.

"Now, young man, let me explain why you should go risk your life on a daring and dangerous rescue mission."

Manny grunted and shook his head, reflexively defensive.

"I'd rather not talk about it right now, if that's cool?" he said. "I just woke up, this place is ridiculous, and I'm not going to decide to go into terrible danger because some old man guilt trips me at a bar."

"Suit yourself," Donald smiled. "I can't imagine how stressful this all must be for you. I'm a little surprised you'd choose to trip balls at a time like this."

"What do you mean?" Manny asked, with growing anxiety.

"That's a White Haze, right?"

"I think Mike said it was a Wheat Haze, but I couldn't really read the labels–"

"Ah shit," Mike cursed, while Donald Farris fought back a laugh.

"What?" Manny asked.

"Mike should've warned you. The Wheat Haze is normal alcohol. The *White* Haze packs about two hits of lysergic diethylacid per pint."

The anxious knot in Manny's gut began to pound and pulse. He looked to Skullfucker Mike, furious, "What the fuck, man?"

Mike winced. He looked genuinely rueful.

"I'm really sorry," he said. "I'm not used to it making a difference. Most people here take two or three hits of acid with their breakfast cigarettes."

"Oh shit," Manny slumped forward and put his head in his hands. He started to hyperventilate. The edges of his vision blurred and Manny couldn't tell if that was from the drugs kicking in or just a consequence of his own panic. He could feel Oscar's face hanging out, just at the back of his mind, afloat on a river of guilt. He didn't want to know what a head full of acid would do with those feelings.

"I gotta get back to the room," he said. "I can't handle thi–"

Donald put a hand on his shoulder. He was stronger than Manny would have guessed.

"You've got a head full of Surprise Acid, boy. The last thing you need is to sit in a dark room and stew with your demons." He exchanged another look with Skullfucker Mike and said, "Brainbreakers ought to be kicking off right now. That's the place for a man in your condition."

"But–" started Manny.

"What the hell is that?" Reggie asked.

"Wait–" Manny continued. Donald ignored him and replied to Reggie.

"It's the best damned party on the continent. Or at least the best one humans can attend and survive."

"I don't really want to–" Manny started.

Skullfucker Mike added his hand to Manny's shoulder.

"You really do. Trust us on this."

In the end, Skullfucker Mike and Donald convinced him to go. Reggie, surprisingly, opted to stay at the bar and continue his work. He said he was "close to something." Manny really wished he'd chosen to come along. He didn't know the journalist well, but Mike and Donald were complete strangers. Manny was not looking forward to the drugs kicking in. He also wasn't sure a giant rave room was the best place for him to be when they did.

As they approached it, Manny realized he'd seen the structure when they'd first arrived at the City of Wheels. Brainbreakers was a three story cube at the top of Rolling Fuck's highest gantry. The cube appeared to have been knitted together from long strands of black metal. Multicolored light pulsed inside it and bled out through gaps in the knitted metal of the sides.

Skullfucker Mike led them down the gantry toward the cube. There didn't appear to be any kind of entrance: the wall on this side was the same knitted steel as every other side. But once they reached it, Mike simply stepped into the wall. The woven metal writhed like something alive and curled back to admit the big post-human. The metal tendrils caressed Mike's body as he walked through. Manny flashed a questioning look at Donald.

"It feels nice," he explained.

Manny sighed, exasperated and furious, "Is this whole damned city built around drugs and fondling?"

"Yes," Donald grinned a spidery old-man grin. "Now, inside with you!"

Manny sighed, swallowed, and walked up to the wall. The metal—which felt surprisingly soft and warm–slithered around him and, mother of god, it felt GOOD. That might've had something to do with the acid percolating in the back of his brain. The sensation was a cross between being tickled and being caressed. He was reminded, uncomfortably, of his mother stroking his forehead when he had a fever as a kid.

And then he was through. It took him a moment to realize he was breathing heavily and covered in cold sweat.

It was then that Manny got his first view of the interior of Brainbreakers. It looked a little like a space station designed by M.C. Escher, with a drunken H.R. Giger as the contractor. There were a half-dozen different stages protruding at various levels from the walls. Three of the stages were currently occupied. One performer was an enormous, seemingly sentient xylophone that pranced about on stage, playing itself with eight knob-ended arms. Another stage held four human-looking individuals. They were naked. And they were all fighting.

Manny watched in slack-jawed awe as they punched and bit and kicked and choked each other. Every impact sent a chorus of warbling sounds pouring out from speakers at the base of the stage. The longer he listened, the more hypnotic the "music" seemed.

The third inhabited stage held a what looked like a normal DJ booth with a presumptive person behind it. Manny guessed that was the source of the bass-heavy rhythmic pounding that filled the square. The remaining stages were empty, for now. But the place was so full of sound Manny couldn't imagine two more acts making things any louder. It was chaotic and confusing and a little uncomfortable. But after a few seconds Manny started to pick up on an overarching rhythm. All three "acts" were making very different music at very different paces but, somehow, it all tied together.

The inner walls of the place were covered in projection art. Giant, human-sized silhouettes stalked the walls, floor, and roof. At times they moved so fast they looked almost like wisps of smoke. But here and there, one would stop long enough for Manny get a solid look. He saw several different figures: a tall, muscular but androgynous person; a small, lithe young woman; a broad, squat man with a bald head. They danced around each other, flittering up and down the walls. Their pace and the nature of their motions varied depending on the tempo and pitch of the music nearest to them.

It was mesmerizing. Manny stared for what felt like minutes. The sensation of his body faded away from him and his vision tunneled in on the dancing figures. Their dance had looked joyous and sensual at first. But the longer he watched the more frenetic it seemed, the more danger he spotted in their jerking limbs, the arc of their necks, the uncontrolled way they spun 'round and into one another. Anxiety started to build in the pit of his stomach.

And then there was a person beside him. Mike.

"Heeeeey, budddy," he grinned. The other man's pupils were the size of dinner plates. He clenched and ground his teeth back and forth, "It OK if I put a hand on your shoulder?"

"Uh...sure?" Manny said, surprising himself.

"Cool," Mike smiled, and did so. His hand felt supportive, comforting.

"How you likin' the party?"

Manny really wasn't sure. It was beautiful here. Now that Skullfucker Mike had pulled his attention from the dancing silhouettes, he'd started to focus more on the crowds of people dancing and drinking and fucking across the assorted dance-floors, cuddle-spaces, and bartops of Brainbreakers.

Most of the celebrants were visibly chromed. He saw a woman with six arms, a couple things he could only describe as "dick centaurs," a man with the head of a dolphin, and countless people in bizarre costumes built of light and fur and liquid metal. It was hard to tell how much of this was real and how much was the drugs. The acid was hitting his head pretty darn hard. Skullfucker Mike squeezed his shoulders and brought Manny back again. The fixer blinked and then finally responded.

"It's, uh...good."

"Good? Fuckin' great. Let's get you some whippits and head over to the fireworks table. They're about to open it up."

"Fireworks? Inside?"

Mike laughed. "It's hardly a party without explosives, brother. Just go with it."

And so Manny did. He and Mike did some whippits, which meshed gloriously with the acid. Then they stood up on stumbling feet and headed over to the fireworks table. Things seemed to be just getting started over there. Manny inspected a few different brightly-colored explosive toys, before something burst next to his ear and he looked up to see Skullfucker Mike firing a massive Roman candle toward the musical punching people on the stage.

The sound of it—*holy hell the sound!* It might have been the most compelling thing his ears had ever heard. *The acid is definitely hitting hard now*, Manny thought, *holy fuck. Holy fuck what IS this?*

The rest of his night faded into a blur of lights and music and strange, indefinable sense memories. It was disorienting and exhilarating in equal measure.

Hours went by. The acid faded. And eventually Manny found himself on a bunch of cushions, sitting around a table with Skullfucker Mike and other Fuckians. He couldn't remember any of their names but, after a few minutes of relative lucidity, Manny was able to piece together that they were all friends of the people who'd been captured. One of the men, a bearded guy with multi-jointed fingers the length and width of rulers, reached over Manny to grab a beer. He pulled it back, took a sip, and settled back into his seat.

"My favorite memory of Marigold," he said, "is from back when we were still building this city, right after we stole the Bagger. She got a hair up her ass that there oughta be a big purple clubhouse at the top, for folks to do cocaine in and watch sunsets. I remember she strapped an armload of wood to her back, grabbed a can of spray paint, took a big rail of meth and just started climbing up the center spindle like she was gonna do the whole damn job herself. She got fuckin' stuck two-thirds of the way up, just hanging out there with her panties in the breeze, screaming like a scared cat."

Mike laughed, "I remember that. Me'n Topaz had to climb up and free her. And then she climbed the rest of the way up and started laying down boards."

Finger Man nodded.

"Yeah, I remember. When I climbed up there an hour or so later she was all frantic and fiddling with nails and bolts and turnt to fuck but like, making progress too. And I asked her, 'Marigold, why are you doing this alone? This ain't a one person job.' And she said, 'I know. But unless I start building it, it'll never be real.'"

There was quiet for a while. Manny could feel the pain in the pause, and see it on everyone's face. He didn't want to say anything. He was pretty sure there was nothing worthwhile he could say. But then he spoke anyway.

"Can you tell me about the others? The other two who were captured?"

Another of Mike's friends, a tall Black woman in a bright blue shark onesie, nodded and replied, "Rick's a little dude, great painter and pretty good pyrotechnician. He's no kinda fighter but he's got a real sweet way about him. He puts people at ease. So he goes out on a lot of these delegations to be a good face for the city. Marigold's always the main negotiator, but we sent Tule out too. She's newish to the city. Used to be an activist in Albuquerque, before the King took over and started boiling people. She's a good talker, we had her studying under Mari so she could pick up some of the load in the future."

"They're all good people," Finger Man added. "Marigold saved my life a few times, back during the Revolution. She helped found this place. It started out as just a big caravan of RVs and mobile hydroponics units. She'd find isolated communities, bring 'em food and such. No government was much use back then, so for a lot of folks Mari's caravan was the line between life and death."

"Ayep," said Skullfucker Mike. "She's the one who found Topaz and me. After the Boss went missing, we were pretty lost. Doing a lot of freelance violence but not making anything. Not building a damn thing. Marigold told us her vision for this big stupid city, got us hooked on the idea."

Manny noticed tears at the corner of Skullfucker Mike's eyes. That felt somehow wrong to him. Someone so powerful and inhuman shouldn't be able to cry and make it look so normal. But there he was, crying.

And then, for the first time in the trip, the thing Manny had most feared happened: he thought about Oscar. He remembered a picnic he'd taken with the stringer, his wife Aisha, and their two kids. It had been a lovely spring day, one of the dozen-ish days a year in Austin where the air felt good on your skin. They'd drank cheap beer and eaten hot dogs and watched the kayakers roll along the Colorado River.

I sent him out there. I sent him there and now he's probably dead.

"Y'know, there's something we share," Mike said, his voice low and somber. "We've both spent way too much of our lives feeling helpless."

Manny cocked a disbelieving eyebrow up at Skullfucker Mike.

"Yeah," the chromed man chuckled, "I know what you're thinking. But you'd be surprised how often the fancy hardware doesn't matter."

Mike's face twitched, and more tears poured down his face. He took a deep breath, fixed Manny with bloodshot, puffy eyes, and spoke again.

"We all spend a lot of life helpless. So when you actually have a chance to *do* something, to make a difference for someone... Personally, I recommend you fuckin' take it."

Manny woke up the next day feeling out of place and vaguely unstuck from time. He could hear Reggie snoring on the other bed. The room was very dark and it was impossible to tell what time it might be. Manny thought about activating his deck, but decided against it. There was something almost nauseating about the thought of being flooded with the outside world right now.

He stood up and went outside to wander the spindles and gantrys of Rolling Fuck for a while. At one point a man walked by with a plate full of breakfast burritos, and so Manny had breakfast. A little later he found a self-serve coffeehouse stationed next to one of the Fondleboats, and so he had coffee. He was just starting to think about turning on his deck and welcoming in the world when Donald Farris found him.

"Manny, my boy! I hope your acid hangover's not too bad."

Manny shrugged, "I actually feel alright. It was a...it was good. It helped me sort some things out."

The older man smiled, "I'm genuinely happy to hear that. There's nothing like a head full of acid to help you see what's important. Now listen, I hate to interrupt your morning, but there've been some developments. Nana Yazzie and I need to talk to you."

Manny went with him, back down into the main roller and that weird conference room where they'd met on his first day in the city. There were more people there now. Nana Yazzie sat in the same spot at the end of the table. Reggie was there, fiddling with one of his screens. Skullfucker Mike sat next to him. And then, at the other end of the table, was a large Black dude Manny had never seen before.

He was muscular, but in the lean wiry way of a construction worker or a particularly swole hobo. He had a long, gaunt face with prominent cheekbones and an oft-broken nose. His hands were big. There was something menacing about them. But his face was the least threatening thing in the world. His eyes were lidded, half-focused, and dreamy. His jaw was just a little slack. He had short hair, stubble really, and a patchy six-day beard. He looked stoned.

"Welcome Manny," said Nana Yazzie. She gestured toward the big man, "This is Roland. If you choose to help us rescue our people, he'll be your escort into the Heavenly Kingdom. And your escape plan."

Donald shut the door behind them, walked around to the other side of the table, and sat down next to Nana Yazzie.

"We've tried to give you time and space on this," he said, "but I'm afraid both of those things are running out. All our intelligence suggests the Heavenly Kingdom is very close to another all-out assault. They'll move on Waco in four or five days. They could be outside Austin in a week's time."

"You are free to make whatever call you want. Our offer to fly you to Austin still stands, mijo," said Nana Yazzie. "But I am afraid we need you to make a decision now."

"I'll do it," Manny said.

Almost everyone looked surprised. Donald coughed. Nana Yazzie's eyes went wide. Reggie did a double-take. Skullfucker Mike just smiled and nodded at Manny. Roland didn't look as if he'd been affected in any way. In fact, Manny was pretty sure he was drumming along to some music only he could hear. It might've been Ronnie James Dio's "Holy Diver."

Chapter 14

Roland.

Once he'd been dismissed, Roland had made it his immediate business to get as high as post-humanly possible before he was needed. This was not a difficult task. Rolling Fuck had been built to keep buzzes going.

The main roller's bar stocked an assortment of beers mixed with LSD, laudanum, dimethyltryptamine, and a half-dozen Shulgin chemicals. Roland started off by sampling them all. He drank until the fireworks show in his head was indistinguishable from the actual fireworks outside. *Are those real, or am I just fuckin' LIT?* Roland decided that answering that question wouldn't make him happier.

He lost himself for a while and drifted from one of the Fondleboats to a dance party in a field underneath the main gantry. After hours of that, Roland had his fill of rhythm, so he found his way to a coke binge in a weird purple house atop one of the spindles. The rest of the night he spent testing the limits of his toxin filters and his tolerance for human contact.

The latter came first. He abandoned the coke party and stumbled through Rolling Fuck until he reached a small booth with baggies of Umm Nylokh, a DMT-based hallucinogen made from synthetically grown giraffe liver.

Things got fuzzy after that. There was a fireworks fight on a spindle that caught a shack on fire. He downed a shitload of mescaline as the sun breached. And then, quite suddenly, it was afternoon and he was lying on his back across the baking hot metal of one of the spindles.

Skullfucker Mike stood above him, naked as the day he was born and holding some sort of frosty, purple beverage in a large tiki cup.

"Hey, man," Mike said as he took a sip. "Nana Yazzie told me to find you. You straight enough to talk to people?"

Roland nodded. He wasn't, really, but he could sober up fast. Maybe "sober" wasn't the right word. His brain could flood itself with focusing drugs to offset the hallucinogens. And he had a vial of liquid methamphetamine somewhere in his pack. *That might do the trick.* Roland sat up, grunted, and waved a hand at Mike. Then he dug around in his pack for the vial. He found it and drained half.

"Alright, let's go," he said. "Let's go to the place and do the things."

Mike helped him down the spindle. Roland's unsteady legs were proof that he'd managed to find himself a worthy drug binge. The satisfaction he felt from that mixed well with the initial meth euphoria. By the time they reached the conference room he was wired as fuck and kinda wishing he'd picked a different drug to spin his mood.

Roland sat down and eased into his chair. A short young anglo fellow entered next and sat down on the opposite side of the conference table. He looked and smelled nervous. Roland paid him little mind. He was too jittery from the meth to want to talk. He decided a nice dose of some downers would help his situation and rooted around for his heroin kit.

At that moment, another young man entered the room. He was short, Hispanic, and about twenty-one years old. Nana Yazzie embraced the kid. Skullfucker Mike clapped him on the shoulder. They started talking, the kid said something that seemed to surprise most of the people in the room. Roland half paid attention to all that while he loaded up his syringe and tied off his arm. He stopped when he realized everyone else in the room was staring.

"Uh, hey. Something wrong?" he asked.

"Roland," Nana Yazzie said in a warm voice as she gestured to the Hispanic kid, "this is Manny. He's going to be your partner for the mission. He grew up in the Republic and he's a skilled negotiator. He'll help you blend in while you do your work."

"Cool," Roland grunted, and returned to his heroin.

"Roland, if you wouldn't mind, Reggie was about to speak," Nana Yazzie's smile was as indulgent as ever. "He's uncovered something important about the Heavenly Kingdom. It might be useful to you."

Roland shrugged. “Unless he’s got a list of which bartenders in Plano make a passable whiskey sour, I can’t imagine caring. But if you let me finish this...” he jiggled the syringe in the air, “I might be able to at least pay attention. Right now I’m too meth’d out to focus.”

The old man leaned forward and sighed. The kid looked horrified. He started working his mouth, in what Roland was sure must be the prelude to some sort of expression of shock or offense. Skullfucker Mike preempted him.

“Let Roland shoot up. Trust me, drugs aren’t going to make him more or less effective here.”

Roland grinned. Skullfucker Mike clearly knew him, even if he could only sorta remember Skullfucker Mike. He went back to tying off his arm and shooting up while the younger Brit stumbled into the start of his speech.

“Yes, well. I’ve, uh, been going over the last few days of successful vehicle-based bombings on checkpoints, from Galveston and Lake Houston and all across the Dallas-Fort Worth area. In total, I’ve identified three-hundred-twenty-one bombings that appear to have been carried out as part of this overall offensive. Two-hundred-forty of those bombings involved autonomous vehicles hitting dedicated autonomous vehicle checkpoints.”

Right on queue, a projection map flickered to life on the wall behind him. Hundreds of red dots populated a map of the conflict-riddled regions of North/Central Texas. It looked like the pattern of attacks you’d want in order to funnel the SDF’s limited resources toward the least defensible chunks of their line. What was weird was that so many bomb-rigged autonomous vehicles had gotten through the scanners.

“So,” Roland asked, “how’d the fuckers do it? A bunch of zero-days?”

Reggie shook his head.

“That’s what I thought at first,” he said. “But these attacks actually started more than a month before this offensive. If they were relying on exploits, the SDF’s IT folks would’ve caught something by now. The most likely explanation is that the Martyrs found some way to make vehicles that aren’t autonomous seem that way.”

“Yeah,” Manny said. “The Martyrs have tried to hide drivers in ‘autonomous’ vehicles before. The SDF watches for it.”

“Which means the Martyrs have figured out something new,” said the journalist, "some way to hide a human driver that doesn't register on conventional sensors."

"And that way is?" Nana Yazzie asked.

Reggie's face reddened. He grunted, swallowed, and then spoke. "I've got no idea. But I think I know where they're putting these new vehicles together."

He snapped his fingers, and the projected image changed to a map of a city called McKinney, in the Dallas suburbs. It zoomed into an aerial shot of one enormous factory building near the outskirts of the city.

"The BBC pays for access to a few independent satellites that overlook this part of North America. We also pay the SDF for limited access to some of their drone surveillance footage. From all that, I was able to trace out paths for seventy-eight of the vehicles used in these attacks. Every one of them started their journey here."

The projection changed again, to what looked like a stock photograph of the front of a large white factory building. The Tesla logo was displayed prominently by the front door.

"It's an old Tesla plant. They finished it about a year before the civil war. It's been in and out of operation since then. As best as I can tell the last normal vehicle rolled off the line three years ago, before the Heavenly Kingdom started cocking things up. McKinney was one of the first parts of the old Metroplex to fall, so they've had plenty of time to fiddle with shit."

Roland raised his arm and realized belatedly the needle was still dangling out of it. The old man sighed again, but Roland bravely ignored him.

"So what does this have to do with your captives?" he asked. "I didn't sign on to help you guys spy, or to blow up a factory. Send this data to the SDF or Austin if you think it matters."

Skullfucker Mike put a hand forward in a placating gesture. "We're not asking you to do anything about this," he said. "But you and Manny will be our only eyes and ears inside the Kingdom. If you get a hint of how they've accomplished all this, it'll be valuable to us and the SDF. We'll find a way to make it worth your while."

"I mean, the drinks are free here right?" Roland asked. "I don't know what else you've got that I might want."

Mike smiled and gestured to Roland's backpack of narcotics, which sat next to him on the big redwood table.

"By my count you've gone through about half your stash since coming out here. If you're able to get us any worthwhile info, I'll make sure the bag's full before you leave."

Roland narrowed his eyes. *It would be a giant pain in the ass to find good Percocet between here and CamelToe.* He sighed, "Alright, fucking fine. If we hear something, we'll look into it. But don't hold your breath."

After the meeting, Skullfucker Mike took Roland down to the city's makeshift morgue so he could steal a dead man's face. Rolling Fuck's militia had found the fresh corpse of some guy Roland's rough height and build. He'd fled Dallas and made it almost as far as Waco before getting hit by a drone attack. The poor fucker'd been gutted by shrapnel, but his face was intact enough for his Chameleon implant. Roland hadn't used the thing in so long he worried it might not work.

He stared down at the man's face and took in his features. The fellow was white, but his skin was burnt a deep reddish brown. He'd clearly spent a lot of time under the Texan sun. He appeared to be in his early forties and clearly hadn't taken many JuvEn treatments. His hairline was fine, but the man's eyes and the edges of his lips were creased with wrinkles. His dead, staring eyes were blue. There were deep, dark bags beneath them. *Plenty of time to sleep now, buddy,* Roland thought.

He closed his eyes, focused on the dead man's face, and felt his facial bones start to tear themselves apart and then reform. He felt the pigments in his skin shift too, which was always strange. The sensation of his pigments opening up and taking in more light felt a little like stripping off a thin layer of clothing.

While Roland did this, Skullfucker Mike ran a scanner over the corpse and located the ID card in its right forearm. Mike used a tool that looked like a long metal straw to suck the ID free and then shoot the tag into Roland's arm. It took a second for Roland's body to pull the data.

His name was Aaron Weathers. He was single. He worked as a mechanic in Arlington for most of his life. He had a clean criminal record, save for a drunk driving arrest in his early thirties.

Roland, now Aaron, left the morgue with Skullfucker Mike and headed for the ride that would take him into the Heavenly Kingdom.

He used the walk as an opportunity to smoke a couple grams of fine Afghan opium. He was still smoking when they reached the battered old pick-up truck on the outskirts of Rolling Fuck's campground. The kid, Manny, was in the driver's seat.

"Hey," Manny said, and stared wide-eyed at him. "You look different," he added with a forced smile.

"Yeah," Roland replied and pulled himself into the passenger's seat. Mike tapped him on the shoulder.

"What?" Roland asked.

"I'm gonna need your bag, man. And that," he pointed to the still-smoking opium pipe in Roland's hand. "The Heavenly Kingdom's got a pretty strict policy on intoxicants. You're not gonna get a backpack full of narcotics through their checkpoints."

Roland growled at Mike. He couldn't fault the other post-human's logic, but he'd be damned if he was going to spend several days surrounded by a bunch of religious nuts AND do it sober. Roland locked eyes with Skullfucker Mike, opened his bag and grabbed a heavy handful of drugs. He swallowed them all, one by one; pill bottles and baggies of hallucinogens and vials of amphetamines. He ordered his gut to reduce its acidity, so he could store the drugs for later regurgitation and consumption. Then he took one last deep hit from his opium pipe and handed it, and the bag, to Mike.

Manny popped the car into drive and they rolled off into the night.

They drove in silence for a while. Roland's hindbrain would've marked the time if he hadn't done such a successful job of pickling it with opium before they left. The quiet got awkward and boring pretty quick, though. He considered putting on music but, of course, his headware was severed from all outside networks. He couldn't connect to the car anymore than he could blink-send an email. He decided to ask Manny to put something on.

"Hey guy? Music? Can you music?" Roland realized he was slurring. And his words were not coming out the way he'd intended. The kid—Manny—looked irritated.

"How fucked up are you right now?"

Roland gave a shrug that meant "very."

"You know, my ass is on the line here too. I'm not made of whatever fucked up science you've got in your veins. I'd appreciate if you took this seriously."

On an objective level, the kid's request was fair. This must be a big moment for him, going off on a dangerous mission to enemy territory, etc. But to Roland this was Tuesday. Or whatever day it actually was. He'd disabled his clock and calendar years ago, because fuck that noise.

"Fuck that noise," he said without meaning to. *Good God, I'm so high.*

"What?" Manny sounded confused and perturbed.

"Oh shit, sorry, man," Roland rubbed his eyes, a little dazed from the opium. "I wasn't talking to you."

"I am the only other person in this car," Manny said.

"Yeah but, y'know. I'm high as shit. Words come out sometimes, and they aren't meant for anyone. They just happen."

The car slowed and Manny pulled over to the shoulder of the cracked old highway. When the car came to a stop he put his head in his hands and breathed in and then out very slowly. It took Roland a moment to realize the kid was going through a panic attack. *He's never done anything like this before, of course he's terrified.* Roland wondered if he should do something to comfort the kid.

"You know," he said, "I've killed about twelve-thousand armed people."

Manny turned to stare at him. He looked shocked, but—Roland noted with satisfaction—the statement had disrupted his panic. "Wh-what? What the..."

"I mean, give or take a handful," Roland continued. "I burned my brain's kill counter out with Krokodil and cheap vodka a while back."

"Why would you tell me this? Why would you think this would help?"

"Because," Roland said, "we're about to go into a very dangerous place together. You're scared you're going to die. And I want you to know, however many armed nutjobs are in that city, I can murder them. All of them."

Manny stared at him. He still looked terrified, and vaguely pissed, but his heart rate was steadier. His breathing had slowed. Roland declared his gambit a success.

"Ok," the kid finally said. "That's actually comforting. Thank you."

There was silence for a beat, and then Roland spoke again.

"That all said, I'd prefer not to kill anyone. I'd really prefer that. I was on a pretty good no-murder streak until a couple days back. I'm trying to stay on the wagon. So, uh, talk well. Be a good face-man. This'll all be easier if I don't have to commit murder."

Manny looked a bit nervous again, but he popped the car into drive and rolled back onto the highway.

"I'll do my best," he said.

They were an hour outside of Dallas when they hit the first checkpoint, and the Kingdom's guards ordered them out of the truck. Roland stepped out with his hands up. Manny did the same. The guards scanned them, verified their status as Republic citizens and then the questioning started.

"What brings you back to the Heavenly Kingdom?" their leader, a fat man with a Kalashnikov, asked Manny.

"We heard about the amnesty," Manny replied, "and we thought it sounded good. We want to live under the rule of God."

"Hmm," the fat man grunted. "So you're both good, God-fearing men then?"

"Yes sir," Manny nodded. "Of course. And Praise be to God for the victories you've won here."

The fat man sniffed at the air and looked over to his partner.

"I'm not wild about another spic in here. Hansen, you think we need any more Mexicans?"

Hansen shrugged, "Orders say the faithful are all welcome."

"Yeah," the fat guy continued, "if they're faithful." He turned back to Manny. "Why'd it take a couple of devout men like yourselves so long to make a break for the Heavenly Kingdom? We've been at this fight for a while, y'know."

"I, uh, I mean we were scared, and we weren't sure what to believe–"

"What you're supposed to believe is the word of God," the man snarled. "And that's clear as day to everyone who lives inside the Kingdom." He'd looked back at his men and smiled an evil wolfy grin. "Hansen, Molloy, I think we might need to question these two more intensively. Radio command and–"

That was the last thing the fat man said, probably ever.

Roland shoved a hand into the Martyr's mouth, pulled downward, and shattered his jaw in four places. Then he leapt into the others. It went quickly. He gouged eyes, broke jaws, severed tongues, and then started in on their limbs. By the end of it, all four men were still alive, but none of them were in any shape to report on what they'd seen.

Manny vomited several times.

"What happened to doing your best, Manny?" Roland asked, more irritated than angry once he'd finished. The kid recoiled. Roland realized Manny had started to shake a little. He also realized there was still part of a man's ear in his mouth. *Aw hell, you scared him.*

"Sorry kid," he said, and squatted down next to Manny. "Look, the odds were always good that this first try was gonna be a scratch. The good news is, they've got other checkpoints. We'll hop on the access road and find the next one. It'll be fine."

"What did you do to–" Manny started.

"I stopped them from talking," he said, very quickly. "No one's dead. They'll be, uh," he glanced down at the burbling, bleeding mess of shattered humans, "...they'll be aight. But we need to move now, before someone else comes along and I've got to break them too."

Roland popped open the cab so he could change into a clean set of spare clothes. He was grateful that Skullfucker Mike had packed them bags to lend their story extra verisimilitude. Manny changed too, and once his hands stopped shaking they rolled off to the next checkpoint. Roland tried not to think too much about the men he'd just broken. It helped that one of them had been an asshole. It helped that none of them had died. But still...

They hit the next checkpoint eight minutes later, and things went much better this time. For one thing, it was busier. There were already a dozen other cars in line when they pulled in. The guy who questioned them was less of an asshole and he seemed to buy Manny's claim.

"We weren't brave enough to make the journey until now. But we prayed all night about this. I know it's the right thing to do."

Roland had to fight to avoid rolling his eyes. The line worked, though. The man at the checkpoint waved them in and issued them a temporary transit pass.

"This is good for six hours," the checkpoint officer said. "That's plenty of time to find the immigration center and report in. If you're caught driving around the Kingdom after that, it won't end well for you."

They drove on, but it was slow going after the checkpoint. The roads into Dallas were choked with ruined vehicles and actual traffic.

It looked as if hundreds of people had taken the Heavenly Kingdom up on its amnesty offer. Roland couldn't fault them for that. The Kingdom seemed to be winning.

As they rolled toward Plano, they were stopped regularly by patrolling Martyrs and asked to present their papers. But bit by bit, they made their way onto and through the packed and crumbling highways of old Dallas. At one point, they found themselves in stalled traffic on Highway 75, overlooking the cratered ruins of the Lakewood Blast.

He felt cold October air. He smelled barrel fires and heard the sharp crack of riflery. He saw flashes of a face—it might've been Jim's—and he remembered the feel of a cold metal handle, attached to something heavy and dense. He remembered yelling too, a small, sweaty hand held tight in his own. He remembered guilt.

"What's up?" Manny asked. He looked over at Roland and his eyes widened. "Dude, you're shaking. Don't tell me you're flipping out now. We're too deep into this thing."

Roland shook his head. "It's nothing," he said. "Just a piece of an old memory hitting me in the face. I think I was in town when that fucker went off.

The young man's pupils grew as big as saucers.

"Ni verga," he spat. "You're full of shit."

Roland shrugged. "I dunno, maybe. It's just a piece of a memory. I might be confusing it with something else. Sure got triggered by seeing the blast site, though."

Manny was not satisfied by that answer. "I refuse to believe that someone could watch an atom bomb eviscerate a city and not have a clear memory of it. I had to take anti-rad pills my whole childhood because of that bomb."

"I don't have any clear memories, kid. None from further back than about, I guess, five or eight years ago. I don't have a lot of clear memories since then either, but that's from the drugs."

"What the hell happened to you?" Manny asked. "I thought you post-humans all had hard drives running through your blood. Were you too cheap to pay for a photographic memory?"

Roland scratched his neck. He wasn't itchy. It was a nervous gesture. He was a little fascinated at the fact that this line of questioning made him feel nervous. He really couldn't remember the last time a conversation had made him feel that way. Weird.

"I got hurt," was all he could honestly say. "I don't remember much of anything from before the Revolution. Hell, I don't really remember the Revolution."

The line of cars started moving again. Manny popped the car back into drive, and they rolled further into the Heavenly Kingdom. Both men were quiet for a minute, until Roland spoke again.

"That's why I'm doing this, you know." He wasn't sure why he was saying all this, but Roland found he couldn't stop himself. "Jim, the guy who brought me on, knows some fuckin' East Coast surgeon who specializes in post-human brains. They think they can give me back my memory. This rescue mission is how I pay for that."

"Are you sure you want those memories back?" Manny asked.

"The fuck do you mean? I don't even know who I am, or was, right now. Wouldn't you want that shit back if you lost it?"

Manny glanced over at him. They locked eyes.

"I don't know," the kid said. "You say you've killed at least twelve thousand people. I've been working as a fixer for the last two years, and I've seen a lot of fucked up eyes. Dead eyes on men who've done too much killing. But none of them hold a candle to what's going on there." He pointed to Roland's face. "I dunno. I got a feeling your past is one big, fucked-up nightmare. Maybe you're better off without it."

Roland was quiet for a while, and Manny didn't say anything else. They crept along in stops and starts and inched closer to Plano as the sun cracked open the horizon. *The kid had a point*, Roland decided. He'd worried about the same thing himself since Jim made the offer. Every hour or so he still found himself thinking about the driver of that technical. The man had reeked of love.

And yeah, the guy'd been fighting to establish a Christofascist hell state. But somehow that didn't mitigate his death in Roland's head. Most causes were shit. Most men who fought for anything fought for nightmares. That guy, and all his friends, had just been doing what felt right based on the shit lives they'd lived. The same thing had to be true for most of the soldiers and insurgents Roland had killed. *How many civilians did you kill, Roland? How many lives did you end just to keep the battle drugs flowing?*

When he thought about it that way, he really didn't want his memories back.

But then, of course, there was Topaz. He loved her so much. Or, rather, the pieces of him that remembered her loved her so much. Roland knew he wanted those memories back. He needed them back. Every time he thought about her face something twisted inside him, as if his guts were being tugged in whatever direction he thought she might be. It was a weird way to feel about a woman he only remembered in fragments.

Roland shook his head in a nervous attempt to shake the thoughts from his mind. Then he stared ahead at the line of cars.

The immigration center was chaotic, crowded, and heavy with the smell of scared humans. It was also a happier place than Roland would have expected. Martyrs in fresh olive drab uniforms with bright golden crosses emblazoned on the arms handed out food, water, and even cups of instant coffee to the adults. They posed for pictures with children. The whole place almost had the air of a party about it. There was someone filming too. Roland guessed he must be a propagandist for the Kingdom, putting together some sort of documentary.

They stood in line for two full hours before it was their turn in front of the intake officer. He was an older man, with a big bushy mustache, red jowls, and a droopy rooster-wattle of a throat. He had a whiny voice that barraged them with questions as soon as they sat down at his desk.

"How many Apostles did Christ have?"

"What was the name of the hill where our Lord was crucified?"

"What is the fifth commandment?"

Manny answered every question while Roland sat there and smiled vacantly like an invalid. They'd decided in the car that "playing dumb" was his best option. He'd probably wind up starting a fight if he talked to the man and, besides, Roland didn't know shit about the Bible. He didn't even have any memory fragments of church services.

"And why is it that you're answering all the questions, young man?" the officer finally asked. "What about your friend here... Aaron, is it?"

"Uh, yeah," Roland replied, "I just, um. I don't test so good. Mom said I ain't a thinker."

"But you are a Christian, yes?"

"Oh yeah, sir," he nodded enthusiastically. "I love God. I'm all about God!"

The intake officer narrowed his eyes at Roland. Manny flashed him a look of fury and then quickly turned it into a smile directed at the officer.

"He's, uh. He's slow, sir. His momma took care of him but she died in a drone strike two months back. From the SDF. I'm just trying to make sure he's OK."

"Mmmh," the man grunted, then looked to Roland. "I imagine that must make you angry, losing your mother."

Roland nodded and put on his best facsimile of an angry face. "They're bad men. I want to hurt them back."

The intake officer chuckled. "Well, I've got good news for you then. The Heavenly Kingdom needs soldiers. I'm sending you both to a training platoon. In a few days you'll be Martyrs, and you'll have a chance to get your revenge."

"Wait," Manny asked. "We're...we're being drafted?"

The officer narrowed his piggy eyes. "The Heavenly Kingdom is fighting for its life, boys. Every person we let in has a job. There are no shirkers here, no layabouts. If you aren't willing to help build the Kingdom of God on Earth, we have no use for you. And I've decided you boys will best serve God in our infantry."

And just like that, Roland found himself inducted into a military for what was (at least) the second time in his life. The intake officer gave them more papers, signed a mustering order, and sent them off with directions to find the barracks that was, apparently, their new home. Manny handled the rest of the interaction well. He even managed to act enthusiastic, after his first startled outburst. But once they were out of earshot, back in the truck, he started to hyperventilate again. It looked like another panic attack.

"Mierda!" he cursed. "This was such a fucking bad idea!"

"Hey," Roland patted the kid on the shoulder, "it's gonna be alright, buddy." Some aspect of his comforting tactic must have gone wrong, because the kid just looked pissed.

"Do you not realize how fucked this is?" Manny shoved Roland back. "We're supposed to be effecting a rescue here!" he yelled. "They're going to have us drilling and training day and night. We'll be surrounded by soldiers. I thought we'd just be squatting in an apartment, saying some 'Peace be with yous' when we went outside. I thought we were gonna track down those hostages in like a day. Now what the fuck are we supposed to do?"

Roland thought about that for a moment. He thought about the Martyrs he'd faced on the battlefield three days ago, in their motley armor and battered, rusted weaponry.

"Look," he said, "if this were a real army, we'd be fucked. But you've seen how these guys fight. They've got numbers, and some professionals, but the bulk of their forces are just poor dumb fucks with a week's worth of training and whatever gun was lying around. We're not gonna be drilling from dawn 'til dusk."

He gestured at the truck's dashboard.

"They're letting us drive our own fucking truck up there. This ain't gonna be like a real army. I guarantee you we'll have time to do our shit. Stay calm. Stick close to me. Do what I do. I'm real fucking good at soldiering. If you follow my lead they'll love us and our job'll be that much easier."

"And what if something goes wrong?" Manny asked. "What if they catch us?"

Roland shrugged.

"If they catch us, then we'll already be in the middle of their army. That'll save me so much time."

Chapter 15

Sasha.

The man on the gurney was the most comprehensively broken human Sasha had ever seen. His jaw had been ripped completely out of its socket and shattered in four places. His eyes had been gouged into horrible smashed-grape looking things. His hands and fingers were all broken, as were his feet and shins. His ears appeared to have been bitten off. His tongue had been severed and the wound cauterized with something that had charred the flesh black.

Sasha hadn't known a person could take such punishment and survive.

The chart at the end of the bed identified him as Sergeant Lufkin, a two-year veteran Martyr who'd been guarding a checkpoint outside of Dallas. He was conscious; every now and then he'd thrash about and let out a burbling moan. But the man didn't appear capable of any sort of intelligible communication.

"Well, these aren't combat injuries," Dr. Brandt said. "These men look almost like they've been in a car wreck, only the damage is too precise and too deliberately targeted. I've never seen anything like it."

It was Sasha's duty to administer the men's painkillers, just a tiny drop of morphine each. It wasn't enough by any proper hospital's standards. The soldiers were all in clear agony. But the Heavenly Kingdom was short on painkillers and this was the most they could afford to spare for "invalids," as Dr. Brandt had called them.

This frustrated Sasha. Her mother's hospital could've restored all four men to full health and vigor with, perhaps, a month of treatment and physical therapy. But the Heavenly Kingdom forbade vat-grown organs and limbs. Cloning contravened the Lord's will. Sasha agreed with that, in theory. She'd fled to the Heavenly Kingdom partly because she believed JuvEn treatments had robbed the AmFed of its humanity.

But still. It seemed so wrong that these men would go the rest of their lives as twitching, insensate lumps of flesh.

The number of things that felt wrong about this place grew every day. The executions had been the first big shock to her system. But she'd accepted Helen's justification. The Bible was filled with decent men doing awful things in times of war. The gallows weren't pretty, but they were hardly without Biblical precedent.

She'd been unable to justify Alexander's actions in the same way. Oh yes, she knew polygamy was condoned by the word of God. She'd read about Lamech and Abraham and Solomon and David and, of course, Jacob, the patriarch of the Twelve Tribes of Israel and apparent namesake for Alexander's "order." She still hated what he'd done to her. Sasha couldn't bring herself to believe that a man as truly good as Pastor Mike would condone their actions.

"Polygamy is a biblically sound strategy for a people on the edge of destruction," he'd written in one of his *Revelator* columns. "But it is not the human ideal. In our Lord's eyes, the most perfect union is one man, one woman, and as many children as they can bear." Had he decided since then that the Heavenly Kingdom was a people "on the edge of destruction"?

After the disastrous meeting with Alexander, Sasha had made her way back to the House of Miriam. Helen was seated at her desk when Sasha barged in. The older woman looked tired, resigned, and almost depressed. It seemed as if she'd been waiting for Sasha.

"Hello, dear," she said with a sad smile, "I assume you just met with Alexander?"

"Yes!" Sasha couldn't help but shout. "What they're doing is vile, Helen. He wanted me as his third wife. He lied to convince me to come down here. He says there's a whole group of Martyrs—they call themselves Jacobians—and they're just catfishing girls down here. We have to tell someone. This isn't OK. This is so wrong. I just, I can't—"

Sasha started to sob. She'd been too angry to cry in front of Alexander. But the House of Miriam was a safe place. Helen was a safe person.

Sasha's grief caught up with her anger and she found herself doubled over on the floor, wracked by sobs. She lost herself in sorrow for a few long heartbeats, and then Helen was there beside her. She felt the older woman's strong arms around her, felt a hand running through her hair.

"There, there, child. It's alright. It's going to be OK."

"We have to do something," Sasha choked out. "Pastor Mike needs to know what's being done in his name."

She looked up into Helen's eyes. She saw pain and anger there.

"Sasha," Helen said, "this will be hard for you to understand. But the Pastor is well aware of what those men are doing. I've spoken to him about it myself."

Sasha stiffened. She pulled away from Helen, and Helen let her go. They sat next to each other, on the floor, in silence, until Sasha spoke again.

"Authenticity is the strongest arrow in our quiver," she quoted. "When did that stop being true? When did it become OK to lie in the name of the Lord?"

Helen sighed and shook her head.

"It is not OK. But so much about this world we live in is not OK. They still murder forty-thousand babies per year in the American Federation. A hundred thousand in the California Republic. Sodomy and cloning are rampant all across the world. We, the faithful, are surrounded on all sides."

Sasha recognized that last line. It was the opening sentence of Pastor Mike's infamous "Sinful Continent in the Hands of an Angry God" column. Sasha couldn't deny the truth of those words. Everything Helen said was accurate. But–

"But how are we any better than them if we stoop to dishonesty to fill the Heavenly Kingdom?"

Helen stiffened and straightened her back. "We are better than them, dear, because our goals are Godly." There was a hint of pride in her voice. "We are fighting for the one singular Truth. You must never forget that the men and women fighting for that truth are flawed. We are all fallible. We will fall short of God's standards. But we are also the only ones trying to meet God's standards."

"And that makes what Alexander did OK?"

Helen shook her head. Sasha saw tears in the corners of the older woman's eyes.

"No, child. Nothing makes it OK. You were wronged. That boy played with your heart. He lied to you about his love. And that's an unforgivable thing. But you're here now, aren't you? And that's what matters most."

Helen held her and talked with her for the next few hours. By the time the other girls came back, she felt better. Not good, exactly, but better. Stable enough to not burst into tears during dinner. She kept quiet at mealtime and was glad that the others seemed too exhausted from their day of labor to say much either.

After dinner they had another hour of personal time. Anne and Susannah zeroed in on her with military precision. Sasha's vaunted poker face hadn't been enough to hide her sorrow. Her new friends guided her to a corner of the room where they'd have relative privacy.

"What's wrong?" Anne asked in a low voice. She and Susannah both laid their hands on Sasha's shoulders. Sasha reached up to grasp both of their hands. It happened automatically, as if by reflex, but it brought her great comfort. She closed her eyes and stood quiet for a moment as her mind and heart calmed down.

"I met Alexander today," she said.

Anne looked confused. Susannah frowned, then laughed and asked, "What, did he have bad breath? Were his eyes all..." she blew out her cheeks and crossed her eyes. Anne laughed, but Sasha stayed quiet. Susannah's smile faded.

"Sash'," she said in a quiet voice, "what happened?"

Sasha looked from Susannah to Anne. She felt a surge of gratitude in her new friends for being there at all. She took a deep breath in and then told them what had happened. She went quickly, in the hope that her clipped recitation of events would make it all seem less devastating.

"Oh Sasha," Anne said, "I'm so sorry. This has to be some sort of mistake."

"Helen didn't seem to think so," Sasha said. "I don't think Alexander lied about the Sons of Jacob being powerful here."

"It's chaos right now, Sash'," Susannah assured her, "maybe a few guys can get away with acting like this now, during the war. But once it's over Pastor Mike won't let them treat us like this."

Anne nodded.

"Kyle gets rotated back from the front tomorrow," she said. "I'll ask him about the Sons of Jacob. Maybe he'll know something we can do."

Sasha knew from the look she'd seen in Helen's eyes that further protest against the Jacobians would be useless. *And besides*, she thought, *the most painful thing was Alexander's dishonesty. He's already hurt me as much as he can.* She tried to convince herself of that, just as she tried to enjoy the company of her friends without dwelling on the face of the boy who'd betrayed her. She was less than successful.

Bedtime came. The girls washed up, said their goodnights, and snuggled up in their beds. As usual, Sasha's mind stayed awake and active. She wasn't having second thoughts exactly—*of course not, never!* But so much about today felt wrong. Alexander and the Sons of Jacob, of course, but also that the brave men she'd worked on that afternoon would never walk or see or talk again. *This is war*, she reminded herself, *a great deal of it is going to seem wrong.*

The next morning and afternoon went by in a haze of industrious activity; breakfast and bandages and preparing medications for doctors and nurses. Sasha lost herself in the work and, for a few hours, wasn't happy or sad.

Her shift at the hospital ended at five. She took her nightly jeep ride back to the House of Miriam, but rather than going right inside, she decided to take a walk around the downtown strip. She had a few ration scrips in her pocket, enough that she could've bought coffee or even a meal in the one functioning restaurant still in town. But she wasn't hungry; she just wanted to walk.

This part of the Heavenly Kingdom looked less like a war zone and more like a functional polis with every passing day. Most of the piles of rubble and spent shell casings were gone now. There was still quite a lot of damage to all the buildings, and very few intact windows to be found, but that strange spoiled milk smell was gone. Some shops were open again, along with a small farmers' market about ten minutes down from the House of Miriam. There were people out too. Not many families, yet, but she saw a lot of sweaty, tired-looking soldiers. They wandered in small groups and clustered around the strip's only functional cafe.

There were refugees too, and new immigrants to the Kingdom. Greeters in blue and white uniforms, the foot soldiers of the Kingdom's immigration department, led columns of them down the main drag and into old government buildings that had been repurposed into housing collectives. Sasha felt herself fill with a strange pride, at odds with all the doubt that still roiled in her gut. From right here, the Heavenly Kingdom looked exactly like what had been promised to her. It was still rough, raw, and unfinished, but it overflowed with the good intentions of Godly men and women.

Helen had been right. Sasha could see that now. As ugly as Alexander's lies were, as detestable as she found the whole idea of the Jacobians, the Heavenly Kingdom was still a thing of beauty. It was still worth fighting for. She just had to accept that it would never be perfect, and–

"Hello, Sasha."

She stopped. The hair prickled up on the back of her neck. Sasha turned around to face Alexander.

Sasha had been lost in thought, so it was hard to say how long they'd been following her. Three other young men were with him. They all wore clean, pressed new uniforms and sidearms at their waists. She didn't recognize the rank insignias on their shoulders. But she did notice that each of them wore a large gold badge in the shape of a lion's head on their lapel. She'd seen a lot of uniformed Martyrs during her short time with the Heavenly Kingdom. She'd never seen a badge like that before.

"Hello, Alexander." She tried to keep her voice cool, but respectful. "Hello, brothers. Peace be with you."

"And also with you," the other young men mumbled by habit.

"Are you walking alone right now, my dear?" Alexander asked. His lips curled up into an unctuous smile. "That worries me. These streets still aren't as safe as they should be. Let us walk with you a while."

Sasha stiffened. There was something dark in Alexander's eyes. She wondered if it had always been there and she'd just ignored it before. Her heart began to race. Sweat beaded on the back of her neck. There were a lot of people around still, but she was away from the most crowded part of the main drag. It wouldn't be hard for three strong young men to move her somewhere less visible.

"I'd prefer to walk alone." She tried to keep her tone even. Sasha felt like they must still have heard the trembling in her voice.

"That's nonsense, Sasha," Alexander said. "No woman wants to be alone when they can enjoy the company of their protectors."

He stepped toward her, reached a hand out, and brushed the hair away from her eyes. Alexander stroked her cheek. His hand drifted down to her shoulder, where he applied firm pressure. Sasha wanted to pull away. But Alexander was much larger than she was. He had a gun, and two friends with guns, and apparently the personal support of Pastor Mike. So she stood still and tried to stop her heart from beating quite so fast.

"Sasha," he said in the gentle, sweet voice that had helped to carry her here, "you deserve to be cared for. I know the full truth was a shock to you, and I'm not angry at your reaction. Really. But you're still holding onto fragments of the secular world. You need to drop that veil from your eyes and accept that God wants this. He wants men like us..." Alexander gestured to his friends, "men with superior talents, to breed and fill the world with more holy warriors."

Sasha closed her eyes. She took a deep breath in, and out, and then another. *Just go with it*, a part of her said, *he won't hurt you if you just tell him what he wants to hear*. She knew that wasn't right, though. She hadn't risked her life to cross into the Heavenly Kingdom just to compromise her morals now.

"I am doing good and valuable work here," she replied in the calmest voice she could muster. "I don't want to be your third wife. I know God has another purpose for me, and I intend to seek it ou–"

His hand clenched tight on her shoulder. Sasha's eyes widened in fear. There was something dull, black, and hungry in his eyes. The two men behind him straightened their backs and started glancing around, scoping out the area.

"Sasha," Alexander said, "I brought you here. You are my responsibility. I don't believe you're thinking clearly. We should take a walk and find somewhere private to talk about all this. I've commandeered a home nearby. Come on. Walk with me."

He pushed at her the whole time he spoke and grew angrier with each passing word, so that by the time he said "Walk with me" his voice had grown tight and cold. Sasha steadied her heart, met his eyes with as steady a gaze as she could manage, and said:

"I. Don't. Want. To. Walk. With. You."

Her heart was pounding so loud she was sure Alexander and his friends could hear it. But Sasha didn't move. She was sure any minute now he'd grab her full on and force her forward. But before he had the chance a familiar voice called for her.

"Sasha! Is that you?"

It was Dr. Brandt. In all her focus on Alexander and his posse, she hadn't even noticed the electric hum of the doctor's jeep as it pulled up behind them on the main street.

"Yes, sir!" she cried, her voice a bit higher and more frantic than she'd meant it to sound. "What do you need?"

"Get in the back, girl. You can flirt with soldiers later. The Heavenly Kingdom needs your skills. We've got a little bit of an issue."

Alexander's face went purple. The two men behind him seemed confused. One put a hand on his gun but Alexander waved him back. He shot Sasha a vicious look and then turned to Dr. Brandt, suddenly composed.

"Any idea how long you'll need her?"

"What are you? A lieutenant?" Dr. Brandt scoffed. "She'll be gone as long as the Kingdom needs her. I don't see a ring on either of your fingers, so I'm fairly certain it's not your place to care how long this takes. Sasha," he beckoned to her with his index finger, "come on now, girl."

"Gladly!" she said with a genuine smile. Sasha darted past Alexander and his men and hopped up into the backseat of the jeep. She tried to keep her head and eyes down while the doctor's driver gunned the engine and sped off down main street.

Once they were under way, Dr. Brandt turned back to her.

"Sasha," he asked, "was anything going on with those young men? Anything...untoward? I ask because you seem positively elated I've picked you up to deal with a problem."

Do I tell him the truth? Sasha wondered. *Do I admit I was lured to the Kingdom by a catfisher? He'll never take me seriously then.* This job was her favorite part of serving the Kingdom. Sasha didn't want to say or do anything that might disrupt it. And besides, Dr. Brandt was a busy man. Lives were in his hands every day. *I can't distract him with this.*

"No, no! Everything's fine. I'm fine."

Dr. Brandt gave her a stern look. Sasha smiled a tense smile in response. He shrugged and turned his head back to the road.

"Alright," he said. And then: "There was a problem with one of your patient's blood tests."

"Oh," Sasha frowned, "I'm so sorry. What did I do wrong?"

"Nothing at all," Dr. Brandt assured her. "But that vile woman, Marigold. She's pregnant."

"Pregnant?" Sasha was shocked. Most adult women in the American Federation had Aphrodite Rings installed. Sasha had refused hers, but the government offered them for free. They provided complete control over reproduction and allowed women to select whether or not they wanted to be fertile. She'd assumed anyone with as many bio-modifications as Marigold would have a Ring as well.

Maybe she just wants a baby. For some reason, Sasha hadn't initially considered that a possibility. It was hard to imagine someone as fallen as Marigold choosing to raise children.

"Yes, Sasha," Dr. Brandt said. "Or, at least, that first test indicated so. False positives do still happen. That's why we're headed back. We need you to administer another test so we can be certain."

"Well, shit," Marigold grunted, "I didn't expect to see you back this soon. You need a friend, darlin'?"

The heathen woman looked the same as she had on their last interaction. Her hair was less greasy, so they must've let her wash. But she wore the same slip dress and sat in the same corner of the same cell.

"Sorry, no." Sasha said. "I'm here to administer a pregnancy test."

Marigold's eyes widened. For a few seconds the woman was speechless. Her mouth opened and closed, she nodded and clutched her left knee with her left hand.

"OK," the captive said. "Right. Where do you want me to do it?"

"Do...?" Sasha looked down at the stick in her hand and realized how these things worked. *I'm sure Dr. Brandt doesn't expect me to watch her pee.*

"You can go over to your...normal...space. I'll just, I'll turn around."

She handed Marigold the test and spun around on her heels, so the other woman wouldn't see how much she'd started to blush.

"Damn, girl. Are you that squicked out by the human body?"

"What?" Sasha asked without turning around.

"Your face is as red as a damn beet."

"I'm sorry!"

"Why?"

"I don't know!"

Marigold laughed.

"You can turn around now. I'm decent, and done."

Sasha turned around. Marigold smirked at her.

"You know," she said, "that instinct to apologize actually might come in handy around here. I'm sure the sort of men who jump in on this bullshit will appreciate it."

Sasha recovered her senses, and felt a bit of anger at Marigold's words. "I don't appreciate you saying those things," she said. "The men here are good and brave and, a–" Sasha's voice caught. It broke, just a little. Marigold saw and heard her doubt. The other woman didn't laugh, like Sasha expected. In fact, her smile fell away. Marigold looked at her with something like pity.

"I know you don't believe that," she said.

Sasha closed her eyes and took a deep breath in. Then she replied, "No men are perfect, just as no women are perfect. But everyone here in the Kingdom tries, every day, to abide by the Lord's will. That's what elevates us above–"

Marigold interrupted, "Does your Lord say women don't get last names?"

"We don't use last names in the Kingdom because they distract us. We can't afford connec–"

"The men keep their surnames. Don't they?"

That was true. Sasha hadn't thought about it much, what with everything else that was going on. But Dr. Brandt went by his last name, didn't he? And Alexander had a surname too. *She's trying to weaken your faith in the Kingdom. Don't give in to the doubts of the serpent.*

"It doesn't matter," Sasha said, and immediately regretted it. Any response would surely just egg Marigold on. And sure enough–

"Oh, it doesn't? Then why is that the rule?"

"Well, it's obviously because we need some way to tell families apart from one another."

"Yes," Marigold smirked now, "and the only lineage that matters is the man's, isn't it? Women are just appendages in your belief system."

"I AM NOT AN APPENDAGE!" Sasha shouted, surprised at her own anger. She heard shuffling feet, and a second later the guard had one hand on the door and another on his rifle.

"Is everything alright, miss?" he asked.

"Y-yes," Sasha called back to him over her shoulder, "I'm fine. Sorry. She's just..." Sasha fixed Marigold with a withering glare. "She's very frustrating."

Marigold smirked at that. Then she held out the test. Sasha hesitated for just a second before taking the strip from the other woman. Marigold smirked at that, too.

"You're pregnant," Sasha said.

"Ayep," Marigold nodded.

"Congratulations," Sasha tried to sound genuine. Marigold's eyeroll didn't help that cause.

"Oh yeah," the other woman said, "this is a real joyous moment for me. I hope your people let me live long enough to know whether or not my kid'll deserve a last name."

"You know," Sasha said in growing anger, "this place isn't perfect, but if you got to know the people here you'd understand. They are the best people I've ever met. I wish you could have seen the welcome I received. I've never felt so–"

"Loved?" Marigold asked. "Like all you needed to do was show up to earn their acceptance?"

"...Yes," Sasha admitted, suspicious.

"Did they, sort of, swarm you? But in a nice way? Everyone hugging you and holding you and offering you safe, physical affection?"

"Yes..."

Marigold nodded, as if she'd just gotten the answer to a longstanding question.

"They love-bombed you."

"What?"

"It's a tactic cults use," Marigold explained. "You sorta overwhelm someone with love and acceptance and camaraderie and all that. It nurtures loyalty. And dependence." She shrugged. "It's a smart way to manipulate young people in your position. You've just fled your home and family for a strange and dangerous land. You're scared and alone and isolated. And then, like magic, you've got a family and a support network."

"You are so cynical..." Sasha had to fight back the urge to say "*damned* cynical." This woman was making her forget herself. She opened her mouth, as if to deliver a tongue-lashing, but the words wouldn't come.

Instead she just narrowed her eyes at Marigold and stared for a few seconds.

"I'm leaving now," she said. "I'm going to go enjoy the companionship of my new family. You enjoy this cell."

Then Sasha turned on her heels and walked out.

She returned late to the House of Miriam. The other girls had already finished dinner. Helen had left out Sasha's plate (a ham sandwich, carrot sticks, an apple, and a small block of cheese) and she took it into the common room where the other girls were talking and winding down from their day.

"Look who finally showed up," Mae sneered when she walked in. "I guess you're too important to eat with the rest of us now?"

"I–" Sasha started to reply. Then she saw Anne and Susannah huddled in the same corner where they'd all sat last night. There were tears on Anne's face, and her eyes looked swollen and red. She made no noise, but her back and shoulders shook as she sat there, half-shielded from view in Susannah's embrace.

Sasha gave Mae a dirty look but turned and moved past her, toward her friends. She heard the other girl scoff and say something to her coterie of friends. Sasha couldn't hear what, though, and she didn't much care. She squatted down next to Anne and put a hand on the back of her neck.

"Hey," she said, not sure what else to say. Susannah met Sasha's eyes and offered up a sad smile. Anne continued to sob. For a few minutes, they just held her. Sasha burned with morbid curiosity over what, exactly, had happened. She knew it must have something to do with Kyle. Anne had been set to meet with him today. Had he revealed himself as a Son of Jacob too?

"He's dead," Anne whispered in a cracked, broken voice. "I went to meet him at the Cafe Clement and there were two Martyrs there, waiting for me. They both," she stifled a sob, "...they both smiled when they told me he'd been killed. They said I should thank God for the blessing of a death in battle."

"I'm so sorry, Anne," Sasha said. "Susannah and I are here, though. We'll take care of you."

She hoped that might comfort Anne a little. But the other girl lost herself in another fit of tears. Sasha's heart broke for her. The pain over her own, comparatively minor tragedy flowed into the empathy she felt for Anne, and soon Sasha was crying too. She was sure some of the other girls were whispering about them, egged on by Mae. She didn't care. After a few more minutes of tears, Anne managed to clear her throat and speak again.

"The men, the Martyrs I met told me the same thing," she said. "They told me I'd be taken care of, that they'd find God's choice for me among the Martyrs. I tried to tell them, I don't want anyone else, not now. I need to mourn but they said, they said..." Anne's voice caught in her throat, and she fought to throttle another sob before she continued. "They said the Heavenly Kingdom might not be able to wait for my grief to pass."

"What's that supposed to mean?" Susannah asked. Sasha didn't say anything, because the only answer that occurred to her was surely unhelpful. She had a strong suspicion that the Sons of Jacob had turned their eyes on Anne.

Sasha stared into Marigold's vagina. She'd seen it before, of course, the first time they'd met. But it hadn't been her focus then, and she'd tried very hard not to look at it too much. Now though, the point *was* to look. Dr. Brandt had picked her up halfway through her shift at the hospital to conduct a pap smear on the captured woman. She'd only had about an hour to practice.

"It's a procedure I've done myself a hundred times," Dr. Brandt had told her, "but that was back in the AmFed. It's a sinful thing for a man to touch a woman other than his wife. That's why the Israelites used midwives. That's why we use midwives. And I think this kind of work might be why God drew you here."

His words made her proud. She liked Dr. Brandt, for all his prickliness. She also liked learning and feeling she had a useful skill that made her special. So she'd paid close attention as Dr. Brandt had walked her through the procedure. It had been fun, and the act of learning had distracted her from her worries about Anne and her own grief over Alexander.

Marigold shuddered as Sasha slid the speculum in past her labia.

"You could stand to be a little gentler. And would it kill you to, I dunno, warm it up first or something?"

"Dr. Brandt didn't say to do that," Sasha kept her voice firm. "This is for the baby's good. I'm sorry if it's uncomfortable. This is my first time."

The woman snorted.

"Oh, well, in that case you're doing a great j– OW! Maybe a little less hard. And mine slopes down. You're going against the grain."

"The grain?"

Marigold rolled her eyes in disdain, but didn't dignify Sasha with a response.

"You're pushing the wrong way."

Sasha readjusted, and Marigold gave a sigh of relief.

"That sucks less, at least. Thanks."

Sasha busied herself with the swabbing and rubbing that came next. She worked slow, methodical, with as much care and gentleness as the instructions she'd received from Dr. Brandt would allow. She did her best to focus, but the other woman kept talking.

"You don't look old enough to have graduated high school. I'm going to guess they don't train teenagers to do Pap smears in the AmFed." Marigold added, "Do they?" with surprising earnestness.

"No," Sasha grunted.

"I'm gonna guess Dr. Whatshisname taught you then? Because why, he's too scared of my demon snatch to come in here and do the job himself?"

Sasha's face reddened. She did not like the word "snatch," or Marigold's casual mention of demons. But she kept her eyes straight and stared into the other woman's vagina. *I have one too. It's not that big a deal,* she told herself.

"It's impressive you were able to learn that. I'm serious. Real props, lady. You're the only woman I've seen do a damn thing around here. How'd you trick them into treating you sorta like a person?"

Sasha's ire rose and rose and rose. *Lord calm my heart*, she prayed. *I know she's just trying to set me off. It's just desperation*, she told herself.

"How long do you think they'll let you keep playing like you've got a real life? I'm gonna guess it won't be too long before somebody puts a baby in you. You know that'll be the end of all this, right? Like, your life, using your brain, all that. You're going to be a brood mare before too–"

"STOP." Sasha didn't yell, but she used her firmest tone and she was quite loud about it. Despite herself, she looked up from her work and at Marigold's face. The other woman didn't look surprised or chagrined. One edge of her lips curled up into a wry grin. Her eyes twinkled. Sasha had never actually seen someone's eyes twinkle before.

"There we go. I wondered where the edge was."

"The edge of what?" Sasha asked without thinking. *Idiot. This is exactly what she wants you to do.*

"The edge of your patience. The point where meekness ends. I was worried they'd beaten it out of you."

"No one beat me," Sasha insisted. "And there's nothing wrong with being meek. The Lord asks us to put on a heart of compassion, kindness, humility, gentleness, and patience. Maybe you wouldn't be in a cell if you'd accepted that for yourself."

"I'm in a cell because I came here to trade. We weren't waging any kind of war. We weren't harming anyone. We wanted freakin' cheetos in exchange for our latest coffee crop. Your people killed the old government and captured us."

Sasha closed her eyes, breathed in and out, and tried to calm herself. For some reason Marigold's words made her feel anxious and angry. She wanted to say the anger was toward the other woman. But that wasn't quite right. Marigold had been sarcastic and catty, but she'd also been complimentary, thoughtful, and far from cruel.

"I'm sure you'll be sent back to your people soon. The Heavenly Kingdom doesn't want any kind of fight with...with your city."

"Yet."

Sasha finished her work. She withdrew the speculum and started gathering up her kit.

"I do hope you're not laboring under the impression that this war will ever end," Marigold said. "Because it won't. Not while your Kingdom exists."

"You're wrong. We'll take Austin soon. And then there'll be peace."

"And what about El Paso?"

Sasha shrugged. "A heathen nation. But they haven't launched any strikes against us. If they'll let us be, we'll let them be."

"'Remain and expand,'" Marigold quoted one of the slogans Pastor

Mike had coined during the early days of the Kingdom. The other woman had a surprisingly deep understanding of their movement. Marigold continued.

"'The Kingdom of God will remain and expand until it reunites this broken land, from sea to shining sea.' That's your prophet, right? Your mighty pastor? Sure sounds like a recipe for eternal war. Mexico, the Navajo, the California Republic, and the King of goddamn Albuquerque don't seem likely to sign up for a theocracy. And those are just the big powers in the Southwest."

Pastor Mike would have had an answer to that, of course. He'd said that as the Heavenly Kingdom grew it would draw in millions from around the world and become "a shining beacon to the fallen people of the world." Fighting would be replaced by peaceful annexation.

She'd believed that once, before she left the American Federation. It had seemed sensible. With Alexander's romantic words in her ear and the fiery prose from *Revelator* in her mind, how could she not believe? But now she'd spent time in the reality of the Heavenly Kingdom. She'd met beautiful people and seen wondrous things, but she'd also helped treat a seemingly endless train of broken men whose bodies had been shattered by war. She'd watched a dozen people be executed by hanging.

Sasha was anxious. And Marigold must have picked up on it. The other woman's eyes changed. There was something almost predatory in them. She leaned forward.

"I know I'm hitting nerves, Sasha. That's because you're too smart for this shit. You got suckered into a fucking nightmare. It's time to wake up."

Sasha kept Marigold's words in her mind as she headed back to the hospital. A fresh wave of wounded men had been sent over from the Lake Houston front, and she wound up working three hours later than normal just to help handle the load. It was a whirlwind of bloody bandages, screaming Martyrs, and irate, exhausted doctors trying to do too much with far too little. By the time she got off shift it was dark outside and downtown was almost deserted.

Her driver dropped her off in a weird spot at the other end of main street. It was a good two blocks away from the normal location, but she chalked that up to the fact that this wasn't her normal driver. She didn't really mind the extra walk. In fact, after an long day under the hospital's florescent lights, a dark walk and some fresh air seemed relaxing.

So she strolled and she tried to forget the faces of the men she'd seen that day. For a few blissful minutes Marigold's words fled from her head and she lost herself in the peace that came at the end of a good day's labor. The streets of the Heavenly Kingdom felt safe. She'd done meaningful work. The Lord must be–

"Hey– HEY! No, please, I really don't want to–"

Sasha heard a familiar female voice cry out in distress. A man yelled something, but she couldn't tell what. The woman let out a brief scream that was muffled by something. Her voice sounded familiar. Very familiar. Was that...Anne?

Then Sasha rounded a corner and saw them. It was Anne, alright. The girl had a bag over her head but Sasha clearly recognized her friend. Two men in black uniforms held her by either arm and forced her to walk forward with them. Two other men walked beside them. They all wore red berets. The man who seemed to be their leader locked eyes with her.

It was Alexander.

"Sasha," he said in a clipped tone. "You're out quite late."

She stopped. Stared. Anne continued to thrash between the men. Her cries were muffled by the bag but far from inaudible. She seemed terrified.

"Y-you, you all n-need to let her go," Sasha insisted. "She belongs at the House of Miriam."

Alexander laughed. "Where do you think we got her from, silly girl?"

Two of the other men laughed at that. They seemed nervous, though. She could see both hunger and a strange sort of anxiety in their eyes. Alexander was all hunger.

"Alexander, please–"

"Please what?" he asked with a wry smirk, "Deny this girl the bliss of serving God? Why would you want that for her? Do you even believe anymore, Sasha?"

His lips, the lips she'd dreamed about for months, the lips she'd watched say such lovely things to her, curled up in disgust.

"Look at you. You're wearing surgical scrubs. You look like a man. You've lost your proper place in the world. It disgusts me that they let you do that work. Have you forgotten what God Himself calls on you to be? Titus 2:5, Sasha. Our Lord wants you to be 'discreet, chaste, homemakers, good, obedient to their own husbands, that the word of God may not be blasphemed.' Remember that, Sasha?"

"None of you are her husband."

Alexander laughed. "That's not true at all!" He put a hand on the shoulder of one of the men restraining Anne. "Tomas here married her today. We're just helping the happy couple to their marital bed."

"Then why is there a bag on her head? Why is she fighting?"

"Because it was a rather abrupt marriage," Alexander frowned. "And her mind is still polluted with ungodly ideas about how a marriage should look. Tomas chose her. The Spirit of the Lord spoke to him when he saw her from afar. It is right and good that they should be wed. And he moves up to the front tomorrow. Tonight will be his first and maybe last chance to help the Kingdom remain and expand."

He held out a seal, a golden badge in the shape of shield with a heavy cross emblazoned across the front.

"This comes from the pastor. I have the authority to grant marriages to any worthy men who wish them."

He smiled again. Sasha's heart fluttered. She felt nausea rise up inside her.

"So back away. Let us pass. And I'd suggest you dedicate some more time to thinking about why God brought you here. When your time comes, I think you'd prefer doing this without the bag. But I'm fine either way, really."

It was past dinner and past bedtime when she entered the House of Miriam. Helen was seated at her desk. She looked up as Sasha entered and, in an instant, Sasha knew there was no use in reporting what had happened to Anne. Helen's eyes were bloodshot and puffy with tears. She knew.

"Sasha," the older woman said, "I have some bad news–"

"I saw them," Sasha said. "Is that what's going to happen to all of us? Is this place just a holding area until we get married off?"

"This place is your home," Helen said in a voice that was almost pleading. "It's here, and I'm here, to shepherd you to the next phase in your life. Don't you believe I want the best for you?"

"I do," Sasha said. Her voice softened. "But Anne didn't want this. She told me so. Didn't she deserve time to grieve?"

"She did," Helen said, "but the Lord demands sacrifices from all of us. Sometimes more sacrifices than seem fair. Anne is in a dark place now but the Lord will send his light to guide her."

Helen seemed to straighten up as she spoke. Sasha saw resolve settle into the older woman's flint-gray eyes.

"So may it be," she said. "May the peace of the Lord be with you."

Sasha started to walk off. She didn't trust herself to stay and talk. She was sure more of her anger would bleed out into the conversation. And she wasn't sure what Helen would do if she got the impression that Sasha's loyalty had started to waver.

"Sasha, dear," she said, and Sasha looked back. "You forgot your dinner. It's in a bag on the table."

Sasha took it and ate in silence, as fast as decorum would allow. Then she cleaned up for bed and headed back into the dormitories. As soon as she saw the light glinting off of Susannah's open eyes, she knew the other girl was awake. Sasha knelt down at her bed and the two shared a long look. Susannah held out her hand and Sasha took it.

"What happened?" she asked.

"They let us out early and dropped us off downtown," Susannah's eyes were wet with tears. "Anne and I had a coffee and we visited the market. It was...nice, normal almost. We headed for the House of Miriam once it started to get dark and," she gulped, "they were just there. Waiting with Miss Helen."

Susannah swallowed loudly and her eyes grew watery, but she didn't cry. Sasha was proud of her friend.

"That was them, wasn't it?" Susannah asked. "Those men were the Sons of Jacob."

Sasha just nodded.

"How long until they take me too?"

Chapter 16

Manny.

The barracks had been a high school once, built to serve several thousand of the Plano area's wealthiest students. The dozen huge, gray buildings were centered around an enormous courtyard that included a practice football field, several tennis courts, and a running track. The compound was boxed in by a high concrete wall, topped in razor wire. What had been built to defend the scions of wealth and privilege from their jealous peers also made the former school an ideal training ground for the Kingdom's soldiers.

Manny could see hundreds of young men just within the courtyard. They ran laps or charged through a makeshift obstacle course that had been assembled over the old football field. Manny's head throbbed just watching them. *I hope we don't have to do too much of that shit*, he thought as he scratched the bandage over his severed deck, *at least not today.*

Dozens of men sat in small groups around the courtyard, reading together from books or cooling down from work-outs in sweat-drenched underclothes. Manny could hear the sharp crack of rifle fire from a shooting range nearby. The whole place buzzed with a sort of busy, nervous energy that might've been contagious if not for the ugly stares Manny attracted.

"You picked the wrong skin to wear," Roland muttered at him as a troop of pale young infantrymen clomped past them. Manny couldn't help but notice that he seemed to be the only person on the training field who wasn't lily white.

"This might be a problem," he said.

Roland nodded in response. He spat at the ground and muttered, "We should'a asked Skullfucker Mike to sew you into some new skin before we left."

Manny frowned. "I'm almost certain that's not how–"

"Martyrs!" A rough voice cried out from behind them. "Turn 'round, boys. Let me see your eyes."

Manny stopped on instinct. He stiffened his back and turned around. Roland did the same thing, but with a heavy sigh and a roll of his eyes. The shout had come from a tall, square-jawed man with hair that had gone a majestic shade of silver-gray. He wore a black uniform shirt with brass cross pins in the epaulettes, black cargo pants, and a big black handgun slung low on his left hip. His nametag identified him as "Ditmar." Manny didn't know enough about the Martyr's Brigades to tell the man's rank.

Roland turned as Ditmar closed the distance between them. He stopped about a foot in front of them, looked Roland up and down, and then turned to Manny. The fixer forced himself to meet the grizzled Martyr's gaze.

Manny wasn't sure how to look like a fanatical Christian soldier. There was no way to fake the manic glint of true commitment. So he chose a different tack. He thought about Major Clark, the defiant set of his jaw and the promise of violence frozen into the ice of his blue eyes. DeShawn Clark was not a fanatic, but he was a warrior. Manny knew he might be able to fake that. So he screwed up his face into his best imitation and hoped it would pass muster.

"Well," the silver-haired old soldier growled and narrowed his eyes. But then his face broke out into a grin. His tone lifted up an octave. "By God," he said, "it's good to have you boys here." He clapped a hand on both Manny and Roland's shoulders and pulled them into an embrace.

"Your souls are safe now, my boys. Thank God for your warrior hearts. Now," he pulled back and straightened up, "I'm Martyr Ditmar. Where are you bound for?"

"Intake," Manny said with more confidence than he felt. "We just arrived today." He glanced down at his papers for a moment and then said, "This says we're infantry. Reserve division."

Martyr Ditmar seemed surprised. "Really?" he asked. "I'd have expected them to put you, at least," he nodded to Manny, "in the Storming Battalion."

"The Storming Battalion?"

"Yes," the elder Martyr nodded. "You've got the right...complexion for it."

Thaaaaat's got to be a bad sign, Manny thought. *Don't press the question too much now. You may not want the answer.* Instead he put a hand on Roland's shoulder.

"Wherever we go, I gotta stay with Aaron. He's strong, but he took a few hits to the head too many. I help him get around."

The Martyr gave a smile that seemed genuine.

"Well, then," he said, "you'll want to get your butts down to cadet processing. It's a hundred meters down that-a-way." He clapped them both on the shoulders. "It's good to see you here. Smile, boys! You're heroes now. Warriors in Christ. Go forth!"

"God bless you, Martyr," Manny said. Roland followed up with his best attempt at honest enthusiasm.

"Yay God!" he said with a too-wide smile.

"We should go," Manny said quickly. "I don't want to tarry on the Lord's time."

"That's the spirit," Martyr Ditmar replied. "I'll see you both on the training field."

They stomped off toward the cadet processing building which, until recently, had been the high school's administrative building. There were posters for school dances and after-school clubs on the walls. It looked like a student body election had been underway when the Heavenly Kingdom captured this place. Manny and Roland queued up behind a half-dozen other confused-looking young men and waited for their turn at the processing desk.

The intake process lasted around an hour. They took his name, his date of birth, and his measurements, and then Manny "helped" Aaron answer those same questions.

It would've been triflingly easy for anyone with a deck and a good connection to find evidence of Manny's career as a warzone fixer. But the Martyr handling their information wrote things down on actual paper. Manny got the distinct impression that many of the Martyrs had disabled their decks. He also knew from experience that data speeds tended to be pretty shit this close to the fighting.

Someone will check eventually, he warned himself. *You'd better be fast about this whole business.*

Roland stayed on his best behavior through the whole process, although he grew twitchier and twitchier as the minutes wore on. Manny wasn't sure if the chromed man was allergic to bureaucracy or just frustrated at having sobered up. Once they were done with the first stage of the intake process, they were ushered over to a room filled with folded stacks of clothing and dense with the scent of mothballs. They were issued uniforms and then bundled off to a locker room to change.

Manny was somewhat nervous about stripping down and changing in front of Roland, a dude he barely knew. If the post-human felt the same nervousness, he didn't show it. Roland pulled off his clothes in a couple of seconds, revealing a body that was tight with wiry muscle and covered in thick surgical scars. Roland started to pull on his BDU pants and noticed Manny hadn't yet started to strip.

"What's up?" Roland asked. "You smell nervous."

Manny shrugged. "I guess I'm a little prude still. Must be the Catholic in me."

"Don't let them hear that," Roland laughed, "these fuckers'll hang you with your rosary beads."

He pulled the pants up and buttoned them. Then he paused again and looked back to Manny.

"Are you still Catholic?" he asked.

Manny shook his head. "No, I don't believe. But my family does."

"Ah," Roland nodded. "You fake belief well. That's a talent."

"It's not a talent," Manny said, "it's a survival skill. Grow up in Texas, and you either learn to fake what you need to fake, or you learn to fight."

Someone knocked on the door.

"Are you ready yet?" a voice called out to them.

"Almost!" Manny responded, and he started to strip his clothing off.

A few minutes and a change of clothes later they arrived on the field where their training unit, twenty-four sweat-drenched young men, were doing push-ups. Manny was surprised to see that these Martyrs, at least, weren't all white: there was one Black man right in the middle of the group. It took Manny a second to recognize the instructor drilling them was Ditmar, the man they'd met on their way into the base. He broke into a broad smile when he saw them.

"God's will is truly magnificent, is it not?" And then he nodded down to the ground. "Fall in and join us, lads. Let's see what you've got."

Manny and Roland dropped down and joined the unit in another set of push-ups. If Roland had any trouble at all with the work-out regimen he didn't show it. The chromed man barely sweated. And Manny had a feeling that his sweat was more for show than the result of an actual biological process. Even with the show it was obvious to everyone that Roland wasn't having any trouble with the exercises.

"God's blessed us with a new Samson," Ditmar said, a hundred or so push-ups in. The rest of the men, Manny included, had collapsed from the exertion. But Roland just kept going. For a while they all sat there, huffing and exhausted and watching him go. Ditmar smiled and shook his head, a little awed at the sight. Finally he waved for Roland to stop.

"You've made your point, son. And we're all blessed to have you here with us. Now, get up—all of you, and sit around me."

Manny stood, shook the soreness from his arms and moved to take a seat in the semi-circle of young Martyrs. Once they were all properly positioned, Ditmar squatted down and cast his eyes around the group, settling on each of them in turn.

"I don't know how you all got here," he said in a quiet, somber voice, "but I know what brought each of you here: the spirit of our Lord and Savior, Jesus Christ." He cleared his throat. "Now," he said, "very soon, you'll all be going into battle. Sooner than I'd prefer. We don't have time for the kind of training you boys deserve. You'll be fighting against men with more experience, better weaponry. It's a scary thought. But I'll tell you all right now, if you go into that battle with the same blind faith that brought you here, you'll do just fine. God won't let any other end come to pass."

It was dark by the time Ditmar led them all into the dining facility. The sight of the high school cafeteria set off a surprising pang of nostalgia in Manny's heart. He hadn't enjoyed school. But something about the gray fabric-covered walls, the colorful posters, and the dozens of identical faux-wood tables made him long for a simpler time. For a second he was almost able to forget where he was, what he was doing, and pretend this was just another day in school.

That illusion was broken when he looked at his "fellow" Martyrs. Hundreds of them had filed into the cafeteria, dressed in a motley assortment of battle-dress uniforms from the old U.S. Army, the Republic of Texas, and even the Mexican Army. Most of them were young, not even into their twenties. Around a quarter of them, though, were old for soldiers, in their forties or fifties. There was no military discipline to their appearance. Many of the men had beards or long, unruly hair.

"These fucks aren't soldiers," Roland whispered to him as they took their seats at one of the fake wood tables on the left side of the room. "This is what cannon-fodder looks like, kid. The Heavenly Kingdom just expects these people to die."

Manny felt a surge of anxiety. He was sure someone else must have heard Roland. But when he glanced around, he saw their table-mates were all deep in conversation with each other. Most of them, at least. Jonathan, the only other non-white person in their training unit, seemed to have been excluded. The other soldiers leaned away from him. The focus of the table seemed to be a tall, square-jawed young man with a Georgian twang to his accent.

"Martyrs!" A loud voice cried from a podium at the center of the cafeteria. The sound of hundreds of bodies on hundreds of chairs turning to face the noise filled the room. The speaker was a tall, painfully thin man clad in a long black robe. An enormous wooden cross hung from his neck. His hair was greasy, unruly, and shock white. He had a patchy beard and the overall look of an unkempt madman. But then he spoke.

"My brothers, it is a blessed thing to have you all here today," he began in a voice that was little more than a whisper. There was a raw rasp to his voice, he sounded almost hoarse. Something about that quality drew Manny's attention.

"In the coming days, your instructors will prepare you for the great battles that lie ahead. You will be given the best arms and armor our Kingdom can provide. But just by being here, each of you has shown you already have a weapon more powerful than any tool in our armory: faith in God Almighty."

His voice raised in pitch now. It was still raspy and hoarse, but it picked up a sharp, booming quality. He spoke faster. His cheeks grew red.

"Put on the armor of God," he cried, "and you will stand firm against the schemes of the devil. Be strong and courageous! Do not panic before the enemy. For in every battle, the Lord your God will go ahead of you. He will never fail you nor abandon you."

At this, several men around the room pounded their fists on the tables. One man in the back let out a "whoop." These outbursts inspired other men to cry out "Praise God!" Manny glanced around, trying to gauge if more or less than half of the room was joining in. He didn't want to stay quiet if that was going to look weird. But then the pastor went quiet. A sense of anticipation filled the room.

There were about four-hundred cadets all dining together in this shift. And, of course, the officer in charge, a tall, gangly red-head with no chin but a strangely beautiful baritone voice, led them in prayer before the meal. Manny repeated the words after him, but he didn't hear them. He *did* have to elbow Roland once, when he saw the big post-human wasn't chanting along with the other soldiers.

Just then, a pair of big doors to the left of the stage slung open. Ditmar walked out, with a hefty brown canvas bag over his shoulder. He was followed by an armed guard, and then two men in shackles.

The captives wore striped white prison pajamas, and they both looked the worse for wear. One of them, a middle-aged Black man, looked familiar. Manny thought he must be a captured SDF fighter. His lip looked as if it had been recently split, and there was a nasty gash on his forehead. He kept his head down and his shoulders slumped. His posture was one of complete resignation. The other man was—Manny's heart skipped a beat—

Oscar.

He'd been beaten too, although not as badly as the soldier. He looked not so much frightened as bewildered, starving, and probably reeling from one or more head injuries.

"Dude," Roland nudged Manny's rib cage and whispered to him, "the fuck?"

Manny realized his mask had slipped. He'd let himself stare in horror rather than the excitement evident in everyone else's face. No one else seemed to have noticed yet, they were all focused on the prisoners. But Manny forced a grim smile onto his face and tried to look, at least, like he was deeply satisfied.

An armed Martyr prodded Oscar and the SDF man in their backs with his rifle and ushered them up onto the stage. Dead silence reigned over the cafeteria. No one spoke. It took Manny a few seconds to realize that he was actually holding his breath. Once the captives were up on stage the armed Martyrs pushed them down onto their knees. Ditmar set his bag down, unzipped it, and pulled out a wooden rod, about two feet in length and as thick around as Manny's forearm.

"Warriors of God," the pastor intoned in a low whisper. Manny felt himself lean into the man's words, even as dread pickled the pit of his stomach. "These men appointed themselves enemies of our Heavenly Kingdom; foes of God." He raised a hand up to Ditmar. His hand shook, but not out of fear. He positively vibrated with excitement.

"Who among you will take up the rod and punish these men?"

The chair-scraping-floor sound of someone standing up very quickly rose up behind him. Manny glanced back and saw that one of the men from his cadet group had been the first to stand. He was tall, with broad, thick shoulders and chest muscles that spoke of a youth spent laboring in the field. He had thin, dirty blond hair, a thick jaw, and blue eyes that shone with excitement.

"What's your name, Martyr?" the pastor asked.

"Eric Friedman, sir!" the young man cried back.

"Martyr Friedman," Ditmar called out as he held the rod up, "come forward and do the Lord's work."

The young man walked forward, stepped up onto the stage, and took the rod from Ditmar's hand. He glanced down at the captives. His eyes passed over Oscar and lingered on the battered Black soldier.

"Strike a blow for the Lord," the pastor whispered. And Martyr Friedman obliged. His first swing was weak, unsure, and poorly aimed. It struck the soldier on his shoulder. He didn't cry out. Martyr Friedman's second strike was harder, surer. He hit the soldier right in the gash on his forehead and the man dropped with a muffled cry. Eric hit him again. And again. And again. Ditmar grabbed another rod from the bag and held it out.

"Step up, men of God," the pastor's voice rose again, to a pitch so high it was almost a shriek, "step up and be the hands of justice!"

Just for a moment, Oscar saw him. Surprise, then confusion, and then anger passed over the stringer's face in the space of about a second. Manny didn't want to think about what Oscar saw in his face.

And then men rushed the stage, and Oscar disappeared in the swarm of Martyrs-to-be rushing in to share in the beatings. Roland took the opportunity provided by the chaos to lean back and whisper a question to Manny.

"What's going on, guy?"

"I know that guy, the one on the left," Manny whispered back. "He's one of my stringers—he works for me. I...he's my friend."

Roland nodded, and then stood up and rushed up to the stage. By the time he reached it, a dozen other Martyrs had joined Eric in beating the two captives. There was blood on the floor, blood on the sticks, and blood spattering the Martyr's new uniforms. Oscar cried out from each blow. It sounded like his mouth was full of blood.

And then Roland took a rod from Ditmar's hand and, in the space of a second, brought it down on both men's skulls with dull, meaty thuds. The soldiers went still. The screaming stopped, and every eye in the room turned to Roland. The chromed man looked out at the crowd. There was an agonizing moment of silence. And then Manny knew what he had to do.

"Praise God!" he screamed out. The room joined in, and soon a chorus of cheers filled the cafeteria.

After that, Roland was everyone's favorite Martyr. Once the men's bodies were dragged off the stage and dinner began, the Martyrs could barely contain their admiration for his strength.

"That was incredible," Eric said. "I can't wait to go into battle with you!"

"What did you do before?" a young man with a thick Oklahoma twang asked. "From the way you cracked those skulls I'd have guessed you've been doing that for years."

Roland gave short, noncommittal responses. His taciturn attitude didn't stop the other Martyrs from talking ABOUT him with supreme glee. Their words sickened Manny, but their focus on Roland gave him a chance to breathe and mourn and avoid looking over at the stage while Ditmar's men dragged Oscar's body away. By the time the excitement had subsided and dinner had ended, Manny felt like he could just barely make it to his bunk without breaking down. He lagged behind Roland and the others as they all filed into the barracks.

Manny was grateful for Roland's ability to draw attention until, during the walk, that young Black Martyr sidled up to Manny and introduced himself.

"I'm Jonathan," he said, "and I'm honored to meet you."

"Why?" Manny asked.

"I think you and I were the only ones who weren't cheering during... that."

"Ah," Manny said with a nod. He took a careful look at Jonathan's face. The other man's chubby cheeks and soft smile seemed almost calculated to make him look guileless. *Whatever he says, he's one of them. Be careful.*

"I understand why it was necessary," Manny said, "but I don't have to like it."

"Neither do I," Jonathan said. "We have to fight them. We're fighting for God here, after all. But we don't have to become monsters."

Manny nodded. He didn't say anything. Jonathan took that as an invitation to say more.

"I think we're going to have a harder time here than the others," he said, and gestured to the very caucasian crowd ahead of them. "We've got a lot to overcome here. But I think that just means God will shower more glory on us for the effort."

Manny was proud that, in his sorrowful and half-panicked state, he managed to avoid shouting "WHAT THE FUCK?" at Jonathan. Instead he matched the Martyr's smile and just said, "Praise God."

Their next morning started with an hour of calisthenics. The work-out was strenuous, but Manny actually enjoyed it. The speed with which they were dragged outside and forced into motion kept him from picturing Oscar's face for a while. After the work-out, they dove into the real meat of the day: a trip to the gun range.

It had been set up on what had once been a marching band's practice field. Dozens of vaguely human-shaped targets had been cut out of sheet metal and set up at varying intervals behind a crude sandbag line. Their group of about two-dozen new recruits were each issued weapons of varying quality. Manny received a janky old Kalashnikov that rattled like a maraca. Roland was given an almost-new G36 assault rifle.

The range instructor was a one-legged old Martyr with a prodigious belly and an equally overgrown white beard. He walked them through the basics of how to operate a variety of different assault rifles ("You can't know what weapon you'll end up needing to use.") and then set them up on the sandbag line and told them to start firing. Manny took aim at a target around a hundred feet in front of him. It was hard to tell if he hit it or not; several other men had aimed at the same target. Again, Manny got the feeling that the purpose of this training was not to make them marksmen. Basic familiarity was all the Heavenly Kingdom had time to provide.

Roland, of course, proved a fabulous shot. He stitched a smiley-face in bullet holes across four of the metal targets and earned genuine praise from the instructor.

"By God, son. You've got a gift."

This only increased Roland's social cachet with the Martyrs. They crowded around him during the walk to the next activity of the day: lunch, and a lecture on assault tactics. This was held in a little concrete amphitheater, something that had presumably once served the school's drama department. Manny tried to sit down next to Roland, but Eric and a gaggle of his friends settled around the post-human first. They babbled excitedly to him. Manny wasn't sure what they were saying, but every time he glanced back Roland looked absolutely miserable.

Manny wound up in the back, seated next to Jonathan. The young Martyr patted his leg. "Don't worry, brother," he said. "It's gonna be rough for us to earn their respect, but once we're all out in the field together they'll stop caring about your skin."

"You sure about that?" Manny asked, happy he was never going to wind up in "the field" with any of these people.

"Course I am," Jonathan said. "I grew up in Atlanta, y'know. I knew it was gonna be rough coming out here. But that's the sacrifice we make for God. I know He's gonna bring this nation back together. Tell you the truth, I'm honored to be a part of that."

Jonathan's eyes shone when he spoke. *He's a true believer,* Manny realized, *there's not a doubt in his mind that he's doing the right thing.* That was scary. And things got scarier still when their next instructor stepped into the amphitheater. This man was old and grizzled too. He had both of his legs, but his right arm was missing below the elbow, and a jagged scar ran up the left side of his face. The skin on most of his forehead was bald and mottled, as if he'd been badly burned.

"Afternoon, boys, and God bless you. I'm Martyr Carruthers. Today you're going to learn how to assault a fortified position."

Most of the strategies he walked them through began and ended with the application of shoulder-fired rockets and incendiary grenades. Manny couldn't help but notice that no time was spent talking about how to avoid civilian casualties. He wasn't even sure Specialist Carruthers knew how to pronounce the word "civilian."

"Remember what it says in the book of Samuel, boys," the older man drawled: "'Now go and strike, and devote to destruction all that you have. Do not spare them, but kill both man and woman, child and infant, ox and sheep, camel and donkey.'" He laughed, which made a few of the young Martyrs comfortable enough to laugh too.

"I don't expect you'll run into any camels or donkeys out in Austin. But there'll be men, women, children, and infants. If they stand in your way, they all equally deserve to be purged."

Manny didn't like the eagerness he saw on the faces of his fellow "students." The pit in his stomach grew throughout the day, while Martyr Carruthers explained how to use the various heavy munitions they might be called upon to deploy. There weren't enough rockets or mortars for them to actually train on any of those things. Manny wasn't sure how good a gist anyone really got. He wondered how much that would matter when these men took to the field.

He ate ravenously at dinner. Thankfully, there were no executions that day. But Martyr Ditmar did take the stage again and announced that the buses were ready to take any interested recruits down to the main drag for a couple of hours of what passed for R&R. One of the older Martyrs handed everyone ration cards and explained they were good for either a cup of coffee or tea, or a small amount of food from one of the few stores that had opened back up.

"Fuckin' tea," Roland grumbled into Manny's ear as they headed out for the buses. "That's what these jumped-up puritans consider a recreational beverage. This garbage country..."

Manny had noticed the post-human growing increasingly jittery and irritable throughout the day. He'd seen Roland cautiously cough up another small bag of pills right before lunch. That had sated him for a while, but considering his post-human metabolism, Manny thought he had to be pretty close to sober.

"I am so fucking lucid I can't stand it," Roland muttered.

"What is it with you people and being high all the time?" Manny whispered back. "Can't you stand being sober for a few days?"

"Not if I can help it," Roland said. He pointed to his head. "There's just too much going on in here, too much input. It's like my whole body itches, but I can't scratch."

"Ah," Manny said, since he wasn't sure what else to say.

The bus hit downtown Plano after twenty minutes or so. It wasn't an impressive sight. There were maybe a dozen little shops and one cafe open, plus a pretty sad looking farmers' market. He could see no signs of any bars, any clubs, anything that even vaguely resembled night life. The main drag was crowded with people, throngs of soldiers and young women in long dresses, and new immigrants to the Heavenly Kingdom.

"Where should we go first?" Manny asked, as soon as they'd filed off the bus.

"Well," Roland grunted, "unless you're in the mood for shitty coffee or some root vegetables, I say we check out that gallows."

Manny had avoided looking too long at the gallows. It was empty now. But just staring at it made him feel sick. There was something sinister and unsettling about the ground beneath it. It was as if he could feel the death radiating outwards.

"What could we possibly learn there?" Manny asked.

The big man shrugged, "Not much. But if they wind up hanging anyone tonight I might be able to sniff out where they're keeping their prisoners. That'd be useful data."

"Well, I'm gonna be useless for that," Manny said. "What should I do?"

"I dunno man. Grab some coffee?"

"What?"

Roland locked eyes with him. He didn't do that often. His gaze was normally as shifty and jittery as the rest of him.

"Look, kid, you've done a great job. Above and beyond the call of, I dunno, duty or whatever. You're good company too. But I've got a half-dozen satellite's worth of sensory equipment in my brain and hundreds of wee-bitty microscopic robots floating around the air feeding me news. There's really not much for you to do here. Chill out. Find whatever passes for relaxation here and do it. I'll get you when it's time to go."

Manny started to protest. But then he thought, *What the hell? He's right. I'm useless. I've earned a cup of flavorless gringo coffee.* So he thanked Roland and headed off in the direction of one of the strip's functioning coffee houses, the Cafe Clement. It looked like it was less crowded than the others. As he reached for the door, someone slammed into him.

She was a young blonde. Younger than Manny, at any rate. She wore baggy surgical scrubs. Her jaw was tight and clenched. Her brown eyes were wide with fear and there were deep bags under them.

"Oh– oh my," she said. "I'm so sorry, sir. Please let me–"

"It's OK," Manny said. "No damage done. Are you alright? You look terrified."

"I'm just... Just. Trying to avoid someone. It's nothing serious."

Manny wasn't sure why, but he pulled the ration cards he'd been given out of his pocket and offered one to the stranger.

"Here. If you want, we can grab a table together and I'll sit with my back to the door. You're not big. I can block you."

She looked surprised, and a little hesitant. But after a few blinks she nodded and said, "I'd actually appreciate that a lot. Thank God for you, sir."

"Uh, yeah," Manny agreed. "Praise him."

They sat and ordered coffee. The young woman kept craning her neck around Manny to peek at the door behind them.

"Look, I'm not gonna ask what's up with you. But can I get your name, at least? That might make this less awkward. I'm Mann– uh, Emmanuel. Manny for short."

"Sasha," she said. "I, uh, I just got here a few days ago. You?"

"This is my second day."

She looked surprised.

"I wouldn't have guessed, what with the uniform."

He laughed. "It turns out they just hand these to anyone who'll hold a gun. I didn't even really have a choice."

"Well, if that's where you wound up I'm sure it's where the Lord wants you. Praise God for that."

She didn't seem like she was joking. But there was something about her tone and the way her jaw never unclenched that made Manny suspect she was a little less than convinced about her own words. For the next few minutes they talked in between sips of mediocre coffee. He learned she was from the American Federation, and enough of a true believer that she'd smuggled herself into the Heavenly Kingdom. She didn't seem like a zealot, though. More than anything she seemed scared.

"How do you like it here?" he finally asked. "Is it what you'd expected?"

She didn't respond for quite a while. Instead, she stared into his eyes. Manny stared back. It was a strange feeling. She must have been trying to search out whether he was trustworthy or trying to trick her into revealing her disloyalty. He maintained eye contact and tried not to seem like a member of whatever the Heavenly Kingdom called their secret police. Apparently it worked.

"Of course I'm happy here in God's Kingdom," she smiled an empty smile. "I've been blessed to meet so many dedicated people. But, um...I've also met some people who, um...I, um, well..." She coughed. "Not everyone here seems to have the Lord in their heart."

Manny almost laughed at the irony in her admitting that to him. But he kept his mouth shut and just nodded. Sasha took a long sip of her coffee. He felt a little bad for staring. She was very pretty. But she was also pretty young. And of course she'd volunteered to join a theocratic murder-state. That was probably another reason he shouldn't get too attached.

"So, anyway," Sasha explained, "I've run into some men I don't like very much. And they keep finding me when I get off from my shift at the hospital. I'm sure they're waiting outside the House of...where I'm staying, right now. I don't want to deal with that yet."

"Well," Manny smiled his most charming smile, "I'm happy to help you wait them out. I've got another hour at least before the buses take us back to the barracks."

And so, for a while, they just talked. She told him about her work in the hospital and he tried to say as little as possible about his two shitty days as a Martyr. Sasha didn't seem to mind that he didn't have much to say about himself. Manny got the feeling she was just happy to have someone to talk with. Most of her words passed over him until she mentioned something about a prisoner.

"She's from one of road people, from some moving city with an obscene name. And she's pregnant. So I'll be seeing her again tomorrow, probably, to do a more thorough examination. I feel weird about it. She was so strange, so different from anyone I've met. But I really don't like–"

"Wait, a prisoner? Is this at the hospital?"

Sasha seemed confused by that question, and Manny worried he might have overplayed his hand.

"Why do you–"

The rest of her question was cut off by the sound of a bullhorn outside. Manny couldn't make out most of what was being said, until he heard, "prisoners" and "SDF" in an electronically distorted southern drawl.

"Oh no..." Sasha moaned.

"What? What are they talking about?"

"It's another execution."

Manny stood up and stepped toward the door. He had to see who it was. Even before he got there, a terrible feeling had started to boil up in the pit of his gut. He pushed the door open, jogged toward the gallows and pushed his way through the crowd. He could see Roland, standing twenty feet off to the left from the wooden platform. But Manny's eyes were focused on the four men and two women in shackles at the foot of the gallows. Five of them were strangers.

The sixth was Mr. Peron.

Chapter 17

Roland.

Roland smelled the execution before it started.

There'd been a lot of strong smells in downtown Plano when he arrived. Gunpowder and sour fear-sweat, the acrid stink of anxiety and the warm, wet odors of grief and confusion. He'd smelled the stale reek of military rations, the sharp pang of anemia and the boiling hot testosterone that wafted from the Martyrs like a jet stream.

But, a half hour into his time downtown, something else had drifted over the packed masses of refugees and pilgrims and militiamen. It was hard to define: a bit of tension, and a bit of anticipation. The odor was faint enough to suggest something unconscious, a collective emotion. The aggregate scent of a crowd of people who weren't consciously aware of how they felt. There was no neurotransmitter, no pheromone he could identify in particular. This scent was more elusive. He was only able to lock it down through the memory fragments it triggered.

Coal gray sky. A biting chill in the air. Hundreds of men and women bundled up, clustered around barrel fires. Everyone talking. Excitement in their voices. Anxiety on the air, mingled with gun-oil and anticipation. Something was about to happen.

A few seconds later, the scent of anxious anticipation started to rise. Roland heard the deep bouncing thrum of heavy rubber wheels on pavement. His hindbrain tied the sound to a particular species of obsolete armored personnel carrier, originally manufactured in Bulgaria.

After following its route for several seconds his hindbrain guessed the APC was bound for the main square.

Roland spent the next few minutes jockeying for a good position close to the gallows. He wasn't certain that's where the convoy was headed. It seemed like a good guess though. And he was quickly proven right when the APC pulled up to a stop just a hundred feet away. The crowd stopped and gawked as the heavy doors slid open. Soldiers in full-body armor stepped out, dragging six men and women in honest-to-god manacles and chains out into the dying light.

The captives were all SDF. Roland didn't even have to make an educated guess on that one. The Heavenly Kingdom had made sure to dress them in their tattered and blood-stained uniforms. They were, all of them, emaciated and broken-looking. The evidence of torture was so clear that Roland's enhanced eyes weren't even necessary. The captives had broken, bleeding fingernails, black eyes, painful limps, and feet that looked like they could barely stand to touch the ground.

One of the Martyrs, a tall man wearing a red beret instead of a combat helmet, strode ahead of the group. He had a voice-amp in one hand. He raised the other up in the air in a prayerful gesture that was matched by most of the crowd.

"Brothers and sisters," the Martyr's voice boomed, "today the Lord and his loyal soldiers have delivered unto you a blessing."

The crowd tightened around Roland. He could see, hear, feel as people rushed out from cafes and shops to watch. The fear and excitement was so thick in the air Roland was sure even unmodified humans could have sensed it.

"Here we have six prisoners from the SDF," the Martyr began. "These men and women were all captured in the last week. Rather than accept their defeat, they chose to fight as insurgents against the Heavenly Kingdom. God and his Martyrs are merciful. But these sinners have spat on that mercy. Now it is our privilege to execute upon them the judgement written: this honor have all his saints. Praise ye the LORD!"

A ragged cheer went up from the crowd. Many of the assembled sounded less than enthusiastic, at least to Roland's ears. But there were still dozens and dozens of voices full of reckless hate. The prisoners marched forward with their escort, ever nearer to the gallows. Roland's ear tingled, and he sensed Manny's presence out in the street now. The kid smelled afraid, with a faint fading tinge of pheromonal arousal. *Huh.*

Roland backed away and escaped the main press of the crowd. In a few seconds, he was behind Manny and he put a hand on the fixer's back. The young man jumped and then shot Roland a furious look.

"What the hell–" Manny caught himself and instead pointed up to the line of doomed men and women. "Roland I know that–"

"Hey!" A girl ran up to them. She smelled scared too. But the scent was much deeper on her, sunken into her skin. She'd been scared for quite some time. She seemed to know Manny, and he definitely knew her.

"Sasha," Manny said, "I'm sorry. I just needed to..." he paused, shook his head, and then put a hand on Roland's shoulder. "This is my comrade, Martyr Aaron. We fled here together, once the SDF retreated from Farmer's Branch. Aaron, this is Sasha."

"It's good to meet you, Martyr Aaron," she said, and flashed him an anxious smile. "I'm so glad God's grace has brought us all together."

"Oh yeah," Roland said in his most convincing voice, "God's so good. I'm really, just–" he gestured toward the gallows, "I'm psyched to see this."

A look crossed over her face. Disgust, mixed with building anxiety. She was dressed to play the part of the Good Christian Woman; her hair done up in a tasteful bun, her face unadorned by makeup, her sleeves long, and her clothing baggy. But her scent didn't lie. It suggested she was pretty far from all-in on this whole "Heavenly Kingdom" thing.

"You're not excited to see God's justice?" Roland asked.

The young woman frowned and shook her head.

"I understand the necessity of such bru...of such extreme measures. But I don't have to like it. Manny, do you–"

She started to ask Manny something, but the young man broke off from their little group and darted forward toward the gallows.

"Oh!" Sasha said, in surprise.

"I'll...go check on him," Roland said. "It's probably best if you wait here, eh?"

She looked confused, but she nodded. Roland followed behind Manny and caught up to him about four people deep into the growing crowd around the scaffold. The fixer's eyes were locked on one of the SDF prisoners, a middle-aged man with a prominent black mustache and a look of courageous resignation in his brown eyes. He stood in the middle of the gallows, calm as a stone in the ocean, while one of the Martyr's fitted a noose around his neck.

"Manny," Roland said.

"That's Mr. Peron," Manny said.

"Someone you know, then?"

Manny swallowed and nodded his head. Tears threatened at the corners of his watery eyes. Roland felt like it would probably be a good idea to get the kid away from the gallows before he did something stupid. Roland's hindbrain helpfully informed him that there were only around sixty armed men in the whole square. But he also knew there were one-hundred-eighty-three armed men within a mile of their current position. If shit started now it wouldn't end for a while. Roland put a hand on Manny's shoulder.

"We have to do something," Manny said.

"What do you want me to do?" Roland asked. "Rush up there, beat that red-beret'd fucknugget with his own sidearm and then cock-punch the rest of them into submission?"

"You can beat them," Manny said.

"Yeah," Roland nodded, "but if I do, that's the end of the mission. And probably the end of those hostages. I can save your buddy, and you, and probably even that girl if she wants to come. But the Kingdom's going to assume some monster-man from Rolling Fuck just terrorism'd them. They'll bury those captives too deep for us to find. And then Austin's as fucked as a blind pussy in a dick forest."

A man in the crowd turned and stared at Roland. *Volume man, volume.* Roland guessed he'd heard just the tail-end of his last sentence. The word "pussy" had probably piqued his ears. Before the man could say anything, Roland pointed toward the gallows and let out a loud "WHOOP!" followed by a "PRAISE GOD! PRAISE GOD!" The inadvertent eavesdropper started cheering along with him and turned back to the impending execution.

Roland turned back to Manny. The boy was quiet, his face controlled, but fat tears ran down his cheeks and his shoulders shook with silent sobs. Roland directed him back, away from the worst of the crowd.

"Mr. Peron baked the cake for my twelfth birthday," Manny whispered. "He showed us Monty Python. He dropped us off at soccer practice."

Manny had started to babble. He smelled on the edge of an outright panic attack. Roland's hindbrain started to identify potential improvised weaponry options among the crowd. He settled on a small, thickset man. *He's got a real dense cranium. Good weight distribution. He'll make a great club.*

Roland shook himself out of it. Then he tried to shake Manny out of it by, literally, shaking him by the shoulders.

"Hey. Listen. Your friend up there is going to die. Or a lot of other people are going to die. Those are the two options. I know it sucks. I know it's shit. But we cannot fix this. If you stay calm though, we can fix something worse. Do you understand me?"

Manny's eyes came unglazed. The flow of tears slowed, then stopped. It was an impressive feat of willpower. Most people didn't have that kind of control over their emotions. Roland had to guess Manny's work as a fixer had, at least, prepared him to function in the middle of a waking nightmare.

"OK," the kid said, "but I have to watch."

Roland wanted to argue. But one look at Manny's eyes made it clear that arguing wouldn't do any good. So instead he stood there, next to Manny, and kept his hand on the boy's shoulder until the terrible thing was done. It was as ghastly as these things always were. Most of the crowd cheered every snapped neck, every jerk of a dying soldier's legs.

Shockwaves of memory wracked Roland's mind at the sight. *He felt warm spring air blow across his cold chest. He saw a small sea of familiar strangers, men and women he'd known once upon a bloodier day. He felt a big gun kick in his hands, he felt a warm splash of blood across his chest and face, he heard the heavy final thump of a tiny body hitting the ground. He saw Topaz. She looked ill. He saw Skullfucker Mike with a hand on her shoulder. He heard Jim's voice.*

"Make sure the cameras catch this next one," Jim cried. "We've got an honest-to-god Cheney with us today!"

Back in the present, Roland watched as Manny's friend's turn came around. Manny swallowed. His face went pale. Tears streamed down the boy's face and Roland felt a sudden, peculiar urge to bury him in a hug. He did not do that, though. Roland just stood still with a firm hand on Manny's shoulder while they tightened the noose around Major Peron's neck and dropped him down to hang until he was dead, dead, dead.

Roland was proud of how straight Manny stood, how the boy held back from sobbing and how, once the sad spectacle was over, Manny turned back around and headed toward the Christian girl, Sasha. She still stood where they'd left her. Roland could tell she'd been crying too, although she'd taken some pains to disguise it. She was hard to get a read on, that one. She struck him as one of the faithful, but she didn't strike him as a nut. Maybe she'd just gotten suckered into this awful place. Roland could certainly understand that. He was pretty sure he'd been suckered into dumber things.

"Praise God," she said, with hesitation.

"Praise God," Manny responded. Roland didn't say much. She gave him *a look*, but not an angry one.

"That was..." she locked eyes with Manny. Roland was pretty sure she'd blocked the rest of the world out. She must've seen the signs of his tears too. She coughed a little and continued, "That was awful. I know it's necessary, but I'll never stop hating that."

"It's a good thing to hate," Manny said. And then, "Look, we have to get back to base. Curfew's coming up soon. But if you're looking to hide from those, uh, undesirables tomorrow, I'll be waiting outside the cafe."

They kept talking, but what they said was beyond Roland's interest. He was busy listening as the prison convoy drove off. Now that he knew the sound of the prisoner transport APC, aurally tracing it back to its origin point was child's play.

"Aaron," Manny's voice jerked his attention back to the conversation happening in front of him.

"We should probably go," Manny said. "The buses will leave soon."

"Oh, shi– uh, sh...surely. Right. Surely right. We should go."

Roland smiled at Sasha, "It was lovely to meet you. Good evening."

He put a hand on Manny's shoulder and, together, they headed off to the buses. Manny only stopped twice to cry.

Manny didn't say much the rest of the night. Roland was proud of him for holding back his tears during the bus ride and the walk to the barracks. The kid broke down as soon as he got into bed, of course, but he kept his sobs silent and Roland was pretty sure none of the other recruits noticed. It helped that they were all exhausted at the end of the day.

Roland puked up, then popped, a handful of Ambien and Percocets and washed them down with a tall glass of the beer he'd brewed in his own guts. He offered Manny some but the boy declined. So Roland had a second glass. And then a third. It wasn't enough to get him wasted, but the cocktail of drugs did a tolerable job of leading him to unconsciousness. He drifted off to sleep an hour or so after the rest of the men in the barracks.

The next day was more army-style bullshit. Push-ups and wind-sprints and a big dumb obstacle course. Roland had to be real careful to act challenged as the day went on. He instructed his body to elevate his blood pressure and temperature, to flush his face red with blood and to send enough sweat from his pores to make a passable imitation of exertion. It was tedious and he hated it. But the first half of the day went by pretty fast.

Then it was time for a close-quarters firefight drill. The men were given actual rifles, sans ammunition, and divided up into assault teams. They spent the next five hours taking turns defending or attacking different rooms in an old apartment complex that had been commandeered by the Heavenly Kingdom. There was a lot of shouting from instructors who sure as shit wanted the recruits to think they knew more about urban warfare than they did.

At the end of one particularly long set of door-breaching drills, one of the instructors dropped to his knees and started chanting in tongues. He seemed to be celebrating that one of his "slowest" squads had finally nailed a textbook entry. Roland wasn't sure what to hell to make of it. The man almost smelled like he was having a schizophrenic break. The heady wash of neurotransmitters wafting off him made it clear this wasn't just some gesture for show. He seemed legitimately overcome with joy.

Other soldiers, and even a couple of the instructors, started kneeling down around him. They were all chanting in some strange language. The first instructor kept repeating what sounded like, "Om nashakallaska, om nashakallaska." Roland's hindbrain knew a lot of languages, but this sounded like nonsense to him. He noticed that the speech patterns of each chanting man were pretty consistent with American English. The actual words were gibberish, though, and–

Manny grabbed him by the shoulder and pushed, gently, down. Roland took the hint and then took a knee. The kid started to chant in a low voice.

"Hila taskilla jeosapha tinshalla..." It was more gibberish, but Roland followed suit. He started to spit out nonsense of his own in a tone low enough that it didn't rise above the din of chanting maniacs. Manny's strategy, he realized, was to make big exaggerated mouth-motions without actually speaking at a high volume. It made him look right without drawing any attention.

The whole weird scene went on for a little over two minutes. Eventually the instructor stopped chanting and lay on his back, sweaty and spent. The other soldiers seemed to have ended their fits in the same way. Roland could tell from their heart rates and body temperature that about half of the men had been faking it, just like he and Manny. The humid stink of guilt was heavy in the air. Roland's heart went out to them. It must be agony to believe so hard in something so dumb that you'd castigate yourself for not buying into it enough.

After that, they filed into the mess hall. They said their prayers, ate their dinners, and then queued up for the buses downtown. The ride was uneventful. And the instant their feet hit the square Manny went off to find Sasha. Roland shook his head in appreciation for the all-consuming power of human desire and then bounded off to check out the presumed location of the jail.

It was about a three-mile jog. At full speed, Roland could've cleared the distance in a few minutes. But a low profile was the name of the game. He stuck to a fast walk and kept to the shadows and alleys as best as he could. Plano hadn't been a very dense city before the Martyrs had taken over, so there were a lot of times where he was basically out in the open. He had to trust that his uniform and the general state of chaos in the newly-founded Kingdom would obscure him.

This was the first look he'd gotten of the Kingdom on foot. Roland decided he didn't care much for it. There was a great deal of foot and vehicle traffic but most of the people seemed to be either soldiers or refugees without anywhere else to go. He passed two checkpoints where twitchy-looking Martyrs performed datascans on decks and personal hard drives. He even saw one soldier sorting through paperback books in the trunk of some poor fuck's car.

Roland noticed several white vans with black crosses painted on the side. They cruised the streets, clearly on patrol for something. He watched one stop in front of a family of refugees, heavy with backpacks and carrying intake papers in their hands. Men in white jump suits with gold cross badges piled out and surrounded the family. Roland concealed himself behind a dumpster and watched as the patriarch of the family handed them his papers and spoke in a frantic, animated tone. One of the men pointed at his daughter, who wore a stained t-shirt and a ragged pair of denim shorts. They were baggy and hardly stylish. But the men in the jumpsuits seemed furious. They pointed and shouted. The man put his hands in the air and tried to say something, but one of the jump-suited men smashed his head with a cane.

Cold rage bubbled up inside Roland. *Fuck this place*, he simmered to himself, *fuck these janky-ass throwback fundamentalists and their fascist bullshit.* He wanted to charge out from behind the dumpster and tear into these low-rent, hisbah motherfuckers. He wanted to shove those thick wooden rods so far up their asses they'd be shitting splinters for weeks. *The mission*, he reminded himself, *the fucking mission.*

And so he watched as the men in white beat the old guy. He watched as they pulled the poor bastard's daughter into a van and forced a hideous gray woolen dress over her head. It didn't fit and it looked liable to give her heat stroke in the late Texas summer. She didn't fight them though.

Roland moved on, reluctantly, and found what his hindbrain suspected was the old jail. The APC's he'd seen last night were parked out front. The compound was crowded and busy. Roland counted fourteen guards just outside. Mind you, they were human guards. No powered armor, no heavy artillery, nothing at hand that could do much more than tickle him. They wouldn't present a danger. But they would cause a hell of a lot of noise if he attempted a daylight prison break.

He scrambled up onto a half-collapsed condo that had been abandoned after a heavy mortar shell gutted the inside. It provided a good view of the jail. For the next hour Roland just watched. His hindbrain mapped the pattern of the guard rotations and noted the security protocols they followed when each new vehicle arrived. He took a lot of deep breaths and, gradually, pulled enough scents from inside the jail to have a decent idea of how many people were in there. He'd never smelled Marigold or the other Rolling Fuck negotiators before. But his nose picked up on three people with a handful of aftermarket modifications. Most of the Martyrs he'd met had been limited to civilian-grade healing suites and sensory upgrades. It was a safe bet that these were their targets, then.

When you've got the message, put down the phone. Roland wasn't sure where, or when he'd heard that aphorism. But it came into his head and, a moment later, he realized the sun was pretty low in the sky. It'd be bus time soon. He headed back through the high shadows and across the cracked and bullet-scarred boulevards until he was able to merge back into the evening crowd at the square. Manny and the Christian girl had moved on from the cafe by that point. He actually ran into them in front of some building with a sign that identified it as the "House of Miriam." They were saying weird, chaste, religious-y goodbyes.

"Oh, hello, Aaron!" Sasha smiled when she saw him. Manny turned around and flashed him a weary smile too. Roland could still see pain in the kid's eyes, but it was at least cut with a bit of arousal. He decided that was a good thing. Ever since Oscar's death, Manny had been riding the line between function and complete emotional collapse. He decided to encourage the fixer's weird little friendship with the Christian girl.

"Hey!" Roland said. "How was the, ah, coffee? Smelled like it was mostly chicory and food dye when I walked by earlier. But maybe they sold y'all the good stuff."

"They did not," Manny said.

"You must be blessed with an exceptional nose," Sasha said, and gave him an odd look. Then she asked, "What did you get up to?"

"I checked out the farmers' market," Roland lied. "I'll tell you what some, uh, some good freakin' cucumbers up in there. That's where I was. Cucumbers."

Sasha's odd look deepened. Manny brought a hand up to the bridge of his nose and kneaded his brow in frustration.

"We should head back to the buses. I'll see you tomorrow Sasha, yes?"

"Yes, of course!" Sasha replied with a genuine smile.

If this was a sane world, the two of them might... Roland shook his head. This was the Heavenly Kingdom, they were surrounded by extremist militants and Sasha probably wasn't even allowed to look at condoms. *Also, she's one of those militants,* Roland reminded himself.

He let the kids say their goodbyes and then walked back to the bus with Manny. The kid seemed unsettled.

"I feel like I'm making a real dumb decision," he said.

"What?" Roland asked.

"Talking with that girl," Manny shrugged. "She's told me all she knows about those prisoners already. But we're supposed to meet at the one shitty cafe in this town tomorrow. I know it's stupid. But I kinda wanna make that meeting."

"Why's it stupid?" Roland asked. They had to drop their voices a little as they drew closer to the line for the buses.

"Because," Manny said, "we're not going to be here long. Sasha confirmed our people are in the jail. And you scouted it out today, right?"

"Yep."

"So we're confirmed twice over. It's time to do this thing and get out. I don't have time to eat shitty food with a pretty girl."

Roland turned and fixed his eyes on Manny's. He leaned in, until their noses were almost touching. And then he poked the boy's chest with his index finger, for emphasis, while he spoke.

"Emmanuel Sanchez, listen to me: there is always time to eat shitty food with a pretty girl. Fuck the war, fuck what's a 'good idea.' Go eat some garbage and stare into her eyes. Do something human in this inhuman place. Late night will be a better time for the rescue anyway."

Manny was silent for several long seconds. Then he said, "OK."

The next day started with more PT, as usual. Then it rolled right into an extra-long trip to the firing range and three more hours of close assault drills. Roland found himself disgusted by the Kingdom's tactics. Their go-to was to dump heavy artillery on any embedded resistance. No heed was paid to the civilian cost. They were fine having untrained kids lob mortars into crowded neighborhoods.

"The Lord will recognize his own," Martyr Carruthers said, over and over again.

That evening, before the dinner prayer, the raspy-voiced pastor came by to speak to all the recruits in the chow hall. Roland missed Martyr Ditmar's introduction of the pastor (he was too busy puking up and surreptitiously eating his last bag of drugs) but his ears perked up when the wild-haired old nutfuck launched into his speech.

"The burdens placed on the Warriors of God are great. You men have sworn yourselves to a ponderous duty. But that duty does not end on the battlefield. If the Heavenly Kingdom is to remain and expand, we will need you to fight in the field *and* with your other God-given attributes."

This elicited a dim chorus of chuckles from the audience. It took Roland an embarrassing amount of time to realize what the preacher was talking about. *Ah jeez, this speech is about fuckin'.*

"The Lord commands us to be fruitful and multiply," the pastor wheezed, "but he also calls us to respect the sacred bonds of Holy Matrimony. In times of war, the times we all live in now, this might seem to create some difficulty. But that's only because most of us are trained to think of marriage in the secular context. The average married couple in the American Federation 'dates' for eight years before being wed. In California, it's closer to ten. Of course, in both those places, 'dating' is more or less a form of cashless prostitution."

Roland had to strain to avoid rolling his eyes. Next to him, Manny listened dutifully. His face was almost unreadable.

"Perhaps people who don't trust their creator need years of time to decide if another person is a suitable partner. Happily, we have the Will of God to guide us. You young men are strong and virile and faithful. Your Lord wants you to find love. He wants you to bring more children into this world. This is why, as the hour of action draws closer, we still encourage each of you to spend time every day going out into the city and mingling with the other sheep of our great flock."

Aha! Suddenly Roland understood. It had seemed odd to him that the Heavenly Kingdom, a state still so unformed and tumultuous, would devote time and resources to busing their military recruits downtown. It made sense now. They wanted all these young men to find women and fill them up with babies before they went off to die. It was grim as hell. But it was also quite logical.

"The truth of it is," the pastor rasped, "marriage is a simple process. When you find the right person, the proper arrangements can be made in an hour or two. That is why I'm here, along with Pastors Sandor, Elsworth, and Biggins. You can find us at any hour of the day—or night—to bless your unions once God shows you to your wives. And there are more pastors at the House of Jacob near the square. I urge you to go out into the Kingdom in search of love and make use of us. Our chief job, and our chief joy, is to help our noble Martyrs find the love and bliss God promises every faithful man. Wives are his blessing to us. Children are our duty to him. Now," the man said with a rakish grin, "go forth, and multiply the flock."

The line for the buses was extra long that day. By the time Roland and Manny actually made it to the square, they were nearly an hour later than usual. Manny rushed right off to find Sasha. Roland made his way to an alley and then darted across town and toward the jail once again.

They'd already confirmed the location of their targets, so Roland's last job was to mark out a good exit route from the city. He didn't expect it'd be a quiet prison break. That would draw attention, and fighters. The good news was that nothing within the Heavenly Kingdom looked particularly well organized. A ton of fighters patrolled the streets, but most of Plano was still pretty war-torn. Their camera grid was far from comprehensive. If they had a sizable drone force it was kept nearer to the front than here.

The quickest route seemed to be to head straight north from the jail, up K Avenue and past an old housing development filled with crumbling mansions. That route would take them past two fortified bases. There'd be a couple hundred infantry to deal with, along with their attendant APCs and a handful of drones. Roland felt confident he could punched a hole through all that on his own, but he expected to have four or five civilians in tow. The odds of one of them taking a stray round were just too high.

Another possible route took him up and to the left, toward an old tollway that seemed to mark the end of the Heavenly Kingdom's static defenses. They controlled a lot of the territory beyond, but the patrols there looked random. There were no fortifications or checkpoints. It was a much longer route than the other but, potentially, one that required a lot less fighting. The last option was to veer right and take Park Avenue to Richardson. The Heavenly Kingdom had controlled that territory for even less time than they'd held Plano, and the fighting there had been heavier. They'd pass a lot of checkpoints, but not much in the way of troop concentration as long as they kept south and away from Dallas proper.

The scouting work itself was exhilarating. Roland had a lot of ground to cover so he spent most of his time sprinting and scaling buildings, leaping from roof to roof and in between shattered windows. His senses were in full use. There were always passing convoys of civilians or patrols of Martyrs or those odd white police vans somewhere nearby. He was close to caught a dozen times and he loved every minute of the work.

By the time he got back to the main square it was quite late, and almost time for the buses to leave. He did a quick loop of the square to see if he could find Manny and Sasha. He caught traces of their scents but neither of them seemed to be out and about. He eventually tracked Sasha's pheromone trail back to the House of Miriam, but Manny seemed to be gone. That was strange. Roland headed back to the buses in the hope of finding him there. But Manny wasn't in line, or on any of the buses.

So Roland headed back to the base and tried to ignore the unease as it blossomed in his belly. *Maybe he headed back early. Maybe the "date" went bad.* That made sense. Sasha seemed nice, for a religious extremist, but you couldn't predict zealots. It was so damn easy to set them off. Manny might've just said the wrong thing and decided it'd be safest to head back to the base and chill in the barracks.

The bus pulled into the school-cum-training-facility's little vehicle depot. Roland noticed at once that Martyr Ditmar and a small bodyguard of armed men were waiting. That was unusual. Roland's hindbrain warned him that this was probably related to Manny's disappearance. He felt a thin drip of adrenaline start tapping on the back of his amygdala. It was the feeling he associated with Shit About To Happen. Roland tried to enjoy it, without letting it push him into action before he knew what was really going on.

"Martyr Aaron," Ditmar said, as he approached Roland. The instructor's bodyguards stayed close behind. "Would you come with me? We've got some news for you."

"Where's Emmanuel?" Roland asked.

"We'll explain everything," the older Martyr said. "Just come with me."

Roland followed him into the maze of buildings and toward a small office occupied by a white-haired man in what looked like the Heavenly Kingdom's equivalent of a dress uniform. It was blue, bedecked with medals, and had a shining silver cross on each epaulet. The fancy man looked very tired. Roland could smell cheap caffeine wafting from his pores.

"This is Commandant Dawkins," Martyr Ditmar explained. "He's in charge of this facility. We've been telling him about you."

"Martyr Ditmar is hard to impress," the Commandant said. "But to his eyes, you're some sort of latter-day Samson."

"The strongest man I've ever seen," said Martyr Ditmar. "He's a darn fine shot, too. Something of a marvel."

"Where's my friend?" Roland asked. "Where's Emmanuel?"

The Commandant gave an indulgent smile. It didn't meet his tired eyes.

"Listen, Martyr. I know you can appreciate how important unit cohesion is during a situation as stressful as combat. We've had to make some changes in order to ensure unity. Emmanuel is one of a number of soldiers we've transferred to special duty."

Roland could read between the lines. He was sure if he checked in the barracks that Manny, Jonathan, and the other handful of non-white recruits would all be absent.

"What kind of special duty?"

Ditmar growled behind him, "Now listen, son. Just because the Commandant called you a Samson doesn't mean you're in charge around here. We're prosecuting a war. You won't be privy to every decision made above you and you're just going to have to get used to that."

The Commandant was a bit calmer. He put his hands forward in a placating gesture and tried again.

"Your friend is fine. He's better than fine. He's going to get a chance to serve his Lord and the Heavenly Kingdom in glorious Martyrdom. You should be happy for him."

Ditmar stepped forward and squatted down next to him. He put a hand on Roland's thigh. A third of a second later, Roland had calculated the best way to rip that arm free of its socket and beat the other men in the room to death with it. But he held still, for now. Manny would have been proud.

"Listen, boy," Ditmar said, "I know you got used to having that brown kid help you talk with people, and I'm sure he did a fine job. I get that you're not much for social graces. But we're going to take care of you now, alright? You've got a whole army of brothers here. Just do what you do best and we'll handle the rest."

"OK," Roland said. He put a hand on Martyr Ditmar's wrist and clenched it hard enough that everyone in the room heard the bones snap. The look of dawning terror on the other man's face was the best high Roland had gotten in days. He savored it for a quarter-second before finishing his sentence.

"I'll do what I do best, then."

Chapter 18

Sasha.

Sasha didn't feel safe out on the street after Anne's abduction. The next day she'd volunteered for four extra hours of duty in the emergency ward. She changed bandages and administered antibiotic salves and delivered food to wounded soldiers until her eyes started to glaze over and Dr. Brandt ordered her home. She'd barely had the energy to eat that night, but by the time her driver dropped her off at the House of Miriam it was dark, and there'd been no one waiting for her.

That strategy hadn't worked the day after that. Dr. Brandt had even tried to send her home early. Sasha had talked him out of it, but not out of sending her back downtown at the normal time. She was sure her driver must've noticed how anxious she was. By the time they reached the main drag she was drenched in sweat. Her hands were shaking. She asked him to drop her off a half-block down from the normal spot, so she could enter the square from the left side and get a good look at who was hanging out near the House of Miriam.

Alexander had been there, of course, sitting out in front of a building two doors down from the House along with one of his friends. Avoiding them had brought her to the Cafe Clement, and then something she could only assume was God's Providence had bumped her into Emmanuel.

He was sweet, and fun to talk to, and it was actually refreshing to have a conversation with someone who didn't constantly quote scripture or Pastor Mike. She was surprised at herself for feeling that way.

A few week's ago, she'd have given anything to have an open conversation about her beliefs. But now that she was deep within the Kingdom it was nice to talk about normal things, with a normal boy.

The next day had brought her back to the hospital, which was filled with soldiers wounded from an airstrike on a troop transport. Sasha had spent nine hours without a break, helping Dr. Brandt cut clothing off of horribly burned young men. She'd applied slick gummy burn dressings and changed IV drips of painkillers.

The day was long, bloody, and brutal. Four men died in front of her eyes and there was no time to really think about it. She knew she should have been more horrified at what she was seeing, but the exposed organs and burnt, shriveled limbs didn't feel like parts of people. Even the screams felt more like road hazards, or bad weather, than damaged pieces of human beings. They were obstacles to be dealt with. She and Dr. Brandt dealt with them well.

A still, small voice in the back of her mind recoiled in horror at the sheer volume of human misery she saw that day. But that voice was quieter than it had been on other days. And it grew quieter as the day went on and the death toll mounted. Sasha had read about Post Traumatic Stress Disorder back in school. She understood the mechanics of it, that people tended to cope with terrifying situations by suppressing their fear. But this didn't feel like that. It felt like she was just doing her job. And she enjoyed her job.

Before she knew it, ten hours had gone by and Dr. Brandt demanded she find a ride back to the House of Miriam and get some rest. That was the first time in the entire day when Sasha felt truly scared. It started in her chest. Her heart fluttered faster and faster until the flutter turned to a pounding so loud it felt like someone was smashing a hammer on the inner walls of her cranium. She pressed her back hard into the seat of the jeep and hoped her growing panic wasn't obvious to the driver.

He dropped her off on the other side of the square again. She didn't see Alexander or his comrades near the House of Miriam this time, but she knew that didn't mean they weren't watching the place. She had plans to meet Emmanuel again, anyway. Sasha half-expected him to have moved on since she'd been so late. But he was there, standing out in front of the Cafe Clement when she arrived.

"I'm so sorry I'm late," she said. He shrugged in response.

"I just got here myself. They dismissed us late. We had a special lecture before dinner, about– ah..." His face grew red and he trailed off.

"About what?" she poked.

"Maybe let's just sit down first, eh?"

So they found a seat and ordered their coffee. Manny tried to change the subject by asking Sasha about her day. But she was curious about his reaction and would not be dissuaded.

"I'll tell you all about my day, if you'll tell me about that lecture and why just thinking about it made your face go red."

He grew redder and stared down into his coffee.

"A pastor came over to lecture us about our duty in helping the Heavenly Kingdom grow. Y'know, our duty."

Emmanuel gave her a significant look. She gathered his meaning. And then she blushed too.

"That's why they bus us out here every day," he continued. "It's so we can, ah, get to know the local women. And then get to know them in the biblical sense."

She laughed in spite of herself. *I think that was the first off-color joke I've heard in weeks.* It felt good, and risqué. It was actually the same sort of thrill she'd gotten back home when she'd sneakily read issues of *Revelator* and browsed the media feeds of various Martyr's brigades.

"You know, Emmanuel," she said, "you're not quite like anyone else I've met here. It's nice to meet someone who isn't afraid to joke. I didn't think I'd miss that."

He was quiet for a little while. Manny stirred his coffee awkwardly, cast his eyes down. He went a little paler.

"You seem different too. I dunno. This place... Maybe it's not exactly what we thought it would be?"

She should have gotten angry at that. It was the kind of comment that could've gotten Emmanuel in a lot of trouble. *Why would he say that to me?* she wondered. *And why am I OK with all this?* Maybe it was Marigold rubbing off on her. Maybe it was just gradual disillusionment, the climax of a process that had started with Alexander's betrayal. But the Heavenly Kingdom no longer felt magical, or even all that holy.

"It's complicated here," she finally said. "I mean, before I came here, I knew it couldn't be perfect. No place is. But yes, it's not what I'd hoped to find, exactly."

Sasha felt a spike of panic as soon as the words left her mouth. *You barely know this man, Sasha. His whole job might be ferreting out potential disloyalty.* She coughed, and tried to walk her admission back a little.

"It's still better than the SDF, or any of the other heathen states. I have to keep telling myself that. What's important is what we're fighting for, not the imperfections we have to live with in this moment."

"Mmmh," he gave a noncommittal grunt. That surprised her. She hadn't expected anything specific, exactly. But that surprised her. He started to say something else. Then his eyes went wide.

"Who–" he started to say.

Sasha heard bootfalls. She felt the presence of several tall men behind her. The heavy, familiar scent of Alexander's cologne filled her nostrils.

"Martyr Emmanuel Sanchez. Miss Sasha. May the blessings of the Lord be with you."

"And also with you," Sasha replied by rote. Emmanuel chimed in a second or two later. He sounded a bit awkward, like he wasn't exactly sure what words to use.

Alexander pulled up a chair and set it against the right side of the table. He sat down, placing himself between them. He rested one arm on the table, but his left arm hung down directly over his sidearm. He looked at Emmanuel, smiled, and then looked at Sasha. She felt a wave of nausea grab her by the guts and tug. His lips curled up, revealing his straight white teeth.

"Excuse me," Manny said, "but who are you?"

Alexander looked back to Manny, his expression unchanged.

"Martyr Alexander Dubois. I'm a friend of Sasha's," he glanced back at her with a wink that curdled her stomach, "...and I'm also in charge of recruitment for the Storming Battalion."

"Never heard of it," Emmanuel said in a gruff, clipped tone. Sasha realized she was shaking a little. Alexander's lips curled up into an even more ghoulish variant of his already unsettling smile.

"There's a reason for that, Martyr Sanchez. The Storming Battalion plays a key role in our success on the battlefield. They've been central in every one of our victories. We don't publicize their work, for various reasons. But I assure you it's a distinct honor to be recruited by me. That's actually why I'm here, Emmanuel. We've chosen you."

By now it felt like the pit of Sasha's stomach was boiling. Something terrible was clearly happening. Even Emmanuel seemed to realize that. His face had gone pale. His pupils were the size of dinner plates.

"I, uh, thank you for the honor. But I'm happy with my unit. I, ah, feel that's where the Lord needs me. My friend Aaron–"

Alexander put a hand up, flat palm facing Emmanuel.

"Your comrade will be taken care of. And we'll be the judges of where the Lord needs you. Trust me, we've got a lot more experience interpreting His will than you do. There's a reason the Cross flies over this entire city."

Emmanuel half stood in his chair. It was a sudden gesture, and a faintly aggressive one. Sasha noticed his hands were balled up into fists. His eyes darted left and right. He seemed to be looking over the heads of Alexander and his men. Alexander tensed. Both the men put hands over their sidearms. But Emmanuel didn't take any further action. After a few turns of his head he stopped looking, relaxed his hands, and sat back down.

"OK," he said, "I get the feeling you want me to go with you now?"

Alexander smiled. It was a vicious, oily thing and it confirmed in Sasha's heart that he had something terrible planned.

"Yes, that's exactly what I want." He cocked his head up and pursed his lips in an exaggerated gesture of consideration, "Well, actually, I want you to go with these men. I need to stay here and have a word with Sasha."

Emmanuel looked into her eyes. He was scared, clearly. But he kept his voice steady when he spoke.

"Sasha, I've got to go do my duty. Find R– Aaron for me, will you? Tell him I, um, wish him the best. And I hope to see him *soon*."

He put definite emphasis on that last word. And then he gave Sasha a very deliberate nod before he stood and stepped toward Alexander's men.

"Take him to the factory for his intake processing. I'll be along shortly," Alexander said. He put a hand on Emmanuel's forearm as the young man passed by and said, "You should give a prayer of thanks, brother. God has blessed you with a great honor."

Emmanuel's smile was as false as Alexander's.

"God bless you, Martyr Dubois. I'll pray that you and all your men grow closer to our Lord."

Was that a threat? she wondered before deciding, *of course it was.* In a more normal situation Sasha would have mulled that over. It certainly was not the sort of comment she'd have expected from a true Martyr.

But just then she was far too consumed with terror, both for Emmanuel and for herself.

Alexander's guards led Manny away, and Alexander took his place at the table. He took a long sip from Emmanuel's cooling coffee and smiled his snake smile again.

"I must say, Sasha, I thought you had better taste than that."

For the first time in her life, Sasha found herself trying to stare daggers at someone. *Oh, if only I could shoot knives out of my eyes*, she thought as she imagined one striking Alexander in the forehead with enough force to burst out the back of his skull. *Is that something "chromed" people can do?* She wondered, and decided she'd ask Marigold if she ever got another chance to talk to the woman.

"Hey!" He snapped his fingers in front of her eyes and she hated him a little more. She was sorta surprised to learn that was possible.

"Look, I know coming here can be disorienting. I know this is a lot to get used to. But him? A fucking spic? It's people like him who filled this continent with their mongrel spawn and tore American civilization to splinters."

"We are all brothers and sisters in Christ," she said. "We are all the frui–"

"Fruit of the same tree. Yeah, I know. I've met Pastor Mike. I know God made us all. And I also know he made some of us better than others. There's a reason civilization reached its peak under white men. And there's a reason it crumbled once we let them take the reins for a while."

It's not worth arguing with him, she told herself. So Sasha decided to ask a blunt question.

"What's going to happen to Emmanuel?"

Alexander smiled.

"Exactly what I said was going to happen to him: he's going to the factory for, ah, 'training,' and then he'll participate in the invasion of Waco. As part of the Storming Battalion."

"And what is that?"

"In a way, it's the luckiest unit in the Heavenly Kingdom's whole military. They are the first ones in. Guaranteed glory..."

He took another long, slow sip from Manny's coffee. His eyes bored into her all the while.

"And guaranteed martyrdom."

Sasha felt a little pride for not crying. Tears threatened at the corners of her eyes.

"Praise be to God," she choked out. Followed by, "I still have duties tonight at the House. May I go?"

Alexander sneered at that. And then he waved his hand in a gesture that was surely meant to be casual and dismissive. It looked calculated, though. Like it was important to him that she feel like this didn't matter to him. For some reason, that observation made Sasha feel a little stronger.

"Go on then," he said. "We'll talk tomorrow. Maybe we'll do more than talk. Maybe not."

She stood up, still fighting back tears, and left the cafe without a response.

Sasha wanted to go to someone, anyone, in the wake of all this. *There's nothing to do,* the smarter, colder part of her brain—the part that always sounded like her mother—warned her. *Anything you say will only make it worse.* She knew that was true. Even Helen couldn't do anything for Emmanuel now. She'd made it very clear that military matters took precedence over everything else in the Heavenly Kingdom. It made sense. And yet...*shouldn't right and wrong be what matter most here?*

She wasn't even sure what either of those words meant anymore. Was this really what God wanted? Was this how a society based on His laws operated? Sasha told herself, over and over again, that she'd made the right decision, that the Kingdom wasn't perfect, but it was the best of all the other options. That voice grew quieter and less convincing as she walked through the doors of the House of Miriam and noticed another missing person.

"Where's Susannah?" she asked Helen, after scanning the dining room for her friend.

The older woman smiled, but it wasn't the warm look Sasha had come to expect. Helen looked strained, tired, perhaps even a little ill.

"Susannah met her husband today."

Sasha narrowed her eyes and fought down an immediate burst of rage. "She 'met' him? Or did he see her and claim her, like Anne's suitor?"

Helen did not like that. She almost growled her next words. "Be very careful with what you insinuate, Miss Sasha. I know this isn't what any of you dreamed of, but you did come here to help further the Kingdom. This is how that looks."

Sasha knew in that moment that there was nothing else she could say to Helen. What would be the point? So she nodded, meekly, and she apologized. And then she ate her dinner like a robot and cleaned up for bed. Throughout all that, Marigold's words rang louder in her memory.

"You got suckered in to a fucking nightmare. It's time to wake up."

Sasha went to bed around nine. She'd had a long and exhausting day. Tomorrow was sure to be more of the same. But she couldn't sleep. Now that she was safely in bed, hidden from the world, the tears refused to stay hidden behind her eyes. It was all Sasha could do to avoid audible sobs. She lay awake for an hour, maybe more, until she heard a *thwack*, followed by a *thump*.

She opened her eyes and rolled over to face the door. In the time it took to complete that motion, she heard the door whoosh open and then a series of thumps so rapid they sounded like one long drumroll. Sasha felt a rush of air, and sensed the presence of a new person the instant before she completed her roll. She looked up to see a man at the side of her bed. He was big, broad, and clad in a torn and bloodied Martyr's uniform.

He had a heavy metal pipe in his hand. Sasha raised her hands up in an instinctive gesture of self defense the moment before she saw the hulking man's face and realized who he was.

"Aaron?"

The man blinked. He looked confused for a moment, and then he laughed.

"Oh, right. Yeah, that's not my name, hon. You can call me Roland."

"What do you– what's happening? Are we under attack?"

"Yes, sort of. By me. I knocked out the old lady." He gestured his head back toward the other girls, sleeping in their beds, "I knocked them out too. Just minor concussions. But they're out cold."

"I am very confused," Sasha said in a flat voice. "And very frightened."

"You're not frightened."

She was surprised to realize that he was right. Sasha knew she should have been scared. But her heart rate didn't elevate. She didn't start to sweat. She did feel confused. But she also felt...calm? *Maybe I've just been so scared the last few days, my body can't handle any more of it. Maybe I've reached the limit of my capacity for fear.*

"I guess you're right," she said. "I should be afraid. This is all so..." she trailed off, grasping for words.

"Yeah, it's fucked," Roland said. And then he pulled up a canteen that had been hanging from his shoulder and took a deep pull. The scent of alcohol wafted over to her.

"You want some?" he asked. "I made it in my guts, filled a canteen as I finished up at the base."

"Wait," Sasha said, "what happened at the base?"

Roland gave another shrug and took another pull.

"The boss guys told me Manny had been reassigned to some sorta, I dunno, suicide battalion. This pissed me off, so I broke exactly half of their bones."

Sasha could hear sirens now, off in the distance. It sounded like there were rather a lot of them. She imagined this was connected to whatever Roland had done.

"I'm going to guess you and Emmanuel aren't really Martyrs, are you?"

He chuckled, "I mean, maybe someday, sister. Just now, I don't see any causes worth dying for. But I get your meaning. And no, I don't give a shit about your Heavenly Kingdom. Manny actively hates it. We're spies. Or we were spies. Now he's a captive, and I'm a terrorist. Again."

"Oh," she said. "I think I would like a drink."

He handed her the canteen and she took a generous gulp. Sasha had only tried alcohol once before. She'd been thirteen, not yet a Christian, and at a party she'd been far too young to attend. She remembered the sensation of gentle warmth spreading down her throat, and the sense of elation and well-being that had followed. She'd taken a few more sips, which had made the world far too spinny for her comfort. She'd vomited not long after. *But,* she figured, *if there was ever a time to try alcohol again, it's now.*

This drink tasted like beer, but it burned like a shot of hard liquor. Sasha passed the canteen back. She felt like taking more would be a bad idea.

"Alright, then," Roland said, "I'm going to make a few guesses. Guess one is that you're a little less than enthusiastic about the Heavenly

Kingdom now that you've seen it up close. Guess two is that you're looking for a way out. And guess three is you know something about where my little buddy went."

"Huh?"

"Emmanuel. Manny. You know where he is."

"I don't..." she started.

"I'll bet you do, even if you don't know you do. I know you were there when he was taken. I could smell it in the street."

"Smell it?"

He sighed and kneaded the bridge of his nose. "This is the time where you explain things. The time where I explain things comes later. Or maybe never." He lifted up the pipe in his hand so she could see how bloody and dented it was, "I have the pipe. Whoever's got the pipe doesn't have to explain shit."

Sasha couldn't argue with his logic. And she did want to see Emmanuel free and safe. "Look," she said, "this...this boy I know, Alexander, he found us at the cafe. We were just sitting down to coffee. He had two men with him and he said Emmanuel had been selected for the Storming Battalion."

"Do you have any idea where they took him? The kid's scent trail goes cold about a mile from here."

Sasha wracked her brain. Of course she didn't know where the Heavenly Kingdom did this sort of training but–

"Alexander said something about 'the factory.'"

And at that, Roland's eyes lit up. He turned around, as if to leave.

"I know where he is, then."

He looked back, and down to Sasha and said, "Moment of truth time, darlin'. You wanna stay here in this shitpile kingdom? Or," he jerked his thumb to the door, "do you want me to break you out? I don't make offers like that often. So take it as a compliment."

This time, it didn't take long for Sasha to make up her mind.

"Yes," she said, "I'd like to go with you."

Chapter 19

Manny.

He knew where they were taking him as soon as soon as the transport exited Highway 75. It took exit 40B, White Avenue. McKinney. He'd visited the town a few times as a kid, before things in this part of DFW had gone entirely to shit.

Manny thought of the satellite photos Reggie had shown them. He thought about that Tesla plant, and what strange mysteries it must hide. Somewhere in that plant was the answer to how the Martyrs had so thoroughly befucked the SDF's defense network. Manny hadn't exactly planned to find an answer to that question on this trip. Now it seemed like he wouldn't have a choice in the matter.

His escorts, Alexander's men, hadn't said much. They'd directed him to the proper transport and, when he asked for an explanation, they told him to keep his mouth shut. Manny did as they asked, because he half expected them to gun him down if he made a real fuss. *Roland's bound to find me. He can find any-fucking-one. I just need to stay alive long enough for him to get here.*

Once upon a time, the Tesla factory had been an immaculate sign of what some commentators called the "Texan Renaissance." After the fall of the old United States, the Republic of Texas had been one of the first functional states to arise in the Southwest. Dallas had been wrecked by the Lakewood Blast but the rest of the state still had tens of millions of people and abundant natural resources. For a while, the hardcore libertarian policies of the Republic had created a minor economic miracle. Tesla had gotten this factory going about three years before that boom went bust.

The first room he was taken to had clearly been some sort of reception area, and probably a showroom, at one point. There were three large oval-shaped plinths that had once held cars and a handful of metal desks bolted hard into the ground. There were also several benches, stripped of whatever they'd once been upholstered with, and a few dozen folding chairs that were clearly recent additions. Manny could see signs that the walls had been attacked at several places in an attempt to strip them of wires. The damage was obvious, but not as extensive as he'd expected. By ciudad de muerta's standards, this building was in good shape.

A dozen Martyrs occupied the room. They wore quality non-powered body armor and toted rifles that must've been looted new from the Republic's armories. One of the desks was manned by a harried-looking young man in an off-white suit. He wore no sign of rank, but did have a white cross armband around his left bicep and a golden cross pin on his lapel. He was balding, baby-faced, and the deep bags under his eyes spoke of severe exhaustion. His face lit up when he saw Manny.

"Another! My prayers have been answered."

"As the Lord wills it," one of Manny's escorts replied.

They brought him to the desk and the besuited man looked up at him. He had a hungry look in his eyes. He'd started to sweat a little too.

"You may call me Isaac. What's your name, young man?"

"M– ah, Emmanuel. Emmanuel Sanchez."

The little man jotted that down on a piece of paper and then continued asking questions.

"What's your date of birth?"

"Do you have any family history of allergies or illnesses?"

"Have you ever undergone surgery before?"

"What biomodifications, if any, are currently active in your system? Do you have any inactive modifications?"

And so on. After about ten minutes of questioning, the little man told Manny to stand up and follow him into an examination room. His tone was cordial, even warm. But Manny tasted doom behind it. He smelled death in this place, and his soul cried out against heading further into its bowels. But there was nothing to do but follow. Alexander's men left after dropping him off, but there were plenty of guards in the front room. Two of them followed Manny and the young man back through the double doors and into the heart of the facility.

They walked through what had once been an open-floor office. There were a few overturned desks and chairs but mostly the place was barren and half-cannibalized for scrap. It was badly lit and derelict.

"What are we doing here?" Manny asked. Isaac put a hand on his shoulder and smiled.

"We're doing God's work," he said. "The same as everywhere in this blessed Kingdom."

"I know that," Manny said in a slow, careful tone, "but I don't understand why I was pulled out of training. Or why I was removed from my unit. What is this place?"

Isaac didn't answer. Instead he walked Manny to a door in the back of the empty office and opened it to reveal a small, well-lit white room with a bench, a weight scale, and a computer terminal built into the wall above a rolling cabinet. Isaac weighed him, marked down his height and then pulled a strange measuring device out of the cabinet. It looked like a cross between a protractor and a pin vice.

"This is a craniometer," Isaac explained once he saw the confusion on Manny's face. "It's for measuring the size of your skull."

Isaac set right to work. He fit the strange device around Manny's head and tightened it until the vice grip bit into Manny's scalp. Isaac jotted down some more numbers on his note pad and removed the craniometer. He looked pleased. That alone was enough to turn Manny's stomach.

"Can you please tell me what this is all about?"

Isaac's eyes darted up from his paper for just a moment. He gave Manny an insincere, distracted smile.

"Everything will be explained soon enough, young man. Right now it should be enough to know you're doing the Lord's work."

Manny was very, very tired of that response.

Isaac finished his notes and led Manny out a back door in the room and into what Manny had to assume was the final step in their journey. The scent of blood in the air was too heavy for anything else to be the case. Manny felt the hair stand up on the back of his neck. His shoulders went tense, and a moment later he felt the strong hands of his guards on either bicep.

This new room was part mechanic's shop, part abattoir. It had once been the main factory floor and it was filled with the half-looted carcasses of robotic autoworkers. Several of those machines had been restored to some level of functional capacity. Manny could see twenty-ish new vehicles in various stages of construction across the vast space. Instead of sleek, consumer-grade electronic cars, most of these vehicles seemed to be very old and worn sedans and trucks. A handful of them were outdated and nigh-obsolete military drones. Pallets of plastic explosives sat outside several of the vehicles. Manny could see human workers packing blocks of it into a battered off-white Kia a few dozen feet in front of him.

None of this was particularly shocking. Vehicle-based improvised explosive devices had been *de rigeur* for terrorist insurrections for the last seventy years. Two things about this factory struck Manny as strange. The first is that none of the vehicles in construction had any armor added to them. Most VBIEDs would be covered in thick slabs of concrete and welded scrap metal to ensure they made it safely to their target. The vehicles here seemed like they would look normal when they finally rolled off the re-assembly line.

The second odd thing was the dozens of surgical tables, and the rather significant amount of red blood coating the floor underneath them. Five of the beds were occupied with bodies, covered by blood-speckled white sheets. The men under them appeared dead.

"Oh God," Manny forgot his cover in the dawning horror of the moment. "What the hell is this place?"

"Watch your mouth, young man," Isaac snapped. "This is a temple of the Lord, where young heroes deliver themselves into the waiting arms of eternity."

A tall man in a white lab coat made his way over to them. He had gray hair and warm brown eyes behind horn-rimmed spectacles. He gave Manny a warm smile and extended out a hand in greeting.

"The Lord be with you, Emmanuel. I'm Dr. Arnst. I'm sure you must be full of questions right now. Gentlemen," he glanced toward the guards, who still had their hands on Manny, "you can let him go now. This young man is a hero, and he should be treated as such."

The hands loosened. Manny heard the men step back. He flashed a nervous smile back at the doctor. *Keep him talking,* Manny thought, *the longer you drag this out, the more time Roland will have.*

"What is going on here? These, um," he grappled for the correct terminology, "...these martyrdom devices seem different. And I don't know what's going on with, with..."

"With all the medical equipment, and the bodies?" Dr. Arnst finished his question without so much as a break in his warm smile. "Yes, God bless him, but diplomacy is not Isaac's strong suit. He gets rather focused on the task at hand."

Manny noticed that the odd little man had already wandered off toward a rolling tray of medical equipment near one of the surgical beds. That set Manny's heart beating even faster.

"Follow me," said Dr. Arnst, "and I'll explain everything."

The doctor led him to one of the shrouded bodies and pulled its covering down, revealing the dead man's face. Manny wasn't exactly surprised to see that it was Jonathan, the young man from Atlanta he'd met just a few days before. Jonathan was, of course, quite dead. A bloody red line ran across his skull, just above the ears. His eyes were closed, and his lips were turned up in a beatific smile.

"You know this man, yes?" Dr. Arnst asked gently.

"Yes."

"Of course you do," the doctor chuckled. "You're both colored men in the Heavenly Kingdom. I'd be surprised if you hadn't developed a connection. It's only natural to gravitate toward your own kind."

Manny fought down the urge to slap Dr. Arnst.

"Jonathan here started on his journey to Martyrdom just a few hours ago. I know he appears dead. But, as it was with our Lord and Savior, appearances can be deceiving. His brain is still quite alert and alive. It's just been moved."

Dr. Arnst gestured over to the Kia. Manny saw that another lab-coated worker was now carrying a peculiar metal box over to the VBIED. The box was about head-sized, and covered with sockets and plugs. A single green light flickered on one side.

"See? They're loading him into his chariot now. And soon he'll pilot this anointed engine of heavenly will to the ruin of our enemies."

Manny thought back to that last day before the invasion, to Reggie's questions about that mysterious checkpoint bombing. *This must be how they did it*, he realized. The SDF's checkpoints were perfectly capable of reading the itinerary of any autonomous vehicle that drove toward them. They'd shoot anything that didn't broadcast its destination. But the Kingdom had found a way to hide a human driver, capable of taking over once the car was past the checkpoint.

His eyes drifted over to a combat drone lying half-disassembled on a table a few yards to his left. It was a hefty beetle-black monster with a heavy, under-slung machine gun. It reminded Manny terribly of the drone that had almost killed him and Reggie a few days earlier. *This explains why the SDF's drone jammers didn't work. The Heavenly Kingdom wasn't really using drones.*

Manny realized, with dawning horror, that the drone's open cavity was likely the intended resting place of his brain.

"Ah," Dr. Arnst smiled, "I see you've already spotted your chariot. Yes, Emmanuel, you are quite fortunate. Martyr Ditmar noted your intelligence and suggested you be implanted into a drone. I assure you, it's a high honor even in this sacred place."

Manny's heart thudded like the tolling of a church bell. For a while he couldn't hear anything else. He felt himself gripped by a sudden claustrophobic terror. The worst thing wasn't even the thought of being cut open, torn apart. It was the thought of being trapped inside that little metal box, forced to kill and die in the name of a cause he abhorred. Manny knew he'd started to shake, but there was nothing he could do to quell the terror. *I wonder if this is how Oscar felt before the end...*

Dr. Arnst put a hand on his shoulder. Manny assumed it was meant to reassure him. It did not have that effect.

"Emmanuel, I know this is quite a lot to take in. But all you really need to know is that you've been blessed—truly blessed—with the chance to play a real role in making the Heavenly Kingdom a reality. The Storming Battalion is God's elite, the holiest of our Martyrs. I'm sure, once the shock wears off, you'll realize what a privilege this is."

Manny heard footsteps. He didn't need to look to know his guards were stepping back up behind him. He felt the noose tighten, and his hope slip ever-farther away. *Where the hell is Roland?*

"I, um, uh," he stuttered, "can I have some time to th– to pray on this?"

"Of course, Emmanuel," Dr. Arnst's smile never looked false or forced. He put a hand on Manny's shoulder. "It will be a few minutes before we're ready to begin the operation. I commend your devotion. This is an ideal time to pray for guidance."

A few minutes? His heart pounded so hard he thought it might beat its way free from his chest. He was sure Dr. Arnst must have heard it.

But if he did, he said nothing about it. Instead, the doctor led Manny over to a small carpeted area that looked to have been set aside as a prayer room for the soon-to-be-martyred members of this "battalion." It consisted of a half-dozen chairs (*at least they're padded*), a three-foot tall, white stone statue of Christ on a cross, and two small end tables, each with a couple of dog-eared Bibles.

Manny sat down. Bereft of any better idea, he grabbed a Bible and flipped it open to a random page.

"King Nebuchadnezzar made an image of gold, sixty cubits high and six cubits wide..."

Manny rolled his eyes. *What the flaming hell is a cubit?* He skimmed the next few verses, until he realized which story he'd stumbled upon. His religious schooling hadn't been intense, but he had gone to church most Sundays for the better part of a decade. He'd listened to enough sermons and attended enough Sunday school classes to know the story of Shadrach, Meshach, and Abednego, three stupid assholes who'd walked into a furnace and trusted in deus ex deus to save them.

"...If we are thrown into the blazing furnace, the God we serve is able to deliver us from it, and he will deliver us from Your Majesty's hand. But even if he does not, we want you to know, Your Majesty, that we will not serve your gods or worship the image of gold you have set up."

It struck Manny that his current predicament had more than a little in common with these ancient men (if they'd ever existed in the first place). The chief difference was that, of course, Manny wasn't praying for the help of a God. He was, however, strongly hoping for rescue from a god-like being. That felt close enough to give him a sense of kinship toward the men in the story.

"The king's command was so urgent and the furnace so hot that the flames of the fire killed the soldiers who took up Shadrach, Meshach, and Abednego, and these three men, firmly tied, fell into the blazing furnace."

He hadn't remembered that bit from Sunday school, the part where the King's soldiers were burnt alive by the heat of his fire. Manny wondered what kind of soldiers would so willing step into a pointless death at some mad king's command. And then he remembered where he was. He looked up from the Bible at the twenty or so armed men stationed around the factory. *I really, really hope someone comes along to burn them to death.*

Manny heard footsteps behind him. He looked back this time and saw Dr. Arnst advancing with two guards and Isaac. The bald little man was visibly excited. An obscene smile played across his features. He held an almost comically large needle in his hands. Manny looked from him over to the doctor.

"Emmanuel," Dr. Arnst said, "it's time."

Manny stood. His mind raced for some sort of delaying tactic.

"I need to, um, pray. More. I need more pray-time."

Confusion passed over all the men's faces. "Time is of the essence here," Dr. Arnst insisted. "Don't delay this important work because you're scared. Trust in the Lord. Open your heart to his will."

"See, I have, I totally have," Manny stammered. "And I'm pretty sure he's actually not down with this. Yeah, I think he wants me to be a soldier. A regular soldier. With a gun. Not a brain in a drone."

Dr. Arnst glanced back at the two guards flanking him. He nodded and they advanced. One man had a Kalashnikov on his back, the other had a holstered sidearm. Both men were much larger and more muscular than Manny. He glanced around for a weapon, as if anything left around would be useful against two firearms. There was still a Bible in his hands. That probably would've been enough for Roland. Manny had no doubt the post-human could kill a dozen men with a book. More if it was hardcover.

"Emmanuel," the doctor's voice was low, soft, and as comforting as a lullaby, "I know this is a frightening thing. But you must trust me, you must trust all of us. The Heavenly Kingdom would not spend your life this way if we were not certain your sacrifice would further the will of our Lord. This is why you came here, Emmanuel. I know, if you listen to God, you'll see what's right."

Manny closed his eyes. He listened, not for the voice of God but for the sound of footsteps. After a few second's pause he heard the guards move toward him again. He gripped hard on the Bible in his hand and he tried not to think too much about what he'd already decided he had to do. The footsteps grew closer until Manny could almost feel the heat coming off the other men's bodies.

"Very good, Emmanuel," Dr. Arnst cooed. "God loves you..."

Manny opened his eyes. The guards were right in front of him now, reaching for him. Manny swung the Bible up, underhanded, into the Kalashnikov man's chin. Then he dove to the right and slammed his head into the other man's crotch with all the force his five foot, ten inch frame could bring to bear. The man howled. Manny half-fell, caught himself, and dropped into a dead run aimed straight for Isaac. Both the bald-headed needleman and Dr. Arnst stared at him in astonishment. Belatedly, Isaac raised his arms up in defense. The gesture did nothing to stop Manny from plowing into him and knocking him to the ground. He punched the other man in the face, hard, and then scrambled back to his feet to–

He felt the pain of the gunshot before he heard it. Or, rather, he didn't register the sound of the gunshot as a gunshot until the pain made it clear he'd been shot. And then Manny was on the ground. His world shrunk to the space below his belly button, which now pulsed with spurts of deep red blood. His hands covered the wound, pressing back against it in an instinctive attempt to protect himself.

He stared in fascination at the spreading red. He watched as his blood turned chunky and thick. The spurting faded away to a slow ooze. The pain caught up to him now and Manny's vision went black for a moment. The world faded back into view after a while. Dr. Arnst, Isaac, and both guards were standing above him. The guard with the handgun had it drawn. A wisp of smoke trailed up from the barrel. Manny watched, enthralled, as it curled up to the sky and gradually disappeared into the air around them.

"You've made a grievous error, my boy." Dr. Arnst's voice was grave now, devoid of all compassion. "You were so close to paradise. It almost brings me to tears."

The doctor was only a few feet away, but his voice sounded distant and muffled. *I'm dying, aren't I?* Manny thought. *No, if that was a kill shot I'd be dead by now. The bleeding's already stopped.* The thought did little to calm his nerves. He'd thoroughly blown his cover. Even if they never guessed his true purpose in coming to the Heavenly Kingdom, he'd be executed for trying to flee.

"This is going to put us even further behind schedule." That was Isaac. His nose was bleeding, but it didn't look broken. *I wish I was better at punching.*

"Take him outside," Dr. Arnst said to the guards, "and make it quick. There's no sense in stringing him up in public for simple cowardice."

So this is how it's going to end. Manny was confused by how at peace he felt with that. Some of it was guilt. Alejandro was dead, Hamid was dead, Oscar was dead, Mr. Peron was dead. This was nothing more than he deserved. He was pleasantly surprised to find that, as the little robots in his blood flooded his system with happy drugs, that sense of guilt began to fade. He felt wonderfully detached from the world. He wondered if this was how Roland felt all the time: disconnected and pleasant in a vague, indefinable way.

The guards bent down. Manny felt their hands on his arms. He felt them lift him up. He felt a terrible, shifting pain in his gut as another rush of clotting blood poured out of him. Manny thought of Mr. Peron; he could almost see his face. *Maybe the Christians were right about the afterlife.* That was a nice thought, actually. He thought Mr. Peron would be proud of him. *I tried to do something, sir, I really did.*

KRRRAK-THUD.

Manny didn't see the source of the noise. It sounded like something heavy falling from a high height onto something soft and squishy. *Someone soft and squishy*, he realized. The guards dropped him. Men started to yell.

Blak! Blak! Blak!

Gunshot! Gunshot! Gunshot! Manny thought, and he giggled a little bit. The sounds of chaos and violence that had erupted inside the factory could only be Roland's doing. Manny lifted up his head with considerable effort and looked over, toward the waiting area where most of the guards had sat idle. It was a mess now. Several of the chairs and one of the big tables were mashed together with a chunky red paste that resembled good salsa. *People salsa!* He thought, and then giggled again.

Manny caught a glimpse of Roland as the chromed man rocketed across the factory floor and into a trio of guards. The men didn't even have the chance to fire their weapons. The first guard burst like a balloon full of jelly. It was hard to tell exactly what happened next, as it occurred under a red cloud of human viscera. Manny slipped—in his own blood—and fell back onto the floor. He stared up at the ceiling for a little while and just focused on trying to keep his breath steady. There was nothing else he could do here, anyway.

"Emmanuel?"

Sasha? He thought.

"Glaaugh?" he said.

"It's OK." He felt her warm hand on his forehead. "Don't talk. You've been shot but you're probably not going to die."

Probably? He had to admire her fundamental honesty.

"I'm going to try and drag you out of here. If you can walk, that would be really helpful."

She grabbed Manny under the armpits and tried to pull him up. He let out a coughing cry at the pain of being moved again. But he also realized, late in the game, that he still had some control over his legs. He pushed up and, with Sasha's help, fought gravity well enough that he soon stood under (mostly) his own power. Sasha wrapped one of his arms around her shoulder and took some of the weight off his weakened limbs. And then, together, they hobbled free of the charnel factory that had almost been his tomb.

An hour later, Manny sat with Roland and Sasha on the roof of an old Bank of America and watched as the Tesla factory burned in the distance. Manny had passed out almost as soon as Sasha got him out the door. He recalled waking up a few times during the run away from the factory. At some point, Roland had met up with them and started carrying him.

He'd come to on the roof of the old bank building, just in time to see Roland dribble a trail of weird-ass blood into his gunshot wound. He'd felt a little revulsion at the act, but it passed once his pain dissolved. *I should really find a way to bottle that stuff*, he thought.

"What happened?" Manny asked, once reality had solidified a little more.

"Roland found me," Sasha said, "after they took you. I told him that Alexander had mentioned a factory and then, well, he seemed to know this must be the factory they'd been talking about."

Thanks for that, Reggie.

"He told me he was going to, ah...," she coughed a little and her cheeks reddened in embarrassment. "To 'feed them their own dicks,' and that I should wait until they were engaged to run in and drag you out."

A loud explosion echoed across the cityscape, and the trio watched a small orange mushroom cloud light up the sky where the Tesla factory had been.

"It's about damn time," Roland grumbled. "The detonators those fuckers stole from the Republic were garbage. Hey," he looked over to Manny, "what the hell was that place, anyway?"

"Yes," Sasha added, "and how exactly did you end up getting shot there?"

Manny related the whole story as best as he could. Sasha's face went pale white with outrage and disgust when he explained exactly how the Heavenly Kingdom had managed to get its suicide vehicles past the SDF's checkpoints.

"Oh God," she moaned, "oh God above, no no NO!"

Roland just laughed. "That's as clever as a two-headed crow, I'll give them that." He clapped Sasha on the shoulder. "C'mon, lady, you can't still be surprised by how fucked the Kingdom is. How many people did you watch them hang?"

Sasha didn't respond. She just sat there, eyes red and watery, and stared out at the burning factory. Manny felt like he should have said something, but his mind was still catching up to his body after the events of the last couple of hours. Staring straight ahead represented the extent of his abilities right now.

"Sorry," Roland said in response to the silence. "I forget you kids aren't used to this sort of shit. I'll tell you, it gets easier."

"What, almost dying?" asked Manny.

"Or being betrayed by the only thing you ever believed in?" asked Sasha.

Roland shrugged. "Both, I guess. Neither is much fun. But hey, y'all popped some cherries today. So it's gonna be nothing but downhill from here on out."

Neither of them responded, but Roland plowed right along.

"I meant 'downhill' in the positive sense of the word. Like sledding, or something."

More silence. Roland sighed and took a loud gulp from a piece of sheet metal he'd bent into a make-shift cup. The beverage inside smelled like another batch of his gut liquor. It burned Manny's nose from three feet away. A minute went by, and then another, without a word. They listened as emergency sirens sounded and drew closer to the site of the blast.

"So, what the fuck do we do now?" Manny asked.

Roland grunted, and then belched.

"Well, we gotta roll back into town. Break those folks out of jail. And then, I dunno. We should probably leave, right?"

Manny rolled his eyes. The casual recklessness of Roland's confidence had been fun and reassuring when he wasn't recovering from a gunshot wound. The events at the Tesla plant had proved to Manny that the post-human's protection wasn't enough to guarantee his safety. Or Sasha's. He was the deadliest thing Manny had ever seen, but he couldn't be everywhere at once.

"Wait, who are you breaking out of jail?" Sasha asked.

"Those three negotiators," Manny said, "from the City of Wheels. The women you examined and their male companion."

Sasha gave Manny a look he couldn't quite parse out.

"What?" he asked.

"Is that why you started talking to me?" she asked. "Because you knew I was working with those women, and you thought I'd be able to get you into the jail?"

"No–" started Manny.

"I mean, sorta, right?" finished Roland. "That was sure as shit a big plus."

Manny glared at the post-human. Roland had all the tact and diplomacy of a chainsaw. *That's why I'm here in the first place,* he reminded himself.

"Look," Roland continued, "there's no point in dressing any of this up. Sasha, you fled your home to join a militant terrorist organization that butchers civilians. Manny, you kinda manipulated her in the hope of getting information. I just beat, like, twenty people to death. Plus I fed Martyr Ditmar his own hand, and I feel genuinely bad about that."

Roland shook his head. "I'm really trying to not fall completely off the murder wagon here, guys. But when I get angry AND the battle-drugs start flowing," he shivered, "I get ugly."

Once again, Roland's words were met with stunned silence. And once again, he plowed forward nonetheless.

"What I'm sayin' is, this whole situation is ugly as fuck and none of us is a hero. But we're probably the least shitty people in this city with any kind of power. So let's all forgive each other's trespasses and use that power to try and save some nice people from being crucified or whatever it is Christians do to the people who piss them off. Is it just hanging?"

"I..." Sasha started to respond, and then shook her head in exasperation. "Probably not," she said instead.

"Alright," Roland clapped and put on a bright smile, "so how do we get in there? I mean, I can just sorta balls my way through the front door, or the ceiling. But since this is an actual jail it's probably reinforced. There's a good chance they'll kill the hostages before I punch my way into the cells."

Manny could almost hear the wheels turn in Sasha's head as she caught her thoughts up with what was now, apparently, her reality. To her credit, she responded in short order.

"That's probably the case," she nodded. "There are armed guards outside of each cell. And there's a real disgust for those captives among the Martyrs. They probably would shoot those women rather than let them escape."

"And what about the guy?"

"I never saw him. I dealt with the women: Marigold and, oh, what was her name... Tule! But I assume he was in the same jail."

"He is," Roland confirmed. "Or at least, he was, last time I sniffed around there."

Manny's mind finally spun up to full speed. The pain in his guts had subsided, as had the light-headed bloodless feeling he'd woken up with. He felt comforted by the mere fact of having a simple problem to solve. At its core, this question was a logistical one, just like the problems he faced every day as a fixer. He needed to deliver his team into a certain location—the jail—in a limited time frame. So Manny's first job was to figure out what connections he'd need to make in order for that to be possible.

"Sasha," he asked, "who can help us get inside that jail? Do you know anyone who has the authority to come and go from there with impunity?"

"Dr. Brandt," she replied. "He's a good man, I think. But he's committed. He's not going to work with us to betray the Kingdom."

"He doesn't need to," Manny assured her. "I'm going to guess he's a smart guy, right? He has to be somewhat worldly to be an actual doctor."

Sasha nodded. "He's not a mindless zealot, if that's what you're asking. Most of us aren't, you know. There was a reasonable case for supporting the Heavenly Kingdom. It just..." She trailed off, and Manny put his hands out in a placating gesture.

"No, no, that's not what I'm getting at. I want to make sure this guy has a sober, realistic understanding of what someone like Roland can do."

Sasha's eyes went cloudy, but she nodded. "He talked about them with me, a little," she said. "I would say he has a healthy respect for post-humans."

"Good," Manny said. "So we find him, and we'll make him an offer. Either Roland tears the heart out of the Kingdom or Dr. Brandt helps us get those captives out of the jail. If he's a sensible man he'll have to see the reason in that."

Sasha didn't look so sure about that. But after some consideration, she nodded and agreed that it was, at least, possible.

"OK. So we find this Dr. Brandt. We use him to get inside the jail, Roland does Roland-things and then we beat feet to get out of ciudad de muerta."

Roland shrugged and took another deep pull from his gut beverage. He seemed on board. Sasha raised another question, though.

"OK, so who are you two supposed to be, then? Every time Dr. Brandt and I visited the jail we had a driver and an armed guard. But you two don't exactly look like you fit the bill, right now. You," she pointed to Manny, "...clearly just took a bullet. And you," she jabbed a finger at Roland, "...look like you just destroyed dozens of people. Which I guess you did."

"Right," Manny clapped his hands, "that's easy enough to fix. It's what, five AM now? The city's starting to wake up. Do you know what shift Dr. Brandt's expected to work today, Sasha?"

"Lately he's been doing seven to seven."

"And Roland," Manny continued, "you know where the vehicle pool is?"

The big man nodded. "Yeah, I tracked that down during my first recon day. It's about thirty minutes away on foot, for you guys. Five minutes for me."

"We'll go slow," said Manny. "Sasha, you'll let us know when you recognize Dr. Brandt's jeep and driver. We'll stop them, relieve them of their uniforms and drive on to the doctor's house. Roland, you think you can take two men out without bloodying up their uniforms?"

He gave another shrug. "50/50."

"Alright," Manny nodded. "That's Plan A then."

"And what's Plan B?" Sasha asked.

"Close your eyes and hide behind Roland."

Chapter 20

Roland.

“That looks like them,” Sasha whispered into his ear.

The three of them were stationed on the third floor of an old office building that overlooked the Kingdom’s vehicle pool. Based on the posters and decorations inside, the people in this office had once helped coordinate for a string of restaurant supply stores. Roland suspected the coming of the war might’ve been a relief to the people who’d been stuck working here.

He was positioned by the window, sitting down so only the edge of his face would’ve been visible to anyone looking in from the outside. Manny had elected to take a nap out of view, behind one of the desks. His ability to fall asleep anytime, anywhere marked him out as a true expert in warzone survival. Sasha had situated herself on the other side of the window frame. Roland had warned her to keep her head out of view until he saw new arrivals to the vehicle depot. He’d called for her eyes six times already, and gotten six negatives. Now it seemed their target had arrived.

“Are you sure?” he asked.

“Pretty sure,” she said, and nodded. “The driver walks with a limp, one of his legs is shorter than the other. I think it’s a birth defect. He must come from some part of the continent where those still happen.”

“Good eye!” Roland was genuinely impressed. The girl had potential.

“So what do we do now?” she asked.

"You rouse Manny. I'll keep an eye on things. When they depart I'll carjack them into unconsciousness and bring back the uniforms."

And that's more or less how it went. The guard and driver departed in a jeep five minutes later. Roland bounded down from one of the rear windows and landed on the hood as they took a right hand turn out of view of the vehicle depot. The "guard" did not do his job title proud. Roland slammed his face into the dashboard and knocked him out. He also knocked out most of the man's teeth, but his hindbrain told him the guy's odds of a fatal brain hemorrhage were only about 6 percent. *Acceptable.* He broke the driver's jaw with a right cross, took the wheel, and steered the vehicle to a stop while he was still hanging outside it.

Roland tossed both men in the back of the jeep and pulled into the office building's underground parking lot. He stripped them both and cursed when he realized the guard's bleeding face had stained the neck of his uniform shirt. He found some bottled water in the trunk and managed to wash out the worst of it, but the stain would still be visible to anyone who really took the time to look. Still, it'd probably be enough to get them through the door of the jail.

He stashed both men in a janitorial closet and dragged an old metal dumpster in front of it to wedge the door shut. Someone would probably find them before they starved to death. He felt a pang of guilt for how little he cared about what happened to those men. *I should feel worse about this.* Roland knew the battle drugs had suppressed his conscience. He knew that the longer they stayed in this dangerous place, and the more fighting he did, the more tempted he'd be to kill outright.

Roland leaned against the dumpster and closed his eyes. He tried to force himself to take long, slow breaths and meditate on the flow of air in and out of his lungs. He hoped taking a breather would prompt his system to reduce the drip. Instead, he found himself flashing back to more violence–

Red siren lights screeched and blinked on walls of institutional white. Men and women in lab coats ran and screamed and died, died, died as he squeezed the trigger of his Sig Sauer. Roland kicked at a locked door and the metal buckled inwards, revealing a room filled with giant glass organ-filled vats–

He shook his head and tried to banish the memories. He'd started flashing back to this place when they'd rescued Manny. But the memories had kept coming, even once the violence had subsided–

"Please Roland!" the old woman begged through blood-stained teeth. He looked down at the hole in her gut, the red blood on her white lab coat. She slid backward on the tile floor until her shoulders hit one of the racks of vat-grown organs.

"Please don't do this!"

Roland shook his head. He didn't know why this was happening exactly. It was likely just a glitch, some unforeseen interaction between the wetware of his hindbrain, the procedural memories stored in his DNA, and the battle drugs that flowed through his system. He questioned, again, whether he really wanted his memories back.

This wasn't the time to ponder that question though. Roland headed back upstairs to grab Manny and Sasha. He led them down to the garage and handed Manny the un-bloodied uniform.

"Dude, that's really obvious." Manny pointed to the bloodstains on Roland's own uniform. "They're going to notice that."

"You think so?" Roland was so used to normal humans not noticing much of anything, he sometimes underestimated their senses.

"I've got an idea!" Sasha said. "Pop the hood."

Roland and Manny were both a little surprised. But he popped it for her. The girl stared at the engine, reached for the dip stick and pulled it free from its slot. She rubbed her hand down the shaft and it came away covered in sticky black grease. She rubbed the grease into Roland's collar, coated the dip stick again and repeated the process two more times. When she was done, he looked like he'd been working on an engine rather than beating a man half to death.

"Fucking brilliant," Roland said.

Manny nodded his agreement. Then he said, "Alright, let's go abduct a doctor."

The abduction itself was easy. Dr. Brandt lived in an undamaged mansion about two miles away from downtown. As one of the Kingdom's few medical professionals, Dr. Brandt had apparently earned himself some luxury. Sasha hid in the trunk so the doctor wouldn't notice anything was off until he entered the vehicle.

"Where's Jerry, and Samuel?" Dr. Brandt asked as he opened the door and sat down inside the jeep.

Manny gunned the engine and peeled away. Roland put a hand on Dr. Brandt's thigh and squeezed just hard enough for the man to feel like his thigh bone might shatter.

"I stuffed them into a closet somewhere," he explained with a smile.

"My name is Manny," the fixer said. "The guy who's about to break your leg is named Roland. We're kidnapping you."

"Ah," said Dr. Brandt. Roland had to give credit where credit was due. The doctor endured the pain with a stony face, and without any signs of panic.

"We need you to help us get into the jail," Manny continued, "where those negotiators from Rolling Fuck are being held."

Dr. Brandt grimaced, either from the obscenity or just due to the continued pain of Roland's iron grip.

"And what makes you think I'll give you any aid?" There was a bit of strain in his voice now, but the doctor's features stayed decidedly neutral. "I may be a doctor, but I'm no less prepared to die for my Kingdom than anyone else here. You might as well just go ahead and kill me."

Roland relaxed his grip. The doctor sighed in relief.

"Yeah, we thought you might say something like that," said Manny. "That's why Roland and I prepared an alternate proposal."

Roland drew the guard's stolen sidearm from its holster. He gripped the pistol in one hand and then crushed it in his grip like he was balling up a piece of paper. The doctor's eyes widened in shock and horror.

"So," Manny said, "my friend's just fulla chrome. High grade stuff. He could walk right through a tank if he wanted. You're an educated man. You know what people like him can do."

The doctor nodded, but didn't say anything.

"Our offer is simple. You help us out and we'll leave with our people. You refuse to help, and we'll get our people anyway. Only Roland here will take a little detour to burn half this city to the ground."

"I see." Roland could smell the fear wafting off Dr. Brandt now, but the man's expression didn't change.

"You wouldn't be a doctor if you didn't see value in human lives," Manny's voice was soft, his reasonable tone wouldn't have been out of place in a boardroom. "If you refuse to help us we won't hurt you, won't harm a hair on your head. But my friend here will break this city, and a few thousand of the people in it. You'll be hale and healthy so you can pick up the pieces. And you'll know that every ounce of that suffering could've been prevented if you'd just helped us out."

"It's true, sir," Sasha spoke up. Dr. Brandt stiffened. She sat up from her hidden position in the back. The doctor was a smart man; he put together that she was not being held as a prisoner. His eyes narrowed in contempt.

"Sasha." Dr. Brandt's voice was cold, "I'm sorry to see you in such poor company."

"Sir, I'm really sorry but–"

"But nothing," he snapped, and now the anger showed on his face. "Have you been a traitor this whole time, or did your will simply fail?"

"Sasha," Manny spoke up, "we really don't have time for this..."

Roland disagreed. His hindbrain estimated Sasha and the doctor could afford a solid eight minutes of emotional closure before they got too close to the jail.

"Is eight minutes a lot of time for you people?"

Everyone stared at him, their individual disagreements forgotten for a moment. Roland realized, late, that he'd spoken out loud.

"Sorry," he said. "That was just supposed to be in my head."

They still stared.

"Well, now you only have like, seven minutes and forty seconds."

"Ignore that," said Manny. "He's a maniac. That's why you don't want us to let him loose in your city."

"Dr. Brandt," Sasha added, "I know you're a good man. The Lord put you on this earth to save lives. This is your chance to do that."

The doctor kneaded the bridge of his nose with his hand. He did an admirable job of not giving too much away with his body language, but Roland could smell the truth. The scent of stress wafting off the doctor faded. It was a sign the man had made a decision: there was something about choosing that calmed the human soul.

"You are correct of course, Sasha. I never approved of us holding those women in the first place. It was foolish, to antagonize things like him," he nodded toward Roland. "If I can avert a massacre, I will. But I sincerely hope you plan to escape with them, Sasha. I won't hide or protect a traitor."

"I'll leave," Sasha said.

The doctor gave a somber nod.

"I won't be able to get you out of the jail with those prisoners, you know." He said to Roland. "I can get you inside, and I can probably get them to send the prisoners into an examination room. But the guards won't let them leave the building."

"I'll take care of that part," Roland promised. "I'm real good at making doors."

Roland was aware of the old saying, "No plan survives contact with the enemy." For some reason his hindbrain remembered the original version of the quote, from an old Prussian General named Moltke: "No plan of operations extends with any certainty beyond first contact with the main hostile force."

People who observed Roland in battle tended to think he just sorta winged it and ballsed his way through on sheer violent potential alone. But Roland was, at his core, a planner.

Having a plan was essential to take maximum advantage of the way his hindbrain worked. A plan was nothing more than a clear set of tactics meant to accomplish a concrete goal. In this case, the goal was "free the prisoners and take his new friends to safety." The plan he constructed to achieve that goal was based mainly on Sasha's recollections and his own espionage on the jail. He knew it would change once the shooting started. But the fact that he had a rubric would give his hindbrain something to focus on while it zeroed in on the best tactics for the evolving situation.

At any rate, the plan Manny and Sasha had cooked up actually did survive first contact with the enemy. Roland and Manny had posed as guards and followed Dr. Brandt and Sasha right through the door. The Martyrs inside were all used to seeing the doctor and his assistant, and they didn't pay a different set of armed guards any mind. When Dr. Brandt requested they send all the prisoners in to the examination room, the officer in charge didn't even blink at the request.

The only thing that had seemed off to Roland was an odd scent of anxiety in the air. It wafted off the guards and hung in a thick cloud above the entrance room. The odor reminded Roland of countless hours spent sitting with nervous men in the cramped belly of an APC or drop aircraft. He assumed this had something to do with the giant explosion he'd caused earlier, or his escape from the training facility.

Of course these guys are on high alert, he thought, *some nutfuck monster-man blew up a factory this morning.*

Dr. Brandt led them into a large waiting room and closed the door. He let out a long, nervous sigh and slumped back against the wall.

"Ok. You'll have your prisoners soon enough, and no one else will need to die. Right?" He looked straight at Roland.

"Right," Roland said. And then added, "Up until you fucks invaded Dallas, I'd gone years without killing anyone. I'm actually pretty good at it."

The doctor did not seem comforted by this fact. Roland opened his mouth again, but Manny put a hand on his shoulder.

"No," he said. And Roland nodded. *I could have avoided so many violent misunderstandings with this kid's help.* Roland mulled this over and wondered if Manny might be interested in an adjoining mountaintop shack. Just then the door opened.

A guard entered. He was followed by the three prisoners and then two more guards. Rolling Fuck's negotiators were all handcuffed to each other. Roland had been shown pictures of all three captives before they'd departed the city of wheels, so it wasn't hard to recognize Marigold, Tule and Rick. But they all looked different. Marigold's bright purple hair was limp and greasy. The sockets on her augmented arm had been filled in with some sort of resinous substance.

Tule, bald in her pictures, now had a head full of peach fuzz. Her necklaces and amulets and rings were all gone, of course. She looked pale and deflated. Roland could see the ghost of an old black eye, likely earned during the initial capture. She walked with a limp, but otherwise looked healthy enough.

And then there was Rick. His wounds were fresh, and extensive. He was covered in bruises and it looked like his guards had cut into him, "writing" over several of his scarified tattoos with a combat knife. His left eye was broken and looked dead. Roland could tell the man's orbital bone had been shattered. And with the slow, juddering way his good eye looked around the room, it was likely he'd suffered at least one concussion.

Dr. Brandt sighed and went right to the injured young man. "Have the others sit down," he told the guards. He started to examine Rick. His jaw clenched, his eyes narrowed. Roland felt the doctor's heart rate accelerate in anger.

"You've been at him again, haven't you?" Dr. Brandt sounded angry. "I told you all this had to stop. He's clearly concussed. You could have killed him."

The lead guard shrugged and rolled his eyes. One of the other guards snickered. Roland could tell by the look of fury on the doctor's face that he was not used to being treated this way.

"Soldier, I am the senior medical doctor of this entire Kingdom. I will bring your superior into this, and I will..."

Roland heard, and then smelled, six new men enter the jail. His mind rocketed downstairs, away from the petty argument, and started to analyze the new arrivals. They were soldiers, he could tell by the sound of their footfalls and the strong smell of gun oil and powder that wafted off of them. One of them smelled familiar, he'd been present when Manny had been abducted to the factory. Roland guessed this was the guy Sasha had told him about during their impromptu rescue mission.

"Huh," Roland said out loud. Manny was the only one who seemed to notice.

"What?" Manny asked in a voice low enough that the guards wouldn't hear it over the sound of Dr. Brandt dressing them down.

"That guy, Alexander. He just entered the building with a squad of armed men."

"What does that mean?"

"I dunno," Roland shrugged. "Probably an ambush."

Roland was a bit embarrassed that it had taken him this long to piece it together. That's why the guards had been so accommodating of Dr. Brandt's unusual request. It's why they'd smelled so nervous. Somehow, the rescue attempt had been spotted before it had gone down. The soldiers of the Heavenly Kingdom must have assumed the doctor was a traitor too.

Roland stood up.

He knew that violence would need to happen here. There were too many decent people's lives at stake for anything else. The instant his forebrain made that decision, his hindbrain started pouring adrenaline and battle drugs into his synapses. He felt the electric crackle of chemical glee start deep in the back of his neck. It spread out to his shoulders, down his arms, to the tip of his fingers. Roland fought back against the building euphoria while he analyzed the situation.

The world slowed down around him. He had plenty of time to watch as the guards started to reach for their sidearms. The word "ambush" had keyed them in. But it didn't matter: they still moved too slow to affect anything. His hindbrain calculated that Manny and Sasha were relatively safe. No one had a gun on them, just now. The prisoners were his priority then. They were exposed, both to the door that enemy reinforcements would soon rush through, and to the guards already in the room. Dr. Brandt was a tertiary responsibility: he seemed like a decent enough guy, in spite of it all.

Alexander and his men are two-point-oh-four seconds from the door. Maybe faster, if they dropped into a dead sprint.

Roland stepped forward, into the lead guard. He grabbed the man by the hair, lifted him into the air, and slammed his skull hard into the second guard's face. Bone cracked. *16.3 percent and 28.7 percent chances of a fatal hemorrhage, respectively.* Roland dropped the first man and plunged his fingers into the third guard's eyes. He gouged deep, stopped just short of the man's brain, and then pulled his hand free.

That man staggered back, opened his mouth, and started to scream. A surge of battle drugs hit Roland's synapses at just that moment and, in a fit of gleeful pique, he grabbed the man by the jaw and pulled. His intent had been to yank the man's head into his knee. But he pulled a little too hard and ripped the whole jaw free. The man fell back, gurgled, bled.

"Huh. My bad," Roland said to no one in particular.

He shoved the jaw into his front pocket, figuring it might make a useful weapon when the reinforcements showed up. In the meantime, he set to work ripping the prisoner's manacle chains apart. It'd have taken too long to remove the manacles. But at least with the chains free they'd all be able to move with–

"What are you... Oh my GOD!

"Roland wh–"

"AHHHHHH!"

Dr. Brandt, Manny, and Sasha finally reacted. Roland had to remind himself that their brains wouldn't have been able to properly process what he'd done while it was happening. The whole altercation had lasted barely a quarter-second. To Manny, Sasha, and Dr. Brandt the violence had been disorienting and almost unintelligible.

The three negotiators from Rolling Fuck were not stock sapien.

They'd reacted faster and gone to ground almost as soon as he'd rushed the first man. At least, the women had. The young man was too dazed and battered to react to much at all, so his friends pulled him down and shielded him with their bodies.

Of the other three, Manny was the first to react. He grabbed Sasha by the shoulder and shoved her down below the window line. Roland was proud. He would have said something about that, but everything went disastrously wrong a fraction of a second later.

Roland had known Alexander and his men were rushing the door. He'd estimated a solid one-point-four seconds before they breached the entry way. That's why he'd occupied himself by checking on everyone. He'd trusted his senses and trusted that the Heavenly Kingdom didn't have any gear he hadn't already seen. That proved to be a mistake, because unbeknown to Roland two men in powered armor hung off the outside wall of the building, directly underneath the window.

Their suits were bleeding-edge stealth technology, utterly absent from Roland's petabytes of memory. His passive sensors had missed them entirely. Roland first realized they were there, and that he'd erred terribly, when they opened fire.

Close to a hundred .30 caliber slugs tore through the wall of the jail at roughly forty-two hundred feet per second. They were fired at such close range, and with such total surprise, that Roland was unable to dodge or prep his sub-dermal armor for impact. Nineteen rounds hit him: fifteen in his center of mass, one in his left thigh, and three in his right shoulder. Two hit Manny, ripping a hole through his left hand and another through his kidney. Dr. Brandt, who'd only half-turned to face Roland at this point, was torn apart in a fusillade of steel. Roland also registered hits on their not-yet-rescued captives: one in Tule's left butt cheek, one that severed Rick's index finger, and another in the young man's shoulder.

Roland staggered back from the impact of the rounds just as Alexander's point man burst through the door. The coordination between the two teams was impressive, as was the fact that the suited men hadn't hit their allies on the other side of the door. On a normal day, Roland would've ripped the shotgun out of the point-man's hands and castrated him with it. But this was not a normal day and Roland's brain was occupied with the damage to his body. The point man fired twice and sent one-ounce tungsten slugs through both of Roland's knees.

He dropped, rolled, moaned. And then the rest of the team was in the room. They moved well. Not like vets, but like men who'd trained a lot for entries like this. They all wore heavy body armor. It wasn't powered, but it provided solid protection against small-arms fire. They mostly packed auto-shotguns. *Smart choice,* Roland thought. *When fighting post-humans, go for tissue damage.*

He was hurt. Nothing fatal, yet. But the loss of momentum and control had cost him dearly. Now six men had a bead on him with weaponry powerful enough to do some real damage. Roland listened as one of the stealth suits smashed the remainder of the window in and crawled inside the room.

This armor was much more subtle than the standard Ares pattern armor. Aside from plating at the chest and shins it didn't look like it added a substantial amount of protection. But the suit was covered in high-definition display panels. The man was hard for Roland to see. He would've been nigh-invisible to a normal human.

"Shit," Roland spat blood and looked up just as a very satisfied looking young man stepped into the room. He was tall, handsome, and well-built. He wore the same armor as his men but lacked a helmet. Instead, he had a red beret with a lacquered gold cross pinned to the front. Roland took one look at the boy's prominent jaw-line and well-tanned skin. He grudgingly agreed that it would've been a crime to cover up that face.

"How new are those fucking suits?" he asked the fancy-man.

"The Republic had some very choice gear in its armory," the youth replied. "My superiors will be happy to hear how well it worked against you."

He sauntered into the room like a conquering king, waving his pistol lazily at the captives.

"Hello, Sasha!" he said with a smile and a cheery wave of his free hand.

"Alexander," she replied in a tone as cold as ice.

The young man, Alexander, stopped in front of Roland, peered down, and grinned the shit-eatingest grin in the history of eating shit.

"You know," he said, "it was rather easy drawing you into this trap. Once you played your hand at the training camp we knew you'd come here sooner or later. I was rather surprised to see you involved, Sasha." He looked over at her. "I wonder: was this your plan all along, or are you merely an opportunist, clutching to these men because my proposition injured your ego?"

He laughed prickishly. Roland wanted to hit him, but the situation merited further analysis before action. Much of the damage done to him in the ambush had already healed, and none of it was substantial enough to impede his deadliness. But his position was rather tenuous. The second armored soldier crouched at the window, adhered to the outside wall. The first stealth suited soldier had one gun trained on Manny and another aimed at Roland.

Alexander's men all had him dead to rights, shotguns leveled and fingers on triggers. He could, perhaps, move fast enough to take out one or two of them. But the others would do a significant amount of damage in the meantime. And, more to the point, Roland could do nothing to ensure Sasha and Manny's safety. He considered their deaths unacceptable.

"I really am a bit disappointed in how easy this all was," the young fuck continued. "I thought we'd be in for more of a fight here. I guess the stories about your kind were exaggerated after all. I suspected so. No amount of scientific tinkering can replace the blessing of God behind righteous men."

Roland sensed movement. Not from Manny: he was frozen still, next to Sasha, under the gun of one of the power-armored troopers. It didn't come from any of Alexander's men, either. It was Marigold. The woman had gritted her teeth and inched her hand toward the body of the guard Roland had de-jawed. He watched as she wrapped her hand around the grip of his sidearm.

Alexander stepped around him and headed toward Sasha. The other soldiers still had their weapons trained on Roland. They didn't seem to have noticed Marigold.

"I warned you, didn't I, Sasha?" Alexander asked, as a smile played across his lips. "I warned you what comes of defying God's will. And then you allied yourself with a beast whose very existence is a sin against our Heavenly Father. If Christ had intended–"

Roland never got to hear the rest of that sentence, because Alexander never got to say it. He was interrupted by Marigold pulling the pistol free of its holster and swinging it up toward the groin of the squad's point man. She fired twice, switched targets, and pumped two more rounds into the unarmored belly of a second man.

Roland was up and off the ground between the second and third shot. He swung his fist hard into the face plate of the nearest soldier's helmet. The plexiglass shattered, and Roland's knuckles pushed shards into the man's cheeks and eyes. The Martyr screamed and fired a shot that went wide, as Roland dove to the left, refracting his fist and pivoting to rush the power-armored man holding a gun on Manny and Sasha.

There were no good options here. Marigold's intervention had given them all a chance. But Roland had been forced to make a choice between going after the armored men and saving his friends, or taking out the entry team and saving Marigold and her friends. He heard her fire two more shots, and heard them impact. But then his attention was consumed by the two men in powered armor.

They'd recovered first, and both men opened up on Roland as he charged. There was no dodging at this distance. It was barely possible to mitigate the damage in any way. Roland took thirty high-velocity rounds to the face, neck, shoulders, and upper chest. Some of them were stopped by his sub-dermal armor. Most weren't. He felt (*holy shit!*) real pain for the first time in what felt like years. Roland's wired nervous system rewarded this with a flood of chemical bliss. As he charged he smiled and "whooped" like a sixteen-year-old railing his first line of blow.

He dove into the first man hands first, grabbed his enemy by the neck and then bum rushed him into the man hanging outside the window. This knocked the top of the second man's body free from the wall and sent him reeling half-back into open air. The man's feet were still attached to the building, but his body flailed free. Roland kept his grip and focus on the first armored man. The Martyr's neck armor had hardened to resist the crushing strength of Roland's grip, so he shook the man's head back and forth and slammed it into the frame of the window as hard as possible.

The soldier pumped another dozen rounds, point blank, into Roland's body. He saw red. He *felt* red. He was numbly aware of the tremendous amount of damage being done to him. But none of it had yet rendered him unable to throttle this motherfucker, so he continued to squeeze until the armor's neck seals failed, cracked, and Roland's fingers bit deep into the meat of the man's throat and crushed his windpipe.

Roland tossed the body aside and went for the second man, still flailing outside the window. He was interrupted when Alexander fired a slug into his temple. The round impacted his reinforced skull and ricocheted off. But the impact, the force of the blow itself, made him see stars. It hurt. Roland staggered back and to the side.

Then several things happened in very quick succession.

Marigold fired another round, her last. It was followed by the sound of the two remaining guards opening up with their shotguns. Roland heard as she was torn apart. Just as his eyes started to focus again, Alexander fired two more shots directly into his head. The man on the wall finally found his grip again, and Roland felt the power-armored soldier steady himself to open fire.

Roland's shaken hind-brain advised him that going for the armored man was probably his best decision. So he surged forward, less steady than before, and hunched his shoulders in anticipation of taking another slug or four to the brainpan. But that didn't happen. For the second time today, Roland was surprised by the actions of a normal human. This time it was Sasha.

She'd gotten up from where she and Manny had taken shelter from the gunfight and crawled over to the body of the first guard Roland had disabled. He'd been dimly aware of this in the semi-conscious way he was aware of the traffic passing outside. His brain had opted to not focus on it since the heavily armed men were a more pressing concern. But then Sasha had removed the unconscious guard's helmet and rushed toward Alexander.

She swung first for his gun-hand. Roland heard her knock the pistol free of his grip. Then she hit him in the face with the helmet, over and over and over again. Roland felt the urge to thank her but, just then, the power-armored man became a concern again.

The fucker managed to get off three more shots before Roland ripped the weapon free from its forearm mount and used it to cave in the armored faceplate. Blood spurted out and the man fell, limp, back out the window. His feet continued to adhere to the outside wall while his jerking, bleeding body dangled in the breeze.

Roland turned just in time to take another two slugs from another two shotguns. But then the men were empty. They'd pumped most of their rounds into Marigold's body. They fumbled to reload, panicked and clearly unused to carrying out the task in a combat situation.

Roland could smell the terror as it wafted off their bodies. Their fear hit his nervous system like an ounce of crystal meth. He loomed toward them, and for a second the only sounds in the room were his footsteps, and the dull "thwhap" of Sasha pounding the helmet into Alexander's now-shattered skull.

Roland whipped his left arm out. A massive blade, not unlike a straight razor, tore through the flesh of his inner forearm and locked into place. The men screamed. One dropped his shotgun and tried to run. Roland tore into him first, using the blade to sever the fucker's arms. Battle drugs and pure liquid satisfaction flowed into Roland's synapses. His dick went hard and he screamed in wordless joy as he slashed downwards and sliced off the man's face. The poor bastard fell away, burbling, and Roland turned toward the last soldier.

He died an equally terrible death.

And then it was done. The battle was over. Quiet reigned. The only sounds audible to a normal human would've been the blood spurting from dead and dying bodies and the sound of sobbing. Tule sobbed for Marigold. Sasha sobbed for, Roland guessed, her lost innocence.

And then, out in the city beyond, came the sound of a hundred sirens. The Martyrs were coming for them.

Chapter 21

Sasha.

Alexander hadn't seen it coming. He hadn't expected her at all. The sound of his furious scream was the most beautiful thing Sasha had ever heard. She hit him again and again and he fell back, and then down to the ground. Blood streamed from his nose and from a gash above his brow. His eyes looked unfocused. His lip was split. He tried to scream, or cry out, or beg her but she didn't give him the time to say one damn word.

Instead she hit him again. And again. And again. She didn't make the conscious choice to dive down on top of him and, in fact, Sasha was rather surprised to find herself straddling the prone, broken boy soldier. But once she was there she kept hitting him until she felt his skull give away and the helmet hit something soft, squishy, and hot that lay beyond.

She sat back and, for what seemed like a year, just stared at the helmet embedded in Alexander's ruined face. Blood pulsed out from around the edges where it met the skin. The way the blood bubbled up looked just a bit like the water at one of the fountains outside the hospital her mother ran. For some reason that similarity did more to raise her hackles than the act of killing.

Her ears still rang, so it was easy to lose herself in contemplation of Alexander's body. Her mind turned to the book of John, and the words of her Lord and Savior, Jesus Christ: "Do not be like Cain, who belonged to the evil one and murdered his brother. And why did he murder him? Because his own actions were evil and his brother's were righteous."

Had Alexander's actions truly been righteous? Sasha knew that, if she searched the Bible, she could find scriptural justifications for everything Alexander had done. That's why she'd come out here in the first place, wasn't it? The Heavenly Kingdom was finally going back to the letter of the Bible, the word of God. Only now that she'd seen what that looked like, Sasha had found she could not abide it.

Am I still a Christian? She couldn't say. Her faith had been such a part of her identity. It had been everything. And now it felt like a lie. *What am I, if not a righteous servant of the Lord? Where do I go from here?*

"Hey, Sash'? Little problem here."

Roland's voice jerked her out of her contemplation. She looked back at the man and her mind recoiled in horror. His skin had been shredded by gunfire; it hung in pale tatters down his face and arms. His clothing had been largely shot away, and the rags that remained were so drenched in blood that they clung to him. He looked almost as if he was clad in a single giant scab. One of his eyes was unfocused, dislocated, and something had happened to his left arm. It looked as if an enormous straight razor had burst out of the forearm.

"Where did you get that?" she asked. Sasha was surprised, and a bit disturbed, by her curiosity. Roland seemed surprised too.

"This?" he looked at the blade. "I really don't know. I'd sort of forgotten it was in there." He lifted up his arm and its blood-soaked blade, and looked at it like a child opening a prized gift on Christmas morning.

Then he flicked his arm down, toward the ground, and the blade slid back into the meat of his forearm with a wet thwack.

"Look," he said, "we've got more pressing shit to deal with right now. You hear all those sirens?"

She actually couldn't. Her hearing had begun to recover from the gunfight, but Roland was just barely audible. A loud tinnitus hum still rang through her ears. Sasha was pretty sure she'd suffered permanent damage.

"I can't hear much right now," she said. "The gunfire, you know."

"Oh," he frowned. "I forgot that can happen to you folks. Well, ah, there's a shitload of cops or martyrs or militia, whatever, a bunch of them are coming. Probably two or three hundred. They got tanks and drones and shit."

"God almighty…" Sasha felt fear rise up in her heart again.

"Yeah, listen, God's not really the dude to worry about right now. Manny's all fucked up. I stopped his bleeding, but you're going to need to get him out of here."

Manny! She'd forgotten all about him. Sasha realized with a start that she'd blotted the rest of the room from her mind. She looked around and took it all in. Manny was still lying where she'd left him, nursing a gunshot wound to the belly. He was pale, sweaty, and he looked to be in terrible pain. But he was conscious and alive. That was more than she could say for Marigold.

The poor woman had been shredded by shotgun fire. Sasha couldn't bring herself to look too closely at the shattered, steaming remains. But Marigold's friends were alive. The young man, Rick, was unconscious and drenched in blood. But most of that blood didn't seem to be his own. His head was in Tule's lap. She'd been wounded in the buttocks, and bled quite a lot, but the wound seemed to have clotted. There were tears, and a haunted, pained look in her eyes.

"Oh my God," Sasha said once her mind started to process the visual stimuli. "Oh Lord in Heaven no, no, no…" *That poor woman. That unborn child. How could this happen? How could this BE?*

"SASHA!" Roland shouted. "This is a very bad time for you to have emotions. Try killing those for a little while."

"How…"

"Just think about the fact that everyone but me will die if you don't get your shit together. And then get your shit together."

Her initial reaction was anger and frustration. *Is he that disconnected from humanity? Does he think people can just turn their empathy off?* But then she stopped herself, listened to him, and tried. She imagined herself putting on a heavy jacket, something that blocked out pain and horror rather than the cold.

It worked.

"OK," she said, "what do I need to do?"

"You need to take Manny. And, ah, whats-her-name. And whats-his-face."

"Tule. And Rick."

"Right, take the not-dead people, run down and out the back door, and find me a car, then you need to–"

"A car?"

He stopped sifting through the dead men's firearms to roll his eyes at her.

"Yes, a car. I'm not going to carry all you lame-bloods out of here on my fucking shoulders. We'll need a getaway vehicle."

"I can't drive," she said. "All the cars in the AmFed are autonomous..."

He shrugged. "You'll figure it out."

Manny moaned just then, almost as if it was in response to Roland's suggestion. Sasha knew it was more likely she'd just been too focused on the big post-human to notice Manny's pained moans the whole time.

"Can he drive?" Sasha asked.

"Sure!" Roland said with sudden cheer. "He's only lost, what, two quarts of blood? I gave him a little of mine. I'm sure he'll be right as rain soon."

Manny moaned again, hand at his blood-soaked belly. He didn't appear to be bleeding still, but he was pale and his face showed agony too obvious to ignore. Sasha doubted he'd be capable of driving a car in the immediate future.

"I can drive," Tule said in a cracked, broken-sounding voice.

"Right!" Roland said. "Well, that's lovely. Get your asses up and get moving. You've got about two minutes before shit and fan start their lovely dance." The post-human's good humor was incongruous in this blood-soaked room, addressed to two people who'd lost a friend today. He grabbed one of the guard's pistols, which he'd shoved in his waistband, and handed it to Sasha.

"Safety's off," he said cheerily, "so once you pull the trigger, stuff'll happen."

Sasha took the gun, then went over to help Manny up. Tule did the same thing with her wounded friend. Neither Manny or Rick were in great shape. But Manny, at least, seemed capable of standing under his own power. Once Sasha got him to his feet he stayed there. She looked him in the eye and, while he seemed sort of dazed and glassy, his pupils fixed on hers and he nodded.

"We have to go," she said.

"Se trata de tiempo de mierda," he muttered.

"What?" Sasha asked.

"I said it's about fucking time."

"Just follow me," she said with more confidence than she felt. "I'll take care of everything."

"Oh fuck that," Manny said. He put a hand on her shoulder and moved as if to push in front of her and shield her with his body. Then he grabbed his side, groaned, and staggered back.

"Alright, yeah. You lead the way."

Men.

Tule was up now. She had an arm around her friend and, together, they moved almost as fast as a single elderly person with bad hips. Manny was not much more mobile. Sasha looked back at Roland.

"Where should we meet you?"

"The next street behind this building is called Alma. Take it and go left until you hit a road named Cross Bend. I should be there by the time you arrive."

"What if we can't find a–"

He cut her off: "Not finding a car is not an option. Talking more is not an option. I have to go kill people; you find something with wheels and get Tule in the driver's seat."

Sasha started to say something, but the sirens had drawn very close indeed. She heard several shouts from outside the front of the building. Roland cursed. He'd already gathered up two of the rifles and slung them across his back. He had a large pistol in his left hand. At the sound of the shouting he brought his right hand up to his belly and dug it deep inside his skin. Sasha watched in horror as he tore a heavy, blood-caked weapon out of his gut.

Roland walked up to the front window of the room and fired the weapon once, twice, three times. Its report was deep and bass-y, like the sound of a heavy drum being struck. There was a brief island of quiet, followed by a trio of explosions that rattled the walls of the jail.

"Look," Roland said as he glanced back to her, "I've got to go be a distraction. Find the car. Get to Cross Bend and Alma. I'll be there innn…" he glanced out the window again and shrugged, "ten, maybe eleven minutes."

"Ok, should–" Sasha started to ask.

"Talking time is done," Tule's flat voice interrupted. "He moves. We move. Now."

She pulled her friend toward the door. There would have been something almost comical about the agonizing slowness with which they actually moved. But the gesture had its intended effect. Sasha took Manny by the hand. She let Tule lead the way the door, but once they were in the hallway the young woman had no idea where to go. Sasha took the lead then and guided her new comrades toward a flashing red Exit sign she knew led to a rear stairwell.

For a brief, passing second she'd been worried that they might encounter other guards or jailers during their flight. That concern proved groundless. Gunfire had torn through the walls of the examination room and ripped apart the interior of the jail. She saw a few gouts of blood by the walls, and one sinister looking pool of it underneath a desk. It all drove an important lesson home for Sasha: bullets don't stop when they miss.

The stairwell was as deserted as the rest of the jail. They hobbled down it as quickly as three wounded people could manage. Sasha stayed in the back, under the instinctive assumption that it'd be best for morale if she didn't rush ahead. Their progress down the stairs was painfully slow, almost every step punctuated by the sound of gunfire out on the street below.

It sounded like a full-scale war had broken out. There was a lot of screaming. Sasha tried not to think too much about which of the nice young Martyrs she'd met in the square were now dying by Roland's hand.

What about Anne? What about Susannah? You're abandoning them. Sasha shook the thoughts clear from her head. There'd be time for self-loathing later.

Tule and Rick reached the bottom floor first. They leaned back against the wall together and caught their breath. Rick was as white as a sheet and looked like he could still barely stand. Tule was doing better but not by a wide margin. When she and Manny hit the bottom floor, he went straight for the exit door. He clearly intended to be the first out, in case anyone had a weapon trained on the door.

Sasha stopped him. That wasn't hard because he was only a little more stable than Tule. She pushed him back, put a hand on the door, and then drew the pistol Roland had given her. She fixed Manny with what she hoped was a firm, fearless look.

"You're in no state to be heroic."

He looked as if he wanted to fight her. But then he looked down to the shaking hand he had pressed onto the sopping wound in his side.

"Yeah, alright. You're down to do the hero stuff, then?"

She nodded.

"Well then, be my guest."

Sasha didn't know how to use a gun. The AmFed banned almost all private firearm ownership. Her grandfather had owned a couple of bolt-action hunting rifles and he'd let Sasha hold them a few times. That was as close as she'd gotten to firearms training. She'd never actually shot the darn things. Once he'd died, her father had sold the guns rather than deal with the hassle (and expense) of a license.

So she burst out onto the street with the pistol held out high in front of her, like she'd seen in movies. It took her a few seconds to realize, sheepishly, that this behavior was more likely to get her gunned down than aid in her defense. Thankfully there'd been no Martyrs watching the rear exit. Sasha waved for the others to follow her out and stashed the pistol under her shirt.

For a few minutes they ran or, rather, hobbled in what seemed like the right direction. The city still rang with the sound of sirens, gunfire, and the occasional concussive blast, but it seemed to be moving away from them. Plano wasn't exactly crowded but there were enough people out on the street to notice the fresh wounds on Tule, Rick, and Manny. No one approached them though. Sasha wasn't sure if they passed unnoticed, but they were able to pass through the city without incident.

Fear and the flight reflex were enough to carry them a few blocks in relative haste. Once they were out of sight of the jail, Rick put up a hand as he slumped back against the wall. Tule continued to hold him up. She was pale, sweaty, and pained-looking. Rick shook and shuddered. His eyes were unfocused and he was clearly in shock.

"He needs to rest," Tule said.

Manny stopped next to them and leaned against the wall as well. He nodded at Tule and then looked back to Sasha.

"Yeah, ditto. I might prefer to lay down and die at this point."

"We need to find a car anyway," Tule said, as she helped lower Rick down to sit against the wall. "If I carry him for much longer I'm going to drop."

Sasha realized everyone was looking at her.

"Is that…my job?"

Manny looked mortified. Tule looked angry. Rick, bless him, was too deep in shock to react.

"Yes," Tule said in a toneless voice that somehow still implied deep disappointment.

"OK then," Sasha said. "When I find the car, I assume you'll know how to hot wire it?"

Tule laughed. It wasn't a nice laugh.

"If you're hiding a real nice deck somewhere in that silly head of yours, or you find a car that's older than my dad, maybe. Otherwise we're going to need something with keys in it."

"What... So I'm supposed to just carjack someone?"

Tule stared dead-eyed at her. Manny gave a pained, helpful smile.

"I mean, you've got a gun..." he said.

Sasha felt the heat rise in her again. *Why not? I've given up every other principle I have today. I might as well commit armed robbery.* The guilt stung her guts, but not as badly as it should have. Perhaps she was still numb from watching Dr. Brandt and Marigold die. *Or maybe it's because I killed Alexander. Maybe I'm evil now, and this is what that feels like.*

There was no time to mull the possibilities. Sasha left Manny and the others to catch their breath and darted down an alley toward a larger street that sounded like it might have traffic. She passed two parked cars and looked inside with the vain hope that, just maybe, someone might have left their keys behind.

It was to no avail. Sasha soon found herself on the cracked and shell-pocked asphalt of Alma Road. The buildings on either side of this stretch of street had taken significant damage during the Heavenly Kingdom's birth pains. There were no people out on the sidewalks, or visible in the windows. Anyone alive had probably hunkered down to avoid the shooting. There was still traffic on the road though. Three trucks and a dented, fume-spewing white Sedan shot by her at the speed of wartime traffic.

Sasha drew her gun, looked at it, and then hurriedly stashed it inside her blouse again when she realized how dumb that had been. *Godly women do not carry guns.* A series of four loud booms sounded in the distance. Sasha didn't know enough about weaponry to guess what those had been, but she knew they had something to do with Roland. *People are dying so I can find us a car and get everyone to safety.*

She started walking down the street, face pointed toward oncoming traffic, hands waving above her head in the international gesture for "Oh God, please help me!" Two more cars zoomed past without even slowing to check on her. It was odd how that shocked her after everything else she'd seen in the Heavenly Kingdom. "The faithful protect and support each other," Pastor Mike had claimed. But not, it seemed, when a half-human monster was on a rampage through their city.

That helped to abate her guilt at least. Or it did right up until the moment a familiar janky brown truck rumbled to a stop next to her.

"S'cuse me, ma'am, do you need..." She turned around and the man's face lit up in surprise, "Miss Sasha?"

It was Darryl, the kindly old foreman who'd driven her to the House of Miriam on her first day in the Kingdom. *Was that really only days ago?* It seemed like years. Sasha felt like an old woman, even though she was just on the edge of eighteen.

"Are you hurt?" He slammed the car into park and opened his door, "One sec', I got a first aid kit in the back. Where'd you get hit?"

Sasha looked down at her chest and realized she looked like she'd been badly injured. The blood wasn't hers, of course, but Darryl couldn't have known that. He thought she was hurt, and he was trying to help. *Am I really going to rob a Good Samaritan?*

She was. Sasha waited until Darryl had closed the door, grabbed his medical kit, and turned toward her. Then she drew her pistol and leveled it at his weathered, grease-stained, and now thoroughly surprised face.

"Wha–"

"I need your truck," she said.

Darryl dropped the medical kit and put both his palms out.

"Whoa now, girl, alright. Why don't you just put that gun down? Darryl ain't gonna hurt you. I'll take you anywhere you need to go. Let's just be real calm, real slow about all this. Did somebody hurt y–"

"I need your truck."

It was so hard to keep her voice even. So hard to do this cruel thing to a man who'd only been kind to her. Sasha could feel white hot tears stream down her face. *I must look like a crazy person,* she thought. *Maybe that will help.*

"Now, Miss Sasha," Darryl said. "I'ma guess you don't know how to drive a truck. Mine ain't autonomous. It's old, stick shift. Please, why don't you let me take you where you need to go..."

Sasha's mind raced. It was the same species of nervousness that had always gripped her during major exams and college admissions essays. She ran through and discarded a dozen different courses of action in her head. *What if he won't give me the keys? What if he takes another step forward? What if–*

He moved. It started with a single glance. Darryl's eyes darted toward the driver's-side door of his truck. She almost didn't catch it. But for some reason, the gesture rose goose pimples on the back of her neck and forearms.

"I need your truck."

Her voice was cold, strong, firm. Darryl nodded at her. His body posture stayed the same. But his eyes changed. There was something hard and haunted in them now.

"Alright, Miss Sasha, I'm just gonna reach in here for my keys..."

He took a step back and moved toward the door. The bottom fell out of Sasha's gut, and she screamed at him to stop.

"DON'T MAKE ANOTHER MOVE!"

He dove for the door, pulled it open, and reached a hand down beside the driver's seat. Sasha saw a flash of metal in his hand and she opened fire. She wasn't sure how many times she pulled the trigger, but soon the gun was empty. Sasha watched as Darryl stumbled back into the truck and then slid to the ground. Most of her shots had gone wide, very wide. She'd shattered two of the truck's windows and put four or five rounds into the vehicle's body. But at least one had hit Darryl right in his throat. A kill shot.

He slumped to the ground, gagged on blood, and jerked like an electrified marionette. Part of her wanted to run to him, to hold him while he died and say she was sorry. Then she saw the gun at his feet. It didn't dissipate her guilt, after all she'd drawn on him first, but at least at least she hadn't shot and killed an unarmed man. She'd killed an armed man.

An armed man who only ever helped me.

Sasha slumped against the hood of the truck and lost herself in a storm of sobs. She didn't realize she'd dropped her gun until it hit the asphalt with a dull clank. She couldn't control her hands or her breathing. Her frantic sobbing had robbed all the air from her lungs. Her legs weakened and she started to stumble to the ground when a pair of warm, semi-strong arms caught her from behind.

"Hey, hey. It's alright. It's alright.

Manny.

"It's OK. You're going to be OK."

Her world went black for a little while. Sasha felt Manny lift her up, heard the sound of the truck's engine rumble back to life. But she couldn't see, and she couldn't move, and she couldn't stop crying. Time lost any sort of meaning. When she came back to herself they were in motion. Manny sat next to her, and Rick next to him. Tule drove. Sasha's eyes were drawn to Manny. He held Darryl's pistol in his left hand. She couldn't help but stare at the four spots of dried blood on the silver slide.

"Are you alright, Sasha?" Manny asked. His question passed through her ears without hitting her mind.

Sasha couldn't stop staring at Darryl's blood. *I did that. I ended him.* She'd ended two men today. She felt no guilt about Alexander, but that was almost more disturbing. It seemed impossible that she'd been a pampered suburban girl less than a month ago. Now she was a murderer. *Whoever sheds human blood, by humans shall their blood be shed.* Sasha felt as if a thick cloud of doom had fallen on her shoulders.

The truck veered off to the right and slammed to a sudden stop. Sasha was flung forward onto the back of Tule's seat. A trio of vehicles zoomed past them, speeding in the opposite direction like several bats fleeing the same hell. Sasha realized, with a moment's focus, that there was an awful lot of traffic heading away from them as fast as possible.

"Cunt!" Tule cursed and fought with the stick shift. The truck lurched forward again and made it back onto the road for a few seconds. Then another speeding car roared into the oncoming lane and she was forced to veer off to the shoulder again.

The sounds of gunfire grew louder. Sasha heard the thrum of helicopter blades too, a second before one buzzed right over their heads. It looked like a military vehicle, painted matte black and laden with weapons. Sasha watched as it zoomed ahead and rose up over a pair of high-rise apartment buildings near the horizon line. There was a loud "krump" sound and black smoke billowed from the side of the craft. It spun around drunkenly in the air for one very long second before slamming into the roof of one of the high-rises.

The resultant blast rocked the truck. Tule veered left and right around a pothole and another speeding truck, respectively. Her knuckles were white; her jaw was clenched. Sasha could see Tule's eyes in the rearview mirror. She looked terrified and angry at the same time. Rick moaned in pain with every shake and jostle. Manny closed his eyes, shook his head, and muttered something low under his breath.

"Are we close?" Sasha asked Manny. He squinted and looked out at the road for a second.

"I mean," he shrugged, "yeah? Probably? I'm going to guess Roland's close to the explosions. And also causing them."

Smoke now dominated the horizon, which grew less horizon-y and more imminent with each passing second. In spite of all that, Sasha's eyes kept being drawn back to the gun in Manny's hand and the dry red-brown stains on the slide. *That was a good man's blood,* she thought. *How did it come to this?*

"Hey. Jesus girl."

It was Tule. Sasha looked up to the rearview mirror and locked eyes with the other woman.

"Buck the fuck up, chica," Tule said. For the first time, Sasha heard real anger and not just cold indifference in her voice. The other woman continued. "My best friend was just shot to pieces. My lover is bleeding out. And you're all fucked up because you gunned down some Christo-fascist shitfuck. Suck your heart into your guts. I don't know where you came from, girl, but you're in a hard-ass part of the world now. It's time to fortify."

Fortify.

Sasha held onto that word like a life preserver. *Fortify. Survive. Then you can lose your head in tears and shame.*

"OK," she nodded. She started to apologize, but was interrupted when the truck screeched to another sudden halt and threw everyone forward. Sasha's head hit the front seat again and her world dissolved into stars.

"SHIT!" Tule cried. Something rammed the rear of the truck. Sasha lost all orientation to reality. When her head and eyes cleared, the first thing she saw was Tule, nursing a broken nose. Blood poured down her face. Manny seemed intact. Sasha looked behind them and saw that a small sedan had dashed itself against the bed of their truck. It must have been following right behind when Tule hit the brakes. Sasha swung her eyes front to see why they'd stopped.

She saw Roland.

He stood maybe ten feet in front of the truck's hood. That arm-razor of his was extended again, but the blade was cracked and half shattered. His other hand held some sort of large black assault rifle he hadn't been carrying in the jail. The pistol-grip grenade launcher he'd been carrying was still with him, but he'd holstered it in an open hole in his belly.

The left side of his cheek had been ripped away. Most of his hair was burnt off and Sasha made out at least one clear bullet hole in his forehead. There might have been more: all the caked-on blood and gore made it hard to discern. His clothing had mostly been shot, burned, or torn away. The dominant colors on his body were red and black, with a few horrible spots of white where bone shone through in the open air.

The city behind him was all smoke and fire. Emergency lights from several vehicles blinked madly in the miasma, but there were no Martyrs or emergency workers visible. At least, none that were standing. Sasha saw several terribly still bodies lying among the piles of rubble.

Roland staggered toward the truck and flung the passenger's side door open. He slumped into the seat, bringing with him an overpowering stink of blood and fire. He leaned back in his seat and took three long breaths. And then he spoke.

"The way ahead's pretty clear," he said. "But you might want to hang a right and then take a left. Avoid the traffic."

Tule nodded, and the truck jerked forward again.

The drive out was so easy it scared Sasha. In fact, it seemed to scare everyone but Roland. Manny's knuckles grew whiter and whiter as they navigated their way out of the old Metroplex. Tule's expression didn't change, but her body shook with nervous energy and her jaw was set so tight that the veins on her neck bulged from the strain. It was a mercy that Rick was unconscious by that point.

Convoys of military vehicles rolled past them, sometimes escorting ambulances and other emergency vehicles, sometimes bringing more soldiers to the chunk of the city Roland had devastated. Sasha's heart leapt up into her throat every single time, but somehow no one stopped their truck.

Roland assured them all that it would be fine. ("I kicked their asses so hard it'll take 'em an hour to find their cheeks.") His only discomfort came once they left the zone of active danger. He seemed to deflate then.

After a half hour on the road, Roland's wounds had mostly healed. The new skin that grew back underneath seemed weirdly dark compared to the skin above it. Roland scratched at it in irritation and then, as casually as if he'd been tossing an apple core, he ripped off his face in one smooth motion and tossed the bloody skin out the window.

"Jesus, dude," Manny said, disgusted. "Could you have waited until we weren't all in the car?"

Sasha stared in shock. Her hands started to tremble and she felt the urge to vomit. But she fought it down, and forced her stomach to an uneasy calm. *You've seen worse than this now*, and that was true. She looked back at Roland and forced herself to take in his new face, which she guessed was really his old face. Neither iteration of him had been exactly handsome. She watched, in queasy fascination, as he picked the rest of the white skin from his hands and tossed it out the window. When he'd finished he glanced up at Sasha.

"What?" he asked. "Please tell me you're not racist. This'd be a very bad time for you to be racist."

"She's not racist, dude," Manny said. "You just ripped your skin off. That freaks people out."

"Oh," said Roland. "Right, sorry."

"It's OK," she said. "This is just my first time seeing someone rip off their own skin."

"First," Roland grunted, "but probably not last."

Sasha didn't have the guts to question him. So she kept quiet for the rest of the ride. So did most of the other passengers. For a long time, the only sounds inside the truck were Rick's unconscious moans and Roland's occasional directions to Tule. He led them through under-populated neighborhoods and around checkpoints, past blackened buildings and wrecks of military vehicles destroyed during the Heavenly Kingdom's first great advance. Sasha was surprised at the emptiness of most of the city. She began to understand why Manny called this place ciudad de muerta.

It took them two hours to escape the city sprawl and finally make their way out onto open plains. They avoided the main highway that linked Dallas to Waco, and instead spider-webbed their way across a series of farm roads. Every few minutes they'd roll past the bones of a rural town. Every town out here seemed abandoned, as dead and dry as the acres of yellow grass that swallowed them up.

A little before dark they rolled over a decrepit bridge across a dry river bed. A bullet-riddled sign identified this area as "Basque County." Roland put a hand on Tule's shoulder and pointed toward a big metal barn on the horizon.

"Take us up there. We should probably stop for the night."

"What?" Tule spoke up. "Why? We could be at Rolling Fuck in an hour."

Roland shook his head. "We got two routes back to the city. Either we find the main highway and deal with Kingdom patrols or we keep riding these country roads. That'll take at least another two or three hours, and a lot of time off-road. In the dark. There's no better recipe for cracking an axle or blowing a tire."

Tule fumed. But she rolled the truck up and through a gap in what had once been the fence line of a farm. There were a lot of farm houses around them, stretched out across acres and acres of fields and pecan orchards. They all looked abandoned, devoid of light, half-reclaimed by vegetation. The barn Roland led them to was just as empty. There were large holes in the sheet metal roof and chunks of the metal walls had been peeled away for scrap metal. The underlying structure had been built from metal girders though. It seemed solid.

They got out of the truck. Roland helped Tule carry her lover across the last few yards of field and into the old barn. The innards of the building were dusty. Rusted tools hung from the wall and boxes of assorted goods littered the floor. Some of them had been ripped open by scavengers but most looked like they'd sat unmolested since the property had been abandoned.

Manny found an old couch inside. Roland and Tule helped Rick onto it. Then Roland walked off into the middle of the barn and started to root around in boxes. He came back a minute later with a load of canned goods in one arm and a handle of brown liquor in the other. He set the whole lot down on the ground next to the couch, held up a can labeled "WATER" in big red letters, and then punched his finger through the top of the can. He handed it to Tule and she helped Rick drink. He was semi-conscious now. Sasha thought there might be a bit more color in his cheeks.

Roland opened three more cans, one of water and two filled with some sort of gloopy beef stew. He ripped the aluminum tops open with his bare fingers and then passed them around. Sasha was still too deep in the throes of depression and adrenaline dumpage to have any kind of appetite. The brown-gray color of the stew didn't help with that. But Manny insisted she take a gulp and, as soon as the food hit her tongue, Sasha realized she was starving. She took two more deep gulps of the salty, mushy mass before passing it along to Tule.

The crew ate and rehydrated without conversation, although not in silence. The sounds of gulping and lip-smacking filled the barn for a few minutes. Roland didn't join in the eating. Instead, he popped open the liquor bottle and drained it dry over the course of about ninety seconds. The big man closed his eyes, a smile crept up onto his features, and he gave a deep contented sigh. When the food was almost gone he stood up and staggered back into the piles of gear to grab two more bottles. These ones were filled with an off-yellow liquid. He sat one down in between Manny and Sasha and immediately began to guzzle the second.

Manny glanced at Sasha, then at Tule, then down at the bottle. He popped the top and took a belt. Then he offered it to Sasha. *If there ever was a time to dive into drinking, it's the day I killed two people.* Sasha took the bottle and stared at it for a second. The label said "Talisker," and identified it as a product of Scotland. The bottle itself was covered in dust.

"Hey, Roland," she asked, suddenly curious, "did you know this place would have food and water? And alcohol?"

Roland paused draining his second bottle and fixed Sasha with his strange blue eyes. He looked tired for the first time since she'd met him. Sasha wasn't sure if that was due to the rampage he'd just carried out or her question.

"I've been here before," he half-mumbled. "Years ago. Back before this whole chunk of dirt was as much of a shithole as it is now."

"Wait, did you used to live here?" Manny asked.

"I don't know," Roland shrugged.

"What do you mean you don't know?" Sasha asked. "You clearly know this farm."

He shrugged and gave a vague wave with his free hand.

"I have memories of this place. Bright lights at night, people dancing, drugs and wine and people and songs. I have memories of packing supplies into boxes. Burying ammunition." He nodded toward the still-locked front door of the barn, "I remember locking that thing up. But I don't remember why, exactly. I might have lived here. It might have belonged to a friend. Either way, I feel like the last time I was here was back before the Revolution."

"His mind is fulla holes," Manny explained. "Something happened to him a few years back. He remembers pieces of who he is, what he's done. But not everything."

Tule kicked Sasha gently in the hip. She gestured to the bottle of whiskey.

"If you're not drinking pass the bottle. Some of us have grieving to do."

On impulse, Sasha took a pull from the bottle. She started to hand it over to Tule, but then the taste hit her and she gagged. It was like someone had lit a fire in her throat, one that tasted of burning peat. She coughed and hacked for several seconds while Tule and Roland laughed. Once she'd regained her breath, Sasha finally handed off the bottle.

"You'll get better at it," the woman said. Her lips twisted up into what might have been a real smile. "Whiskey's an acquired taste, like cigars. And anarchy."

Tule took a very deep pull and sighed in satisfaction. She handed the bottle off to Manny, and started gently petting Rick's face. The wounded man was asleep, but he seemed much healthier than he had been a half hour earlier.

"How are you doing, Sasha?" Manny asked. His eyes met hers, and Sasha saw deep concern in his gaze.

"I'm...fine," she said, not really meaning it.

"She's all fucked up over the guy she killed for the truck," Tule grunted. "You shouldn't be. Fucker picked the wrong side."

"So did I," Sasha tried to keep the anger out of her voice. "At first. Darryl was a good man. He didn't deserve to die."

"Neither did Marigold," said Tule.

"Neither did Major Peron," Manny added in a quiet voice. "They hung him on the day you and I met."

"The whole world's full of good, dead people," said Tule. "My advice? Don't cry over someone you shot in self-defense. That's a karmic freebie."

"The guy had a gun," Manny added, "it seems like you just did what you had to do."

Roland was quiet through all this. He kept drinking, but his pace had slowed. His face took on a dark cast and he slumped down into his chair. He seemed to collapse in on himself a little.

"Look, chica," Tule said. There was a slight drunken slur to her words now. "I know I gave you a hard time, and it was dumb-as-fuck a'you to move to this 'Kingdom.' But I give you credit for breaking free, and for helping us escape. You might be a little dumb. But you aren't bad people in my book. Don't beat yourself up over doing what you had to do."

There was quiet for a little while. Manny passed the bottle to Sasha. She took another gulp and managed to hold it down this time. Tule nodded in approval when Sasha passed the whiskey on. Sasha found her eyes drawn, once more, to Darryl's gun. It was tucked into Tule's waistband.

Roland cleared his throat and gave a loud, phlegmy cough. Sasha looked back at him.

"You didn't ask me for an opinion," he said, "but since everyone else is weighin' in I might as well: There ain't nothing wrong with feeling bad about murder. Even justified murder. But personally, I don't think that's what's fucking you up."

"What do you mean?" she asked.

He drained the last of the whiskey bottle and tossed it off into the darkness. It landed with a clank.

"I got real good senses, y'know. I can't turn 'em off. So I heard your heart rate. I smelled the neurotransmitters running through your synapses. I can taste the guilt wafting off you. But that's not the only thing I taste."

He locked his unsteady eyes on hers. Sasha stared into the cold blue of his pupils. A chill ran down her spine. Sweat beaded on the back of her neck. When he spoke next, his voice was barely above a whisper.

"Back at the jail, when you crushed that guy's skull with a helmet. You enjoyed yourself. You liked it."

Sasha broke his gaze. She stared down at her lap and struggled to find a reply. But there was nothing for her to say. Roland was right.

Chapter 22

Manny.

Rolling Fuck was as bright, shiny, and chaotic as it had been when he'd left. But Manny could see a real change among the citizens themselves. Gone were the lounging crowds of half-naked people. Instead of the perpetual party, a war camp spread out around the great superstructure of the city.

Hundreds of men and women were busy donning armor, applying war paint, and checking over stacks of weaponry. Manny saw crates of guided mortars, piles of rocket launchers, boxes of high-velocity ammunition, and enough firearms to equip every citizen a dozen times over. There was no discernible Rolling Fuck "uniform" that Manny could see. Some of the city's warriors wore powered body armor, painted in garish colors and bedecked with various quotations. "Fuck yer day" seemed particularly popular. Many of them wore pieces of pop-culture costumery mixed in with their gear. Manny recognized Darth Vader's helmet, Hellboy's Red Right Hand, and a surprisingly number of people with Mickey Mouse's face spray painted on their chest armor.

An equal number of Fuckians wore no armor at all. Some of them were dressed in their normal flowing lounge garments. The weapons they wore were the only signs that they had plans beyond debauchery. Others were naked, or mostly so. He saw one man wearing the helmet of a Greek hoplite and carrying two Viking axes on his back. He saw a woman with a Dragunov rifle on her back, an old German Stahlhelm on her head, and Ottoman mirror armor on her chest. She waved at them, excited. It took Manny a second to recognize Topaz's face under the helmet.

"They're here! They're–"

She stopped. Tule had stopped too. She cast her face down. Manny could see the shimmer of tears on her cheeks. A crowd gathered around them. In a few seconds, they were encircled by dozens of heavily armed post-humans in a dizzying array of war costumes. Skullfucker Mike, a good head taller than anyone else in the crowd, pushed his way to the front and ran up to embrace Tule. Manny was surprised when she started to sob. The big man held her tight but looked to Roland.

"What happened?"

Roland gave him a look that said, "You know damn well what happened." But then he spoke anyway.

"Your friend didn't make it."

Skullfucker Mike's jaw went tight. His eyes bulged and he held onto Tule a little tighter. Manny thought back to the night they'd spent in Brainbreakers, and the things he'd said about Marigold. Manny hadn't really known the woman at all, but he could tell Mike had cared deeply for her. He looked around at the crowd closing in on them, the dozens of half-human god-monsters with helpless rage carved onto their faces.

"What. Happened." Mike demanded.

Roland opened his mouth to speak, closed it, and ran a hand over his bald head. He opened his mouth again, managed to squeeze out an "I..." before he slumped his shoulders and hung his head.

"I wasn't fast enough," he said, finally. "They had better gear, newer suits than I'd expected."

Skullfucker Mike stared at him. Behind him, Topaz slid down to the ground and buried her head in her knees. Murmurs swept the crowd. And then Sasha spoke up.

"Your friend saved my life."

Mike looked over and seemed to notice her for the first time.

"And who are you?" His voice was not unfriendly. It wasn't exactly warm, either.

"My name is Sasha," she said, her voice clearly on the edge of a sob. She looked from Mike, to Tule, to Topaz, to the crowd, and then back to Manny. He saw panic in her eyes, barely held in check by a cage of steely resolve.

"I...made a mistake. I left my home for the Kingdom. I thought it was the right thing to do. I met Marigold while I was there and she helped me see how wrong I'd been." She pointed to Roland. "I tried to help him free your people. We all tried. But they were ready for us. They shot him," she gestured to Roland, "...they shot him a lot. They had us all dead to rights. And then Marigold, I don't know how, but she got a gun. She shot two of them. And then they shot her. She died saving us."

The silence that followed was louder than any artillery barrage Manny had ever sat through. Finally, Skullfucker Mike nodded at her. There were tears in his eyes and, Manny soon realized, tears on every face in the crowd. Some people fell to their knees. Others embraced and held their friends. One voice, hoarse and heavy with pain, howled out in anguish. It was met by another voice, and then another and then another as Fuckian after Fuckian tilted their head back and roared their grief out to the empty blue of the Texas sky.

Rolling Fuck preferred to mourn through activity. The wailing and gnashing of teeth over Marigold didn't stop the city's medics from taking Rick and Tule to whatever building served as their equivalent of a clinic. Topaz stayed behind with the gathering crowd of mourners while Skullfucker Mike gathered up Manny, Sasha, and Roland.

"There'll be time to process later," he'd said as much to himself as to them. "There's a war council soon, and they'll be wanting to debrief you."

"Fine," Roland said, "but I'm stopping at the bar first. I need some opium and some goddamn tequila."

Manny expected Skullfucker Mike to be angered by that, given the circumstances. But the other chromed man just nodded and said, "I could use a drink or nine myself."

They headed for the lift underneath the Main Roller. Manny started to prepare himself for the meeting with this "war council," whatever that term meant in a place like this. *Whatever happens, it's bound to be weird.* They reached the lift. Skullfucker Mike opened the door and gestured for everyone to enter.

And so, less than an hour after arriving back in the City of Wheels, Manny, Sasha, and Roland found themselves seated around the same redwood table where Manny and Reggie had first met Nana Yazzie and Donald Farris. The room was more crowded this time around, with two new people he didn't recognize. One was a shirtless man with writhing snake tattoos across his chest and a pair of chaps that did nothing at all to cover up his junk. It didn't help that the man's legs were spread as wide as possible. He seemed to be deliberately showing off.

Manny looked away and found himself staring at a very tall, very muscular young-seeming woman with a mohawk made from thick chrome spikes. She had light brown skin, and her cheeks were covered in several long, thick, diagonal scars. The woman's eyes had no pupils. They looked gray at first, until Manny realized that they were actually just filled with static. When Manny finally pulled his gaze away from her, he was met with the biggest surprise of the day.

DeShawn Clark was seated two chairs down from Nana Yazzie.

"Major Clark!"

"Manny," the Major's lips cracked open into a wide-mouthed grin. The left side of his face was still covered in hemostatic gauze, and the edges of the skin around the gauze looked black and burnt. His right hand was a smooth, angry pink color, a sure sign it had been severed and regrown in the recent past. Major Clark was bloodied, but unbowed.

"It's damn good to see you, Manny. I can't tell you how proud I was to hear you'd volunteered for this mission."

"Mr. Peron..." Manny started to say, but Major Clark put up his hand.

"I know," he said.

Donald Farris "ahem'd," which Manny took as a gentle reminder that now was not the time for personal business. The old Brit gestured first to the man with the writhing snake tattoos.

"This is Jim Shannon," he said. "He heads up a small mercenary outfit."

"I'm the guy who roped Roland into helping," Jim said with a wink.

"And this cheery lass," Donald pointed to the woman with the chromehawk, "is Kishori. She's been the city's elected War Leader for the last three years."

"And who might this young lady be?" Nana Yazzie asked, nodding at Sasha. The old woman stood and stepped forward to greet Sasha with a hug. Sasha tensed up. She looked scared to return the embrace. So Nana Yazzie backed off and favored the girl with a warm smile.

"I'm sorry, child. I didn't mean to pressure you. I'm just happy you're here with us."

Sasha relaxed at that, but she still didn't step forward.

"Her name's Sasha," said Roland. "She used to be with the Kingdom. Now she's not." He paused a second, considered his words and added, "She beat one of them to death with a helmet."

"Oh my. Oh dear..." Nana Yazzie tsked and shook her head. "I'm so sorry, Sasha. That must have been a terrible experience for you."

"She enjoyed it!" Jim said with a harsh bark of a laugh. "I'm sure Roland smells it too. Isn't that right, hon? You loved killing whoever-the-fuck you killed, and you feel shitty about that. Well, let me s–"

"You'll stop right now or you'll leave this room."

Nana Yazzie's voice was firm, but devoid of any anger or heat. To Manny's shock, Jim stopped. The post-human nodded and said, "I apologize, Sasha. That was a real dick move." And then he lowered his eyes, just a little, in contrition.

Nana Yazzie offered Sasha a seat and then busied herself in the corner making Sasha a cup of tea. Once that was done, and they were all settled in, Nana sat back down and looked to Manny.

"What happened?" is all she asked.

Manny started talking. He told her, and by extension the whole table, everything that had happened since he and Roland left Rolling Fuck. He told them about their trouble with the checkpoints on the way into town. He walked them through the intake process, his and Roland's few days as Martyrs-in-training and what he'd seen in the few sections of Plano he'd been allowed to haunt during his time there. The woman with the chromehawk was particularly interested in what he and Roland had to say about the Kingdom's preferred assault tactics.

"They're not gonna be kicking in doors and fighting house-to-house," Roland explained. "They'll just start shelling at the first sign of resistance. They don't care about civilian casualties."

When Manny explained what the Kingdom had been doing at the old Tesla factory, almost everyone looked horrified. Donald Farris spat at the ground. Most of the others cursed, or at least shook their heads. Nana Yazzie teared up. Jim, though, seemed almost enthusiastic about the revelation.

"Fascinating," he muttered just loud enough for Manny to hear.

Once everyone was caught up, the table fired off a few questions at him and more toward Roland. They seemed mostly curious as to what they'd been able to glean about the number of recruits in the Heavenly Kingdom. Manny didn't have much useful there. So he shut up, leaned back and let Roland give the answers. An awkward silence descended on the table after a few minutes.

"Well," Donald Farris said, finally, "I suppose we were fools to hope for much more than what you got. As it stands we're left grappling to try and account for the sheer number of men the Kingdom has deployed to assault Austin."

"Twenty thousand martyrs," Jim spoke up. "Give or take a grand."

Manny's blood went cold. The SDF, at its height, hadn't been more than six thousand fighters. And those were spread out across the serried battlegrounds of North Texas. The whole Free City of Austin didn't have more than five thousand people in its full-time Defense Corps. Twenty thousand men was...

"Impossible," he said. "That's fucking impossible."

"I'd be inclined to agree with you, kid," said Jim, "if my own men hadn't double-confirmed the count for us. The Kingdom has already marshaled half of that force on the outskirts of DFW, near Lancaster. They'll be in Waco tomorrow if no one stops them. Hell, they could be pounding Austin with artillery by dark."

Donald Farris nodded. "Mr. Shannon here," gesturing to Jim, "has agreed to lend a hand, along with several dozen of his mercenaries. Add that to the warriors of Rolling Fuck, and we've got seven-hundredish post-humans. It's large enough force to hold Waco. And badly bloody their nose."

"But," Kishori spoke for the first time. She had a deep, gravelly voice that sounded like she'd been eating cigarettes for the last ten years. "Rolling Fuck is not in the business of volunteering for our own Vietnams. My people aren't signing up for a war."

"I can guarantee our presence on the battlefield for up to forty-eight hours. Enough time for vengeance," she continued. "After that, you're herding cats."

"Is that a problem?" Manny asked. "I mean, I saw Roland lay waste to half a city. Six-hundred of him..."

"There's only one of him," Kishori said.

Jim nodded in agreement and fixed Manny with his uncomfortable gray eyes. "See kid," he said, "me or any one of Rolling Fuck's warriors is good for a few dozen normal troops in a straight fight. More if we're talking half-trained partisans. But nobody's like Roland."

Manny looked over to Roland. The big man seemed distinctly uncomfortable with all the attention. He stared down at his hands, which seemed to be occupied with tearing up a paper drink coaster.

"The Martyrs have a lot of half-trained partisans, but they've also got tanks, artillery, suits... The resources of a nation state. Or close enough. Rolling Fuck can hold that off for a while, but without Roland the best they can do is delay the inevitable.

"Now WITH Roland," Jim continued, "this is a two-hour fight, tops. We set up our troops in some little chunk of the city and start dropping mortars and rockets on their vanguard. They pull up, encircle us, and start deploying their artillery to bomb us to Kingdom Come. Then, when they're good and packed together, we drop Roland on their asses."

Kishori nodded. "Yes," she said, "he'll hit them and disrupt their whole order of battle while our cavalry rolls around to their flanks and charges. That should be enough to make them panic. Then we chase them down until they lose cohesion."

Roland's head stayed down. He didn't speak. Manny looked from him, to Jim, to Nana Yazzie and Donald Farris.

"So what's the problem?" Manny asked. "If Roland and Rolling Fuck are all-in, this should be a walk in the park."

"Roland," Nana Yazzie said, "prefers not to fight."

"But I just saw him..."

"You just saw me break a long streak of not killing people." Roland's voice sounded odd, hollow and dry, and utterly without any of the mirth or mischief Manny had come to expect from the chromed man.

"I did that to get my memories back, Manny," he shrugged. "And I did it for you, because you're my buddy. But I got no stake in Austin."

"But you know what the Heavenly Kingdom will do if they take the city!" Manny protested. "You've seen what they did to Plano. They'll do that to millions of decent people if they can. You have the power to stop that. You're telling me you won't?"

Roland met his eyes and just said, "Yes."

"You son of a bitch," Manny felt the anger well up inside him. It merged with his grief over Major Peron's death, Oscar's death, and his rage at the Heavenly Kingdom, the Martyrs, and every other group of assholes who'd helped turn his young life into a parade of nightmares.

"You absolute son of a bitch. You fucking coward!"

Manny didn't think. Couldn't think. He pulled back his fist and swung as hard as he could for Roland's face. The chromed man didn't move, didn't even blink. Manny hit him right on the nose. He was softer than Manny would have guessed. It didn't feel any different from punching a normal human. Manny swung again and again, until he felt something crack in his knuckles. He cried out from the pain and pulled back to nurse his wounded hand.

For a few seconds Manny forgot about the rest of the room. He closed his eyes and let his thoughts dissolve into an ocean of physical pain. The agony of his broken hand was almost soothing. It was better than thinking about Mr. Peron. It was better than thinking about Alejandro, or Oscar. It was better than thinking about his soon-to-be-shattered home.

Manny felt a hand on his shoulder. The sensation pulled him out of his spiraling thoughts. He looked up and saw Nana Yazzie. She smiled her sad smile and said, "Manny, everyone here understands your pain."

"Not me," said Jim, "I've never been a big fan of Austin. Too damn–"

Roland threw his empty pint glass at the other post-human's face. It shattered on impact, embedding shards deep into Jim's cheeks and forehead. His head snapped back, and he blinked in shock a few times.

"Sorry," he said, "I deserved that."

"And I deserved that," Roland said to Manny. "No hard feelings. I get why you're pissed. But kid, you've got to understand something. Austin is home to you. To me it's just another city, held by just another side. Half my remaining memories are of one cause or another asking me to go murder in their name. I'm fuckin' done with it."

Manny looked to Major Clark. The SDF officer's eyes were lit by a familiar cold fire. He spoke in a tone of barely controlled anger.

"That is your right, of course. You can choose to leave, just as I will choose to fight and die. I wonder, what will Manny choose?"

Manny hadn't really settled on that himself. Before he could stumble through his response, Sasha spoke.

"I'll fight," she said. "I don't know much about guns. But I'll do my best."

Roland slumped back in his chair and tossed his arms up in a dramatic show of frustration.

"Et tu, Jesus Girl?"

"I'll fight," Manny said to Major Clark, doing his best to talk over Roland. "I'll choose to fight too."

"This isn't going to work, you know," Roland said. "I'm not going to be shamed into fighting again. It's just not going to fucking happen."

Jim leaned in. He fixed Roland with a look that seemed almost hungry.

"I think it will happen. I think the peculiar arc of your moral compass won't let you leave these kids to die." He seemed surprised by the revelation. "Huh! Fascinating."

"Enough of that," Donald Farris sounded angry. "I won't stand to see this man badgered and pressured into fighting against his will. We might as well dissolve the council for now and reconvene without Roland."

"Good!" Roland stood up and stomped over to the exit. "If that's all you people need from me, I'm going to get good and pissed and start my walk back to Arizona." He flipped his middle finger out at the room and slammed the door behind him as he left.

All eyes turned to Manny.

"I should...probably go talk to him."

"Don't do anything you're not comfortable doing, Emmanuel," Donald said.

"Fuck that," Jim said. "The bastard is on the ropes. Shame him! Shame him good."

As he headed for the exit, Manny looked to Major Clark. The old soldier's one good eye was narrow and focused.

"Manny," he said, "if he didn't want to talk he wouldn't have gone up to the bar. He'd have just left. There's no honor lost in another conversation. Another try."

Roland was three beers in by the time Manny reached him. And knowing Rolling Fuck that could mean he'd already ingested enough acid to kill a large octopus. The chromed mercenary was already wavering in his seat by the time Manny pulled up a seat.

"Hey," Manny said.

"Heeeeeey buddy," Roland replied in a voice that was just...super stoned. "Sorry about getting angry back there." The post-human spun his empty pint-glass around on the bar table. It was a strange sight to see. Manny had gotten so used to seeing Roland as something akin to a Greek God. He certainly wasn't omniscient, or omnipotent, but he was unspeakably powerful and just as irresponsible to leave out around humans.

And yet here he was, fiddling with an empty pint glass like a nervous college freshman standing at the back wall of some house party. Manny felt a surge of sympathy.

"It's OK, man. I actually think I get it," he said. "Like, I've had plenty of chances to join either the SDF or the Austin Defense Forces. I never did. Maybe some of that's because I'm scared. Hell, up until like...a few days ago, my plan was to get the fuck off this continent as soon as I could afford it."

Manny paused and bit his lip. It was an instinctive gesture, his gut's reaction to a sudden burst of self-awareness. Manny hadn't thought about any of this before.

"I dunno," he said. "This shit's been going on basically all my life. I can't remember a time when I wasn't scared of something like this happening. I didn't understand any of it as a kid. But I can remember being seven or eight years old and just being so angry at the soldiers. Even our soldiers. I thought, if all you assholes would just refuse to be led into battle, none of this could happen."

"But you know that's not how it works, right?" Roland asked, as he turned away from Manny and waved at the bartender.

"We love this war shit. At least some of us do, those of us who are... Oh!" The bartender arrived. Roland ordered "a mai-tai mixed with a margarita and one of those, whaddya goddamn call 'em, oh yeah a fuckin' MO-HI-TO."

"Roland," Manny's voice was gentle but firm, "how many beers did you drink before I got here?"

"Not beers," Roland said in a casual voice, "Mushroom rum. Sweet, but not bad." He licked his lips while he watched the bartender work through the Herculean task of crafting his requested beverage.

"Roland," Manny said. And the chromed man turned back to him.

"Ah, sorry. It's been too long a stretch of sober for me. I got excited. What the fuck was I saying?"

"That war is fun."

"Oh, yeah. As long as you don't think *you'll* die. That's why all throughout history you had so many generals and politicians kickin' off conflicts. Because they felt safe, and when you're pretty sure you'll live, war is an absolute hoot. That's the problem with me and fighting."

"The problem is you like it too much?"

Roland grabbed his hand. The chromed man moved so fast Manny didn't even see the motion-blur. Roland's hand was just wrapped around his wrist, immovable. He squeezed, hard enough that it hurt. Roland's eyes bulged out and stared into Manny with a manic intensity that was frightening.

"I. Fuckin'. Love. It. It's like sex on heroin and bungee jumping and getting rammed in the ass and that first shot of liquor you sneak when you're fourteen, all at once and mixed with the best actual battle drugs the most bloated military budget in history could buy."

He loosened his grip and turned half away from Manny.

"That's why I shouldn't do it. Because I'll get carried away, like I got carried away in Dallas. Maybe this time I won't be able to stop when it's time to stop."

Manny kept his eyes on Roland's. The big man turned a little further to the left, but he didn't look away.

"How do you know that your intervention won't make things better?" Manny asked. "Maybe if we can kill enough of the Martyrs their power will be broken forever. Maybe your intervention will be the first step toward making this a more livable part of the globe."

Roland laughed. It started as a low chuckle that then cascaded into a series of rolling, rib-cracking howls. Manny didn't get the joke and couldn't find any humor in his words. So he sat tight until Roland's mirth subsided and the chromed man had recovered enough to explain himself.

"Sorry, sorry," he said between chuckles. "It's just...ah shit, kid, you're too young to know how funny that is." Roland straightened up and wiped a tear from his eye. "See, you're talking about me the exact same way people talked about the U.S. Military back when I was a kid."

The bartender came by and sat down Roland's drink, an enormous jug filled with a multi-hued mix of alcoholic beverages. The post-human took a deep pull from his maitaigarito. Manny took the chance to ask a question.

"I thought you didn't remember anything further back than a few years ago?"

"I don't remember anything clearly," Roland said. "But I do remember bits and pieces. And I remember being a young man and watching the news break in an off-base bar. Some election had gone bad in Bolivia. The president announced he was sending in more soldiers to help keep the peace."

"Did it work?" Manny asked.

"I dunno, kid. What'd your school teach you about Bolivia?"

"That there was a genocide in– oh," Manny said as Roland's point sunk in. "Right."

"Ayep," Roland grunted and took another, deeper gulp from his ridiculous beverage.

They were quiet for a while. Manny took the opportunity to take a long look at Roland. His face held only a few lines around his eyes and lips. And yet he still looked old, positively ancient. There appeared to be a tremendous weight to the man's eyes, accentuated by the deep wrinkles underneath them. It looked as if the chromed man's face was sagging underneath the weight of what he had seen.

"Roland," Manny asked, "do you have any idea where you came from?"

"I think I was born around Mississippi, b–"

"No," Manny interrupted, "not like where you were born. But how you became what you are today. You said you've been disconnected from the Internet for the last ten years. I've got to guess your implants are even older than that. But the way everyone here talks about you, you're still King Shit."

"Oh," Roland said. "Yeah. That. I got no real idea what happened there. I know I was in the Army. I'm pretty sure that's when the tinkering started."

"Sure," said Manny, "but didn't a lot of the Road People start as ex-special forces who went rogue? Why are you special?"

"I got no clear answer to that question, buddy." He smiled as if he'd just remembered something good. "I guess I've got that surgery coming up. Once I get my memories back, I'll let you know what I find out."

Manny laughed too, but his was cold and bitter. "Sure. I'll probably be in a refugee camp at that point. Or dead."

"Damn, kid," Roland said.

"Yeah," Manny said, "I'm really not trying to manipulate you here. It's just–"

"No, I get it," Roland waved him off. "It's fair. You've got every right to be pissed. I just can't..." he trailed off. Manny put a hand on Roland's shoulder. He didn't understand how the post-human felt. How could he? Manny couldn't even conceive of having that kind of power. But he could see why it was a difficult choice.

There was a part of Manny, a dark manipulative chunk of his soul, that knew he was on his way to changing Roland's mind. This was essentially the same strategy he used on the job. You built empathy with people through a combination of shared experiences and regular engagement. That empathy paid dividends when you needed some Lieutenant's approval to cross through a checkpoint. It would pay dividends here if he was careful and consistent.

That's fucked up man, he thought. *You're manipulating your friend into killing a bunch of people.*

"You know what," Manny said, "I'm sorry. I didn't mean to–"

Roland drained the rest of his mug, belched, and looked over at Manny. He looked unsteady, half-conscious. The chromed man put his left hand over Manny's hand while it rested on his shoulder. He fixed Manny with his half-focused eyes and nodded.

"Fuck it," Roland said, "I'll fuckin' help you. I'd be a dick if I didn't. Sasha might do OK, picking up a gun. But you're a damn bullet magnet. Can't let that happen again."

"Thank you," Manny said with a nod. "I know–"

"Don't say anything else, kid. I really don't want to think about what I just promised to do."

Manny found Sasha sitting around a fire pit, outside the city proper, deep in conversation with Donald Farris. Sasha sat on the ground, legs splayed out wide with her butt in the grass. Donald sat in a folding chair. It wasn't cold outside, precisely, but it had cooled off a great deal from the heat of the day. The air held just the barest hint of winter. It was shaping up to be one of those odd September days where Texas seemed on the verge of an actual seasonal shift.

One look at Sasha's face told him she was at least as unsettled as Roland. He didn't want to crowd her so he squatted down on the other side of Donald.

"Emmanuel," the old man's voice was as smooth and rich as Manny remembered from the narration of his documentary. "It's good to see you. Sasha's been telling me her story. She actually just turned to the subject of you."

"Yeah?" Manny asked.

"Yes, she was telling me how she met you and Marigold, and how you both helped her find her way free of the Kingdom."

"Oh," he said, and looked to Sasha. "I never really met Marigold. I didn't realize you knew her well."

Sasha shook her head. "I only knew her a little while. I was just supposed to be administering tests to her. But I couldn't stop her from talking and...she made sense. She made more sense than what was going on out in the Kingdom every day."

Sasha stared down into the fading embers of the fire.

"I feel stupid for ever believing in that place."

"And what do you believe in now?" Donald asked.

"I don't know," she said. "It seems arrogant to decide that God doesn't exist just because I let myself get taken in by a cult."

"Mmm," the old man nodded. "The good news is, you're young. You've got plenty of time to figure things out again." His cheeks turned up into a smile and his face blossomed with wrinkles.

"Now," he looked up at Manny, "what have you been up to, my dear boy?"

"Talking to Roland," Manny said. "He agreed to help, by the way. He's going to fight."

Donald Farris's smile turned into a frown. Manny hadn't been expecting that.

"How did you do it?" he asked in a somber, grave voice.

"We just talked for a while," Manny said. "He explained why he didn't want to fight. It sounded very reasonable..." Manny paused, and then made the choice to lie just a little. "I wasn't trying to change his mind. I didn't ask him to help." That last part was true, at least. "I do feel bad, though. I'm sure he changed his mind because of me."

"Is it really on you if he chooses to fight?" Sasha asked. "I killed two men. Both of those deaths are on me. But you didn't order Roland to do anything."

"No," Donald Farris agreed, "but I doubt Roland would've made the decision to intervene if Manny hadn't pressed."

"That's probably true," Manny admitted.

Donald looked from Manny to Sasha.

"There's a war ritual, peculiar to the men and women and whatevers of this community. I think you'd benefit from seeing it."

"A ritual?" Sasha asked.

"Not a religious one, I assure you. But yes. They call it their war ritual." He extended a hand out to the field around Rolling Fuck. Manny looked out at it for the first time since coming out here and realized that people seemed to be packing up.

"Right now," Donald said, "the citizens are packing up their tents and their RVs and preparing the city for departure. It's moving out with their army. They'll drive that thing," he jerked a thumb in the direction of the City of Wheels, "right up to the damn battlefield. It'll be behind them the whole time they're fighting. I think they stole the idea from the ancient Celts."

"Anyway," he said, "once the city is in position, they'll open up these little boxes that look quite a lot like bee hives and they'll let out a swarm of about a thousand little drones. Those're mostly just facial-recognition cameras attached to wings and a wee engine. They'll record everything and send data on the faces of every enemy fighter to a central computer in the city."

"What good does that do?" Manny asked.

"It gives us a chance to identify those men, or women, so we can scrape their social media profiles and display pictures and videos from their lives, once they die. The whole city, everyone who isn't fighting, turns out to watch that."

"That sounds fucking terrible," Manny said. "What do we gain from watching the home movies of dead men?"

"A memorial."

Manny didn't understand, but he could see that Donald Farris was revving himself up for an involved explanation. He let the old man talk.

“I was a small child when my country invaded Iraq, along with the United States and a few other nations. The war was news, yes. But that’s all it was. Even our own soldiers were more numbers than real people. I’d hear that two Royal Marines had died in a roadside bombing, and it meant less to me than when my neighbor broke his leg slipping down the stairs.”

“War isn’t like that for us,” Manny said, “I don’t know anyone in Austin who hasn’t lost a friend, or family, to the fighting. It affects us all.”

“So it does, my boy. So it does. And if any of our warriors die today, you can bet it’ll effect everyone in this social experiment we call a city. But you didn’t let me finish. The thing that was truly toxic about my childhood knowledge of war, is that it erased the other side. Our boys didn’t do body counts. So there were seldom reports on how many civilians we killed, how many enemy fighters died. That information was out there, but you had to look hard. Most people never did.”

Donald Farris shrugged, and then winced from the motion.

“It’s easy to get people to care about their own soldiers. But if you want to stop wars, or at least make them less common, you’ve got to get people to give a shit about the soldiers on the other side. That, my young friend, is where your people are even worse than my own. You’re close enough to the war to not just feel indifferent about these Martyrs marching off to die. You actively want them to die. That’s understandable. But it’s also poisonous. When you dehumanize others, you become less human yourself.”

Manny nodded, not sure of what to say.

“In my youth,” Donald Farris continued, “the country that occupied this continent was the most powerful nation on earth. They held the keys to the deadliest military machine ever constructed. It was easy to get Americans to support involvement in a thousand little conflicts, because each only required a small fraction of the nation’s military power. It only risked a few American lives. But millions of people around the world died. Women and children and old men and dumb, young boys from Yemen to Turkey to Guatemala. To justify those murders Americans had to make those people less than human. And once they’d done that, it wasn’t such a great jump to do it to their neighbors.”

He stared up at the setting sun, and Manny saw tears in his eyes.

“What you’re going to see tomorrow is the best attempt I’ve seen, so far, to bridge the empathy gap between a people and their foes.”

Chapter 23

Sasha.

Rolling Fuck trundled forward, crunching its way over the Texas plains and leaving a carpet of flattened grass and broken trees in its wake. And Sasha Marion, situated in a little purple building atop one of the city's tallest spires, couldn't quite believe her eyes. In spite of its many wheels the city didn't look like the kind of thing that should be able to move. It was as if the Empire State Building had taken up jogging.

Sasha had only really talked to Donald Farris and Manny since the war council had concluded. She'd wanted to go up to the bar with Manny and Roland, since they were the only people here she even sort of knew. But their conversation had seemed a private sort of thing. At first she'd thought that her hosts had made an oversight in leaving her unwatched. Surely they wouldn't let someone who'd been their enemy just a few days ago wander freely through their home? But as the hours went by it became clear that's exactly what they'd done.

So Sasha explored. It had been exhilarating, actually. Every inch of the city was different and strange and new to her. Across the gantries there were numerous market stalls with fresh meat and produce. At first she recognized all the foods. But the higher and further she went, the stranger everything seemed. The meat went from beef and chicken to alligator and zebra and mammoth and, eventually, something Sasha thought might be from an actual dinosaur. She was sure it was all lab grown. And the produce was certainly gene-modified. At one point she came across a kiosk filled with fruit that had been tweaked to take the shape of gigantic, erect penises. There were penis watermelons, penis oranges, penis apples, and even bags of tiny penis-shaped grapes.

She knew she should have felt disgusted. Two weeks ago, Sasha would have been horrified. But somehow she just...wasn't. She felt a vague sense of unease, awkwardness at the sight of so many genitals. But after all she'd seen in the Heavenly Kingdom, it didn't exactly horrify her either. How could it?

The Fondleboats were another matter. The sight and the strange musky sweet smell that wafted out the grinding, groping crowd inside it made her queasy. *This is exactly as depraved as Pastor Mike said it would be,* she thought. But she also thought, *is this really worse than all that violence and death? Who are they hurting?*

The Lord, said a shrill, small voice in the back of her mind.

Why would God hate this, and not the hanging of good people? Sasha wondered. *Why would this make Him angry but not the butchery inside that factory?*

You know what the Bible says, Sasha. There was no getting around that. The scriptures were clear.

Well, maybe they're wrong then. Maybe they've always been wrong. Or maybe I read them wrong. Maybe they didn't say what I thought they said.

It was odd how freeing that thought was.

She made her way past a Fondleboat and, for no reason beyond curiosity and the desire to stretch her muscles, Sasha started to climb upwards. The gantrys that made up the bulk of Rolling Fuck's walking space were fairly easy for a human to traverse. They had high walls, so even the very drunk were unlikely to fall, and in spite of the city's clutter and bustle, its designers had done a good job of making two clear lanes for foot traffic. But the gantrys only gave Sasha access to a handful of the strange, glittering buildings that dotted the city's rolling superstructure.

So she left them, and she climbed up.

It was not an easy climb. Here and there she found small sections of ladder or knotted rope to ease her passage. For the most part, though, she climbed hand over hand up the criss-crossed metal girders. She passed several buildings filled with people, drinking and partying. Sasha didn't stop to talk. The climb was hard but at least it allowed her to avoid awkward conversation with whatever manner of creatures lived in this place.

By the time she reached the top of the spindle, Sasha's body was drenched in sweat and her arms were too sore to pull her up one more foot. She was grateful to whoever had decided to cap this spindle with a tiny purple shack, and she was even more grateful that the shack appeared unoccupied. Sasha pulled herself inside and collapsed on the floor. For a while, it was all she could do to regain her breath.

She wondered, in a vague sort of way, if she'd just broken into someone's home. Nobody had warned her that there would be certain places she couldn't travel here. But no one had told her much of anything at all after she'd arrived. Sasha took stock of her surroundings. The interior of the room was plush. The walls were carpeted in thick, cushiony velvet. The floor below her seemed to be some sort of black shag. There was a framed picture on one wall. Sasha didn't recognize the artist, but it looked like a cross-section drawing of a handgun with fetuses as the bullets. The sight of it made her feel a bit sick, but there was also something about the art that drew her eyes.

The center of the room was a low, flat table that appeared to be made entirely out of mirrored glass. There was a pile of white powder on the center of the table along with a strange rectangular piece of green paper. Sasha picked up the paper and stared at it. It took her a moment to realize what it was.

"Money," said a voice from behind her. "Or, it used to be. Once upon a time."

Sasha froze. Stiffened. She turned around, not sure what to expect but with an apology already spilling out of her mouth.

"I'm sorry, sir, I didn't–"

Something in the man's smile, and the relaxed slump of his shoulders made her stop talking. He stood in the doorway of the little building, just a few feet in front of her. She had no idea how he could have climbed up and in there without her hearing him. She didn't remember the man's name, but she recognized him from the war council. Those writhing snake tattoos identified him as clearly as a nametag.

"I'm..." she trailed off. He smiled at her. There was something about his eyes that seemed off, wrong. She couldn't place it. His pupils were somehow different than they should have been. When he spoke, though, his voice was warm and friendly.

"You are Sasha Marion. The girl who was brave enough to flee her home and family for the Heavenly Kingdom, and then brave enough to leave it when she realized what it truly was." His head dipped down into a slight bow. "I'm Jim Shannon. It's an honor to meet you, Miss Marion."

Jim squatted down on his haunches and dropped his arms in between his legs. It was a casual motion, but he executed it with almost mechanical precision. There was something to his movements that spoke of terrible potential energy, kinetic force just waiting to be unleashed. Sasha found that almost as unsettling as the sight of his bare penis.

"It's nice to meet you," she said, because what else could she say?

Jim's smile didn't change, but his eyes did. His pupils contracted and then changed shape, from a circle to a spiraling rounded star.

"No, it's not," he said. "Let's not lie to each other, eh Sasha? I'm weird. I move wrong. My eyes," as he spoke his star-pupils started to spin in a hypnotic spiral, "are wrong. They don't look human. I can hear your heart-beat elevate as we speak. I can smell cortisol in your brain and elevated levels of blood glucose. I can see in your eyes that me saying this has made you even more nervous."

"Yes," she admitted, "yes, you're right. You scare me."

"That's perfectly normal, Miss Marion. It is not an act of weakness to admit fear. Quite the opposite. You feel better now, don't you?"

She actually did. There was a queer sort of relief in admitting her fear and discomfort in this man-thing's presence.

"I do feel better," she said. "Why is that?"

"Admitting fear is the first step to conquering it. You don't strike me as someone who wants to live in fear, Miss Marion. You do strike me as someone who seeks control. Strength. Power over your own life."

"I..." she sputtered, "I don't know. A week ago I'd have told you God was in control of my life." Sasha looked down at her lap, suddenly embarrassed. "It wasn't very long ago but it feels like a lifetime. It was so peaceful, just handing over control."

Jim nodded and leaned his head forward a few inches.

"That didn't end well though, did it?"

Sasha shook her head.

"You traveled to the Heavenly Kingdom with a certain set of beliefs about the universe. Those beliefs met reality. Reality broke them into little pieces. There's no shame in that. It happens to all of us. Now you're a bit older and a few bits wiser."

She looked up at him. His smile seemed somehow softer now. She felt like opening up, confiding in this stranger. Sasha wondered if that was another aspect of his modifications, some alteration of his body chemistry and physical appearance that allowed him to seem more familiar and trustworthy to her. She opened up anyway.

"I just don't know what to do now. I guess I could go home but I don't think I was wrong in leaving home. I don't want a life in the American Federation. I know that. I just..."

"You don't know what's right," Jim finished, in a voice that was gentler than she would of guessed he was capable of sounding.

She nodded as she struggled for her next words.

"I know I can't go back. I don't know where to go next. I don't have any money, or really any useful skills, so I can't go to California or Cascadia. I doubt this place will take me," she gestured down at the rolling city below them, "and even if they would, I don't really feel comfortable here either."

"Mmmh," Jim nodded, and leaned back. "Perhaps," he said, "you should worry less about where you want to end up and more about what you want to end up doing."

"I don't have any options," Sasha said, fighting down a rising panic that tickled the back of her throat. "I didn't even finish high school. I've spent the last two years preparing to join the Kingdom. I don't know how to do anything useful."

"That's where you're wrong," Jim said in a firm voice. "You lied well enough to hide your intention from your parents and AmFed law enforcement. You did that for years."

Sasha wanted to argue that she hadn't lied, not according to Pastor Mike's definition of the word. But she stayed silent while he spoke.

"You escaped from one of the most fortified borders in the world," Jim continued, "and you did useful work in a medical facility. Then you helped facilitate the escape of several prisoners from a Kingdom jail. You functioned effectively in a firefight and killed a trained soldier in hand-to-hand combat. Then you killed another man and stole a vehicle to aid your comrades in an escape. Am I missing anything?"

Sasha looked down again. She didn't speak. She felt bad about taking praise for murder, especially for Darryl's murder. She did, however, feel a tiny swell of pride at Jim's words. It was immediately accompanied by a flood of guilt.

"Killing is not something to be proud of," she said.

"Oh, I disagree," Jim chuckled. "Killing is a highly technical skill. And you've proven yourself a talented amateur. With some training, and a spot of chrome, you could really be something..." He trailed off. Sasha was quiet for a moment. She looked into Jim's eyes and tried to read something in them. That proved a fool's errand. There was nothing in those orbs but cool confidence, and even that might be false. What did any gesture or look mean from a man who could control every aspect of his body, right down to his pupils?

"I don't want to get better at killing," she told him. "I don't want to fill my body with unnatural...things. Just thinking about it makes me feel ill."

"And yet," Jim said.

"What do you mean, 'And yet'?" she asked.

"And yet, that thought intrigues you too. It's no use hiding it. I can taste deceit."

Sasha shuddered a little at that. But she couldn't deny that he was right. As much as the idea repulsed her, she'd spent too much time powerless to not crave power.

"I'm not looking to push you into anything, Sasha. But I would like to provide you with a unique opportunity."

"What do you mean?" she asked.

He smiled, plopped down on his butt and swung his legs in to sit cross-legged on the shag carpet. He draped one elbow over his thigh, a casual motion that also served to let him cover his groin from view without making a big deal about it. Sasha appreciated that.

Jim stuck a finger into the thick black fibers of the carpet and started tugging at them. It was an idle, nervous gesture, and Sasha found it oddly endearing. Part of her suspected that had been his goal.

"I mean that I would be willing to take you on as a project."

"A 'project'?"

He nodded. "My organization has access to skilled surgeons, military-grade augmetics, and vat-grown organs. I'll front the bill. And I'll train you. And in return, you'll work for me."

"Forever?" she asked. Jim laughed. She felt a little annoyed by that, and it must have shown on her face because he stopped.

"Sorry," he said. "It's just, that'd be debt-slavery. You must not know this, but I helped kill the last country that lived on this land to end that sort of thing."

"So how much time would I owe you?" Sasha asked.

"Five years," he said.

Sasha's heart trembled with excitement at the offer. When she thought about the way the adrenaline had coursed through her during the fight in the clinic, she wanted to say yes. But when she thought about Darryl bleeding out next to his car, the shame inside her overwhelmed everything else. Sasha knew she couldn't handle more weights like that on her conscience.

"I don't want to kill people," she said in a tiny voice. Shame dripped from every syllable.

"That's fine," Jim said, his grin widening. "We always need medics, you've shown an aptitude for that already. I have a feeling you'll take well to combat engineering. There's plenty for you to do without pulling a trigger."

"If I work for you," Sasha said, "I have a feeling I won't be able to avoid pulling triggers."

"Not entirely," Jim shrugged, "but any shooting you'd do would be in immediate self-defense. And you'd have the right to refuse any missions that violate your moral code. I know that's important to you."

The way he said that last bit set the hackles on her neck arise.

"Is it not important to you?" she asked. "Morality, I mean."

He swung his hands out to the side, palms up, in a vaguely Buddha-like pose.

"When I was a young man, not much older than y'self, I knew a lot of gallant men who claimed to live by codes of honor. Such things were fashionable in the warrior culture of a dying empire. None of those codes stopped the men I knew from serving that great beast we called a state. When you see enough good, moral men enable war crimes, you stop seeing value in the term 'morality.'"

"So what matters to you?" Sasha asked. "What do you believe in?"

"Change, Miss Marion." He smiled, revealing rows of pearly white teeth. The snake tattoos on his chest and shoulders writhed in excitement. "I believe in change. I grew up in a time when the climate changed, and my home became a deadly broiler. Politics changed, and democracy became a dictatorship of capital. For a time, I believed in the promises of change handed out by progressive politicians and centerfold revolutionaries. But every one of them was either co-opted by the system, or killed by it."

He shrugged, and cast his eyes down to the carpet. For a moment, just a moment, his mask slipped. Sasha saw a deep yawning pit of despair in the tight lines at the edge of his lips and the subtle twitch of muscles below his left eye. It passed, and a black velvet smile took its place.

"Then I met a man who showed me the way. Nothing new could grow on this continent until the weeds of the old were pulled out by the root and tossed into the compost pile of history. So, he said, forget the old debates about what system should replace capitalism. Kill the state, and the seeds of a thousand new worlds will sprout on its corpse. You've seen two of those sprouts already."

Sasha shook her head, "If you're referring to the Heavenly Kingdom...it's a nightmare. The old U.S. can't have been worse than that."

Jim shrugged. "Depends on your perspective, I suppose. Tell me, Sasha, you left the AmFed, the old U.S.A.'s most direct successor state. Why was that?"

"Because it's a soulless pit," she said, the words almost leaping from her throat. Jim smiled at that.

"This isn't though, is it?" he gestured out at the City of Wheels below them.

"No..." Sasha said. Whatever else it was, Rolling Fuck was not soulless.

"Neither is the Navajo Nation," Jim said. "Or Cascadia. The Blackstone Nation. Even the Mormons are up to some interesting things these days. One faction, at least."

"So which do you believe in? Who do you fight for?"

He grinned again. "None of them, child. As I told you... I fight for change, to cast down the ossified bones of the old world and make space for the new. I owe allegiance to no nation or god, save, perhaps, Lady Eris."

"Who?"

He smiled. A bit of smugness leached into the expression; she could see it clear as day right around his eyes. It should have repelled her more than it did.

"Eris was the Greek goddess of discord, back when people cared what the Greeks believed. She set the spark that lit the Trojan War. I know it's a bit silly, reaching back to that old mythology. But I can't help myself. There's something about those old gods that calls to me. I can identify with them."

He leaned in. There was an eagerness to his posture, his tone, his eyes. The snakes jerked and spun on his muscled chest and arms.

"I'm offering you a chance to join us on Olympus, dear Sasha. You've spent your time in worship. It's time to embrace your own Godhead. Leave your antique books behind and rewrite the world with your own will."

"I don't know if that's what I want," Sasha said in a still, small voice. She tried to ignore how much part of her ached for what he promised. The thought of killing again nauseated her as much as it excited her. But the thought of having power, the kind of power she'd seen Roland exercise...that was intoxicating. She hated how badly she'd started to want it.

"Well you don't have to decide now," Jim shrugged his shoulders and gave an amiable smile. The floor rumbled underneath them, and there was a loud, clattering whine as the whole structure of Rolling Fuck came to a slow stop. Jim waited for the scrunching noise to cease and said, "Come and watch what we do today. Then make your call."

ROLAND.

Dawn broke just as Rolling Fuck pulled to a long, slow stop by the shore of Lake Waco. The city had taken the long way around the reservoir, which had added at least an hour to their journey but also put a sizable water barrier between Rolling Fuck and the advancing forces of the Heavenly Kingdom. It had been a tight fit at several points, and Roland had enjoyed watching the wheeled city crunch over several abandoned homes and many a street lamp. But eventually the pilots and navigators had found a suitably large public park and brought Rolling Fuck to rest there.

"It's a nice sunrise," Manny said. The kid stood next to Roland, on a wooden deck built onto the side of the Main Roller. Skullfucker Mike had assured them this spot provided the best vantage point to watch the rising sun. It looked like he'd been right in that. The sky around them was a heady blend of red and orange that brought up fragmented memories of Mai Tais and fireballs in Roland's head. Clouds clustered at the tip of the horizon, ripe to bursting with the color and light of the new day's sun.

Roland nodded. "Yeah."

"It's a shame no one who lives here gets to see it," Manny said. "I've never seen the city this empty."

Roland looked over at his young friend. The boy had seen a lot for his age, and Roland could see how much it pained him. Sorrow had a scent all its own. The plunging levels of norepinephrine and serotonin brought out the sharp stink of cortisol and the greasy odor of opioids. Lurking just behind those smells was the odd spicy tinge of the IL-18 protein. Roland could almost hear it weaken the valves of Manny's heart.

"I imagine this sucks extramuch for you. I mean, you've been where they are, right?"

"Twice," Manny said.

Roland nodded. "I can't exactly recall," he admitted, "but I expect I had something to do with the first time."

Manny looked over to Roland. Chemically, it was clear the kid was battling a melange of sadness, trauma, and anxiety. His actual thoughts, though, were just as hidden from Roland as they would be from any stock human. Perhaps more so. There were moments when Roland feared he was losing the ability to read human emotions, or even display them properly on his face.

"What's that look you're giving me?" he asked, finally.

"What do you mean?"

"I can't tell what the look on your face means," Roland explained. "And I'm curious. Are you angry at me?"

Manny shrugged, and then he sighed. His shoulders slumped. His head drooped forward and down just a bit.

"No," he said. "I'm not angry. What would I even be angry about? If you can't remember what you did back then, are you even the same person who did those things? And even if you are, maybe you were doing the right thing. I assume someone was, at some point, in that fucking mess of a war."

"Maybe everyone was," Roland offered.

"I know the Heavenly Kingdom think what they're doing is right," Manny said. "I also don't give a shitting dick what they think. They're murderers. They can all sit and spin."

"You're confident that me murdering the lot of them is the right thing to do, then?"

"I'm confident that it's better than letting them win," Manny said.

Roland nodded quietly and stared out at the rising sun. The red had faded and the orange had grown brighter. He could see the shape of the sun behind the clouds. Mist rose off the field in front of them and, across the lake, a low light fog rolled in over what appeared to be an old golf course.

"You're probably right about that," Roland said. "But where does it end?"

"It ends when they're beaten, and Austin is safe." Manny's words were forceful, but he looked down and away from Roland when he spoke.

"You know that's not true," Roland said. "I forget my own name a lot of the time and I still know you're full of it. Killing these fucks buys Austin time. And probably not a lot of it. There are still millions of guns and millions of pissed off, desperate people in this ragged chunk of country."

"So what are you saying, Roland? It'd be better to just let the one place around here that isn't terrible get eaten by darkness?"

"No," Roland said, "but read the writing on the damn wall. This place," he waved his hand out in a gesture that encompassed the whole horizon, "is fucked. Don't stay here and die with it."

Manny crossed his arms in front of himself and leaned forward onto the railing of the deck. His head slumped into his hands and he was quiet for a while. Roland knew the army of the Heavenly Kingdom was less than forty miles distant. The scent of that vast, ramshackle horde had grown more prominent over the last few minutes. His nose took in the stink of diesel, the ozone odor of discharging batteries, and the cumulative reek of hundreds of vehicle's worth of engine oil. Behind those prominent smells lurked the foul, gangrenous stench of ten thousand men sweating stress and fear out of every pore.

Roland looked down, over the deck onto the yellow grass that led up to the shores of the lake. The warriors of Rolling Fuck had started to assemble themselves there. A large group of men and women had started to unpack dozens of Quadrophracts. The four-legged robots had been built by Boston Dynamics, back before the fall of the old U.S. They'd been meant to ferry men and equipment up steep Afghan mountainsides. Roland stared at them, and–

–he stalked through the lab, a razor-sharp machete in one hand and a machine pistol in the other. The air reeked of blood. Ahead of him, he could

smell the fear-sweat wafting off two engineers as they hid beneath an overturned metal table. Pieces of robotic equipment were scattered on the floor. Roland reached out his senses, and felt that these were the last two people alive in the facility. He stepped forward, swinging his blade in an arc that he knew would end in flesh–

Roland shook his head and pulled himself out of the past. The flashes of memory were growing more frequent. Guilt came with them. It took some effort to force his mind to focus again on the world around them. Roland looked back out at the mustering yard.

Warriors donned armor—a fantastic array of old-fashioned polished steel plate mail, ultramodern powered body armor, antique flak vests, and a significant number of costumes. He watched as a man in armor that mixed the aesthetic of a Polish Winged Hussar with an Imperial Stormtrooper helped a woman in a crop-top neon green ghillie suit as she locked a pair of rocket launchers onto the flanks of one of the four-legged robots.

Over to his left, another group of warriors had started to assemble the city's vehicle pool. Ramps had descended from garages in the bellies of the rollers. A slow, steady stream of armored vehicles motored their way down the ramps and into ragged lines on the field.

The bulk of Rolling Fuck's vehicles were either modified APCs or armored motorcycles sporting portable field guns or automatic grenade launchers on side-cars. There were tactical arguments for the use of such vehicles in open field combat, of course, but Roland suspected they'd mainly been picked because they were fun to drive. Almost every vehicle's engine had been souped up well beyond any potential battlefield benefit. Most of them also had nitrous oxide tanks although, Roland suspected, those were more for huffing than they were for speed.

"Where did they get all this stuff?" Manny asked Roland.

"I've got no idea," Roland said, "but when the old government fell it left behind a lot of equipment. Bases and bases full of moth-balled ordnance. My guess is these guys got in early, before the rush, and grabbed whatever they could."

At that moment Roland caught Sasha's scent moving down one of the spindles above the Main Roller. His hindbrain guessed she was headed to the deck he and Manny occupied. Roland couldn't smell Jim—who was good at staying hidden—but he knew that Sasha couldn't have known where they were on her own. That meant Jim had likely sniffed Manny out, and made the same assumption about Roland's location that Roland made about Jim's.

It wasn't long before the sliding metal door slid open and Jim and Sasha walked out onto the deck. Jim was in his familiar battle-gear. His blood-red chaps almost shone in the blinding light of the morning sun. He had a smug, self-satisfied grin and gigantic pupils that spoke of recent drug use. Beside him, Sasha looked disheveled and exhausted but jittery. He could smell the coffee wafting from her pores.

"Hey fucknuts," Roland said. "Hey Sasha."

She looked confused for a moment. Jim just nodded and said, "Hey shitbird. Hey Manny."

Manny waved vaguely at them without turning his head to meet them. He continued to look out at the army assembling in the field.

"It's a pretty cool show down there," Roland said. "I kinda wish I had some dissociatives, and maybe a blunt. Now would be the time for one."

"Awwwww shit," Jim said. "Just so happens, I got both." He stepped up alongside Roland, extended his forearm and then tapped his left index finger to the back of his right wrist. The tip of that finger detached and rolled up onto his knuckle. A line of white powder poured out onto the back of Jim's other hand. He offered it to Roland.

"Sure," Roland said, and railed the line.

Ketamine wasn't Roland's favoritest of drugs. He preferred MXE if he was going to snort a dissociative and, in all honesty, a big bottle of DXM-heavy cough syrup mixed with vodka was even more his speed. But hey, drugs was drugs. Once Roland had finished, Jim poured out another line and offered it to Manny.

"No, thanks," said the fixer.

"It's pretty good stuff," Roland said in a helpful tone. "Ketamine goes well with unspeakable violence. It might be fun to watch the battle that decides the future of your people from inside a K-hole."

Manny looked offended.

Roland shrugged. He glanced at Jim, who gave him an I-don't-know-why-you're-looking-at-me look.

"I'll try some," Sasha said, "I mean, f– fuck it. Why not?"

It was a little cute, how she stumbled over the fuck. Roland found it endearing. It seemed Manny did too. The cocktail of dopamine, testosterone, and oxytocin that wafted off him made his feelings as clear as day.

"Hell yeah, girl," Jim said with an exaggerated Southern twang, "get on over here and rail this."

"That means 'snort it,'" Roland said, helpfully.

Sasha approached Jim's arm. She looked him in the eye, then looked over to Roland and, last, to Manny. Then she stared down at the powder as if she was hoping it would say something to her. It didn't, but she leaned in anyway and snorted about half of it before she sneezed, and then retched and then staggered to the side of the deck and vomited over the side.

Jim and Roland laughed in sheer joy. Manny, being a good person, moved to hold her hair back and help her deal with the pukey aftershocks. While the humans engaged with their frailties Roland and Jim did a couple more lines each.

"That was terrible," Sasha said, a few minutes later.

"Yeah," Jim chuckled, "it takes some getting used to."

And then the door slid open again. Skullfucker Mike walked out onto the deck.

"Oy, asshats," he called out. "We're about to war up. You should get down to the field ASAP if you want to see the face-taking."

"What?" Manny asked.

"Excuse me?" Sasha said at the same time.

Mike just laughed and clapped them both on the shoulders.

"I'll explain down in the field. Get a move on." He nodded to Sasha and added, "There's a puke-wash station just inside and to the right, next to the bathroom."

"Right," Jim rubbed his hands together in excitement, "why don't you kids go roll with Skullfucker Mike. I've got to get Roland over to my mechanic so we can suit him up."

Roland didn't like the eagerness in Jim's eyes, or the excitement in his voice when he said that. There was something indecent about it. But a promise was a promise. So Roland nodded and gave Manny a little squeeze on the shoulder.

"I'll see you soon buddy. This won't take long."

MANNY.

"Skullfucker Mike?" Manny asked as the chromed man led them through the gantrys and toward the elevator. "What exactly is so special about Roland? I mean, he's a nice guy, but what makes him so much scarier than other chromed folks, like you and Topaz?"

"What do you know about Roland's past?" Mike asked in return.

"Very little," Manny admitted. "He doesn't seem to remember much. I've sussed out that he was in the Army, back before the Revolution. He's talked about fighting in Turkey. But also in Dallas and Denver and a bunch of other American cities."

Mike nodded. "Yeah. We met in Dallas, back before it was ciudad de muerta. I'd just been dishonorably discharged from the Marine Corps for..." he frowned, shook his head, and continued. "It doesn't matter what for. I was broke and I had a body fulla Uncle Sam's chrome. He wanted it back. I wound up taking shelter in the White Rock Commune. Roland was there too. He was pretty political back in those days, always quoting Bakunin and Öcalan and Red John."

"Did you guys actually know Red John?" Sasha asked. Up until that point she'd walked quietly in the rear of their little group. The few times Manny had glanced back she'd had her head down, stuck in her own little world. But now she was alert and engaged. Manny guessed it was hearing the name of the famous revolutionary that had done it. *That's odd,* he thought.

"I never met the guy," Mike said. "But Roland did. He was in real deep with that whole circle. So was that weird fucker, Jim. I was tight with Roland but I never got into the political side of things. I liked smashin' stuff and they needed stuff-smashers."

"How does this relate to why Roland's...Roland?" Manny asked.

"Well, I've known ol' Roland for a while, back when he was still fully himself. He was always cagey about his background. But we had our theories. And mine was that he'd been part of Project Orange."

"What was that?" Sasha asked.

"Holy fuck," Manny said.

He'd heard of Project Orange, although he wasn't surprised Sasha hadn't. The AmFed was the closest descendant of the old United States. They'd have kept most of the bad stuff out of their history books.

"Well y'know," Mike said, "through the '20s the military struggled with declining enlistment numbers. All the little resource wars that climate change sparked created the need for a capable, nimble force that could project power without requiring a public commitment of force. So back in the late '30s the U.S. military started fuckin' hard with gene-editing tools and biomods. At first it was just basic upgrades to select combat units, early versions of the healing suites y'all both have now. Then they moved on to carbon-fiber-laced bones, bullet resistant skin, nano-healing suites. The end result was Project Orange, the best warriors in the entire military loaded down with experimental, self-adapting neural and physiological upgrades."

"Yeah," Manny added, "it was a real success right up 'til they wiped out a whole city."

Skullfucker Mike nodded and looked back to Sasha. "He's talking about the battle of Incirlik."

"I've heard of that," Sasha said. "A U.S. airstrike hit a giant munitions cache. Like ten thousand people died."

Skullfucker Mike gave a noncommittal grunt.

"That was one version of the story," he said. "The story I heard, the story everyone told back then, is that it was Project Orange."

"They blew up the city?" Sasha asked.

"They didn't blow it up," Manny said. "They just...butchered everyone, mostly in hand-to-hand combat."

"The DARPA guys miscalculated," Mike nodded to Manny. "They'd entirely revamped the endocrine systems of these soldiers. It made them immune to exhaustion and gave them perfect situational awareness, but it also made bloodshed..." He trailed off and frowned while he searched for his next word. "Addictive."

"So what happened to Project Orange?" Sasha asked.

"Well," said Mike, "the scientists did what scientists do. They refined things. They revised their hypotheses and tweaked their creations until the Joint Chiefs had another job for the Orange Team. They must have done well for a while. Incirlik was '39, and no one heard shit from them until '41, when they hit that protest in Denver."

"Six hundred dead," Manny said, reciting the facts he'd memorized a half-dozen times during his elementary education, "including a sitting senator."

They reached the lift doors, which slid open once they got close. Sasha and Manny stepped in first and Mike followed. He fiddled with the control screen on the wall for a moment–

"I'm just making sure this thing is set to normal human speeds. We don't want any more puke from y'all today." Mike winked at Sasha as the lift doors closed. There was a soft "klump" sound, and Manny felt the lift descend.

"So yeah," Skullfucker Mike continued, "the President deployed the Orange Team against a fortified camp that had blocked off access to most of downtown Denver. They cleared out the camp, sure enough. After the bloodbath, some hackers with the Jester Collective took close to a terabyte out of the Pentagon's servers. It contained a few files on Project Orange and a partly redacted report on the Incirlik Massacre."

"And then?" Sasha asked.

Mike shrugged.

"And then they disappeared. They weren't used during the Revolution, and they'd have been pretty damn handy for the old U.S. at a couple points. Midway through the war, we recovered some intel that they'd been wiped out, some terrible accident in orbit. Only..."

"Only Roland," Manny said softly.

"Ayep," Skullfucker Mike nodded. "That was certainly my suspicion. Still is. But the fucker's never confirmed it. Or denied it. Not that he remembers now, anyway."

The lift reached the ground with a gentle bump. Its doors slid open to reveal an army. Six-hundred people in three large clumps out by the shore of Lake Waco. To the left was the city's vehicle pool. In the center were the infantry, bedecked in a ridiculous melange of medieval weaponry, small arms, and hand-held field artillery.

And then, to the right, were the Quadrophracts. The sight of them took Manny's breath away. There were well over a hundred of the strange, horse-like robots. Most of them were still being fussed over by the riders: having bolts tightened, weapons belted onto their chassis or, in a few cases, old time-y leather saddles strapped onto their backs. Manny saw one saddle with what looked like a large purple dildo attached to it.

The Quadrophract riders were the most uniform group of warriors on the field. While Rolling Fuck's infantry wore everything from Roman Legionary armor to bikinis made of bullets, the cavalry wore nothing. Even from here, he could see that every nipple in the group was hard as diamond. They were all covered in the same sort of LED tattoos that Jim wore. But where his took the form of ever-writhing snakes, theirs appeared in blotches of gray-black static all up and down their bodies.

"What are they?" Sasha asked, voicing Manny's thoughts too.

"The elite," Skullfucker Mike said. "The best of the city's warriors. Real tough mother-fuckers, mostly former soldiers who augmented their government-issue upgrades way back in the day. Some of 'em have five or ten thousand hours of combat experience stored in their bodies."

"Why aren't you out there?" Manny asked.

"Eh," he grunted, "Quadrophracts make my ass look big. Besides, Topaz is a sniper. She keeps to the rear. And I keep to her. It's not as fun as fuckin' shit up at the fronty-front," his lips curled up into a wistful smile, "but we all gotta grow up sometime."

While Sasha and Manny gawked, the Main Roller's other lift descended. The doors opened just twenty feet to their right. Nana Yazzie was the first one out. She moved slowly. Some of that was surely due to her advanced age, but there was also a note of ritual to her movements. It was something in the arc of her spine, the cadence of her step, the way she held her head. The enormous gold-bladed knife in her hand didn't hurt either.

Behind her walked the citizens of Rolling Fuck. There were around fifty of them in the lift. But as that group walked forward, ropes and ladders began to roll out from all around the enormous wheeled city. Within a matter of minutes hundreds and hundreds of people had descended. More continued to disgorge from the lifts under the Main Roller and the Rear Roller.

The riders had all formed into ordered ranks. They stood at something very much like a military attention. It was the only time he'd seen post-humans do anything in an orderly fashion.

Nana Yazzie stood in front of the cavalry, and the human civilians clustered behind her in a big semicircle. The other warriors gathered behind them. Mike maneuvered their little group to a hill that overlooked the whole scene. It took almost twenty minutes for the entire city to gather.

"What are they doing, Skullfucker Mike?" Sasha asked, only stumbling a bit over the curse word in his name.

"This is what I wanted you to see," he replied. "She's about to take their faces."

ROLAND.

The process of getting ready for war made the bile rise up in his gut. That was curious. Roland's stomach didn't still produce bile, not the same kind of bile it had when he was human. It had been years since his nervous system had been natural enough to respond to anxiety with any kind of physical symptom.

And yet, there it was. The bile, or the hallucination of bile, curdled at the bottom of his stomach while Jim's men strapped him into the murdersuit. The armor they'd constructed was altogether different from the powered armor he'd faced a few days ago in Dallas. It was also different from what little he remembered of the armor he'd worn as an American soldier. That made sense, of course. Roland's wetware got better with time and experience. Gear did not age so well.

He watched while Sardar, Jim's mechanic, bolted a gauntlet into place over his left forearm and hand. He could tell it was made of boron-nitride carbon tubes, but the weapon's blister carried a sextet of tiny rockets that were not familiar to him.

"Sar', what are these things?"

A smile split the little man's dark, handsome features.

"Scatter rocklets," he said with relish, "each of them contains twelve guided solid-fuel warheads. The left hand are all antipersonnel, built to blow up big. The right hand rocklets," he tapped the second gauntlet, which sat on the work table next to him, "those pack a tiny bronze dart. One'll penetrate a Leopard Mk5's front armor, no problem."

Roland sighed and looked around at the workshop of death that Jim had flown out here. From the outside it had looked a bit like a shipping container, but painted a glossy white. It's edges were rounded and smooth, and the whole thing looked slick enough that it could have been an Apple product.

Inside, the box was wall-to-wall weaponry and armor. Jim's personal stash. Roland couldn't actually name any of the weapons inside. Most were similar enough to older weapons systems that he could make an educated guess as to their capabilities. But there were strange new things on the walls that he'd never seen before.

Jim sat in a comfy chair at the rear of the workshop and watched Sardar work while he sipped scotch out of an enormous ram's horn.

"So is this, like, your man-cave or what?" Roland asked him.

Jim took a deep gulp and then smiled.

"I find it relaxes me," he said. "I've spent a lot of time curating this collection over the years. I spent a lot of time working on that suit, too, so don't fuck it up."

Something tingled at the back of Roland's mind. The suit had clearly been built to his specifications. That suggested Jim had been planning this for a while. But Roland had been retired at CamelToe until very recently. So how–

"Hey man, I need your port," Sardar said.

The squat mechanic held up a pair of fiber-optic cables that terminated in peculiar boxy plugs, not unlike an old ethernet cable. They were connected to a metal breastplate on the table. Roland pointed to a pair of lumpy white scars on his lower back.

"The input sockets are in there. They've scarred up, you'll have to cut them back open. But it should still fit. The nice thing about DARPA engineering is that a bit of blood and skin never gets in the way."

Sardar set to work carving the sockets back open. Roland felt the pain as a distant sort of itch. He was having a hard time focusing his senses on his immediate surroundings. The smells of the advancing army presented an almost overwhelming flood of data. Roland had loaded up on ketamine and vodka to quiet his hindbrain, but all that interfered with his introspection.

"You built this thing for me to wear, Jim. How long have you been planning this?"

"Years," Jim said. His forthrightness surprised Roland.

"Your pacifism is a mistake," Jim continued, "brought on by your overactive conscience. There is so much more you need to do in the world. I figured at some point you'd realize that yourself. So I kept my men working."

Sardar lifted the heavy metal breastplate up over Roland's head and settled it over his shoulders. The weight was comforting. A cold electric shock ran through his body as the armor connected to his central nervous system. Roland felt parts of himself wake up that he hadn't truly realized were asleep. Something in him had missed that feeling, and he felt guilty for that.

"I'm taking this thing off the instant the fight's over, Jim. You wasted your money."

Jim's smile only deepened. "You've forgotten how fun it is, Roland."

"And you've forgotten what it's like to be a fucking human," Roland countered. "Have you always been a sociopath? Is this what I was like, back before whatever took my memories?"

Jim's amused smile didn't shift by so much as a nanometer. Roland felt a spike of irritation before he was distracted by Sardar.

"Raise your hand, please," the mechanic said. He lifted up a four-barreled machine gun on a circular frame and slid it around Roland's right arm. Sardar bolted the weapon into place while he explained.

"It's a stacked charge machine gun, magnetically fired. Similar to the old Metal Storm weapons. But this fucker's capable of putting out twenty thousand rounds per second."

"How long can it fire?"

Sardar laughed, "A little less than a second."

The mechanic turned back to his table and Roland tried to direct his wandering mind back to the conversation with Jim.

"You're going to love it," his old friend said. "I know you've BEEN loving it. When you fought your way out of that city I could smell the dopamine wafting off your brain from all the way out here."

Sardar snapped a cuisse around Roland's thigh. The armor also sported a bulky weapons blister on its outside edge.

"Gas grenade launcher," the mechanic explained. "It should go great with the frag rocklets."

"Oh, so we're committing war crimes now?" Roland asked Jim with more indignation than he really felt. Jim rolled his eyes.

"It's just tear gas," he said, "mostly, at least. I may have included some aerosolized LSD in there. I've been on a big psychochemical warfare kick lately."

For a little while Sardar worked in silence. Jim drank and Roland stared near him, but not at him. The self-inflicted haze in his head had cleared a bit. That meant his hindbrain grew louder. By now it was all but shouting about the approaching army. Roland felt a trickle of adrenaline, oxytocin, and endorphins. His left hand twitched involuntarily. He felt the power of the weapon's system around him, and he felt the power in his own body. Something like arousal gripped him. Roland fought it down as best he could. But it lingered there at the edge of his consciousness.

"I've been remembering more," he said to Jim, as much to distract himself as out of a desire to get it off his chest.

"Mmm?" Jim cocked an eyebrow in interest.

"I've had a few big flashes of memories. Once, when we drove into Dallas past the site of the Lakewood Blast. I remembered–"

He locked eyes with Jim and Jim nodded back. His eyes said "I know," so Roland moved on.

"The memories come most intensely when I'm in combat. I remembered hiking with Topaz. I remembered burning the TAZ in Denver. I got flashes of you and me in Mexico and...a lot more. I'm still sorting through it. It's confusing, because there's no timeline for any of this, just dissociated memories I know happened at some point."

Jim leaned forward. His eyes flashed with excitement.

"Interesting," he said. "Tell me, have you been able to draw any conclusions about who you were from what you've remembered? Have you gotten any insight into the old Roland?"

Roland frowned. He'd been so focused on trying to remember his old life that he hadn't given much thought to what the memories he had said about the man he'd been. As he pondered, Roland's mind lingered on the memory of shooting the Cheney boy in the back of the head.

"I think I used to be a lot more like you," Roland said.

Jim grinned. His lips curled up to reveal long rows of white, straight teeth.

"That's true," he said. "Why else do you think I've missed you so much?"

SASHA.

A part of Sasha had believed that, after the Heavenly Kingdom, nothing she saw would ever shock her again. That part of her was proven wrong when Nana Yazzie's aged, arthritic hand began to messily carve at the first warrior's face. Her target was the young woman with the chrome-hawk Sasha had seen in the war council. The carving was a messy thing. It took the better part of a minute for her to slice and peel the skin free. Sasha noticed that there was very little blood. It was messy, but not as messy as it should've been.

Once she was finished, Nana Yazzie stepped back with the woman's face in her hand. As she did, dozens of citizens stepped forward. They pulled out daggers, swords, straight razors, and switchblades of their own. Each civilian paired off with a warrior and began to carve.

Some of them were quick and practiced. The motion of their hands reminded Sasha of an autopsy video they'd watched in one of her pre-med classes.

But other citizens were cruder with their cutting. A few verged on brutal, hacking and slashing at the faces and necks of their persons. None of the post-human warriors showed any signs of pain or discomfort. They just stood unmoving and, without their faces, seemingly without emotion.

"I don't understand," Sasha said. She hadn't expected to say it out loud; the words just slipped out.

"It's a symbolic thing," Skullfucker Mike explained. "Before they leave, the city's warriors give up their identities to the group. They leave their humanity behind in bloody tatters in the hands of their friends and loved ones. It's a way of making sure the city's civilians don't leave a war without blood on their hands. And–"

"And it makes them look fucking terrifying," someone said from behind them. Sasha turned around. A short, fit man approached them. He had a thin build, but his body was girded with lithe muscle. There was something familiar about his face, but Sasha had met so many strange new people during her brief time in Rolling Fuck. The man smiled when Sasha saw him, revealing pointed metallic fangs. *Hey, wait a second...*

"Hey, Topaz," Skullfucker Mike said.

Manny looked shocked as well. He stared at the man in surprise.

"Topaz, what...happened?"

There was a woman with those exact same teeth yesterday, when we arrived at the city. Sasha hadn't gotten the woman's name. But she'd born a striking resemblance to this man.

"I felt like a man today," Topaz said, "what with the war and all."

Sasha finally realized what had happened. *Of course*, she thought, *these people can change their physiology on a dime.*

"Ah," Manny said with a nod.

Skullfucker Mike walked up to Topaz and the two embraced, and then kissed. They twined their arms together and, a few seconds later, Topaz seemed to finally notice Sasha's presence.

"Sorry," he smiled as he spoke, "but I don't believe I got your name."

"Sasha. Sasha Marion."

Topaz stepped closer.

"Well, Sasha Marion," he said in a low voice, "how are you liking our strange ways and customs?"

"They're...erm...interesting," Sasha said, diplomatically.

"Do you find this place more to your liking than the Heavenly Kingdom?"

Topaz stepped closer. Sasha took a step back and then another. The man's expression was friendly enough but there was a sort of queer menace in the set of his shoulders. It may have had something to do with the very large rifle slung across his back.

Sasha started to sweat. Fear gripped her mind.

"Topaz, back off." Skullfucker Mike's voice was devoid of anger, but firm. "You're scaring her."

Topaz stopped and stared at Mike. His expression went from placid smile to rage and then back to a smile almost faster than Sasha could process.

"Sorry darlin'," he said in an artificially chipper voice. "I just wanted to make sure our guest was enjoying her stay here." He looked to Sasha again. "You are, aren't you?"

"Y– yes."

"Gooooooooood," Topaz purred. "Hopefully you won't be joining any more extremist groups that get my friends killed."

He turned immediately to Manny and, with barely a pause for breath, embraced him and kissed his forehead.

"I'm proud of you, buddy. As far as I'm concerned, you're family."

Manny mumbled his thanks and returned the hug. But he glanced to Sasha, and they shared a "what the hell?" look. Skullfucker Mike seemed to want to plaster over the awkwardness.

"Yep," he said. "We've made some wonderful friends these last couple of days." He pantomimed looking down at his watchless wrist and checking the time.

"Oh my goodness!" he said, in mock surprise. "Look at the time! Topaz, we've got a war to get to. You kids had better find some decent seats."

Topaz smiled at Skullfucker Mike. His eyes lingered on the big man's face, and then drifted back to Sasha.

"Enjoy the show," he said with an empty smile.

ROLAND.

It was windy on the landing pad. He and Jim stood next to a heavy black VTOL aircraft, the steed that would carry him into today's massacre. Roland could taste the dying summer and the faint stirrings of a North Texas fall in the air. It was cooler than he'd have expected at this time of the year. Grayer, too. A gust of chill wind blew across his face, and Roland found himself falling back in time again.

He was shorter. The world seemed sharper, even though his senses were dim and unenlightened. Roland felt a hand around his own. It felt big, powerful, and comforting. He looked up and saw a woman standing over him. She was tall, a giant. Her hair was brown and straight and long and clear as day in his mind's eye. But her face was blank, obscured even in memory. His head turned to track the passage of a blowing leaf. He felt chill, winter air on his arm, and he watched as a red sedan rumbled past them, spraying water into the air as it hit a puddle on the asphalt–

"Roland, pay attention."

Jim's voice snapped him back to reality. The other chromed man held a paper-thin tablet in front of Roland's face. That memory flash had been the most immersive yet, although not the longest. He was a little confused at that. Why that moment? Had it just been the similarity in weather or–

"ROLAND."

Jim was angry. It was actually somewhat refreshing to see genuine emotion on the other man's post-human face. Veins bulged at his neck, and his eyes were fully open. Roland caught a harsh whiff of methamphetamine from his breath.

"Alright, alright, fuckin' chill," Roland groaned. "What am I looking at?"

He needn't have asked. Once he focused on the tablet it was obvious that it displayed a map of the area around Lake Waco. Rolling Fuck's warriors and vehicles were displayed in little blue pin-points. Jim scrolled up a few inches and Roland saw a swarm of red. It was half-over the Brazos right now, and it crept millimeter by millimeter toward their position.

"The river slowed them down a bit," Jim said, "but the bridges there were still intact. I'd say they'll hit Rock Creek in about ten minutes."

Roland nodded and asked, "Couldn't we have killed those bridges, bought some hours?"

Jim gave a careless shrug. "Why would we want to slow them down? We're ready enough. No sense in dragging this out."

There was a strong smell of ozone as the VTOL aircraft next to them woke up. Red lights glowed on the missile pods slung under its belly. The chaingun on its nose cycled. The whole thing hummed with potential energy. It was too modern for Roland to know the make and model, but it reminded him of the Russian Coba assault transport, which had been state-of-the-art back in the mid-40s.

"So what's the plan?" he asked Jim.

"Well," his friend said, "we know they've got at least a half-dozen mobile anti-air batteries. Old U.S. Patriot IIIs. Inaccurate garbage. Nothing I'm worried about–"

The name conjured up the ghost of another memory. *A big Patriot battery wheeled around on its truck-sized chassis. He heard the machine whine of the motors and then the reek of fear hit his nose, as rich and heavy as Texas thunder. There were missiles in the air, aimed at him as he fell. They were child's play to dodge in his suit. He descended as fearstink rolled up toward him from the soldiers below. The poor fuckers–*

"Roland!" Jim shouted. "Am I going to have to find another murder-gorilla to take your place?"

"Wha– no," Roland shook his head. "Sorry," he said, "just memories."

Jim gave him a long look. "Anything you need to talk about right now?"

"No," Roland said. "It's just…the memories are coming at me faster now. It's distracting."

"That makes sense," Jim said. "I'd imagine stimuli that reminds you of your past could prompt your brain into sudden healing. Hmm," he said as he reached into a bag at his hip. It looked like a standard dump pouch, meant for half-spent magazines in the heat of battle. But Jim pulled out a fully loaded crack pipe. Even unlit, it smelled like burning tires.

"Eighty-nine percent pure," Jim held the pipe up to Roland.

"Aight," Roland grabbed the pipe and lifted it to his lips. Jim reached out and flipped on the lighter built into his index finger. He held it under the glass bubble of the pipe. The rocks vaporized into white smoke. Roland inhaled and felt the vapor dissolve into his bloodstream through his mucous membranes. There was a tingle as the crack reached his brain's ventral tegmental area and said, in essence, "Y'know how much dopamine you were planning to produce? Make a shitload more than that."

The happy chemicals flooded Roland's mind. His anxiety at the recently churned-up memories faded, as did the memories themselves.

"Better?" Jim asked.

"Super good," Roland said. "Can I...?"

Jim waved, "Sure man, keep the pipe. In fact..." he pulled his index finger free from his hand and gave it to Roland. "Keep that, I'll grow a new one."

"Cool." Roland took the finger, flicked it alight and took another deep pull of burning crack.

"So," he said as he exhaled a plume of cracksmoke, "the plan?"

"Right," said Jim, "like I toldja, Rock Creek is where we plan to hit 'em. The *Edmund Fitzgerald* here," Jim banged a hand on the side of the VTOL craft, "is gonna take you up to around fifteen thousand feet and then drop you right on their heads. I expect we'll take some flak afterwards but this bird can handle it. And besides," he raised his voice and jerked his head toward the cockpit, "Anderson's piloting it today, and it's not like I give a shit if he dies."

In response, the nose-gun wheeled around on its mount and locked onto Jim. There was a clanking sound as it ratcheted a round into its chamber. Jim rolled his eyes.

"Fucking pilots. Anyway, me'n my people will be with the Rolling Fuck folks, getting shot at." He tapped Roland's helmet, "When we're ready for you, I'll ping you both, and Anderson can drop you on top of their asses."

"So," Roland asked, "I've just got to fall on top of a hostile army and start shooting?"

Jim nodded.

"Right then, let's get started."

MANNY.

Years ago, in what now seemed like another life, Manny had gone to a watch an outdoor movie at Zilker Park in Austin. *Ghostbusters*. He was pretty sure it had been *Ghostbusters*. Hundreds and hundreds of people had shown up, families with children and couples on dates and so, so many dogs. The sound hadn't been great, and the projectionist could've been better, but he remembered the evening fondly.

Rolling Fuck before a battle reminded him of that experience. The people were different. Very few of them were children. But clusters of citizens, friend-groups and families and families of friends, had set up little viewing nooks across the wheeled city itself and in the field in front of it. The whole scene would have been idyllic, if they weren't about to watch a battle.

The vehicles, cavalry, and infantry were already almost out of view. He could just barely see shapes out on the horizon, setting up firing positions on top of buildings in Rock Creek. *They move so damn fast.* Manny didn't think he'd ever get used to the pace of post-human life. He knew Topaz and Skullfucker Mike were somewhere out there. He knew where they'd be soon and, in spite of their confidence, he worried for them. More than anyone, he worried for Roland.

"Drinks for everyone," Donald Farris said. He had a tray full of drinks in his hands, fresh from the bar. He sat down next to Nana Yazzie and smiled. Manny and Sasha sat on the opposite side of them, in a booth in the Main Roller's bar, looking out over Waco.

Donald started handing out beverages. First, familiar-smelling, bubbly drinks in long brown bottles.

"Coca-Cola," the old documentarian said. "Not the stuff they still sell all over. The original recipe, with cocaine and alcohol. It's great shit, we go through gallons of it every day."

Nana Yazzie took a sip from hers and smiled. "It's quite good," she said, "and the intoxicating effect is mild. Our chromed comrades have a stronger variant, of course.

"We're all humans here," Donald smiled, "more or less."

Manny took one of the cokes, sipped it, and nodded to Sasha. "It's really good," he said, "you should try it."

It was good. And it didn't seem like it was too strong. Manny took another sip and smiled as Sasha grabbed her bottle and took a gulp. She seemed to like it.

There was a loud "pop" sound from somewhere up above. Manny tensed up. But then he tracked its origin to one of the landing pads that extended from a gantry tower at least a hundred feet above them.

Dozens of small black shapes flitted out from it and soared forward, off in the same direction the army had gone.

"Spy drones," Donald Farris explained. "They'll be at the front by the time the fighting starts."

"This all seems...so weird," Sasha said. "I think I read about people doing something similar during the Civil War. They'd set up picnic blankets on hills overlooking the battle."

Donald Farris grunted and shifted a bit awkwardly in his seat. Nana Yazzie smiled and said, "It is a bit like that. The difference is that we're not doing this to be voyeurs. We won't see much fighting."

"What will we see?" Sasha asked.

"Just watch," Donald Farris said, and reached for a tiny shot-glass filled with a yellow-brown liquid. "But have a drink first. It'll help."

Manny took one of the shot glasses and moved to belt it down. But Nana Yazzie put her hand on his.

"That's fine tequila, son. I'd recommend sipping."

So he sipped it. And it *was* good. The burn rolled down his throat and mixed with the cocaine and alcohol from the cola. A comfortable warm haze settled over Manny. He was about to encourage Sasha to try some when another sound intruded. The high hum of drones filled the air. Manny fought down an irrational surge of anxiety. He wasn't sure he'd ever feel comfortable with the sound of drones again.

Each of these drones was the size and rough density of a rottweiler. They flew in pairs, connected by what looked like a thick, bendy white tube that hung between them. Several pairs settled in front of the Main Roller's bar in a stable hover. With a whir and a click, the white tubes in between them opened up and unfurled into screens. A second later the screens lit up.

Manny took another sip of truly fabulous tequila and looked back across to his new friends. Donald Farris looked somber, as solemn and gray as a granite wall. Nana Yazzie seemed almost excited, as if she'd reached the first jump scare in a good horror movie. Sasha hadn't touched her liquor. She didn't seem to have taken more than a few sips from the coke. Manny found himself wondering what would happen to her after all this.

What am I going to do after this? Manny realized with a bit of shock that Oscar's wife was the only person he'd messaged in almost a week. He hadn't sent anything to his family, or his friends back in Austin.

He'd had the excuse of his deck being deactivated when he'd been inside the Kingdom. But now that he was back, and his deck was functional, his lack of communication felt less and less defensible. Just thinking about Aisha, and the terrible news he still had yet to deliver, brought a spike of anxiety that was somehow worse than his fear over the coming battle.

There's a certain sound that happens when a very large group of people all notice something at the same time. That sound shook Manny out of his contemplation and alerted him to the fact that something had started to happen on the screens. He looked up and he saw that all the screens scattered around the city and hovering over the field now shared the same images.

One side of the screens displayed a video feed of a man in full tactical armor, his eyes covered by goggles and his head protected by a black helmet. He was seated in the cupola of an armored vehicle, rolling fast over the highway. Next to that video feed was a picture of the same man, sans armor, in more peaceful days. He was fair-skinned, with red hair and an easy smile. He wore a shirt that, Manny guessed, signified his appreciation for some sports team back when he'd lived in the AmFed. The images sat there, alone, for a second.

Thump. Thump. Thump.

Manny looked out at the horizon toward Rock Creek, where Rolling Fuck's soldiers had embedded themselves. He saw three black-gray contrails rush out from an old office building and toward the highway. The Heavenly Kingdom's forces were just barely visible to his naked eye, tiny ant-sized tanks and transports. All three rockets hit, and the black smoke of their detonations obscured the head of the vehicle column.

And then, on the video feed, a rocket burst right above the man in the cupola. Manny watched as he was torn apart in a hail of shrapnel. The video, and the still image of his smiling face, were replaced a second later by a looping video of an older man playing with a baby girl. He picked her up and spun her around and the camera zoomed in on his joyous smile. Another video played, of a younger man attending his high school graduation. More videos and still images popped up, displaying gentle moments in the lives of at least a dozen different men.

And then all the screens cut, violently, to video of an exploding

APC. Manny jerked back in surprise. He saw that Sasha had reacted similarly. Nana Yazzie just sat and stared, her face unreadable. Donald Farris frowned. And when he noticed Manny looking back at him, he waved a gentle hand toward the screen and mouthed the word, "Watch."

Manny turned back to the screens in time to see them populate with more faces and more looping videos. He watched as children opened birthday presents and celebrated graduations. He saw young men pose with teammates or hug their kids. He saw pizza parties and Christmas mornings and laughter and love and then–

Another vehicle detonated. The screen cleared. And then it populated again with scenes from four more lives, next to video of a detonating Leopard Tank. The parade of shattered lives went on as rockets, mortars, and now gunfire lashed out from Rock Creek and toward the vehicle column.

Roland isn't even there yet. This is just the beginning. Manny stared out, numb and queasy, and watched as the Heavenly Kingdom's armored spearhead changed direction and began the drive to Rock Creek. They were firing now too, pouring explosive shot and long-range rockets into the neighborhood.

This is what you wanted, he reminded himself, as the parade of death sped up.

ROLAND.

It was downright cold at fifteen-thousand feet. Roland relished the bite in the air and stared out the *Edmund Fitzgerald*'s side window as he hit Jim's crack pipe for the last time. His synapses bubbled with dopamine now. He couldn't stop his lips from curling up into a grin as he looked out onto the distant fields below.

"Five minutes to drop point," the pilot's voice echoed throughout the cargo compartment. Normally it would've held an array of smart bombs or close-assault drones. Today it held only Roland. He stepped forward, toward the rear bay doors of the craft. The feeling of the cold deck under his feet and the elevated hemoglobin levels in his blood brought the threat of another rush of memory to Roland's mind. The dizzy glee of the crack high helped him shrug it off.

Combat soon. Battle. And battle drugs.

He tried to temper his excitement. He didn't want to crave that high as much as he did. *It'll just take a few minutes*, he told himself, *and then I can disengage.* He could already feel the Heavenly Kingdom's army, far below, settling in. Their nose had been bloodied by Rolling Fuck's rocketry, but they'd suffered relatively few casualties so far. The plan did seem to be working. Dozens of vehicles and thousands of men had already moved into position around the Rock Creek neighborhood. Roland could hear the sound of their mortars, recoilless rifles, and assault guns opening fire.

He reached out with his senses and tried to find Topaz and Skullfucker Mike in the mess, but their scents and heat profiles were obscured by shellfire and smoke. Roland was able to locate Jim, as well as Bigsby and his assault team. They were hunkered down at the edge of the neighborhood, embedded in an abandoned apartment complex and engaged in a furious firefight with the Heavenly Kingdom's vanguard. Roland could smell the dopamine rushing into Jim's synapses from fifteen thousand feet in the air.

His heart began to beat faster. He felt his left hand start to shake. Not in fear, but in delirious anticipation of the battle drugs. Another flash of memory took him, and–

–his hand shook so bad he could barely hold the needle straight. He'd already missed the vein twice. "God dammit, god dammit!" he cursed before taking a deep breath and preparing himself to try again–

"Sixty seconds to drop," the pilot's voice pulled Roland back into the moment. That memory had felt weird. It had been blurry in his mind's eye, but Roland's hands and arms had felt smaller then. *Was I shooting up dope as a teenager?* He knew the answer, based on his current predilections, was *probably*.

Roland shook his mind away from the past and focused, again, on the war downstairs. The Kingdom had moved quickly; he guessed around four thousand of their men were already in position. These would be the elite, their most veteran fighters, the soldiers wearing power armor or riding in real armored transports and not up-gunned trucks. He could feel the rest of the Kingdom's army flung out far behind them, in a long tail that stretched back to the Brazos. *How many of these men will die today? How many are already dead?*

"Ten seconds!"

His nose caught the distant gasoline reek of a flamethrower opening up on a squad of advancing Martyrs. *That's got to be Jim, right?*

"Five seconds!"

The jump light turned from red to green and the bomb bay doors opened with a rush of air and wind that cracked the uncovered skin on Roland's face.

"Three," said the pilot.

He stepped out to the ledge and planted his feet. The world whipped by around them at a maddening speed. Roland looked down, focused, and saw the Heavenly Kingdom's army underneath him. Dozens of vehicles and thousands of men had taken up position in a large park and in several buildings surrounding Rock Creek. Two large gatherings of mortars and a trio of Leopard tanks made up the bulk of the artillery now pouring onto Rolling Fuck's forces. There were also several large field guns and rocket batteries, currently being bolted into place in an old parking lot behind the park.

Competent. Roland was impressed by how the Kingdom's soldiers had parked their armored transports to help complete a fortress wall around one side of Rock Creek. They'd sent a few probing attacks of power-armored troopers but, he could tell, they wouldn't launch a full assault until they'd flattened the neighborhood.

"Two."

A trickle of endorphins and serotonin joined the soggy mush of dopamine in Roland's synapses. He closed his eyes and, with a thought, activated the sundry weapons systems that Sardar had wired into his body. The missiles in their pods hummed and the barrels around his right arm chimed in readiness. Lyrics from a half-remembered song flitted through his mind. *Time, time, time, for another peaceful war...*

"One."

Roland stepped off the back of the craft and into the sky's embrace.

SASHA.

The faces flashed by, along with video clips and curated posts from social media and of course, scenes of death. Some of the men died from sniper fire, cut down as they ran for cover. Others died in long-range fire-fights or from shrapnel. The pace of death had gradually risen over the course of the battle.

Some of that was due to the fact that the Martyrs had sent in several assault teams, to test the mettle of the defenders. Those men had died fast, and badly. Many of them had been burnt alive. The sight of it all should have horrified her. She wanted it to horrify her. Everyone else at the table had tears in their eyes. Even Nana Yazzie was crying, and that lady looked like she'd been through some shit.

Since when do you curse like that?

Sasha felt a pang of guilt at how easily the swear word had come to her mind. Then she felt really, really stupid. She was literally watching people die. She'd killed two human beings fewer than forty-eight hours ago. *What the fuck does cursing matter?*

But still, the guilt was there. Perhaps what she felt was a betrayal of her past self. Or maybe she was just dumb. Sasha shook it off. She tried to focus on the carnage. It was horrible, she knew that in a detached academic sense. She couldn't quite feel the horror, though. It was as if shooting Darryl had opened up a great, gnawing hole inside her heart and that hole had spread, like a black film, over her entire body. All her feelings seemed so distant now.

She wanted to cry about Darryl. She wanted to cry about this. She wanted to cry for Susannah and Anne, left alone in that living hell of a Kingdom. She wanted to cry for herself, too. But she couldn't. And so she didn't. Instead, she sat and watched as the warrior gods of this strange city helped the Martyrs earn their title.

Sasha looked out at the citizens of Rolling Fuck. Most of the people she could see were crying, and even those who weren't looked shaken, horrified. The perpetual party atmosphere she'd come to associate with the City of Wheels was gone. It had been suspended to allow for pain. Sasha wanted to hurt with them.

But instead she thought about the offer that man Jim had made. She thought about the squicking sound of the razor blade flipping out of Roland's forearm. She'd seen the way he fought. She longed for the high that had come with the violence in the clinic, but she couldn't stand more of the guilt that killing Darryl had brought her. *I could be a medic*, Sasha thought, *Jim said so.*

She looked up to the screens again, at the parade of death. She wasn't sure if any of the dead had been Rolling Fuck's soldiers. It didn't look like it. But as she settled back in to watch, something glitched on the screens. The stream of faces sped up, well past the point where she could focus on any of them. Then the flow stopped, sputtered, the picture glitched out and then righted itself.

Whatever algorithm handled the show eventually stabilized, and the individual images on each screen shrank to accommodate many, many more people, a flood of the dead and moments from their lives. The nature of their deaths changed, too. Most of the first wave seemed to come from a sudden burst of explosive detonations. But the explosions stopped and the dying continued, and whatever was killing the Martyrs now moved too fast to be clearly seen.

"What's happening?" she heard Manny ask. "Is something wrong?"

"No," the old man said. "That's Roland."

ROLAND.

Forty-five seconds after his feet hit the dirt, Roland had run out of ammo. He'd managed to do a tremendous amount of damage in that short span of time, decimating their mortar batteries with cluster rockets and clearing the Martyrs away from their field guns with a mix of gas and fragmentation grenades. He'd emptied his machine gun in three long bursts, mostly aimed at the infantry who'd been clustered behind the APC barricades when he landed. Then he'd taken to scavenging rifles from the dead and emptying those into targets of opportunity.

By the one-minute mark, Roland's hindbrain estimated he'd killed or wounded close to a thousand men. The sheer ferocity of his initial assault sent the Kingdom's forces reeling and cleared a roughly two-hundred meter circle around him. Roland finished gunning down the crew of a Patriot battery and ran for an abandoned anti-tank rifle lying next to a pile of bodies.

Bullets smacked into him from all sides: diversionary fire, meant to distract him from the up-armored Mattis APC that suddenly gunned its engine and barreled toward him. *They think they can run me over*, Roland realized with something like glee. So he slowed down, reducing his sprint to something like a normal human running speed while the vehicle closed the gap between them.

He jumped at the last moment, landed on the APC's roof, and punched a hole through the top armor with both of his fists. Then he gripped the ragged metal at the sides of the hole and tore the APC open–

–the smell of fear hit his nose as he tore through the concrete wall. The room held a dozen men, a mix of guards and officers. One man in the middle wore the stars of a general in the United States Army. Some of the soldiers screamed. A few opened fire. But the general just stood there while Roland killed. He didn't even blink. No fear poured off him.

"It's our fault," the general said, once they were the only men left alive in the room. "This is all our fault, Roland. I'm–"

A bullet hit his face and Roland snapped back to reality. The men in the APC below him were dead; it looked as if he'd shredded them with his bare hands. But while he'd been lost in a memory, two more APCs had roared up and disgorged a dozen power-armored soldiers.

They shot him with big guns, weapons meant to hurt monsters. He avoided some of their rounds, but not most. Roland lost the better part of his right hand, a chunk of his skull, and his left knee. It hurt, but that didn't stop him. He leapt off the Mattis and soon he was among them, ripping off armored plates and shattering bones with his bare hands.

The battle drugs poured into his brain and lit his synapses up like the New York skyline. Roland let out a terrible whooping cry that was half laugh and half scream and he tore into the men as they tried, in vain, to do him real harm.

It took nineteen seconds to eliminate them all. As the last man dropped, Roland realized with some surprise that he could hear Jim's voice, distant but getting closer. His old friend was charging, screaming out war whoops, and firing those big dumb pistols. Then he heard the familiar crack of a Dragunov sniper rifle—*Topaz's rifle!* He remembered it now. The sound was as familiar to him as the voice of his own mother.

Holy shit! Roland realized that, for the first time in years, he could remember the sound of his mother's voice. Her name and face were still lost in memory, but all this violence was clearly knocking things loose. He took a step back, behind one of the intact APCs, to avoid a spray of heavy machine-gun fire and take stock of the situation. Now that he focused, he could feel the hoof beats of Rolling Fuck's cavalry. He could sense that many of the city's infantry had charged out from their positions in Rock Creek to meet the Martyrs in hand-to-hand combat.

The Heavenly Kingdom was not in flight, not yet. But they would break soon. Roland knew it. He could smell it in the air. *Time to stop now. Time to let Skullfucker Mike, Topaz, and the others finish the fight.* He'd done enough, he knew he'd done enough. And yet...

The drugs. Even after just a few seconds out of direct combat, the high was starting to fade. And Roland wanted more. He thought about cracking another skull and his hand itched. He heard one of the Martyrs open up with an automatic grenade launcher, and thought about how good that gun would feel, bucking against the meat of his shoulder. The man with the grenade launcher was close. Roland could close the distance between them in two, maybe three seconds.

No. You don't need to do this. Stop. Fewer people will die if you just–

Roland charged.

MANNY.

Manny had seen nine people killed by bullets or bombs. He'd seen a good deal more fresh corpses, in the aftermath of firefights. He had a strong stomach and he was not easily distressed by gore. The opening stages of this battle, and the war ritual, had been unsettling, but not because of the violence.

That changed soon after Roland landed.

"He's just tearing people apart..." Manny said, without really meaning to say anything at all. Donald Farris replied with a grim nod.

"It's hard to watch," Nana Yazzie admitted, as another dozen lives ended messily on the screens before them. "It'll be over soon, though. They can't take much more of this."

"I haven't seen any of your people die yet," Sasha said. "Is that abnormal?"

"No," Donald's voice was grim. "There'll be a lot of injuries, but I don't expect Rolling Fuck will lose a single warrior."

"Good," Sasha said.

"Is it?" Donald asked.

"Of course it's good, you silly fuck," Nana Yazzie snapped. That was the first time Manny could recall hearing her angry.

"I disagree," the old man grumbled. "We're on a precipice here, the edge of a deep cliff. Every time this happens we get a little closer to falling off."

"What do you mean?" Manny asked.

"He means," Nana Yazzie replied with a bit of drunken slur to her voice, "that he doesn't trust the people of this city. He thinks they'll get a taste for war and this whole experiment will turn into a nightmare."

"You can't trust the dark," Donald Farris insisted, "and we're in the dark here." He waved out at the field and the hundreds of people, in tearful silence, watching the faces of the dead. "Right now we've managed to lash together a chain of rituals that keep them peaceful. How long can that last?"

Nana Yazzie glared at him, and then shifted her gaze to Manny. She pointed a finger at Donald.

"He thinks we should have let your people die," she said. "I think we have a responsibility to intervene."

"I'm not saying we don't," Donald Farris insisted. "I'm just saying, I've seen how this story ends. History may not repeat itself, but it does rhyme."

"Pithy," Nana Yazzie said, "but– Oh!"

She stopped mid-sentence and stared out into the screens. Manny looked back just in time to watch the flow of dead faces speed up again. The screens jerked and shuddered to accommodate the new flow. Once they adjusted, Manny was shocked again at the violence on display. He saw men run through with lances, gutted by scimitars, burnt by napalm, and trampled under the spiked hooves of Quadrophracts.

"Oh god," he moaned.

"Ah yes," Nana Yazzie sighed, "that would be the cavalry. It won't be much longer now. They're here to finish the job."

ROLAND.

The Knights of Rolling Fuck were a sight to see, truly. It wasn't often that Roland came across something that registered as completely new to the deep, battered banks of his memory. But there was no déjà vu here, no sense that he'd watched anything like it before. Rolling Fuck's riders worked in two- and three-person squads, mostly using a mix of hand-grenades, small arms, flamethrowers, and melée weapons for shock value.

Their timing was exquisite. One-hundred riders hit the Martyrs at the same time. They didn't seem to have specific targets, or goals beyond causing mayhem. But they did this expertly, spiking armored vehicles and field guns with white phosphorus charges and scattering any clusters of Martyrs they could find.

The woman, Kishori, rode past him, her face skinned and weeping blood, as she lobbed a hand grenade toward a group of Martyrs hunkered behind the shattered remains of a public restroom. She pulled a macuahuitl, with an iron trunk and gleaming obsidian blades, free from her belt as her steed leapt over the burning wreckage of a jeep and bounded toward the survivors. Roland followed her, tearing a piece of rebar free from some rubble as he charged.

The restrooms were at one end of what had once been a giant playground in a public park. It had been derelict for more than a decade, but the corpses of swing sets and remnants of slides were still visible. Several hundred of the Martyrs had fallen back to this position trying to create some kind of defensive line. Panic and mass death had robbed them of a lot of cohesion, but they still managed to pour a lot of fire into Roland and Kishori as they charged.

A rocket-propelled grenade hit the chest of her quadrophract and burst, ripping off one of the machine's legs and sending the chromed woman tumbling to the ground, gravel and rubble embedding itself into the red musculature of her bleeding face. Roland didn't stop for her. He charged ahead, absorbed a few dozen rounds of small-arms fire and dodged a handful of rocket-propelled grenades.

He hit a group of twenty-three men, hunkered behind a long Stihl-glass barricade and several heavy, metal crates. These Martyrs had been trying to get a trio of anti-tank guns back into the fight. They gave up on that once Roland closed to about twenty feet. One of them, an older man with a spine, shouted words of encouragement and charged forward, firing, with a dozen of his men.

These soldiers weren't wearing powered armor. They weren't good enough to hit more than one in twenty shots. They wore old upcycled body armor. Only a few of them had bayonets. They presented no real threat. *Twenty seconds and I can put every one of these fuckers down for the rest of the fight. No one needs to die.* His hand twitched. The river of dopamine in his synapses shrank to a babbling brook. Roland felt a craving rise. *Maybe just a few more.*

He was among them. Roland found that brave old fucker, picked him up by the skull and used him as a flail until the bones of his face came loose in Roland's hands. He deployed the razor in his wrist and started slicing off hands and ears. He moved on to slashing tendons and muscles and, eventually, just hacked at his enemies like a drunken butcher. One boy dropped his gun, tried to back away and fell on his ass as Roland stalked toward him–

–the protesters screamed and screamed. They swung sticks and tried to bash him with their shields and he knocked their clumsy strikes aside and waded into the mass. Roland didn't even consider drawing a gun. He tore. Every fistful of human flesh sent a wash of orgiastic glee bubbling through his brain. A young woman screamed and tried to run. He grabbed her hair and pulled, and the sound of her neck snapping almost made him shriek with joy–

"Please–" said a different man, before Roland shattered his skull against the pavement and leapt up to chase down a trio of fleeing Martyrs.

–he was back in Incirlik, bloody and injured and almost snow blind from the battle drugs. Roland shoved his way through the door and into the air raid shelter. He'd already pulled a grenade free from his harness when he found himself face-to-face with a room of women and children, old men and young boys; civilians. Unarmed.

And, with sudden shock, Roland realized he didn't care about that last part. His synapses screamed for more. Roland obliged them.

"My God stop, STOP!"

He came back to himself and realized he was on the ground and locked into a pretty darn good half nelson. It took him a moment to realize that woman, Kishori, was the one holding him.

"Oh," he said.

"What the FUCK, man?"

Roland looked around. None of the Martyrs near him were still standing. It was hard, even for his hindbrain, to identify how many people had fallen around him. He guessed south of a hundred, but not far south. The number was shocking, it implied a longer blackout than any others. What was scarier was the sheer violence evident in these men's death. Most of them were in more than two pieces.

"Are you gonna flip out if I let go?"

Roland shook his head, and Kishori released him. He turned around, still seated, and looked at the young woman. She was filthy with grime and blood, some of it her own. Her skinless face wept red but, even so, he could still see the judgement in her eyes.

"That was not fucking necessary," she said.

"I'm sorry, I..."

"Roland!"

It was Skullfucker Mike. Topaz trailed behind him at a sizable distance, sweeping the field with a rifle. Roland tried to catch his eye. Topaz avoided Roland's gaze for a second or two but then they connected and–

–she stared at him with those big, brown, tear-stained eyes.

"This isn't what I wanted, Roland. This isn't what we said we were fighting for. This is just butchery."

He felt anger at her, blind rage that warred with his love.

"Of course it's butchery!" he screamed. "The world is built by butchers!"–

"Dude!" Kishori slapped him, hard, and Roland came back to himself. Skullfucker Mike was closer now. Roland looked for Topaz, and found him. He was closer too, and looked worried, but he didn't say anything.

"Is Roland alright?" Mike asked Kishori. "Was he hit?"

"Sure, but that's not the problem. He just went bugfuck on, like, a company of those guys. Ripped them apart with his bare hands."

"It's a fuckin' relapse," said Skullfucker Mike. He knelt down in front of Roland and put a hand on his shoulder. "Buddy," he said, "it's done. They're starting to run. Whole army will be routed in a few minutes. You just sit here and catch your breath and–"

Routed? Roland looked down and realized his hands were shaking. He felt a vast, throbbing emptiness in his synapses. He realized that the emptiness was always there, and had been for as long as he could remember. Most days he hid it under a haze of narcotics but now that he'd had it filled—*for just a minute!*—its emptiness hurt like an amputated limb.

He looked out and saw that, yes, Skullfucker Mike was correct. Several pockets of Martyrs still held out, but the bulk of the vanguard was either dead or fleeing for the line of transports and technicals that stretched back to the Brazos. It felt like the rest of the army had started the slow process of halting, and reversing its advance. The Kingdom had decided to pull back.

Are you done or not, Roland? asked an evil voice in the back of his skull. *If you're not done, if you want more, you'd better go get it.*

Roland leaned back. He looked from Skullfucker Mike, to Kishori, and finally to Topaz. Then he reached behind him, grabbed a busted rifle he could use as a club, and stood up.

"Roland, no–" Skullfucker Mike started to say. Roland didn't hear the rest. He bolted off, as fast as he could run, in the direction of the fleeing Martyrs.

SASHA.

It was amazing how much she could tell about the course of the battle just from watching the faces of its casualties. The pace of the killing had escalated to a certain level, and then started to slowly fall. More and more of the men died with their backs to the enemy, running. Sasha guessed that meant the army, or at least a lot of it, had started to break. The pace of death slowed to a trickle.

"Well then," Donald Farris grumbled, "it seems like that's more or less settled. I'm going to get us another round. I think we've all eaten enough guilt for the–"

He stopped. His jaw dropped.

"Oh no."

Sasha turned back to the screen to see that the roll of the dead had started to increase again. These men were running too, but most of them weren't dying to ranged weaponry. They were being grabbed from behind, ripped apart or clubbed to death by something moving far too fast for human eyes to focus on.

"Roland," Manny said in a dull voice filled with sorrow.

Sasha scanned the faces of her tablemates. Manny looked almost overwhelmed with guilt. His eyes were watery and he just kept shaking his head and muttering to himself. Nana Yazzie's mouth was closed. Her face looked tight and frozen in horror. Donald Farris was quite clearly furious. His face was so red Sasha worried his heart might give out.

And yet she felt nothing.

That's weird, isn't it? Sasha could remember how angry she'd gotten as a girl, when she read some story about anti-Christian brutality in Turkey or Illinois. She remembered being horrified by the executions she'd witnessed. But she could only picture her emotional state in those moments from a great distance, as if she were staring at it through the fogged up lens of a telescope.

Why am I not angry? Why am I not horrified? Her concern over this fact actually generated a stronger emotional reaction than anything happening out on that battlefield.

Sasha stared out at the cameras and the continuing parade of violence. She heard Manny cursing under his breath. She heard Nana Yazzie fight back a sob. But Sasha felt nothing. Save, perhaps, a bit of jealousy.

ROLAND.

The scene out by the Brazos felt less like a battlefield and more like a playground. *This might be the highest I've ever been*, he thought as he broke a man's neck with the back of his hand. Bullets whizzed by as a few of the braver soldiers tried to cover the retreat of their comrades. Most of them, even the drivers, had abandoned their transports. Hundreds of men were already wading into the river, tearing off their armor and tossing aside their weapons as they plunged in.

The Heavenly Kingdom's army would not rally anytime soon.

A Martyr turned and drew his knife in a feeble attempt at resistance. Roland caved in the man's sternum with a fist and squashed his heart like a junebug. Ten meters ahead he saw three soldiers, preparing to make their stand behind an overturned flatbed truck. As he ran, Roland grabbed a discarded rifle off the ground. *A Thompson submachine gun*, he realized. It didn't feel like a reproduction either. Roland brought the gun up to his shoulder–

–the Thompson gun bucked in his hand. Roland laughed as he danced through the charnel house that had once been a forward operating base. Most of the National Guardsmen were dead, but his nose told him one of them was still in the game. Roland turned past a Hesco and saw the young man, half propped up against a pile of sandbags. The boy held a hand to the bleeding hole in his gut. His black face was bloodless-pale and young. SO young. Roland didn't know if he'd

ever seen a soldier who looked that young. There was something familiar about the boy's face.

"R– Roland?" the kid said. And recognition dawned in Roland's eyes–

–and then he was back. He was about fifty yards further ahead than he'd been before he blacked out. The Thompson gun was still in his hand, pointed at a man twelve yards to his left who was scrambling to get a wire-guided rocket launcher into a firing position. Roland put a bullet through his brain. He turned, past the burning wreck of a semi truck. A dozen bullets impacted his chest and side. Then three Martyrs charged him, their bayonets fixed–

–the hit wasn't bad. Nothing but a flesh wound. Skullfucker Mike looked worse; he'd lost most of his left arm. Topaz had taken three rounds to the dome but she was still firing her Dragunov. Roland's mind stretched into the city of Dallas around them. There were a lot of men coming their way. But those men were mostly police, SWAT officers. Nothing substantial. No one who could stop them from getting this bomb where it needed to–

"*–go!*" Roland screamed as he broke his Thompson gun over the skull of another Martyr. Then he reeled back and dropped the gun. That last memory had felt different, like he'd unlocked something. Roland shook his head. The last Martyr in front of him broke and ran. Roland didn't even think to chase him. His head hurt, in a way he couldn't remember it ever hurting before. *What the hell is going on?* It had all started the second he'd thought about–

"The bomb is small as nukes go. Just about one megaton. It matches the ones at Fort Leonard Wood. The Guardian already released the hacked documents, showing the government considered bombing several of the separatist camps. I think we can trust the American people to put two and two together."

Jim smiled. Roland did not. This was his plan, but he didn't like it. He knew, though, that it was the only way forward for the Revolution.

"There has to be another way," said Skullfucker Mike. "This feels wrong. Really really wr–"

The floodgates of Roland's mind opened, and a tidal wave of memory swept him away. He dropped to his knees. The Martyrs around him had fled, too shocked and awed to take advantage of his vulnerability. The battle drugs were gone now, or at least he couldn't feel them anymore. Hundreds of memories assaulted his consciousness. Thousands.

For the first time in years, Roland knew who he'd been. Who he was again.

I'm back.

Roland stood. He took one halting step forward, and then another, and then he leaned against the frame of a broken APC for a little while as he pictured his mother's face and voice for the first time in years. He wanted to sob. But there was no time.

He knew who he was now. And he knew what he was bound to do if he stayed this way. Roland's conscience wouldn't allow that. So he trudged forward until he found the right tool; a hand-held automatic grenade launcher, clutched in the dead hands of a Martyr.

He took the weapon and sat, cross-legged, in the blood-soaked Texas dirt. Roland looked up at the sky one last time and allowed himself a long moment to remember his parents, and his brother, and the day he and Topaz had first met.

And then he closed his eyes and pulled the trigger.

MANNY.

Nana Yazzie, Sasha, Donald Farris, and Manny had all rushed to a transport as soon as Roland's face showed up on the screen. It seems the drones either didn't know, or didn't care enough to separate dead friends from dead foes. Maybe that was the point.

Nana Yazzie drove. It took about six minutes for the shiny green jeep to make its way over the broken roads and toward the site of the battle. No one spoke.

They reached the battlefield. *There are so many dead people.* Manny had seen a lot of carnage in his life, but nothing like this. The stenches of burning flesh, opened bowels, and burning fuel were so overwhelming they almost knocked him down. Donald Farris and Nana Yazzie looked just as queasy. Only Sasha weathered the sights and smells with calm. She stayed focused enough to spot Skullfucker Mike in the mess and direct Nana Yazzie his way.

Rolling Fuck's soldiers were out in force. They stalked through the killing fields in groups of four or five, searching for survivors or just looking for loot. Mike stood with Topaz and Kishori and a couple of chromed who Manny didn't recognize. Most of them were seated by a handful of large metal crates in the center of what had once been a large playground. *Oh god.*

The dead men here had been torn apart. There was so much blood, more than Manny had ever seen. It sluiced around on the concrete like some sort of macabre kiddy pool. The jeep came to a wet stop in front of the group. The act of braking sent a spray of gore out across Skullfucker Mike's legs.

"Hey," he said, "what are you all doing here?"

"Roland!" Manny said. "What happened to Roland?!"

Mike looked confused. Topaz raised his head to look at them. Manny was surprised to see tears rolling down his face. His lip trembled a bit, but when he spoke there was steel and fury in his voice.

"He decided to keep killing. I'm sure he's still killing now."

"No," Manny said. "He's dead...or that's what the drones said. We have to find him."

"Get out of that seat," Mike said to Nana Yazzie. "I'm driving."

In an instant, Topaz's tears stopped and, before Manny could say anything, Topaz hopped in the back seat of the jeep.

"Fast," Topaz told Skullfucker Mike as he took over from Nana Yazzie. "Go very fast."

It didn't take long to find him. Roland's route through the army was painted in red. Hundreds of dead men, maybe more than a thousand, made a clear path with their corpses. That path didn't end until they were almost at the Brazos, and they saw where Roland had fallen.

Roland's armored body was splayed out limp, next to the carcass of an old semi truck. There were two very dead men directly in front of them, but neither of them looked to have done him in. Roland hadn't gone down to enemy fire. He'd jammed a very large gun in his mouth and blown the top off of his head. To all signs, and to all logic, he looked dead.

Donald Farris shook his head and muttered something. Sasha just stared. Nana Yazzie put her hand on Manny's shoulder.

"He was–" she started to say. But she was interrupted—as Roland lifted his ruined head to look at them. His eyes were still unfocused. Blood drooled down his nose, out of his mouth, and down from the gaping exit wound in his forehead. He spit out several teeth. Manny saw daylight through his skull. But still, Roland was able to speak.

"Who the fuck are you people?" he asked.

Epilogue

Manny stumbled out of Aisha's house at around 7 PM. It was still bright outside, the scorching boil of the day had faded a bit, into more of a humid simmer. The normal stark, blinding blue of Texan September had been replaced by the oily gray-white of cloud cover. It looked, and felt, like a storm front was moving in.

He took a few steps forward, just to get away from the door. The meeting had gone awfully. There'd never really been any chance of it going well, of course. Manny had opted to be as blunt and honest as possible. He'd told her that Oscar had been captured and executed by the Heavenly Kingdom. He left out that Roland had mercy-killed him, as he'd left out his own little stint in the Kingdom's militia. It would've taken too long to explain.

She'd reacted with rage. Aisha had hit him a few times. She'd screamed at him off and on for more than an hour, in between bouts of collapsing into his chest and sobbing.

"If you hadn't talked him into this fucking job, he'd still be alive," she'd spat at him. Manny hadn't argued in his defense. Aisha had been right, after all. There was nothing for him to do but endure her rage, soak up her pain, and transfer tens of thousands of AmFed dollars into her bank account.

Before the bodies at Rock Creek had gone cold, Manny had made up his mind to hand Aisha every penny he'd saved. Skullfucker Mike and Topaz had assured him that the cash would be all but useless in his new life on the road with Rolling Fuck. And more than that, it was the right thing to do. He couldn't bring Oscar back, he couldn't make anything OK, but the money he'd saved would mean Aisha had one less worry in the immediate wake of the tragedy.

He stepped off her porch and tried not to focus too much on the muffled sounds of her howling cries behind him. Ahead, parked across the street, was an old beat-to-shit Jeep Wrangler. It had no doors, no top, and Tule Black Elk sat in the driver's seat, legs propped up on the dash and a fat cigar bleeding smoke into the air around her. She glanced up as he approached, and favored him with a lopsided grin.

"Hey, kid, how'd it go?"

Tule had seemed less than friendly on their initial meeting. Given the circumstances, Manny couldn't blame her. She'd warmed up to him in the two days since the battle, and had thanked him repeatedly for saving her and Rick. Manny had tried to brush off her thanks, but she'd ignored his every effort. When it came time to take his last trip into Austin she'd volunteered to drive. Her mods were all minor enough that she was still legal inside the city.

"It went the way it went," he replied. "She's fucked up about it and she hates me. Probably always will."

Manny hopped into the passenger seat and looked around for a seatbelt before remembering that Tule's jeep had none. He settled back into the seat and looked over to her. The woman took two more deep puffs of her cigar, then put the nub out on the side of her vehicle. She exhaled, belched, and then fixed him with a weary smile.

"Is that it, then?"

Manny had already visited his father. It hadn't taken long. The old man was happy to see him alive, proud of what he'd done, and livid that he planned to flee Texas to live with a bunch of weirdos in a moving city. He hadn't fought Manny on the matter though. Life in Austin didn't exactly promise a bright future—for anyone.

The city's defense forces had counter-attacked the Martyrs coming up from Lake Houston at the same time as Rolling Fuck and Roland had made their stand. That battle hadn't been as one-sided, but the Martyrs had been pushed back. Rumor had it that the SDF forces around Lake Houston were sallying out now, sending gunboats with pocket artillery into the flooded parts of the city to shell Kingdom forces in the suburbs.

The Heavenly Kingdom had withdrawn from Waco. They'd probably pull back from around Houston soon. But they still held Dallas, Galveston, and hundreds of miles of territory besides. Word was the

Canadians and Californians were sending in more military advisors, the Choctaw and Navajo were sending in special forces. The UCS had recoiled at all this foreign intervention; they were threatening to send in ground troops to protect the faithful. Texas would not stop bleeding anytime soon.

"Yeah, that's everything," he told Tule. "Austin's got nothing else for me now."

"Good." She reached over and squeezed his shoulder. One look at her eyes told Manny she'd been crying while he'd been inside with Aisha. It was odd, but he appreciated her grief. She hadn't said anything about Marigold, but the fact that she was also clearly wracked with pain and guilt made his own burden easier to bear.

Tule popped the jeep into drive and, together, they rolled forward and out of the subdivision where Oscar had lived, and Aisha still did. Without really thinking about it, Manny opened the glove compartment. His time with Rolling Fuck had taught him that there had to be drugs squirreled away somewhere inside. He was right: a full, clear plastic hip flask sat next to a ziploc bag filled with blunts. Manny grabbed the flask and fished out one of the blunts.

"You got a light?" he asked.

Tule snorted in laughter.

"What kinda fuck'n question is that? Course I got a light."

She handed it over. He lit the blunt, hit it, passed it off to her, and then unscrewed the top of the flask and pounded back a shot.

"You're learning," Tule told him, as she took a sharp right turn onto South Congress Avenue.

"Learning what?"

"Learning that the world's too fucked to take on with a clear head." She passed the blunt back. Manny took it, and handed off the flask.

"When I first came to Rolling Fuck," she started, "I didn't get why everyone was so damn wasted all the time. I'd been an activist back in Albuquerque, y'know. I thought having a clear head would help me fight."

She laughed, took a deep belt of liquor and then continued.

"It turned out my clear head and my hard work didn't stop home from going to shit. After a couple weeks with Marigold, Topaz, and Skullfucker Mike, I realized something."

"What?" Manny asked, already kind of sure he knew the answer.

"The world's gonna be more-or-less exactly as fucked up, no matter how serious I take it. So I might as well enjoy the shitshow."

Manny nodded. He gulped down more of the liquor, took another hit from the blunt, and stared off into the sun, which had started to set over the Colorado River. It was a beautiful day. He thought it was fitting that this would be his last day in the city of his birth. It was like Austin had dressed up to say goodbye to him.

"I never really thought I could fix the world," Manny said, "but I thought I might be able to fix my own life, you know? Be clever enough, good enough, to escape to somewhere better."

"Yeah?" Tule grinned. "Did you give up on that? Or did you decide Rolling Fuck is 'somewhere better'?"

"I dunno," Manny said, "but it's definitely somewhere different. I think right now, that's enough."

Rolling Fuck had moved south since the battle, to Georgetown. Tule pulled onto Highway 35, waved her way through a handful of checkpoints, and tore ass until they reached the outskirts of the camp. By then the flask was long empty, and the blunt burnt down. That was fine, though. Manny was a bit of a lightweight, and he felt pretty wasted as they pulled up to the greeter's station. Skullfucker Mike and Topaz were waiting for them.

"Welcome home, pal," Mike said, and wrapped him in a rib-crushing embrace. Topaz kissed his cheek and gave him a smile that didn't reach her eyes. She was still fucked up, he knew, over Marigold's death, and over whatever had happened with Roland. So was Manny, for that matter.

Roland's brain had reknit within about an hour of his injury. Manny had expected things to go back to normal then, or as normal as Roland ever was. But the post-human had been left with no clear memories of Manny, Sasha, or anything that had happened inside the Heavenly Kingdom. He remembered Mike's name, and he talked frequently about a shack on the top of some mountain in Arizona, but that was it.

Manny tried not to dwell on it. Together, he, Mike, Topaz, and Tule started to walk toward the enormous modified strip-mining machine at the heart of Rolling Fuck. Mike put a hand on Manny's shoulder and squeezed.

"Got some bad news for you, bud."

"What?" Manny asked, hyper-vigilance spiking anxiety into his brain.

"Sasha left," said Topaz, her voice as gentle as it ever got.

"What?" he asked. "Where? Back to the AmFed or..."

"No," Mike replied. "She went with Jim, in that stupid aircraft of his. I think he offered her a job."

"Is that bad?" Manny asked. He wasn't sure how to feel. He'd wanted to get to know her better. But he'd also gotten the distinct impression she wouldn't be happy in Rolling Fuck.

"Depends on your perspective," Topaz said. "Jim can give her a lot of the things she might need right now. He's also the worst person on earth." She paused for a moment, then reconsidered.

"Okay, second worst."

"You talking about Roland?" Manny asked.

"Fuck you," she replied.

"Kid's got a right to talk about him, Topes," Mike said. "They went through a nightmare together."

"Yeah," Topaz said, looking up at Manny, "and now he's left you alone with the shit you did together, while he wanders off into the desert to get wrecked, hasn't he?"

Roland had, in fact, started his walk to Arizona about a day ago, laden down with several backpacks full of painkillers and psilocybin. He hadn't bothered to say goodbye but, then again, he hadn't remembered Manny at all.

"He can't help it," Manny told her. He'd been thinking about this a lot. "Roland warned me, before he went out there. He told me he couldn't handle the guilt, the killing. He made it clear how much it fucked him up. And I still asked him to go anyway."

"Sure," Topaz said, her voice icy and sharp. "And you don't have guilt over anything that happened out there? You think Mike and I don't have blood on *our* hands?"

"Skullfucker Mike," Mike gently insisted.

"We spent years fighting alongside Roland," Topaz continued. "We shed a lot of blood together. He told us he'd always be there, to help us deal with whatever came after."

"And then one day he was gone," Mike said in a dull, haunted tone. "He left us just like he left you." The big man shook his head, as if to clear out the darkness inside. "I don't hold it against him. It's just how he is."

"Fuck that," Topaz spat. "He doesn't get to do that and not be a son-of-a-bitch. The rest of us have to live with our consciences. He takes a bullet-train to Forgetsville, and that's fine?"

"It's not fine," Mike said, "but it is Roland. We have to take him as he is."

"You do, maybe. I'm happy cutting the fucker out of my life. You'd do well to do the same, Manny, when he comes back next time."

"You think there'll be a next time?" Manny asked.

"Of course."

"Alright, cut the shit," Tule said, as they reached the lift that would lead them up to the Main Roller. "Manny's here for good now. We've all got plenty to sniffle over, but it's time to properly welcome this dumbass to the city."

"What's that look like?" Manny asked.

"We'll probably take some MDMA," Mike said.

"And I've got a couple dozen pounds of dynamite," Topaz added. "Explosives are stupid fun when you're rolling."

"We can toss it while we do donuts in the jeep," Tule said. "I'll crack open a case of whippits. We'll make a night of it."

Skullfucker Mike squeezed Manny into a bear hug. Topaz joined. And, after a few seconds, so did Tule.

"This is gonna be the best party of your life," he said. "At least, 'til whatever we do tomorrow."

Afterword

From 2013 to 2017, my wife and I made a series of questionable decisions that ended with heads full of PTSD and a busted marriage. *After the Revolution* was written as an act of therapy. Every day I would run a half-marathon and then bury myself in my laptop, writing until I could no longer keep my eyes open. As a result, this book is primarily about trauma, and the different ways people process it.

At the moment, I suspect trauma will be at the center of every book I write. Getting PTSD is a bit like dropping food dye in a glass of water. Just a little bit changes the color of everything around it. The same is true on a larger scale, when we talk about how trauma impacts vast populations of people. I'm writing this now in the second year of the COVID-19 pandemic, too early to say how the collective trauma of this plague will change the world, but far enough along to know I will not live to see the end of the shockwaves.

My grandmother, Cleo, was a survivor of the Great Depression. She and my grandfather were both very poor. By the time she died, they'd accumulated enough money to own a couple pieces of property, which my grandma had dutifully filled to the rafters with junk. It was stuff she was certain she'd need when the bottom fell out from the world again. As a kid, watching my mom and her sisters deal with grandma's mounds of crap, I didn't really understand what I was seeing.

I recognize it now as PTSD and, if I'm totally honest, a healthier coping mechanism than my own, which heavily resembles Roland's. The only reason I made it out the other side intact was because I'd surrounded myself with good people. There's really no replacement and no better treatment for trauma than letting the people you love know you're hurting.

Anyway, thanks for reading the book. Try to avoid getting PTSD, if possible.